The INFIDEL and the GHOST of MOSCOW

David Tanner

Embram Galaxy Press

The Infidel and the Ghost of Moscow

Copyright © 2023 David Tanner. All rights reserved. No part of this book may be reproduced or retransmitted in any form or by any means without the written permission of the publisher.

Published by Embram Galaxy Press

ISBN: 979-8-9870992-0-9 (paperback)
ISBN: 979-8-9870992-1-6 (ebook)
LCCN: 2023901107

Cover design by Damonza.com

To Linda

Prologue

July 1940, German forces complete their occupation of Britain's Channel Islands.

On the desert motorway, a black Mercedes saloon roared past a vehicle bearing diplomatic plates. The hot wind blew grit against Mark Russell's battered '34 Ford as he watched the Mercedes crest a small hill and disappear. At the top of the hill, Russ saw it skid through a patch of sand, blow through a left curve, and careen into the berm. The car lost contact with the packed gravel road and rose as if in slow motion, then rolled to its side and hit hard on the desert floor. Russ sped up, stood on his brakes, and jumped from his vehicle.

The Mercedes's left front tire spun, and the motor purred. Russ clambered to the top. Blinking back tears from the gasoline fumes stinging his eyes, he peered inside. Russ heard pops and hisses as fuel touched hot metal. Blood streaked the forehead of the man crumpled against the passenger side door.

"Sir, sir. Look up. I'm here. Can you move?"

The man turned and nodded.

Russ wrenched open the driver's door and extended his arm. "Quick. The fuel line's ruptured. Grab my hand." Kneeling on the door pillar, Russ pulled hard on the man's wrist. "You must help me. Push up with your legs!"

He hoisted the man to the pillar and jumped down. "Swing your legs over and fall forward." The disoriented young Kuwaiti just stared. "Come on, I'll catch you."

Staggering under the man's weight, Russ swung him across his back and stumbled toward the Ford. When the fuel tank exploded, Russ dropped the other man and flung himself across his body. Shards of hot metal peppered Russ's neck and back. The fireball cooled, and Russ dragged the man to his coupe and pushed him into the front seat.

The injured man cradled one arm with the other. He gazed through the blood running into his eyes at the flames licking his Mercedes with a searing crackle.

Russ slammed into gear and raced back toward the city. His passenger moaned as the Ford bumped over potholes and dodged donkey carts on Fourth Ring Road.

At the clinic, Dr. Husayn stitched the gash at the Kuwaiti's hairline and set his broken right arm. His nurse assisted the young man onto a nearby bed as the doctor turned to Russ.

He pulled the tattered shirt away from Russ's back and shoulders. The doctor dropped bits of metal into a silver pan while his patient grimaced in pain. "Allah smiled on you today, Mr. Russell." He held up the final shard. "This was very near your carotid artery."

The young Kuwaiti propped himself on one arm. "I owe you my life. Thank you."

"You're welcome."

The other man winced as he watched Russ replace his shirt. "That looks bad."

"Excellency, this is Mark Russell from the American Legation. I know you wish to speak with him, but you have a concussion, a broken arm, and a deep cut on your temple." Dr. Husayn gently pressed his patient against the bed. "Mr. Russell's back is burned, and he has many punctures from the hot metal. Both of you must rest now."

Russ followed the doctor into the waiting room. "You called him 'Excellency,' Doctor?"

"Yes, he is Khalid Ali, the director of research for our Kuwait Oil Company. He is our amir's favorite nephew."

Chapter 1

September 1941. Under pressure from the USSR and Britain, Reza Shah Pahlavi, the shah of Iran, passes the throne to his son, Mohammad Reza.

NESTLED AGAINST A cliff above Gulf Boulevard, the American ambassador's white marble mansion basked in the afternoon sun. Mark Russell stood on the mansion's patio and squinted at the thermometer inching past 130 degrees Fahrenheit. To the north, Kuwait City's mud-brick buildings shimmered in the heat.

A sultry gust blew across the patio. Russ turned in apprehension toward the Persian Gulf, where a dark squall line rode the horizon. On a late summer day, the breeze should have come hot and dry from the great desert to the west. Russ remembered the evil winds on the Great Plains and shuddered, recalling the last time he saw Angie's face. What would she look like if she'd lived beyond childhood?

The American flag whipped in the thickening air. Russ moved along the low patio wall and paused at a crevice in the rocky slope just below the wall's rim. Strange that he had never noticed that odd cavity. Car tires crunched on the gravel driveway, and he turned to see a motorcar pull up next to his coupe in the parking area. Catherine Cushard stepped out and walked up to the patio, a cablegram dangling from her hand.

"Sorry, Russ. You didn't get promoted." She handed him the cable. "Neither did Malcom. George did. I wanted you to know before you ran into him."

Russ bent over, hands on knees. "My two chances are now one."

Catherine dabbed his brow with her hankie. "Don't despair, cutie. This is your year." She squeezed his arm. "Gotta run."

He watched Catherine return to her car. She was pretty, with chestnut brown hair, tinged auburn in the right sunlight. There was plenty of sunlight in Kuwait.

Russ startled at the voice of the residence manager, who joined him on the patio. "Sir, were we finished with the preparations list?"

"I think we're in decent shape, Mohammed." He pulled out his notes. "There's still five days before the new ambassador arrives."

"Yes, sir." Mohammed flashed his perfect smile. "All will be good."

Russ eyed the short, thin Egyptian who had risen from house-boy to servant supervisor over his thirteen-year tenure. The man's deference struck Russ as thinly disguised contempt. "On another day we'll audit your books and check the inventory."

"As you wish, sir." Mohammed inclined his head, but his smile had dimmed. He bowed slightly and turned toward the kitchen doorway.

Russ glimpsed Mehmet, the chief assistant in General Services, standing in the doorway's shadows. *Odd. What would bring Mehmet out to the residence?*

Leaving the shade of the house, Russ glanced up at the mansion's roof water tanks. Rank sure had its privileges. As he approached the steps to the parking area, Russ sighed as a tall, slender man with an Errol Flynn moustache strolled from the parlor and stopped under the awning. The pallor of his face was highlighted by his wavy black hair glistening with pomade. *Just great. George Lander.*

"Hello, Russ." Lander nodded. "Thought that was your car in the lot."

"Yep." Russ imitated Lander's disdainful expression. "Going over preparations for the reception with Mohammed."

"Well, enjoy the calm." Lander groaned. "Once Milbourne gets here, we'll all be busy."

Russ's head snapped up. "You know him?"

"Yeah, back in the twenties, I was his admin officer in Tunis. And he'll take care of your promotion problem. He writes a good evaluation." He smirked. "I should know."

"Right, my promotion problem. Anyway, congratulations to you." Russ replaced his Ray-Bans and headed to his car.

He drove through narrow lanes bordered by mud-brick houses with second-floor porches shaded by wooden lattices. Rooftop wind towers called *bagdirs* collected the occasional breeze and directed it to the rooms below.

Russ parked in the shade of a lofty date palm and nodded at the Egyptian guard sitting beside the Legation compound entrance. White stucco walls, tiled floors, ceiling fans, and potted palms created an illusion of interior coolness. He waved at the marine stationed in the lobby.

"Well, Mr. Russell, you're back early." Sergeant Temple checked his wristwatch. "Heading to happy hour?"

"You got that right." Russ rolled his eyes. "I'm sweaty, sunburned, and parched. I need a cold beer."

They turned to the sound of heels clicking on the central stair.

"Hi, guys." Catherine's hijab draped her arm. "Listen, Russ, I left your mail and a few messages on your desk. There's one from your friend Khalid."

"Going to the Marine House?" Russ nodded in the opposite direction.

"Nope, I have a dinner invitation." With a swish of her gaily printed cotton skirt, she headed for the gate. "You boys behave now. Ta-ta."

Russ pulled open a steel door at the top of the stairs. He stepped into the secure second floor which was accessible only to Americans. In the front office, he waved at Mariah McCarry, deputy chief of mission, who was on the phone. Russ scanned Khalid's message.

A month after Khalid's accident, Minister McNulty and Russ

had trailed a servant through carved teak doors into the amir's reception room at Dasman Palace. Amid handmade carpets and sandalwood incense braziers, a Bedouin warrior occupied an ornate chair. Camel bags, called *mizwidah*, splayed their long tassels across the floor, and a curved silver dagger, or *jambiya*, hung from a wooden screen.

Wearing leather vests over shoulder holsters with British-made six-shot revolvers, Royal Guards manned the doors. Behind silver buckles, each warrior wore his own jambiya.

An imposing figure, the amir of Kuwait wore the white robe of summer, the *dishdasha*. The *bisht*, a black wool cloak embroidered with golden thread, covered his shoulders, and a gold-banded *aqal*, or cord, bound his keffiyeh head cover. "Welcome, Minister McNulty." A smile spread across his sun-weathered face, and he extended his hand to the head of the American Legation. "This must be the man I've heard so much about."

"Yes, Excellency, my assistant, Mark Russell."

The leader of the desert kingdom ran his eyes over Russ before offering his hand in a strong grip. "So, this is the brave one."

Two waiters offered mint tea, fruit, British biscuits, and goat cheese.

The amir gestured to chairs. "Minister McNulty, I asked you here to thank Mr. Russell for saving the life of my nephew. His deed was heroic."

Khalid slipped into the room, his right arm still in a sling, a red welt marking the laceration to his forehead. Of medium height and slender, he was about Russ's age.

His uncle continued. "The desert is a harsh and dangerous place. The motorcar compounds its hazards." The amir included Khalid in his smile. "The code of the desert instructs one man to care for another. The owner of an oasis shares its water with travelers because he risks the wrath of Allah if he allows them to die of thirst." He turned to Russ. "You placed your life in danger to help Khalid. We are grateful." He nodded to his nephew, and Khalid lifted the jambiya from the screen and placed the dagger in the amir's hands.

"Mr. Russell, the jambiya symbolizes the desert warrior. Khalid commissioned our best silversmith, Ibrahim, to design this one. Ibrahim was inspired by the tale of the American diplomat who disregarded his own life for that of a stranger. After twelve days, the silversmith completed his task."

The amir presented the dagger to Russ.

"Thank you, Excellency. My mother taught me to help others in danger. This beautiful dagger will always remind me of the friendship between our two peoples."

While McNulty and the amir chatted, Khalid steered Russ toward a side door. Their path wound through a sandy courtyard. Bleached seashells, an ancient security device, crunched beneath their feet.

Khalid paused in the shade of an archway. "Kuwait Oil Company is developing a more comprehensive drilling program. We'll need the expertise of Western petroleum technicians and marketing professionals. I'd like to discuss our plans with you."

"Of course, Khalid. I'd be happy to meet whenever you want."

"Good. I'll be in contact." The young Kuwaiti bowed his head. "I am in your debt. May Allah grant me time to repay your gift. I bid you a good day."

In the year following this visit, Russ had met Khalid on several occasions. When Russ called the number left by Catherine, Khalid wasn't in, so he scooped up his mail and headed out.

Detachment Commander Gunnery Sergeant Grady stood at the door of the Marine House, wiping sweat out of his eyes. "Say, Russ, is your brother still enjoying the waving palms out there in Hawaii?"

"Yep. When he's not in the radio shack, he's playing baseball with the other marines."

"Lucky guy."

"Got that right." Russ signed the register and entered the bar.

He gave his eyes a moment to adjust to the dimness, then headed to the corner on the far side of the bar where Malcolm Lodge sat in a corner nursing a Scotch. A forty-six-year-old Foreign Service Officer, Lodge had transferred to Kuwait the previous summer. Earlier assignments in Tunis and Damascus had honed Lodge's excellent Arabic. The burly man with a goatee and graying hair pushed out a chair. "Well, you've had a nice relaxing summer."

"Yeah, but Lander informed me that's about to change. And if Milbourne helped Lander get promoted, I'm not so sure I can hope for a good working relationship." Russ leaned forward. "Do you know him?"

"I do. I've been in this business for twenty-four years and new ambassadors don't excite me, but I'll hate ending my career under Milbourne."

"Yeah, I saw the promotion list. Sorry, Malcolm." Russ sat back in his chair.

Lodge frowned. "You're not tenured and I'm out of steps in my pay grade. We could be selected out without a good promotion. It's a tough situation."

Russ tipped his beer. "So, how do you know Milbourne?"

"When I was young and on the secretary of state's staff, we went to Jerusalem. Duncan Milbourne sat on the Palestine desk, so I worked with him in preparation for those trips." Lodge sipped his Scotch. "He's old-line Virginia. Fairly well off, but not like his wife, Bitsy. She's serious money. Her family owns the Wythe Dock Crane Company in New York."

"What's his corridor reputation?"

"He enjoys the trappings of seniority. He'll protect himself before he helps you." Lodge smirked. "Be careful. He's been known to skirt the ethical edge." He tilted his glass to Russ.

"I see. That might explain Lander's comment about Milbourne writing a good evaluation. How else would Lander make it to the top of admin?"

"Exactly my point." Lodge sneered. "Anyway, Milbourne's well-connected socially and in the Department. He's one of the original Black Dragons. Ever heard of them?"

"Sure. They're the assistant and deputy assistant secretary types who really run the Department no matter who the secretary of state is."

At that moment, Mariah shuffled to their table. She was a frail woman in her mid-forties with mousy brown hair framing a pale face. Lodge and Russ exchanged looks.

Russ stood. "Can I get you something to drink?"

"A bourbon on the rocks, please." Mariah fell into the chair Russ offered.

Muslim law forbade the consumption of alcohol, but the palace permitted the Americans to import liquor for the Legation's exclusive use. They referred to it as tea sales.

Lodge shifted in his chair. "How's the chargé business?"

Mariah had barely learned the peculiarities of her new assignment as deputy chief of mission when McNulty left post. With his absence, she'd become chargé d'affaires.

"Awful. I'm swamped, and I'm still miserable with this low-grade fever."

Russ handed her a glass. "Have you seen Doris?"

The Legation relied on Doris Lander, the administrative officer's wife and a registered nurse, for minor health problems because the nearest hospital, run by the American Colony in Jerusalem, was in Palestine.

"Yes, this morning, and she gave me pills."

"Anything we can help you with?" Russ ignored Lodge's glare.

Mariah swirled her bourbon. "Before he left D.C., Duncan had lunch with Senator Billy Dalton of the Foreign Relations Committee. Dalton's heading a congressional delegation reviewing this region. Duncan invited the senator to add Kuwait as another stop."

"Great, a CODEL." Lodge's Scotch landed with a thud. "When and how many?"

"In three weeks. Two congressmen and two staffers. I need a control officer, yesterday, to manage our side." She leveled her gaze at Lodge. "You have the experience."

"I'll take the control officer's job." Russ smiled at Lodge. "Don't look so startled. You don't have the time, and I handled CODELs in Moscow."

Lodge eyed Russ. "He has a point, Mariah. I am busy."

"Are you sure? Dalton's wife and Bitsy Milbourne are close friends, so Duncan will be very particular about the arrangements."

"I can do it. I need points to beef up my next evaluation."

Lodge nodded. "Okay, I'll help you set up their appointments."

"Great." Mariah clicked her bourbon to Russ's beer. "I'll give you what I have so far."

They traded stories about previous ambassadors until Lodge yawned. "That does it for me, I'm headed home."

"Me too." Mariah pushed herself out of her chair. "I'm exhausted."

At home, Russ pulled a yellow envelope from his stack of mail and headed up the courtyard stairs to the roof. Lounging on a reed mat, he held the envelope under his nose hoping for a faint scent of orchids. He closed his eyes and pictured Rhonda sobbing in his arms. He felt her hand on his chest. His heart quickened. He was back in Moscow.

Chapter 2

*August 1938. The Nazis order Jews to add Israel or
Sara to their first names for ease of identification.*

RHONDA PIERSON TAPPED her toe against the marble floor. "C'mon, Preston. You're making us late." She was eager to assess the recent arrivals and see how they mingled with the rest of the diplomats. Knowledge was power.

"First you didn't want to go to this newcomer function and now you're rushing me." Her husband patted his hair in front of the hall mirror. "I must look the part of a chargé."

She scanned the streets of Moscow as their embassy limousine rolled toward the Wyman apartment. Couples strolled in the soft light of a peaceful evening. She recognized a black automobile she'd spotted outside the apartment and earlier near the embassy. When she glanced at Preston, he was oblivious.

Horace met them at the door. "Welcome, Preston. Rhonda, this is my wife, Sadie."

Rhonda eyed the leggy brunette who stood to the right of her husband. *Well, she's an unexpected breath of fresh air. How did this young beauty get hitched to that dour old man?*

"You're the last to arrive." Grasping Rhonda's hand, Sadie pulled her into the party. "I wouldn't blame you if you'd decided to skip it." Sadie rolled her eyes. "Just look at my husband handing yours around to the other men. Poor Preston. They treat him like a hot potato." She giggled at Rhonda's expression. "Sorry, that was rude. Don't tell Horace."

Rhonda laughed. "No offense taken because you're absolutely right." She snagged a red wine from a passing waiter. Touching her goblet to Sadie's, she toasted, "To smart women."

"I'm going to like you, Rhonda Pierson." Sadie led her guest to a pair of women.

"Rhonda, meet Nadine and Bree, our new secretaries." Sadie pointed across the room. "And the good-looking young man with the wavy dark hair is Mark Russell. These single gals are sizing up him up as the most eligible guy in town." She waved away their protests. "Honestly, even an old married woman like me finds him interesting. Wouldn't you agree?"

Rhonda studied Mark Russell and nodded. "Yes, he is indeed."

When Sadie moved on to her other guests, Rhonda wandered to the buffet table where she surveyed the desserts. She sensed someone at her side and turned. Mark Russell held a plate piled high with food. "Any suggestions, Mr. Russell?"

His blue eyes briefly met hers. "Yes, ma'am, everything's good." He hefted his plate. "I live alone, so I'll eat anything I didn't cook."

She gave him her most dazzling smile. "Well, I never turn down a good dessert." She selected a triple-layered chocolate confection. "That's quite an accent. Kansas, or maybe Oklahoma? Oh, don't look so stricken." She smiled again. "I like it."

"Kansas, ma'am. I know I don't fit the diplomat mold. But I'm learning." He popped a cheese appetizer into his mouth. "I'm more used to horses than people."

Rhonda laughed and moved away from the buffet. She selected a seat on the sofa where she could view the room and listen in on conversational flow. It amused her to hear what even seasoned diplomats let slip when they relaxed among associates.

Nadine wobbled by. Too much wine, too little food. Preston still conversed with the men. He hadn't even introduced her. Typical. Sadie had kicked off her heels. Good for her. A breeze drifted through the open door. Rhonda rose and moved to the railing. In the gloaming, she inhaled the smells of her new city. Winter was coming.

The sharp, jagged crash of broken glass shattered her revery. She spun back toward the room. Nadine, pale and sweaty, stared at the broken wine goblet at her feet. Mark Russell moved to her side and guided her down the hallway. He waited outside the bathroom until a more composed Nadine emerged. Sadie called a taxi, and Mark escorted Nadine to the curb.

When Mark returned, Rhonda joined him at the buffet table. "Not much left, is there?"

"No, shoulda brought a sack." He laughed. "Oh, well."

"I'm sure Nadine would give you dinner as a thank you for helping her out tonight."

"She might want to forget that. She's probably a bit over-whelmed."

"Mr. Russell, what a gracious thing to say. I'm impressed."

"Please call me Russ, ma'am. My mother taught me to help those in distress."

"That's good to know. And please stop with the 'ma'am.' I'm Rhonda."

Russ stuck out his hand. "Nice to meet you, Rhonda."

She held his hand in her own until Horace walked over.

"Getting to know each other? Rhonda, Russ is my youngest political officer. Rhonda is Preston Pierson's wife." He nodded to Rhonda's husband amid the group of men. "Let me introduce you." Taking Russ's arm, he steered him away from Rhonda.

Sadie waltzed up, a smirk on her face. "Never mind him." She patted Rhonda's arm. "His first wife bumped up against several other men before dumping Horace and making off with their two kids. I'm amazed he worked up enough nerve to ask me to marry him. He's a good man, but he sometimes forgets how much fun life can be."

"No harm done."

Back at the balcony railing, Rhonda spotted a slender brunette in a dark print dress beside a black limousine. She leaned against a lamppost with an open newspaper. When Rhonda waved, the woman inclined her head and smiled. A pleasant enough first encounter with the NKVD, the Russian security service.

Once again at their apartment, Pierson fell into bed while Rhonda sat at her desk.

Now that we're settled in Moscow, I've begun my study of available young men. I identified someone at the newcomer reception who may make the ideal candidate for my initial foray into our little experiment. He could not be more perfect. He's been spotted by several single women, so I'll have to act fast if I want to get his attention. I'm working on a plan.

I've heard him voice well-reasoned opinions among the men, so he's smart enough to understand what we're trying to accomplish. And his Midwestern upbringing is very charming. So refreshing after our stuffy husbands!

I've pulled out my notes from our various discussions to refresh my memory: Be dispassionate and objective. Guide him to learn more about himself, become a better man, and form lasting relationships with the woman in his future.

I'm glad we agreed to correspond about our progress. Otherwise, I'd be second-guessing myself out here in the middle of the steppe. I can't wait to hear from you. Hope you've had some success in finding a young man.

Chapter 3

September 1938. British prime minister Neville Chamberlain arrives in Bad Godesberg, Germany, for more talks with Adolf Hitler on the Sudetenland crisis.

RHONDA EXITED HER taxi and stood before a massive pile near the Bolshoi Ballet. When the doorman held open the door, she stepped into the Metropol, Moscow's premier hotel. Rhonda scanned the lobby just before Sadie breezed in.

The younger woman caught Rhonda in a brief hug before pointing to the dining room. "I'm glad you found a moment to meet me for the best food in town."

The maître d' seated them at a table near the fountain beneath the ornate glass-tiled ceiling adorned in yellows, reds, and silvers.

Over their lunches of stroganoff and pelmeni, Sadie nattered on. "I know I'm gossiping, but my fellow Americans can be so entertaining. Besides, there's not much else to do, is there?"

Rhonda laughed. "You're so right. Besides, even gossip holds a kernel of truth."

"Are you ready for your first Moscow winter? They can be treacherous."

"I've heard that. My Peugeot 402 just shipped from the factory in Sochaux, France. Once I learn to navigate the ice and snow, I plan to enjoy the countryside."

"Oh, you drive. Good for you." She darted a look at Rhonda. "You aren't the typical wife, are you?"

"No, I'm not." Rhonda's eyes twinkled. "But then, neither are you."

"I am not." Sadie tossed her curls.

"How is Nadine? I hope her new-arrival nerves have settled down."

"She's fine." Sadie frowned. "Horace tore into her at the office. I know the NKVD is always watching us for a misstep, but he should have given her a break. What's wrong with showing each other a bit of kindness, especially in these outposts of civilization?"

"You're right. We all need comfort and friendship." Rhonda tasted her dessert. "Has one of the single women snatched Russ up yet?"

"I don't think so." Sadie chewed her lower lip. "We invited him for dinner like we do with all the bachelors and marines. He's very new to Foreign Service life. Just an easygoing ranch hand who likes baseball and exploring. Very focused on making his mark in the diplomatic world. He seemed kind of lonely."

"Well, if you feed him, he'll be faithful forever." She touched her napkin to her lips. "Me, too. That was delicious."

At the street, Rhonda turned down Sadie's offer of a ride. "I'm like Russ. I enjoy exploring my surroundings." She hugged Sadie and waved goodbye.

At the corner, Rhonda jotted down the license number of the black limousine idling nearby. She strolled along and then entered another large hotel where she waited in the lobby.

When the brunette arrived, Rhonda smiled. Rising, she approached her NKVD minder and extended her hand. "I'm Rhonda Pierson."

The startled woman glanced around the lobby before she allowed herself to touch Rhonda's hand. "Elena Zhukova. Pleased to meet you, Rhonda Pierson."

Rhonda tucked her arm beneath Elena's. "We can get to know each other on the way to my embassy."

Elena ignored the gaping limousine driver and followed Rhonda into the back seat. After a few minutes, Rhonda broke the silence. "So, Elena, why follow an embassy wife?"

The Russian NKVD officer glanced at the driver. "We must know the diplomats who live in our city. That way, we can watch out for them."

"I see." Rhonda followed Elena's gaze to the back of the driver's head. "We need caring for, is that it?"

"Of course." She looked at the driver again. "You understand, yes?"

"I do."

At the embassy, both women stood at the curb. Rhonda quietly said, "Sometimes a woman needs to go alone." She met Elena's eyes. "I'll not need caring for at those times."

Elena nodded. "I understand."

"Good. We've reached an accommodation that will make both of our lives easier." She offered Elena a card with her name on it. "Thanks for the ride, Elena Zhukova."

Later at her desk, Rhonda touched a drop of orchid perfume to her yellow envelope before lifting her pen again.

P.S. I may have met the perfect woman to join our little experiment. Her name is Sadie.

Chapter 4

WASHINGTON, D.C. FACED another hazy, hot, and humid day. Tourists trudged across the Ellipse to gaze at the White House beneath a dishwater sky. A family from Cincinnati posed near the south fence while a passerby snapped a picture with their Kodak Brownie.

Beneath the colonnade outside the Oval Office, a tall man with white hair checked the shine on his brogues, glanced at his Longines wristwatch, adjusted his French cuffs, and smoothed his silk tie. Duncan Milbourne III had an appointment with the president.

President Roosevelt's assistant appointments secretary, Jonathan Wembley, fidgeted with his sheaf of papers by Milbourne's side. "The president's late."

Through steel gray eyes etched with crow's feet from years spent squinting in the Arabian sun, Milbourne watched Wembley recheck the time. "Don't concern yourself with what you can't control."

At the sound of sirens, Milbourne turned away from Wembley as two motorcycles hurried toward the southeast gate. He watched a heavy limousine negotiate the narrow opening and stop before a

Navy steward, who positioned a wheelchair. As two broad-shouldered agents lifted the president into the wheelchair, Milbourne pasted a smile on his face and stepped forward.

FDR clasped Milbourne's hand in his own huge hands. "Good morning, Duncan."

"Mr. President, it's good to see you again."

The steward wheeled FDR into the Oval Office. Wembley had vanished.

"Please bring us a pot of coffee, Hernando." FDR waved Milbourne to a sofa.

"It's been a while, Duncan. Catch me up on what you've been doing."

"I retired a few years back to our Virginia farm. I lecture at Georgetown University and serve on a few corporate boards. Mostly, Bitsy and I enjoy the country and our horses."

"An admirable life. I look forward to working on my stamp collection in retirement at Hyde Park. Maybe I'll write some. I've many stories about the characters I've met in this town."

FDR stubbed out his cigarette. "Remember that European trip I made as assistant secretary of the Navy, and you escorted me around Paris? Now when I hear Gershwin's *American in Paris*, I recall that trip in 1918."

"Yes, Paris is a city like no other. Perhaps we can return some day."

"I'd love to. One last ride down the Champs-Élysées. Let's do it!" FDR chuckled as Hernando returned from the tiny pantry. "This man makes real Navy coffee.

"Reminiscing is fine." The president's face clouded. "But Winston and I must stop the Axis powers before anyone can return to Paris. I hardly need the distraction from our domestic recovery, but the United States will certainly enter this war. I must be prepared for the future." FDR held Milbourne's gaze. "I want you to come out of retirement."

Milbourne struggled with his composure as he recalled how he had arrived at this moment.

They had finished breakfast on their patio. The *Washington Post* lay across the table. Milbourne studied the international news while Bitsy read the *Style* section.

She was relaxed after the worry of settling her father's estate. She had distributed her large inheritance among several different accounts, all of them in her name only.

When the telephone rang, Milbourne rose to answer it in the kitchen. He was not expecting a call from the White House.

Back on the patio, Milbourne dropped into a chair. "That was FDR's assistant appointments secretary. He wants to see me in two days."

"Did he suggest the topic?"

"'A particularly important assignment. The president will explain when you see him.' As usual, FDR didn't elaborate. He's a secretive fellow."

"Yes, I'm aware of that. I've known him far longer than you have."

Milbourne frowned. "Yes, yes you have."

"We're retired. You gave up that life for this one." She waved her hand across the lawn. Beyond the white fence, the pasture ended at the run of pine trees that sloped up to the foothills of the Blue Ridge Mountains. Her gaze rested on her Arabians. "Did this underling mention the assistant secretary position? I know you still want to oversee our Middle East policy."

"No, nothing about NEA."

Bitsy simmered at his side. "This better not be another posting to a two-bit Arab country. I'm sick of the Foreign Service with its petty bureaucracies, weird embassy personalities, strange foods, awful climates, and dreadful diseases! We did our time overseas. Let's enjoy our life here. Refuse the offer."

"Darling, war is coming. You know FDR values loyalty above all else." Milbourne smoothed his thinning white hair. "Besides, I'm young enough to serve in some capacity."

"I know war is inevitable, and families all over the country will suffer." She slapped down her paper. "But this was supposed to be our time to renew our marriage. Rekindle the flame that burned in Hong Kong and Buenos Aires."

Milbourne sighed. "I've served my country since 1907. If the president asks, I'll not turn down what I hope is a short assignment. I'd like your support."

"Why? No matter what I say, you'll do what you want." Bitsy crossed her arms.

"If it is an overseas posting, maybe you'll join me. Consider it a second honeymoon."

Her face softened, but her green eyes remained stormy. "I've always been the dutiful Foreign Service wife, ready for wherever the bureaucracy dumps us."

"Admit it. You enjoyed the Middle East with the suqs, the archeology, and the romance of the sands." He immediately regretted his final words.

Bitsy's face darkened as thunderclouds of his past indiscretions swirled in her eyes. "Don't forget how you buckled under the strain of overseas life. You'll return to the bottle and end up with one of your floozies, like that Jessup woman in Baghdad. Then, we're through!"

She jumped up, glowering. "Don't forget who has the money in this family. I'll use the company's lawyers to sink your pompous, two-timing ass into a tar pit of litigation. One misstep and you'll be selling pencils on a street corner. Think about that, buster!"

Milbourne shook the memories from his head and focused on the present. "I'll do what I can for you, Mr. President."

"Excellent." FDR rubbed his hands together. "I know Hitler is drooling over the British Isles from the French coast, but his invading the Soviet Union really concerns me. If Hitler beats Stalin, he'll move into the oil fields of the Middle East. Then he'll take England at his leisure. America would be next." FDR took a drag on a new cigarette. "And this Wehrmacht fellow Rommel keeps pushing the Brits back in North Africa. All we'll need is the Japanese crossing South Asia toward the Middle East."

Milbourne was on the edge of his chair. "How am I involved?"

"Winston and I agree Marshal Stalin must remain in the game if we're to defeat Hitler in Europe. The Red Army is poorly supplied with war matériel, so we must provide military aid. There are three ways to accomplish this. Each route has its own perils."

FDR held up a finger. "The North Atlantic is rife with German U-boats." He raised a second finger. "The northern Pacific route transits Japanese waters before crossing Siberia. I'd hate to ship a bullet halfway around the world before it's fired at a German."

Milbourne shook his head. "Neither of those routes will work."

"Right." FDR wiggled his third finger. "So, we'll send convoys around the Cape of Good Hope and up through Iran.

"Let's head to the residence, and I'll show you exactly what Winston and I are thinking." FDR pressed a button on his telephone. "Wembley, we're going to the Map Room. We'll be done in twenty minutes."

"Of course, sir. Don't forget your luncheon with the British ambassador at noon."

"Thank you, Wembley." Annoyance clouded FDR's face. "Have him wait upstairs in the Oval Room."

Wembley motioned to the agent on post in the corridor. A seven-year veteran of the Secret Service, Nicholas Pastorini had started his career by chasing counterfeiters in the boroughs of New York City. Nick gave his boss an easy smile and stepped behind the wheelchair.

Milbourne followed them into a small parlor decorated in the colonial period. He turned in a circle to absorb the glut of cartography.

"What do you think of my war room? I got the idea from Winston. Both of us love our maps! Once a month, the National Geographic Society sends over a cartographer with the latest issues." FDR paused as Milbourne moved toward a wall map of Allied and Axis forces. "Those colored pins and ribbons you're looking at tell me the location of every player and the direction he's headed." Settling himself behind a long table, FDR pointed at a map rack. "Please bring us the binder labeled Middle East and Central Asia."

As Milbourne retrieved the sheaf of maps, FDR pressed a buzzer. Pastorini opened the door for a cook's helper. "Jasper, we'd like some coffee."

"Certainly, sir. I got a fresh pot brewing right now."

FDR opened the binder to a map that included North Africa on the west, India on the east, western USSR on the north, and the Arabian Peninsula on the south. He moved a finger around the eastern edge of Africa and up the Persian Gulf.

"We'll funnel the supplies for the Red Army through ports at the mouth of the Tigris and Euphrates. In Iran, that would be Bandar Shahpur on the Gulf or Khorramshahr upriver."

He glanced at Milbourne. "Wondering where you fit in? Bear with me while I provide some background.

"Remember, Germany was Iran's biggest trading partner. The shah allowed so-called German archeologists and tourists unimpeded access to Iran. The British and Russians have neutralized that threat by taking over the country. The Russians control the north while the Brits have the south. The elder shah abdicated in favor of his son, who may be pro-British."

On the map, FDR moved his finger past Iran's river access to the Gulf and tapped a tiny triangle of land south of Iraq and northeast of Saudi Arabia. "This is Kuwait, a British protectorate with one political agent. The British army secures the entire area, but they're fighting Rommel's panzers in North Africa. They don't have time for any new activity in Iran."

After a soft knock, Jasper brought the coffee and FDR poured for both.

Milbourne continued to stare at the map. "A young, untested shah in Iran and a British garrison won't keep the Germans out of the Gulf once they learn about the supply line."

"That's why I want you to take over our small Legation in Kuwait as soon as possible."

Milbourne remembered visiting Kuwait, a land of traders and seagoing merchants, in the early thirties. His rising enthusiasm dipped. "Mr. President, perhaps I may be of greater assistance in a bigger post or here in the Department."

The president gave a thin smile. "I know you want to be the assistant secretary of NEA, Duncan, but your experience will not be wasted in Kuwait. Our Legation will become a major listening post for the coming supply corridor. This is something we can do to aid Britain. Our Legation will be our hidden ace for the entire supply effort to the Soviets."

FDR moved his finger down the Gulf to where the waterway narrowed between Iran and Oman. "It's vital that our Legation in Kuwait keep close watch on everything that's happening from Iran, down through the Strait of Hormuz, and even approaching the strait from the Gulf of Oman. That includes Axis agents in the area, Kriegsmarine vessels cruising the Gulf, and panzer incursions from the desert to the west."

Milbourne wiped his forehead. "How will a small Legation accomplish such a huge job?"

"You've been in this business a long time. You'll manage." FDR finished his coffee. "I've already talked to Secretary of State Hull and Secretary of War Stimson. Cordell and Henry know I expect them to support you in any way they can."

Milbourne thought about parlaying this assignment at a sleepy Legation into the NEA job. That could certainly lift the cloud from Baghdad and restore the crown to his career.

"What if I sweeten the deal by upgrading the title from minister to ambassador?" FDR waggled his eyebrows.

Milbourne straightened his shoulders. "Well, that would make it difficult to refuse, sir."

"Making you an ambassador would also secure the help of the palace. The amir and foreign minister will be flattered at our regard for the importance of their country."

"Count me in, Mr. President."

"That's what I wanted to hear!" FDR thumped the map table.

"If I spot a threat to the supply line, how do I neutralize it?"

"Sound the alarm and we'll come running." FDR shook his fist. "With all the damn firepower we can muster!"

"With your help, I can do this." Milbourne clenched his own fist.

"See Cordell for your briefings as soon as you can. Now, let's talk staff. You'll be plenty busy, so you can keep the assistant that's already in place. I'll add two intelligence boys from Bill Donovan's new Coordinator of Information spy agency."

FDR ignored Milbourne's frown. "A Navy captain is already there as military attaché. He'll monitor the sea lanes of the Gulf. Winston will assign a man from his Secret Intelligence Service to assist our COI fellows. His SIS man will have our security clearances. Your code room will have enough commo fellows for twenty-four-hour service. And you'll have your own cable channel, called Falcon Wing, to communicate with me directly."

Milbourne's deepening scowl finally stopped the president. "What is it, Duncan?"

"I hate attachés and spies in my mission. They aren't professional diplomats."

"We need our spies to catch their spies. How else are we going to do it?"

"Give them offices in town, not in my building. Let them operate as businessmen."

FDR met Milbourne's eyes. "They need diplomatic cover to protect their activities and use your code room. If you can't agree to them, I'll find someone who will."

Milbourne lowered his eyes. "Yes, sir. I'll make it work."

"We must catch Axis agents before they do damage. Consider the attachés and COI as assets to your ambassadorial authority." FDR smiled. "I'll make sure Bill Donovan sends his most capable intelligence officers to Kuwait."

"I'd appreciate that, sir."

"Look, use Falcon Wing to tell me about Iranian infrastructure, British cooperation, anything and everything. I value information garnered from unofficial sources. I'm depending on you to be my eyes and ears at the top of the Gulf."

"I'll do it." Milbourne relaxed into his chair. "I'm sure you know that a high-quality crude oil was found in Kuwait a few years back. As worldwide demand for oil increases, this might be an opportunity to stake our claim to their fields."

FDR held up his hand. "Concentrate on securing the military supply line. Besides, their wells will be plugged to protect the fields from Wehrmacht advances. Get involved in Kuwaiti oil only, and I repeat only, if a concession is handed to you on a silver platter."

"Certainly, sir."

"Look at this map one more time. The Nazis will probably aim for Stalingrad here on the Volga River." FDR touched a town north of the flat terrain between the Black and Caspian Seas. "Hitler would like nothing more than to take the city named after Uncle Joe.

"Strategically, it's a straight but rugged shot from Stalingrad south to the republics of Azerbaijan and Georgia, Stalin's birthplace. In the west, Rommel's panzers are pushing the British back in the desert. If the Imperial Japanese army gets out of China and moves across northern India, those three vanguards could meet in Iran, a place none of us can afford. Then the Axis powers will have oil, and the United States will be standing alone like the British are now.

"That cannot happen." His fist hit the map table. "Iran is the key to success! If we can't stop the Axis forces in Russia, you'll be running for your lives from Kuwait. Winston and I fear that the Eastern Front will collapse without Lend-Lease aid and Stalin will negotiate a separate peace. If that happens, Lord have mercy on all our souls."

"I'll not let you down, sir."

FDR pushed away from the table. "Use the east gate exit so we can avoid questions from the newspapermen. Keep your part in this mission as closely held as possible." He shook Milbourne's hand. "Give my regards to Bitsy. After the war, we'll visit Paris. Godspeed, Duncan."

"Paris it'll be, Mr. President."

Still damp from a refreshing shower, Milbourne sat in a white robe and slippers before the remains of his room service lunch. Fingering his wine glass, he realized he was still smiling. *Now that I have FDR on my side, I can put Baghdad behind me. Stay away from the women. Ease up on the alcohol.*

His mind filled with thoughts of the Axis coalition, the backwardness of Iran, and, most of all, his return to the fiery heat of the Kuwaiti desert.

Better write all this down before I forget. He moved to the desk where he pulled out pen and paper, then jotted down the key points from his meeting with the president.

I think that's everything. Damn shame I couldn't get Franklin to budge about putting spies in my mission. I used to be better at this. Maybe I'm getting old. Bitsy certainly thinks so. Ah, Bitsy. She'll rage about this posting. He rose and walked to the portable liquor cabinet.

With a healthy two fingers of single malt in a crystal tumbler, he returned to the desk. *Time to make a list of everyone I'll need to see before I head home. Quite a list. Better begin calling for appointments. But first, Bitsy.* He returned to the liquor cabinet.

He paused in the act of refilling his tumbler, and the smile that lit his face was so bright it made his eyes shine. With his Scotch in hand, he returned to the desk where he lifted the telephone and moved it to the lamp table nearest the bed, the long cord trailing behind. Sitting on the edge, he dialed a familiar number. While he waited for the exchange to pick up, he pulled the pillow from the empty side of the bed and placed it against the headboard over his own pillow. *Might as well be comfortable.*

"Put me through to Marvella Jessup in the secretary's office. Yes, I'll hold."

He kicked off his slippers and sat back against the pillows.

"Hello, Marvella. Guess who's back in D.C. for a few days? I've a lovely corner suite at the Willard." He listened for a few moments. "Yes, I'm here for consultations on a new position. And I'm alone.

"No, you'll have to wait until dinner tonight to hear my title and learn all about my responsibilities. Franklin was very persuasive." He felt the first stirrings in his groin.

"In the meantime, why don't you go over and close the door to the hallway? We wouldn't want anyone to overhear our conversation, would we? When you come back, you can tell me how much you've missed me and what you plan for our entertainment."

While he waited for her to return to the phone, he switched the receiver to his other ear. With his free hand, he pulled open the front of his robe and smiled.

Chapter 5

September 1941. German Jews are ordered to wear yellow stars.

IT WAS 108 degrees in the shade. With Russ standing at her side, Mariah sat in a rickety chair beneath a tattered canvas awning outside the Shuwaikh harbor master's office. A tired ceiling fan pushed stagnant air around the room. Flies lumbered in the heat.

The first of the water dhows arrived from the Shatt al-Arab River, seventy-five miles northeast along the southern border between Iran and Iraq. Handlers urged their white donkeys alongside to receive animal bladders and tins full of water, a cargo more precious than pearls.

"The seagoing dhows remind me of the angle-sailed feluccas of the Nile."

Mariah followed Russ's eyes as he watched the donkeys climb the beach. "They remind me how backward Kuwait is. How long can they keep importing water from Iraq?"

"But they can't afford a filtration plant." He turned his gaze to the *boums* and *battils*, the largest cargo ships on the Gulf, resting at anchor. The Kuwaitis imported everything from India, Iraq, and Iran. "How does a country exist without railroads, rivers, or paved roads?"

"Where are their cranes and berths? The Kuwaitis are so far behind their neighbors, they'll never catch up," Mariah said. "A few days ago, the foreign secretary told me, yet again, how oil will improve the life of every Kuwaiti. He's banking their future on oil."

"He's fighting an uphill battle given Kuwait's culture."

"Oh, he knows the tribes hate talk of constructing a water filtration plant, paving roads, and bringing in European oil technicians. 'Must stop the infidels from contaminating our religion and way of life' and all that. But he seems determined."

"Well, good luck to him. You know old traditions die hard in the Middle East."

She nodded. "Oil won't necessarily bring prosperity. The amir and his brother will find it hard to force modern times down the throats of a nomadic people."

The pair resumed their study of the scene. The din rose as the day's heat slowly subsided. Merchants shouted orders at stevedores while water sellers haggled with house servants who came to fill their containers. Russ mopped his brow and held his handkerchief by its corners to dry the sweat in the faint breeze.

"Miss McCarry, the ambassador's ship is here." Bassam, the Legation expeditor, pointed at a small steamship docking along the breakwater farther out from the dhows.

Stevedores and laborers jostled the two diplomats as they followed Bassam to the dock. The stench of shallow water mingled with the reek of animals and men hard at work under a sweltering sun. Mariah clung to Russ's arm as she stumbled over the uneven surface.

At the top of a gangplank, a tall gentleman appeared to disregard the frantic world around him. Duncan Milbourne III coolly considered Russ and then turned his gaze to Mariah. He descended the wooden walkway with deliberation. "Hello, Mariah. I hardly recognized you."

"Welcome to Kuwait, Mr. Ambassador. I hope your trip wasn't too taxing in this heat." Mariah flicked her fan a few times. "This is Mark Russell, your assistant."

Milbourne touched Russ's hand with his fingertips. "Hello, Mr. Russell. Have you arranged my reception for this evening?"

"Yes, sir. Everything is set. The guests will arrive at seven o'clock."

"Excellent. I'm sure it will be a pleasant evening." His lips approached a smile and settled into a frown when his gaze fell on the stains darkening the armpits of Russ's suit coat.

Mariah's cheeks flushed, and she wilted against Russ. "Shall we go?" She pointed the way toward the car. "Mr. Ambassador, won't Bitsy be joining you?"

A veil dropped across Milbourne's features. "She remained in Middleburg. She and her brothers have recently inherited the family business in Manhattan. They need to settle a host of matters with the company attorneys. Then she must ready our farm for the caretakers."

Milbourne looked around the harbor. "The long voyage here was merely tedious in earlier times, but now we must zigzag across the ocean from Miami to Cape Town to avoid hostile ships." He swept his arm across the scene. "All to get to this miserable little country!"

"We still have a role to play, even here in tiny Kuwait," Mariah said.

"Well, the Legation is about to undergo a major change." He smoothed his lapels. "I've been charged with one of the Allies' most critical operations, and Franklin has promised me plenty of support." At her doubtful look, he added, "I'll provide more details tomorrow at country team."

Over his shoulder, he asked, "How do you feel about the coming conflict, Mr. Russell?"

"We can't let Hitler and Mussolini make Europe their personal playground. Nor can we allow the Japanese to move across Asia from China." Russ strode on the balls of his feet in his enthusiasm. "I'm grateful that I can serve my country right now."

Pondering his assistant through narrowed eyes, Milbourne considered how to rein him in. This novice must not distract him from his diplomatic comeback.

Hassan, the chauffeur, bowed Milbourne into the limousine and then held the other rear door for Mariah. Russ slid into the front seat.

They moved slowly through the crowd surrounding the automobile. Except for the Al Sabah royal family and employees of the Kuwait Oil Company, most Kuwaitis moved about on horses, donkeys, and camels.

Milbourne shook his head. "How quickly one returns to the primitive life."

Glancing at Hassan, Mariah said, "You'll present your credentials to the amir at Dasman Palace the day after tomorrow. Have you met the amir?"

Milbourne shook his head. "Only his brother, who's now the foreign secretary, correct?"

"Yes. The amir is charming, but he remains very formal in his dealings with us."

"Like most Arabs. They chafe under the power we and the Brits hold. They assume they can manipulate us by wielding their oil potential."

Russ turned in the front seat. "They're certainly interested in improving their country by marketing their oil. But since the American and British oil workers have evacuated, that might be a moot point."

Hassan crept around pedestrians and donkey riders before turning onto Gulf Boulevard. Dust drifted through the baked air and settled on the limousine's occupants.

Later that evening, Russ climbed the driveway to the ambassador's residence. Despite a change of clothes, he was still rumpled and sweaty in the ninety-degree heat.

Mohammed bowed and smiled. "Mr. Ambassador is resting. His luggage is unpacked. All is okay."

Russ surveyed the rooms. A bartender arranged fruit juices and iced drinking water. The Americans and their guests would conform to Islamic law forbidding alcohol until the Kuwaitis departed. He moved on to the patio as the sun dipped behind the peak. Garden torches and a gentle breeze lent a tropical air to the reception. He recognized several waiters from previous functions. All were relatives or friends of Mohammed. He wandered into the entry hall, reading his notes from the back of an envelope.

"Good evening, Mr. Russell." Dressed to impress, Milbourne strolled down the stairs.

"Good evening, sir. Please call me Russ."

"I approve of your invitation list." Milbourne walked out to the patio. "I plan to make a good first impression with my guests tonight. When will my staff arrive?"

"In about fifteen minutes. As you greet the guests near the front door, Mariah will direct them to a table. Important guests will be escorted by a member of the staff."

"Should I be aware of potential difficulties with anyone on the list? I dislike surprises."

"No. The Kuwaitis are congenial, and they're ready for a strong American presence. They want the protection we offer their country and know we'll strive to keep their oil out of Axis hands. Politically, they're very astute."

"That's a good analysis, Russ. What's your specialty when you're not my assistant?"

"Political cone, sir. I strive to look at the big picture, even here in a country unknown to most Americans. After the war, it could become important in world affairs."

Opera music drifted across the patio as members of the American staff trickled in. Milbourne acknowledged them with a nod and turned to take up his place at the door.

"Hi there." Catherine Cushard touched Russ's arm. "Everything okay out here?"

"So far." He looked her over and smiled. "How do you stay so cool?"

"Talent." Her own smile flipped to a frown. "I'm going to check on George. I saw him heading for the liquor cabinet in the parlor."

Promptly at seven o'clock, a Mercedes saloon stopped before the entrance. The foreign secretary, Sheikh Abdullah Al-Jaber Al

Sabah, brother of Ahmad Al-Jaber Al Sabah, the amir of the State of Kuwait, stepped out. The sheikh was a burly six-footer with a bristly beard and skin burnished to the patina of saddle leather. Khalid Ali paused at the rear.

Milbourne extended his hand. "Welcome to my home, Excellency."

"Mr. Ambassador, thank you for inviting me."

"How is the health of the amir and his family?"

"My brother is a strong man, even after twenty years as leader of our country. He is eager to talk with you about your president's plans."

"I have much to tell him. Miss McCarry will show you to your table now."

The ambassador turned to his next guest. "Welcome. Have we met before?"

"No, Mr. Ambassador, I am Khalid Ali Al-Jaber Al Sabah, nephew of the amir. Welcome to our desert kingdom. You have an excellent staff, and I enjoy working with them."

"Those are kind words, Mr. Ali. One of my staff will escort you to a table."

"Thank you, but I'll walk over to talk with my friend Russ."

Milbourne observed Khalid and Russ until the next person in the reception line cleared his throat. He turned to greet a tall gentleman in his forties dressed in a Savile Row suit. He was accompanied by a small, rosy-skinned woman in a flowery dress.

"Alan Smythe, Mr. Ambassador." Bright eyes gazed at Milbourne from a bronzed face with deep-set wrinkles. "I'm His Majesty's Political Agent."

"Mr. Smythe, good of you to attend. Secretary Hull asked me to meet with you as soon as possible. Perhaps sometime in the next few days would be convenient?"

"I'm sure that can be arranged." Smythe turned. "This is my wife, Jane."

She offered her hand. "I'm so pleased to meet you, Mr. Ambassador. We really like your residence. It has the best view in town."

"Why, thank you, Mrs. Smythe. You and your husband are always welcome here." Jane lowered her eyes under Milbourne's gaze. "In fact, when my wife arrives, we'll enjoy dinner some evening and watch the changing colors on the Gulf."

"Oh, she didn't make the journey with you?" Jane asked.

Milbourne's smile tightened. "No, family matters detained her departure." He bent over the hand he held in his fingers. "When she arrives, I'll tell her to call on you first."

George Lander lounged in his shirtsleeves on a boulder behind the house, a Lucky Strike in one hand and a full tumbler in the other. A partial bottle of Scotch sat in the dirt.

He turned when he heard someone approach. "Ah, Catherine. Shouldn't you be welcoming our guests instead of snooping on me?"

"I was hoping for some fresh air." She waved away the cigarette smoke. "Why aren't you out front doing your dazzling imitation of an interested diplomat?"

"Yeah, right. I'm too tired to dazzle."

"That doesn't look like mango juice, George." She tilted her head toward his bottle.

"Scotland's finest single malt. Want a sip?" Lander blew smoke rings into the air.

"I'll pass." She leaned against the boulder. "Don't you want to meet the ambassador?"

"Nah, I already know all about him. I was his admin officer in Tunis back when."

"Ah, interesting. Will we be able to get along with him?"

"I'm going to get along with him! I can't get buried in another hellhole like Kuwait." Lander tossed back his Scotch. "I've got to make it work this time."

"You're off to a good start, George." She turned and sauntered off.

Khalid stood with Russ along the low wall surrounding the patio. "We may have found a new oil field in the western desert. Inshallah."

"That's good news." Russ leaned in to hear above the guests' chatter. "Where?"

"Twenty miles west of Kuwait City, on the dirt road to the oasis at Al Jahra, then forty more miles to the west of Ar Ruqʻī."

"Past Ar Ruqʻī? Isn't that part of the An Nafud wilderness held by Bedouin shepherds and other desert traders? Wait a sec, that's in Saudi Arabia! How can you explore on land that doesn't belong to Kuwait?"

Khalid laughed. "The House of Saud relies on our tribe, the Al Sabahs, to watch its northeastern lands. Those lands are a long way from their capital in Jeddah on the Red Sea. The Saudis appreciate our crossing into the desert past Ar Ruqʻī to report on the desert tribes."

"Reporting on desert tribes and taking oil from Saudi land are two entirely different matters." Russ lowered his voice. "Do they even know about the oil?"

"Not yet. It's desolate out there. The Saudis have concentrated on their oil fields farther inland and to the south." Khalid lowered his own voice. "I'll make it work."

After the last guest departed, Milbourne held up his hand. "Everyone, gather around me for a minute. Thank you for the success of my first social event. Your excellent contacts in the government and in the diplomatic community will benefit us in the days ahead."

Milbourne looked at Malcom Lodge. "Malcolm, please draft a cablegram to the Department discussing what we've learned tonight. Tomorrow morning, we'll have our first country team meeting at nine." He waved his hand. "That's all."

Lodge rolled his eyes at Russ. "Cocktail chatter. Think Washington's gonna care?"

Mariah joined them. "Make something up for me. My fever's back and I'm heading home."

In the den, Russ located a Paul Whiteman album featuring a young crooner named Bing Crosby. Through the window, he watched Doris Lander guide her unsteady husband down the driveway. He felt Catherine's arm slip around his waist and squeeze.

"Wait until you hear about my chat with ol' George."

Brisk footsteps fell on the flagstone leading to the room, and Catherine smoothly withdrew her arm.

"I hope I'm not interrupting." Milbourne raised an eyebrow. "What can I get you two to drink?" He jiggled his Scotch on the rocks.

"Same but no ice, sir." Russ turned to Catherine, who nodded. "And for her."

When the ambassador returned, he hoisted his tumbler. "Here's to the diplomats who may win the war in this unknown theater without firing a shot."

Catherine squared her shoulders. "Sir, I strongly believe we're up to any task you and the president may assign. We're Foreign Service professionals, and this is our job."

Russ smothered a grin. It was unwise to mess with Catherine in her patriotic mood.

Milbourne covered his own grin. "Let me assure you, Catherine, this post will figure in a complicated plan to help win the war."

She clicked her tumbler to Milbourne's, drained it, and handed it to Russ. "I'd like to chat all night, but tomorrow will be a busy day. Good night."

"She'll be an asset to the front office." Milbourne turned to Russ. "But Mariah concerns me. She's very competent, but she's much frailer than I remember."

"Yes, sir, she is. She's been fighting a bug for a long time. Maybe she'll be better soon."

Drinks in hand, the men strolled to the wall where glittering constellations held sway over Gulf Boulevard, the beach, and the Persian Gulf beyond.

Milbourne inhaled deeply. "Ah, the smells of the Middle East. Saltwater, dust, spices, coffee, and old leather. Sample the wind at each new post, Russ. Your memories will awaken each time you encounter the same smells."

Russ recalled a land far to the north. "Moscow had its own smells. Unfortunately, I recall cabbage, cigarettes, sausage, and unwashed bodies."

Milbourne forced a thin smile as he sipped his Scotch. "Kuwait isn't where I hoped to end my short-lived retirement. But the president called. He stressed the strategic importance of Kuwait to our allies. I hope all of you are up to the task ahead."

Russ sought inspiration in the bottom of his own glass. "Sir, the Legation has been a small operation with a limited portfolio. But I believe we can meet the president's expectations."

"We'll be getting some help, such as it is, with staff from other agencies." Milbourne frowned into the Scotch he swirled in his hand, then pushed off the wall. "Come in early tomorrow to prepare a short list of urgent items for country team. We'll review your job requirements, say at four o'clock."

"Certainly, sir."

Milbourne raised his eyes to the stars. "The next year will test us all."

"I'm ready to help our country, even if we're a long way from a battlefield."

"You might be surprised to learn how close we may come to a battlefield."

A gust of wind trailed up the rocks from the waters below.

Chapter 6

September 1941. Nationals from Axis countries are ordered to leave Iran.

CATHERINE WALTZED INTO the office suite to the clatter of typewriter keys. "Good morning, Russ, you're here early." Her eyes widened. "And you're typing?"

Russ squared up his papers. "Yes, I know it's shocking, but this is a list of post issues for the ambassador's review before country team."

"Ha! Did you include a rest and recuperation trip away from this broiler?" She tapped a finger to her chin. "Give me a minute and I'll think of more."

"It's supposed to be short. Your list would run to several pages!" He smiled innocently.

She mimicked his smile and then shook her fist at him.

Mariah strode in, and Russ handed her the list. "Not my choices, but it'll do."

"You're still pale. Are you any better?" Catherine stood to the side as Mariah hung up her hijab and opened her safe.

"Not really." She handed her mug to Catherine. "I'm not up to briefing a new ambassador, but it's got to be done."

Catherine cradled the mug. "Russ and I will help. Don't try to do everything yourself."

"Thanks." Mariah touched Catherine's hand. "I don't know how much longer I can last with this damned bug."

Milbourne strolled toward his office. A mahogany desk and a stunning silk rug from the Iranian town of Qom dominated the room. A private bathroom was tucked into one corner, and French doors opened onto a balcony with a view of the Persian Gulf.

"Was Hassan there on time, sir?" Russ stood just inside the office.

"Yes. We had a nice drive in. George Lander met me at the door, but not Mariah."

"Sir, Mariah arrived just a few minutes ago. She's still not feeling well."

"Well, she better mend quickly." Milbourne came around his desk. "Ah, Catherine. Your position is particularly important to a smooth-running front office. You needn't come every week, but I'd like you at the country team this morning to hear what I have to say."

"Of course, sir. I'm very curious about our new mission."

Milbourne checked his watch. "Do you have my list of post issues?" He took the document from Russ. "Ceiling fans and staff housing: Lander issues. The Dalton visit: discuss with Mariah. Delay of consular officer Burton: old news." His finger stopped. "Post security: an important topic for country team." He nodded at Russ. "Good work. Shall we?"

When Mariah fell in beside them, Milbourne gave her a measured look. "Any better?"

"No, but the work won't wait until I'm well."

Country team was the weekly meeting of section chiefs held in every Foreign Service post around the world. Milbourne took his place at the head of the table. Russ stood with Catherine along the wall.

"Good morning, everyone. Please be seated. Let's quickly go around the table. Remind me if we've met before. Unless your section has an urgent issue, I'll use this time to tell you about my meetings with the president and Secretary Hull." He nodded toward Lodge.

"Malcolm Lodge, Political/Economics. We met when I was on the secretary's staff, and you worked on the Palestine desk."

Milbourne nodded. "Certainly, I remember."

"George Lander. I was your administrative officer in Tunis."

"Thanks, George. Those were good years."

Lodge shifted his bulk to gaze at Lander.

"Captain Kimball, Military Attaché. I'd rather be on the high seas, sir, but I'm making the best of it here."

Milbourne nodded to a tall, slender Yalie with a mop of blond hair.

"Sir, Radley Spencer, COI. I look forward to this opportunity. May we talk later?"

Milbourne frowned. "I'll get to you in the coming days after I meet with my regular staff. My secretary will call to set up a convenient time.

"Well, Mariah, have you anything to say to this distinguished gathering?"

"No, Mr. Ambassador. I'd like to hear about our expanded duties."

"Very well. In August, I met with the president, Secretary Hull, and the top officials in the War Department, COI, and Navy. I'll summarize those consultations."

Milbourne opened a leather binder.

"Last month, the president and Prime Minister Churchill met in Placentia Bay, Newfoundland. They reviewed an extensive list of issues related to our entry into the war.

"As part of aid to the Allies, we will deliver military supplies to the Soviets. Our ships will steam past the Cape of Good Hope, sail through the Indian Ocean and the Arabian Sea, and proceed up the Persian Gulf to Iran. The supplies will be offloaded and transported to the Soviets via the Iranian railway or by truck overland."

Milbourne barely glanced at his notes before continuing.

"It's our mission to support and protect that supply corridor. We'll secure the lands on both sides of the Gulf and the waters from the Strait of Hormuz to the ports of Iran and Iraq. Our concerns will be Nazi commerce raiders and U-boats patrolling the Gulf as well as Axis sympathizers who live along its shores."

Milbourne looked at each of their faces. "Against the horrors of a war already gripping Europe, we're but a small outpost of the Foreign Service. We might be forced to evacuate if the Axis powers draw near. Our labors might never reach fruition. Let's make sure that the fault for failure lies with others, not with us.

"The president and Secretary Hull, along with COI's Colonel Donovan and Secretary of War Stimson, will support me in any way they can. But for now, I must make do with the resources that already exist here."

The ambassador turned to a new section in his presentation binder.

"Captain Kimball, you'll be responsible for monitoring the entire Gulf. Mr. Spencer, COI will monitor the land approaches to the ports at the head of the Gulf. You'll need assets along our side of the Gulf, plus the entire southern coast of Iran. That's roughly one thousand miles." Milbourne glared at Kimball and Spencer. "I hope you two are up to this task. We'll coordinate with a new British SIS man on recruiting resources in this region."

Pausing once again, Milbourne drew a deep breath. "This Legation has been designated a hardship post. You'll earn that extra pay. We may have to revert to living on the local economy. I want this to be perfectly clear. We're in for a long, hard pull."

Catherine reached for Russ's hand along the side of their chairs. She turned in his direction and bit her lower lip.

Milbourne continued. "We're in a war, even if it's undeclared. Monitor your conversations, especially in front of local employees. Be alert to your surroundings, both at the office and at home. Report any suspicious activity immediately to George or the marines."

He turned to Lander. "We must review our security measures, particularly document security. How many security violations have there been in the last few months?"

Lander's head jerked up. "Three in July, four in August, and two already this month."

"Too many." Milbourne's eyes snapped. "Either you're not paying attention, or you've lost your mental discipline. I will not tolerate it!" Milbourne's fist thumped the table. "George, stop by my office to discuss protection of our secrets and duty officer responsibilities. We must be ready for telephone calls from Washington or visits from walk-ins."

Milbourne stood. "Questions?" He closed his binder and strode from the room.

Lodge turned to Russ and Catherine. "Like that performance? He's good at demanding the most from us while making himself look good." He shook his head. "Lander positively glowed when Milbourne recalled Tunis."

"Yeah, I saw you move to the edge of your chair to get a better look at him."

Catherine sighed. "If George and the ambassador are old pals, we might as well give up on having our homes repaired."

Lodge paused in the hallway. "Come to me if you have trouble, like with the Dalton visit. Document everything you do." He held Russ's arm. "I'll support you in any way I can. I'm sure you'll do fine, but if you have a question, ask me, not Milbourne."

Back at the front office, Mariah was seated in front of Milbourne's desk while Catherine stood behind her, clutching her steno pad.

"I understand, Mariah. But I've decided to present my credentials to the amir first, followed by a meeting with Alan Smythe at the British Political Agency."

"Fine. Who'll accompany you to the palace?"

"How about just you and me? Malcolm has enough to do."

"A woman at court may not be the image you want to present tomorrow. Besides, I'm not sure I could handle a court visit."

Milbourne leveled a gaze in her direction. "Remember, you'll be the chargé d'affaires in my absence. Never feel you can't do your job in this country because you're a woman. However, in this instance, I'll defer to you."

Russ walked into view. "Sir, perhaps I could be of assistance. I've been to the palace."

Milbourne looked up. "Come in. Was it a presentation of credentials ceremony?"

"No, sir, but I'd certainly enjoy that experience." Russ stood next to Catherine. "I've met the amir. He's an imposing figure with the regal bearing of a leader. I think you'll like him."

"Your visit was an official call, then?"

"Not really, although I went with your predecessor." Catherine and Mariah turned. "In brief, I rescued Khalid Ali, who was in a motorcar accident. You met him last evening. The amir thanked me with a gift. That was about it." Russ studied his shoes.

"Always take credit for your accomplishments, especially helping a member of the royal family." Milbourne tidied the papers on his desk. "Well then, it'll be you and me. Have Hassan put a shine on the car before we leave for the palace.

"Catherine, we'll meet at three o'clock today to work up your job requirements statement for your evaluation. Mariah, we'll do yours on another day.

"And Mariah, I will address the locals. Let's say the day after tomorrow at three o'clock here in the lobby. Then I'll meet the American staff and their families at the residence about five with a small buffet on the patio afterwards." He spun the dial on his safe. "Well, I'm off to my residence for lunch. I'll be back about two."

Chapter 7

September 1941. FDR orders the U.S. Navy to protect merchant ships from Axis vessels.

"Well, he likes a schedule." Russ leaned against Catherine's desk. "What'd you think?"

She tapped her pencil. "He knows his job. But he needs to relax. He's too intense."

"Maybe he's just trying to impress us on the first day. Malcolm told me to be careful since he does everything to his advantage. And I know he doesn't like surprises. Everything must be choreographed." Russ shrugged. "We'll see. Want something from the snack bar?"

"No, thanks. I brought my lunch today."

"Okay. I left my safe open. Remember, security."

"I'll be here, cutie." She blew him a kiss.

Russ walked down to the dungeon of a basement. Bare bulbs in metal baskets lit the gloomy corridor. Paint peeled on the walls. Grease fumes tainted the air.

The galley kitchen consisted of two refrigerators and one freezer. They struggled against intermittent power outages to keep the food from spoiling. Six small tables, faded posters of American national parks, and a weary ceiling fan defined the dining area. Ossama, the chief cook, and Ali, his helper, were the sum of the staff.

The menu leaned heavy on Middle Eastern and American dishes. Baklava and local bakery bread rounded out the offerings. Still, the prices were reasonable.

While Russ waited in line, he made eye contact with Radley Spencer, the COI officer, who pointed to an empty chair. Russ nodded and turned to place his order at the open window.

Ossama wiped his hands on his greasy apron, adjusted his paper hat, and shifted the cigarette dangling from his mouth. "The meat loaf is very good today."

Russ added a cucumber salad and a slice of hot bread before joining Spencer.

"Interesting meeting, huh? Get the impression he doesn't consider COI part of his operation?" Spencer grinned.

"Yeah, there's his staff and then there's you and Kimball. Too bad." Russ tested his meat loaf. "You've been here a few weeks, Radley, and I've hardly seen you."

"Busy organizing office space and other stuff. Please, call me Trick."

"Trick, huh? Where'd that come from?"

"When I was a kid, I had a sweet tooth. Halloween was my favorite day of the year."

Russ chuckled. "How do you plan to secure both coasts?"

Spencer ran a visual sweep of the room. "Not sure. It's a vast area. Maybe my new deputy, Trent Hedges, will have some ideas. He arrives next month.

"To be honest, I'm still figuring out my job. COI's a brand-new agency, so we need to succeed or we'll remain poor cousins to you guys in the overseas business. If we falter, we'll get less funding, less trust in our product."

Around a mouthful, Russ said, "We need an agency like yours. If I can help, you know where to find me."

"Thanks." Spencer grinned again. "I might need you to run interference for us. Some stations are having trouble with ambassadors. Milbourne seems to be that kind."

"Surely he'll cooperate. He wants the work done."

Spencer wiped his mouth and nodded toward the door. "Let's go for a walk."

The COI man reminded Russ of Rhonda and Moscow. Always guarding his conversation and looking around. He wondered if Rhonda had been hired by the new COI.

"About office space. I'm on the second floor, but I need a Dutch door at the hall so no one can walk in unannounced." Spencer stuck his hands in his pockets. "And a small darkroom."

"You develop photos?"

"Part of the business. Any suggestions?"

"Sure. There's a closet on Malcolm's side of the hall."

"Perfect, because on paper I'll work for Lodge. Trent will be in consular."

"Piece of advice." Russ slowed. "Don't tell George Lander about the darkroom."

Russ headed toward the rear entrance. "I need to pick up a few office supplies for the ambassador." He saw Spencer bite down on a smile. "Yeah, I know. Glorified errand boy."

At the corner of the building, Russ stopped. Just ahead, a man smoked a cigarette on the back step while he bent his head to another man standing below him.

"Mehmet and Ali whispering together."

Spencer peered over Russ's shoulder. "Is that an odd pair?"

"Well, as the big boss under Lander, Mehmet supervises all GSO local employees. He would normally never bother with a guy as lowly as Ali, a mere assistant cook." Russ snapped his fingers. "Hold on. Mehmet was at the residence last week. I assumed he was with Lander, but now I wonder if he was waiting until I was done with Mohammed, the residence manager."

"So, what could the three of them have in common?"

"Ali does extra duty in a storeroom next to Mehmet's office in the warehouse." Russ scratched his head. "We store commissary items there. And our booze."

They watched Mehmet slip a piece of paper to Ali before he

returned to the warehouse. Ali tossed his cigarette butt into the flower bed and disappeared through the rear door.

Spencer and Russ rounded the corner. "So, Russ, what did we just see?"

"I'm not sure, but I bet it involves that storeroom."

"If you think something fishy is going on, I could run record checks on those two."

"No, their chat may be entirely innocent. And we're supposed to report any suspicious activity to Lander. I don't want to involve him in something that could be harmless."

"Part of my job is counterespionage, the protection of the staff from internal spies."

Russ chewed on his lower lip. "Okay, but let's hide our real interest in Mehmet and Ali with a routine check on all the locals. It probably hasn't been done for a while. You can get the list from Lander but whatever you do, don't mention my name."

"I'll be careful," Spencer said. "I'll also run the names with the police."

"You have liaison with the police? I thought that was Lander's job."

"He does the criminal police while I do Special Branch at the Interior Ministry."

❦

Hassan dropped Milbourne at the residence. Lander was already standing on the patio with a drink in hand. "Mr. Ambassador, the morning meeting went well. You haven't lost your touch."

"Why, thank you, George. It's been a while since Tunis."

Over lunch, Milbourne quizzed Lander. "Are my staff up to the responsibility given to them by the president?"

Lander raised his eyes as if seeking biographic material from the heavens. "Lodge is stoic, but capable. Kimball's good with languages and likes meeting his local counterparts. Spencer's some sort of East

Coast preppie, too young for the job. Catherine's perfect for the front office, although a bit feisty at times."

Milbourne sat back as Mohammed appeared with a kitchen cart stacked with fresh fruit, lamb, and rice. After opening a bottle of French Beaujolais, he placed a basket of hot bread next to the gilt-edged chinaware embossed with the seal of the Legation. Then he disappeared.

Milbourne raised his goblet. "Remember, your priority is this residence, followed by the office building. My assistant placed staff work orders on his list of talking points for the country team. I don't want to hear about those kinds of things. I'm sick of whiners at my posts."

Lander sipped his wine. "Yes, sir."

The ambassador leaned in. "I want this post to run like clockwork. That means you'll have to watch the bottle. You can't afford another Tunis."

"Tunis is behind me." Lander pushed his peas around his plate. "You'll see."

"At least Bitsy stayed home this time."

Lander waited while Mohammed served coffee and baklava. "When's the new consular officer arriving? I'm covering that section right now."

"Piper Burton's on a medical hold. When the other COI guy, Hedges, arrives next month, he'll be under consular cover. He can take over for you then." The ambassador pushed away his dessert plate. "Tell me about Russell."

Lander frowned. "Well, he's not East Coast."

"You're from Columbus, Ohio, George. Not the sort the Foreign Service dotes on."

"True, true." Lander swallowed. "Russ is full of energy, always looking for work to make his evaluation look better. But he gets under my skin. He's there in the front office, right in the middle of things, but he holds himself apart. Not much of a team player."

"You're one to talk. You come to social functions only when you're forced to."

"I guess Russ is friendly with Lodge and some of the marines, but only them."

"What about women?"

"Dunno. I don't get out much." At Milbourne's raised eyebrow, Lander sighed. "Okay, there's no women as far as I can tell. Catherine's too old for him." He scratched his head. "There's a secretary at the British Political Agency and a few gals from the American oil companies. But they've been evacuated." He shrugged. "There's really little to choose from out here in this big sandbox."

Milbourne stirred his coffee. "He's certainly enthusiastic. Mariah said he volunteered for the Dalton CODEL. What do you know about him and the palace?"

"There was something about a royal kid last year, maybe a car wreck." Lander shrugged again. "He never talks about it, so I'd guess that was the end of it."

The ambassador stood and looked down at Lander. Memories flashed through his mind. *George knows about Tunis. Mariah knows about Baghdad.* He smiled. He had enough information on both to keep them in line. Knowledge was power.

"Remember, George, you take care of me, and I'll take care of you." Milbourne turned on his heel and left.

Lander fell against the chair and reached for the last of the Beaujolais.

⸙

Lander turned onto Gulf Boulevard and sped along in a hot breeze. Milbourne hadn't changed. His memories of Tunisia might be blurry, but he knew he hadn't been drinking alone. Milbourne had been right there with him. Did Milbourne remember how he lusted for Bitsy?

If Milbourne got testy like in Tunis, Lander knew enough to protect himself. The old reprobate would not blackmail him this time. Knowledge was power.

Chapter 8

September 1941. Twenty-six crew members perish when a U.S. freighter is torpedoed in the Atlantic.

CATHERINE SHOT RUSS a smug look when she strutted from Milbourne's office.

"Please come in, Russ." In a concession to the heat, Milbourne had removed his suit jacket. Even though Russ had rolled his sleeves to the elbow, he sweated through his shirt.

"Catherine and I finished a little early, so let's get started. I like to discuss staff responsibilities as soon as I arrive. You have rather a unique job as my assistant."

"Yes, sir. I'm more of a generalist than a specialist."

"Exactly. By being available for anything, you provide more value to the mission."

Russ nodded. "I'll do anything to advance my career."

Milbourne leaned back in his chair. "That's admirable."

"I wasn't promoted in Moscow. This is my last chance if I'm to stay in the service."

"I see. What happened in Moscow?"

Russ hesitated. Milbourne probably knew Preston Pierson, the DCM in Moscow, and maybe Horace Wyman, the Political Section chief. He'd be honest but avoid mentioning Rhonda.

"I needed to improve my report writing. But I had some successes, like handling visits by the secretary of state and several senators. To be blunt, I was robbed."

"No one likes to recall their shortcomings; just don't repeat your mistakes here. If you're careful, I assure you your evaluation will reflect what you've earned."

"That sounds fair." Russ put his steno pad on his knee.

"You'll work in the classified area of security for the supply line from now on. To cover this work, we must use unclassified language. So, we'll add the phrase 'and other sensitive duties as directed by the chief of mission' to your job requirements. Okay?"

"Certainly, sir." Russ nodded with enthusiasm.

"And finally, you'll report on local issues that fall outside the purview of the other sections. That could include shipbuilding, water filtration, and medical care. Being a control officer for visits will let you prove yourself beyond being my assistant.

"I gave one of your old jobs, organizing receptions, to Catherine." Russ glanced up. "That doesn't reflect on your work last night, which was quite good. But from now on, you'll plan whom to invite and why, not how much juice to order."

The muezzin began his afternoon call to prayer, and Milbourne stood. "Let's move to the chairs on my balcony and enjoy the cooling air while we continue. What do you want to discuss?"

Russ took a deep breath. "Well, sir, I'd like to research Kuwait's petroleum and how U.S. companies could obtain future concessions."

"Our primary mission is protection of the supply line. The president's only interest in oil is preventing the Axis powers from getting it."

"But when the war is over, oil will flow in earnest. Kuwait won't make improvements without oil revenue. Buying their oil will help both our countries."

"I see." Milbourne tilted his chair back. "How would you do it?"

"I'm not sure. The American companies evacuated their employees. What's left is a refinery at Al Ahmadi for gasoline and some lubricating oils. Just local use."

"So, what's to report?"

"I have a source inside KOC who's trying to reach me." Russ leaned forward. "I think there's something going on in the desert."

Milbourne lowered his chair. "Who's your source?"

"Khalid Ali, the man I told you about this morning, the one in the car wreck. Khalid's the director of research for KOC. Some say he's the future of Kuwait's oil industry. He's also the amir's nephew."

Milbourne inhaled sharply. *So, Lander's wrong. Russ has a strong connection to the palace. Khalid Ali would know everything that goes on over there. Now, how to use Russ's inside information to enhance my impact as ambassador?*

"Your contact with Mr. Ali could benefit our mission. I'll tell Malcolm you'll be covering oil."

Milbourne rose and walked to his credenza. "Want a drink?"

"Scotch and water, sir."

Milbourne passed a tumbler to Russ. "Tell me how you came into the Foreign Service."

"After college, I worked at Commerce for a year. I passed the Foreign Service exam in '35, and I've had assignments in the Department and in Moscow."

Catherine stepped onto the patio. "I'm leaving. Mariah called to say she'll try again tomorrow. Do you need anything else?"

"No, enjoy the rest of your day. Are we locked up?"

"All the safes are secure, sir, except the two of yours. The marine will be in shortly."

Milbourne stepped into his office and placed a few documents in his inbox. He put the box in his two-drawer safe and scanned for classified material. "I lock up in the same manner each evening, Russ, especially when I'm in a hurry." He spun the dial on his safe.

He returned to the balcony and sipped his Scotch. "My experience was a bit different. My father was career Foreign Service, so I grew up in many countries. I studied international relations, French, and Arabic at William and Mary before getting my master's in Arabic and Middle Eastern Studies at the University of Virginia.

Later I took advanced Arabic at the American University in Beirut. Now I'm retired on a horse farm in Northern Virginia."

The muted chatter of the Legation employees rose to the balcony as they strolled out the main gate. A breeze riffled the palm fronds, cooling an ancient land seared by the summer sun.

"It must have been hard to leave retirement to come here." Russ tasted his Scotch.

"Well, the president values loyalty. He places his friends in positions of power so he can receive the unvarnished assessments he favors." Milbourne sighed. "I told Bitsy I'd come out of retirement only for the assistant secretary job in NEA. But when the commander in chief asks, it's hard to look him in the eye and refuse. To be honest, I'm not sure I made the right decision."

The marine knocked on the door. "Ready for the evening security inspection, sir?"

"We'll be done shortly." Milbourne checked his wristwatch. "Come back in a few minutes."

He knocked back his Scotch. "Well, we have the palace presentation tomorrow morning and the meeting with the Brits after lunch."

"Of course, sir. Anything else?"

"Have Hassan devote more time to the interior of my limousine. I don't appreciate having to brush dust from my suits."

Russ glanced at the clutter spread across his desk. Time to better organize his tiny space. He dropped into his chair and watched the marine start his inspection while he thought about the details of securing a thousand miles of coastline bordering three countries. Grabbing a pencil, he jotted down a few ideas about who would be involved, equipment required, command structure. Studying an area map pasted to his wall, he circled the great wasteland of the An Nafud Desert. Tapping his pencil against his notepad, he finished off his Scotch. Then he sighed and tossed his pad in the safe and spun the dial. He needed to let the muddle of questions settle before tackling them again. Kuwait was no longer an insignificant country on the edge of nowhere.

Chapter 9

*September 1941. British RAF fliers arrive in Archangel
to train Soviet pilots on Hurricane fighters.*

With less than a quarter of an hour before the new ambassador was set to arrive, Khalid Ali had to present his uncles with a well-reasoned summary. They had listened so far, but he could tell they were unconvinced. He paused in his pacing and faced them.

"Uncle Abdullah, you spent a small fortune to educate me at Oxford. I learned much about oil, oil research, oil refining, and oil marketing. I'm good at what I do. You've trusted me to manage our oil industry thus far. But I can't bring our country into the future without more financial resources. Simply put, I cannot make money without having money to invest."

"Khalid, Khalid, we've been over and over this," the foreign minister said, his voice rising. "You know I keep a careful eye on our country's finances, and you know that our treasury is nearly without funds. I must keep our schools running, our roads in repair, our water importation…" He stopped at the amir's calming wave of a hand.

"What my brother is trying to say, Khalid, is we hear you and we understand. But you must also appreciate that I rule with the trust and compliance of the many tribes that make up this country.

Many of the tribal chiefs would balk at cooperating with European infidels and resist moving Kuwait into a more modern system of banking and governance. They still live a nomadic life with their tents and camels. They care little for schools, roads, and ports. I can't risk a confrontation over my rule."

Khalid resumed his pacing while his uncles sat back in their chairs. "I understand your tenuous position with the old men clinging to the old ways. I do, Uncle, I do. But I've lived in the Western world and seen how it works. We can do so much better for Kuwait."

Again, he stopped pacing and spread his hands in a final appeal. "Today you'll meet the president of the United States' personal representative. Please consider broaching the topic of our treasury situation and our future in oil. That's all I'm asking." Khalid dropped his hands. "Please."

With a final glance at the clock, the amir and foreign minister of Kuwait stood. "We will assess the ambassador and decide what to do." With a glance at his brother, Ahmad Al-Jaber Al Sabah, amir of Kuwait, said, "Agreed?"

Sheikh Abdullah Al-Jaber Al Sabah nodded.

"Thank you, Uncles." Khalid bowed his head and retreated.

⁂

The U.S. flag fluttered from the fender of the limousine as it stopped at the entrance to Dasman Palace. Milbourne nodded to the amir's private secretary, who led them to a small parlor where a waiter presented a sterling silver tray with glasses of guava juice.

The door opened. "Gentlemen, the amir will see you now."

They passed through teak doors that resembled the planks of a dhow. The amir and the foreign secretary stood. "Mr. Ambassador, welcome to my home."

"Excellency, thank you for inviting me to your beautiful residence. Your hospitality will be long remembered. And how is the health of your family?"

"They are very well, pray to Allah. And your family, Mr. Ambassador?"

"Excellency, they are also in good health."

"I believe you know my brother, Sheikh Abdullah." The amir gestured to the foreign secretary. "It is important to find work for family members, even if it is only a lowly government job." He chuckled with the deep voice of a big man.

Milbourne gave a tense smile. "I'm sure this strong man is capable of handling any position you choose to offer him."

The amir took Russ's hand in both of his. "Mr. Russell, you're always welcome in the house of Al Sabah."

"Thank you, Excellency. You are kind to receive me today."

The amir gestured to low divans before turning toward Milbourne. "Mr. Ambassador, your Mr. Russell saved my nephew from certain death last year. We know the story from your Bible of the Samaritan who helped a traveler on the side of the road. Mr. Russell behaved like your Samaritan. Allah says He will provide if we believe in Him. My nephew is a true believer, and Allah sent Mr. Russell to protect him." The amir smiled once more in Russ's direction.

Russ reddened as he gauged Milbourne's reaction.

"Excellency, Mr. Russell learned lessons of personal behavior while young. I'll instill in him the lessons of the world of diplomacy. They're not always the same."

The amir blinked and slid his eyes toward his brother, who picked up the ceremony.

"Mr. Ambassador, it is our tradition to offer food and drink to all travelers. Today, we welcome you from the United States, our ally against the demons of fascism." The sheikh reached for the *ibrik*, the distinctive brass pot with a spout shaped like the curved beak of a bird.

Milbourne cued Russ to hand him the lambskin portfolio. "If it is convenient, Excellency, I'd like to present my credentials." He passed the portfolio to the amir.

The amir read with deliberation and raised his eyes. "Your president is concerned for the welfare of all peoples, rich and poor. As a world leader, Mr. Roosevelt faces immense troubles every day. I have read many of his speeches and believe he is a modern-day Samaritan."

"The president has never wavered in his support for the unfortunate, either in our country or in the Middle East. He understands that friends often need a helping hand."

"Well said." The sheikh nodded with approval.

"With your permission, Excellency, I'll read to you a letter from the president."

Excellency, I send these greetings with my representative to your court, Duncan Milbourne III. He is an experienced emissary and a trusted friend. In recognition of the importance of your beautiful country to the return of world peace, I have elevated his rank from minister to ambassador. I trust this will meet with your approval.

With hostilities raging in Europe, North Africa, and the Far East, the Axis forces could march toward your country from many directions. Although I pray we'll never fight a defensive battle on your land, the Allied powers will support and protect your country.

We plan to supply the armies of the Soviet Union with war matériel to help them maintain a strong Eastern Front. I have charged my diplomatic personnel in your country with securing the supply channel to the Soviets. We must vigilantly monitor land and sea approaches to the ports of Iran. With your cooperation, we will increase the size of our Legation staff. But we will need your assistance in our protection plans. Ambassador Milbourne will meet with you in the coming weeks and will convey your excellent ideas to me.

I extend hearty good wishes for today and for the future. May Allah bless our joint endeavors against the forces of evil.
Sincerely,
Franklin D. Roosevelt

"Excellencies, the president holds strong beliefs in the rights of all men to live free from fear and want and aggression."

The amir placed the president's letter on a silver tray, and the sheikh resumed the lead.

"Mr. Ambassador, we have heard the Allied powers wish to seal the oil wells of the region to prevent an Axis takeover. Do you know these reports?"

"Yes, I do. Possession of your petroleum would embolden General Rommel's Wehrmacht, or even the armies of the emperor of Japan. Since the enemy is only fifteen hundred miles away as the falcon flies, I strongly recommend that the wells be plugged now, rather than trying to accomplish the task with the enemy at your door."

The amir stroked his beard while the sheikh continued. "We're a poor country in dire need of revenue to modernize life for our people. Our trading and commerce will suffer if the battles come closer. If you plug our wells, we will face unbelievable hardship."

"Excellency, death and destruction are but a few of the perils faced by many countries. Kuwait is fortunate to have escaped these. The Allies in London will expect your cooperation in denying oil to the Axis forces." Milbourne's jaw tightened. "Besides, how can you maintain production after the evacuation of the European oil workers?"

The sheikh's face darkened. "We'll focus on a few wells in the Burgan field. We'll supply ourselves and sell limited amounts to support the Allies. We must keep the wells open."

The men glared at each other. Russ cleared his throat. "Excellencies, Ambassador Milbourne has asked me to monitor the progress of your oil industry. I know he does not wish to offend your hospitality by spending so much time on a technical question." He glanced at Milbourne. "With the ambassador's permission, I have a suggestion."

Milbourne's eyes narrowed. "Please proceed, Mr. Russell."

"Perhaps Khalid and I can meet to discuss the various solutions. After we've studied the matter, we can present our recommendations to the three of you. Inshallah."

"An excellent suggestion, Mr. Russell. My nephew will welcome this opportunity. You and Khalid are the future leaders of our countries. I trust you will offer a good resolution to our concerns. Perhaps now we may talk of more pleasant topics. Brother, what do you say?"

The sheikh waved his hand. "A lowly clerk is not permitted to speak for the court."

When the amir smiled, Milbourne exhaled. "Mr. Russell has expressed my exact thoughts. Proper guests should not be concerned with problems best handled by two young aides who need experience in solving such issues. We'll await their report."

Russ stared at Milbourne in astonishment, then lowered his eyes.

"More refreshment?" The amir gestured to the fruit and cheese. "Mr. Ambassador, when the weather cools, please join me for a trip into the desert. Looking at the stars is one way I relieve the strains of my job. We'll both need this relaxation soon."

Wiping away the distaste that wrinkled his brow, Milbourne struggled with a smile. "I would be honored, Excellency. You're kind to invite me."

"Very well." The amir rose. "Thank you for the letter from Mr. Roosevelt."

As Russ followed Milbourne to the limousine, Khalid stepped next to him and said, "I have no time to talk right now. I'll call you later about coming to my *diwaniya*."

"Well, that ended rather abruptly." Milbourne took a deep breath as the limousine pulled away. "We'll try the diplomatic way to resolve this issue, but the U.S. is in control here. While I appreciate your effort to resolve the impasse, Kuwait will do what is best for the Allies. The time will come when they realize that."

He smoothed his lapels. "On another topic, you led me to believe that your interaction with the palace was brief and incidental. Now I witness the warm greetings the amir bestowed upon you. Do not deceive me in the future. What did Khalid want?"

"He's going to call me. That's all I know." Russ turned to face

Milbourne. "I didn't deceive you about the palace. I told you I had been there with McNulty one time. I have no relation with the amir or the sheikh, only with Khalid. If you wish, I'll take up the oil well issue with Khalid. Otherwise, I'll step away from oil and the palace."

Milbourne turned hooded eyes to his assistant. "Nice speech. Continue with the discussion of plugging the wells. Don't botch it. I'll not be made a fool in this two-bit country."

The ambassador turned away from Russ, and they continued to the Legation in silence.

An hour later, the amir fingered his lustrous string of worry beads. They reminded him of simpler times, when pearl divers supplied the jewelry merchants with a bountiful harvest. He turned when Khalid entered the room.

"How was the meeting, Uncle?"

"Not good, I'm afraid. Unlike the amiable Mr. Russell, Mr. Milbourne is unpleasant. We wish to avoid conflict with the United States and its allies, but we'll not tolerate subjugating ourselves to another power, especially through such a disagreeable lackey."

"I'm sorry to hear that. What can I do to assist you?"

"Mr. Russell proposed that you work with him to find a solution about plugging our wells." He held Khalid's gaze. "Can we trust Mr. Russell?"

"Absolutely. Russ never asks anything from me. He's sensible and smart."

"We must protect our security in these dangerous times. There are many who would do us harm." The amir fingered his beads. "My brother agrees that the new ambassador isn't someone to count on. I'll not endure another meeting with that man until you've better assessed the situation with Mr. Russell."

Khalid inclined his head. "Uncle Ahmad, thank you for your trust."

"I'm sorry to say we didn't discuss our finances with Mr. Milbourne today. Once we saw his disdain for Kuwait, we withheld our appeal. I'll not subject myself to his ridicule or put my brother in the control of the United States through this man."

"Am I to understand that you wish me to also discuss a loan with Russ?"

"Yes. A monthly loan from the United States. We're risking much by trusting an infidel, Khalid. Guard against your regard for Mr. Russell. It can lead you into a position of weakness. We cannot have the ambassador telling untruths to Mr. Roosevelt."

Khalid took a deep breath. "About the oil seep."

The amir bristled. "This is not a good day to persist in this matter."

"But it's pertinent to all we've discussed. I investigated our agreement with our Saudi brothers. Nothing is written about the neutral area. If I approach them in the right way, I believe they'll be unconcerned if we drill some exploratory wells there. I'll sweeten the request by offering to report on the tribes that wander that area and present the results to the Saudis." Khalid inclined his head. "With your permission, of course."

For the first time since early morning, a smile broke out on the amir's face. "Of course."

"Thank you. I'm eager to begin. We're losing too much time."

"Please restrain your exuberance, Khalid. Be patient."

"The world is an impatient place. We can't have the sands of time shift below us."

"Remember, we're still a British protectorate. They control our foreign affairs and our oil company. We must not offend them." The amir clicked his worry beads.

"But the Americans are deeply involved with our oil now. We need to reinforce their interest in purchasing from us."

"That's why the man President Roosevelt sent to us disheartens me so. Wendell Fox will say the same thing."

"About Fox." Khalid wiped a hand across his face.

"Stop! I hear enough about him from my brother."

"As you wish, but you know I'm concerned where his loyalties lie. Remember your own advice to me about Russ. Don't let your regard for another cloud your judgment of him."

"Enough." The worry beads disappeared into the amir's robes.

Khalid stood to leave, then paused and turned back. "About the British protectorate. Most of my college professors supported the British colonial system, but a few believed their empire was a symbol of a bygone era. In the peace, the predominant power may be the one without a costly empire. That is America, not Britain. The United States will need our oil more and will pay the better price."

"Yes, yes, my brother says the same. And we must consider our Arab brothers. Once Allah blesses us with oil, will he also curse us with aggressive neighbors? The desert is a vast and dangerous place."

Across the courtyard, a sudden gust of wind created a small dust devil. The amir shifted in his chair. "Allah sends a strong message to beware. The swirling winds of turmoil have begun to churn in the minds of men."

Chapter 10

September 1941. Kiev, Ukraine, is encircled by two Wehrmacht army groups.

ALAN SMYTHE LED Milbourne and Russ into his office at the British Political Agency. An older man with close-cropped gray hair rose. "Ambassador Milbourne, Russ, I'd like to introduce Reginald Heath-Fleming, our agency's new SIS man."

Overweight with thick eyeglasses propped on big ears, Heath-Fleming gripped a meerschaum pipe between his teeth. "Glad to meet you."

Milbourne nodded in Heath-Fleming's direction but made no effort to shake hands.

Smythe waved everyone to a chair and sat at a desk covered in files. Behind him a wall map of the Persian Gulf was almost lost in memorabilia from Smythe's career. Photos of him in native garb, oryx horns, the hide of a Bengal tiger, and tribal spears decorated the other walls.

"Roosevelt and Churchill have given us a tall order, Duncan. Keep keen eyes on hundreds of miles of coastline and seaward approaches, not to mention neutralizing German spies in Iran and Iraq. Would you care to begin?"

Milbourne threw a quelling glance at Russ. "Yes, Alan, we have a daunting task before us. Captain Kimball is the natural choice for protection of the sea lanes. Frankly, I'm most concerned with those extensive coastlines. We must enlist coast watchers among the tribes, after gaining the cooperation of their chiefs."

Heath-Fleming nodded. "We'll also need help from the fishing and trading fleets. Their sailors will spot any vessel that's a stranger to these waters. Since we can't monitor all the ships that come and go, I suggest we enlist the aid of the Shuwaikh harbor master's office. They can be our focus with the captains of the ships."

"I understand that, Reginald. Kimball's operation can overlap with the fleets." Milbourne turned to Smythe. "I appreciate that we'll be going it alone because of your commitments at home and in the region, but this is a large expanse of water. We'll supply naval vessel silhouette cards to both land and sea watchers to help them identify the different enemy ships."

Russ watched a shadow cross Smythe's face at Milbourne's rebuke of his SIS man. He took a breath and shot up his hand. "May I comment?"

"Certainly, Russ." Smythe gestured for Russ to take over the floor.

"We may wish to concentrate our resources right here." Russ approached the map and pointed at land jutting into the Persian Gulf. "Here at the Strait of Hormuz, the sea lane is only forty miles across. Every ship from the Gulf of Oman must pass this point."

"That's right. Narrow our lens on that point." Heath-Fleming joined Russ at the map. "If we don't catch an enemy at the strait, we'll lose him in the larger expanse of water."

"I considered that idea last night." Milbourne folded his arms. "Catch the enemy at the bottleneck before he gets lost in the Gulf."

Russ gaped at Milbourne as the ambassador stepped in front of him at the map.

"Need we worry about Germans still living in Iran? Sleeper agents? This is, after all, British territory."

Heath-Fleming tamped tobacco into his pipe. "Sir, we control all Iranian telegraph and telephone services. A spy will have to rely on long-range radio transmissions to Jerusalem or Cairo. We'll set our technical chaps on triangulating any signals they pick up."

Smythe focused on Milbourne. "Our coastal networks will need telescopes, radio gear, and the like. Our forces in Iran are unwilling to part with their equipment."

Milbourne met Smythe's eyes. "Understood. Russ will jot down your list and pass it to Kimball and Spencer, who can cable it to their respective headquarters."

"Smashing! Not bad for our first meeting." Smythe smiled. "Reginald, meet with Kimball and Spencer soonest to draw up a tactical plan. When you're ready, we'll meet again."

"We've solid ideas on how to proceed." Milbourne relaxed in his chair. "After our next meeting, we'll visit the amir to gain his assistance with the tribes and the fleets."

Russ returned to the map. "Mr. Smythe, where's General Rommel right now?"

"Blimey!" Smythe smacked his forehead. "We forgot our backside."

Milbourne flushed. "Yes, Russ, we must consider panzer incursions from the An Nafud Desert."

Heath-Fleming took Russ's place. "Today's SIS summary puts Rommel right here in the Libyan desert. If the Luftwaffe can keep him supplied, he'll have a go at Cairo. Then he's due west of here on practically the same latitude, perhaps a thousand miles as the falcon flies. German tanker trucks average two hundred miles a day on flat desert." He tapped the map at Kuwait. "If Rommel takes Cairo, his advance units could be here in a week."

Milbourne gasped. "Good lord! The Wehrmacht from the west and the north and the Japanese from the east. A three-pronged attack!"

"Rommel could use the old caravan track from Aqaba right here in Trans-Jordan, straight across the sands to Kuwait City." Smythe traced the route across the top of the An Nafud Desert.

Heath-Fleming chewed his pipe stem. "General Rommel is an exemplary student of tactics. He'll send his recon unit to identify all the obstacles. If he takes Cairo, he'll start for Iran, Iraq, and the Arabian Peninsula. Just think of all that oil.

"If Rommel takes Cairo and moves against Kuwait, there'll be no supply shipments to the Soviets. The Russian front will collapse. The Wehrmacht will head south, marching between the Black and Caspian Seas, straight here."

"This calls for a beverage." Smythe pulled four tumblers and an unopened bottle of single malt Scotch from his credenza.

Russ retrieved his notepad from his suit jacket. He gave it a quick scan and waved his tumbler at the map. "If the Russian front collapses, Hitler will be free to throw everything he's got at Britain. And if Rommel controls the Persian Gulf," he continued, "the Kriegsmarine will have a protected harbor from which to attack the Jewel in the Crown."

"India!" Heath-Fleming motioned for the Scotch.

"And don't forget, gentlemen, if the Japanese take Ceylon, the Imperial Navy could attack our convoys as they make the turn toward the strait." Russ shuddered.

"Bloody hell!" Smythe shook his head. "I've given my adult life to the service of the Crown. The British Empire has always been, and His Majesty has stated that it will always be. I will not consider losing the Raj!" He thumped his desktop.

Milbourne turned to Russ. "I'm going to give my assistant the lead on this. Please, Russ, tell them how we view our choices on this matter."

With all eyes on him, Russ faced the map for a moment. He moved his hand along the caravan route from Aqaba to Kuwait City. "Rommel won't move his army in our direction unless he's verified the route with recon teams. If they perish in the vastness of the sands, he'll have to reconsider."

Russ turned to face his audience. "I've had several conversations with a Kuwaiti friend about the Bedouin nomads who roam this area. I learned a lot about how the tribes interact." He pointed to the top of the Arabian Peninsula. "The Saudis allow the Kuwaitis to watch over this part of the desert because it's closer to Kuwait City than to Jeddah."

"That means we can deal with this area of the An Nafud without involving the Saudis?" Smythe pointed at the map.

"That's right. We could ask the palace to enlist the aid of the Bedouins in monitoring the caravan route. If we supply them with carbines, field radios, binoculars, and telescopes, they could surprise even mechanized units with an attack. Trained and armed, the Bedouins could overcome Rommel's recon unit. Attack at dawn, with the sun behind them."

Heath-Fleming struck a match to his pipe. "Even if they don't stop the recon, the Bedouins can still raise the alarm. We could send in planes to strafe mechanized infantry lined up against the sands."

"This plan rests on the cooperation of the palace," Smythe pointed out. "Without the goodwill of the amir, the Bedouins will be out of reach. We'll have to convince the foreign minister that any plan we devise will be to Kuwait's advantage. Any ideas on how to broach this topic with him?"

Milbourne smiled at Smythe. "I've got that handled, as it turns out. I've already assigned Russ to ingratiate himself further with his friend at the palace." He nodded to Russ. "Why don't you tell them about Khalid Ali?"

Russ's thin smile did not reach his eyes. "Khalid is the friend I mentioned earlier. You know he's the amir's nephew and a chief at KOC." He turned to Smythe. "Once you settle on a plan, I'll approach Khalid. If I can convince him, he'll work on his uncles."

"Okay, let's meet again with ideas on monitoring that section of the desert." Smythe raised his tumbler. "To keeping the wolves at bay. We have no alternative."

Chapter 11

September 1941. The siege of Leningrad commences.

Everyone in Kuwait City gravitated to the suq. Rows of mudbrick stalls bordered the main concourse. Overhead, angled mangrove thatching provided sun-dappled shade. Wooden shutters secured the shops at night. By day, the same shutters served as racks from which the merchants hung their wares.

At either end of the suq, food and spice vendors worked at open-air stalls. In the labyrinthine alleys off the concourse, merchants sold sails, coffee, and *arfaj*, or brushwood.

The Safat was an open marshalling yard near the suq. Bedouin herders waited there with their sheep and camels while others in their tribes traded animals and arfaj for goods.

The marketplace brought together townsfolk and merchants, sailors and Bedouins. It was alive with commerce and diversion. Everyone wanted to hear the news from the desert, the villages along the Gulf, or the faraway lands of the Indian subcontinent.

Russ parked near the Safat and immersed himself in the sights, sounds, and smells of the suq. Butchers shooed flies from meat hung on hooks under the awnings. The odors of hot tea, oiled saddles, warm bread, and ground spices mixed in the close air.

"Welcome, Mr. Mark. Please come and sit." A merchant struggled to rise from his stool. Although stiff from age, the man's keen mind and artistic talent drew the attention of many. Khalid had chosen this artisan to design the dagger given by the amir to Russ.

"I'm happy to see you, Ibrahim. Your health is good?"

"Well enough. Mr. Mark, let us enjoy mint tea while we talk." Ibrahim looked around. "Where is that boy?" He ambled toward the tea café in search of a chai boy.

When the old merchant returned, Russ surrendered the stool. "Yesterday I introduced our new ambassador to the amir. He's a gracious host."

"Yes, the amir and I are from the same tribe. He's a true son of the desert and knows his duty to a guest. Does the ambassador understand our country?"

"Very well. Ambassador Milbourne has been here before, speaks fluent Arabic, and wants to help the amir protect Kuwait from the Axis powers."

A boy hurried up with a silver tray connected by three straps to a ring in his hand. When the child left, Ibrahim tasted his chai. "How was the amir?"

"He's worried about Kuwait's oil fields and General Rommel in North Africa."

"The amir should be concerned. But how can our cavalry, armed with swords and daggers, fight infidels who have tanks and huge guns?"

"Everyone can help by using his eyes and mind. For instance, you know many people. You might recognize a dishonorable stranger asking questions. He may be a spy."

"Bah! I'm too old to chase spies in the alleys." Ibrahim spat into the sand.

"But you could alert the palace. You and your many friends here in the suq could be a valuable resource to your amir and his brother."

"Perhaps you're right." Ibrahim's eyes twinkled. "We fought our enemies in the past, and we'll fight them now. This time, we may need to be a bit more devious."

"I'd also like to know about any suspicious activity you observe. Okay?"

"Ah, my friend wants to be a spy, too." Ibrahim slapped a knee. "Good enough.

"This war presents many problems for my country. We must rely on infidels to protect us against other nonbelievers." The old merchant wiped a hand across his brow. "But I'm an old man who talks too much. Tell me how to reach you with our reports."

Russ took a card from his wallet. "Keep this telephone number for the Legation. When you need me, call and say, 'Your jewelry is ready.' I'll come as soon as I can.

"And talking of jewelry, I need something for my mother's birthday."

The silver seller flipped a switch to illuminate his glass case. He chose a filigree pendant with a lustrous black onyx at its center. "A sister-in-law of the amir has eyed this bauble for weeks. I need customers to buy my pieces, not admire them."

Russ hoped he had enough dinars. "What's your best price?"

"The last customer of the day is a sign of good fortune. For you, only one hundred fifty."

The pendant was worth every dinar, but Russ knew he was expected to bargain for a better price. "It's a stunning example of your superior craftsmanship, but I'm only a lowly civil servant earning a mere pittance. Unless Allah provides me with a more prominent position, I can offer only seventy dinars."

"Mr. Mark, I toil each day to make trifles that are unworthy of your patronage. Alas, nobody wants jewelry with the war nearby. For you, my dear friend, only one hundred thirty."

"My mother lives more than seven thousand miles from here in a little house in Kansas. Her friends will coo with envy when they see your beautiful pendant. Would you accept ninety dinars?"

"One hundred twenty."

"One hundred."

"Mr. Mark, let us each give half. One hundred ten dinars."

"Agreed." Russ's hand sealed the deal.

The old merchant polished the pendant one last time and dropped it into a green silk bag. He tightened the string with a flourish.

Ahead of Russ, grit swirled high into the heated sky. He lowered his head and aimed for his motorcar. A commotion among the camel herders drew his attention. Russ heard retching, as if someone suffered from heat exhaustion.

A European, as white men were known, knelt in the middle of the Safat. Russ waded into the crowd to help. He stopped when he recognized George Lander's glistening black hair and pasty white face. Drool smeared a brown stain across Lander's shirt.

Russ bent to him. "C'mon, George, help me get you to my car." He turned his head to avoid the stench when Lander lifted his face.

"I don't feel so good."

He maneuvered Lander into the seat and lifted in his legs. Lander's head rolled, his mouth hanging open, as Russ threw the car into gear.

"This'll be all over the suq within the hour, to the palace by evening. The ambassador could get a call from the foreign secretary tonight. We could lose our tea sales because of your public drunkenness. What's the matter with you?"

"It was the heat, I swear-r-r." Lander fell against Russ when they turned a corner.

"Don't you have more to do than get drunk in the middle of the afternoon?"

"Doris is mad at me. She needed a trinket to make her forget."

Russ wove his way toward Lander's home. He had never been inside.

"When I get home, I'll alert the ambassador to expect a call from the palace."

"Don't call him. He'll call me, and I can't deal with him now."

"You should've thought of that. You'd better brace yourself for a storm."

"Don't tell the old man. If you do, I'll get you for it. Don't think I won't!"

"Get your stinking ass out of my car." Russ reached across Lander and opened the door.

Lander hit the hot dust and promptly threw up.

Back home, Russ held the receiver away, admiring Milbourne's choice of profanity.

"George has jeopardized our tea sales and our good liaison with the palace. You should have left him for the police. If the Kuwaitis raise an uproar, I'll send George packing." There was a pause on the line. "I might send him home anyway."

"Yes, sir."

"I'm glad you called. As representatives of our government, we should be above such behavior." Milbourne exhaled sharply. "It's one thing to indulge in private, but not in public."

After Milbourne hung up, Russ fetched a beer from his tiny icebox, sniffing the interior for spoiled food. He dug through his hoard of American provisions and came out with Campbell's bean with bacon soup. He dumped the soup into a pan on his two-burner hot plate.

He finished a letter to his mother and started one to Emil Fairfax, a classmate now on the staff of the deputy secretary of state. While eating his soup, he thought about Emil's great connections within the Department and around town.

He tidied up and headed out to the courtyard with a pitcher of water. He looked at his lonely rosebush drooping in the sandy soil. It reminded him of the yellow roses his mom kept in a vase on her kitchen table. He glanced at the empty half of his two-family house, wondering if he'd ever get a neighbor. He gathered his bedding and a reed mat and climbed the stairway to the roof, where he slept in summer. Leaning against a bagdir, he gazed at the stars. Stillness suffused the desert, and he closed his eyes.

As he drifted to sleep, Rhonda filled his dreams. He floated away from his rooftop in Kuwait to his flat in Moscow. The fragrance of orchids wafted around the edges of his longing.

Chapter 12

December 1938. Nazi SS Chief Himmler calls for a final solution to the Gypsy question.

AN OLD MOSCOW landmark, the U.S. embassy building contained offices and housing for the marines and some staff. Russ lived three blocks away in a one-bedroom cold-water flat. On the Wednesday after Christmas, he nursed a beer at the Marine Bar. Two officers sitting beside him railed against life at the embassy.

"Admit it. You got it easy living here. By the time I get home, I've lost toes to frostbite, and my eyeballs are frozen open." Russ watched it snow through the grimy windows.

"Yeah, but you don't have to listen to your coworkers move about their bedroom. And I don't want to even think about fire. It'd roar up the stairs faster than I can run down 'em."

Russ turned away from the grousing. A few couples danced to a phonograph recording of Artie Shaw and his band. A code clerk and a marine threw darts through the blue haze of cigarette smoke. In the adjacent dining area, staff members and their families ate greasy hamburgers and fried potatoes.

As he served Russ another "revolutionary beer," the sergeant behind the bar remarked on the new arrivals. "Well now, look at that. The DCM and wife with Mr. Wyman."

Russ watched the trio scan the crowd before settling into a corner of the dining room.

Horace Wyman came into the bar. "Hello, Russ. Pretty small crowd."

"Yeah, it's the holidays. But it sure beats sitting alone in a cold flat. I haven't seen you here before, sir. Can I buy you a drink?"

"No, thanks. I'll get this round. You're right, happy hour isn't for me, but I thought I'd come for the sake of morale." Wyman ordered two beers and a third for Russ.

"I guess you're stuck here for Christmas since we still don't have an ambassador."

"Yeah. Preston's chargé. We're both doing double duty. Got to keep that paper flowing into the big vacuum tube to Washington. Couldn't you escape Moscow?"

"I'm saving up to get home to Kansas. Only six months left here."

"That's right. Care to join us?" Wyman waved toward the Piersons.

"No, thanks. I'm leaving pretty soon. Appreciate the beer."

Russ drained his glass and stood, fishing in his pocket for a tip. He dreaded picking his way over the grimy sidewalks coated with black ice, known among the staff as perma-slime. He mused about the vast size and complicated nature of a country that spanned eleven time zones, stitched together by the Trans-Siberian Railway. Not even the treacherous winters stopped the people of the Union of Soviet Socialist Republics.

The scent of orchids cut into Russ's reverie. When the bartender cleared his throat and shifted his eyes, he looked around. Her smile made him think she'd been standing there awhile.

"Hi, remember me from the welcome party at the Wymans'?"

"Sure do. Rhonda Pierson."

"You should be more aware of your surroundings, Mr. Russell. Remember your security briefing?" She scolded him with a wagging finger.

"Sure, I remember. What can I do for you?"

"You can buy me a red wine."

Russ glanced through the doorway into the dining room. Pierson was just out of sight, but Wyman appeared to be watching them. Russ nodded to the sergeant.

"I don't recall what you do here at the embassy." She smiled. "If I didn't know better, I'd think you were someone's kid visiting for Christmas."

"I'm a political officer." He leaned against the bar. "And I'm twenty-five."

"I know. Just teasing." She wore a pout, but her eyes twinkled.

Medium height, early thirties, a tad pudgy around the hips, great legs. Hair he thought they called auburn. Eyes the color of maple syrup, and just as warm. She appeared to be studying him. Russ was baffled. He wasn't used to confident women. He wasn't used to women, period.

The bartender placed her wine on the bar and changed the record. Bandleader Paul Whiteman's sweet symphonic jazz rose above the chatter. "If you're done with your inventory, let's dance." She grabbed his hand.

The bartender and Russ's fellow officers watched this tiny drama with great interest.

Russ allowed her to move them out of Wyman's view. "I'm not a very good dancer."

"You're trainable. The best men are."

"Trainable?"

"Yes." She pulled back to look into his eyes. She traced her fingers along his muscled shoulder. "I hope you haven't anything against older women."

When she stepped back into him, he mumbled, "You don't look older to me."

"Thanks." She ran her hand down his arm.

He tried a little separation, but her curves followed without effort. At the end of the record, she remained on the dance floor. Russ shot a glance toward the dining room.

"Ah, the men. I can handle my husband, but your boss, Horace, is another story. His wife, Sadie, said he's very old-school when it comes to relationships." She led him back to the bar. "We have plenty of time."

"Time for what?"

"Oh, just a little project of mine. You may want to help me with it."

Wyman's appearance behind Rhonda stopped Russ's reply. "What charming dance partners." Wyman eyed Russ. "Let me carry your wine." He steered Rhonda by her elbow back to her husband.

The bartender stopped polishing a glass and leaned across the bar, waggling his eyebrows at Russ. "She's been to happy hour a handful of times, but I've never seen her act like that."

"Good for you." Russ gathered his coat and Russian fur hat. As he headed out, he glanced into the dining room. She flashed him a cute grin.

At the end of the slippery sidewalk, Russ nodded at the burly police guard watching from the warmth of his booth. Even the NKVD had some miserable jobs.

In the vaporous light of a lamp pole, ice crystals danced in the coal-smoke haze. He negotiated the glazed pavement with care. Frost nipped his lungs and numbed his toes. Two and three-quarter blocks to go.

No one else was out. His NKVD minder was probably snug at home. The Soviets had finally realized he wasn't a spy, so his intimidation was only sporadic.

At his building, he struggled to hold his key with frozen fingers. Scratchy radio music drifted into the corridor through the concierge's open door. She was the Party's block chairman and, Russ suspected, an informant of the NKVD, paid to watch the building's residents.

In his freezing flat, he shed his clothes and quickly washed up, thoughts of his dance with Rhonda running through his mind. When he closed his eyes beneath a pile of blankets, he felt her move against his body. As he drifted into sleep, her smile lingered in his memory.

Chapter 13

September 1941. Bletchley Park code breakers reduce Allied shipping losses.

"No, you may not sit down. I'm not done talking to you."

Lander leaned on the patio chair, whiskey and vomit staining his shirt front. He lit one cigarette from another. Beads of sweat dotted his thin moustache.

In linen trousers and a crisp white shirt, Milbourne finished his breakfast. "Your eyes are bloody spiderwebs. Your hands shake. You slept in your clothes. What does Doris say?"

Lander wilted in the direct sun while Milbourne adjusted the patio umbrella.

"She kicked me out. I slept in the courtyard. I haven't eaten since yesterday." Lander mopped sweat from his face. "Maybe my marriage is over."

The ambassador poured water over his glass of ice chips. "Is that what you want?"

"No, I guess not."

Milbourne took a long drink. "Fix your problems at home so you can do your job." He dabbed moisture from his lips with a napkin. "How are you drunk if Doris wouldn't let you in?"

When Lander hesitated, Milbourne smacked the tabletop with the flat of his hand.

The sound ricocheted inside Lander's head. "I had a bottle hidden in a flowerpot."

Milbourne raised his voice. "I will not tolerate behavior that reflects poorly on me."

Lander cringed. "If you send me back to the States, I'll never get another chance at a bigger embassy. Then Doris will leave me."

"You should have thought of that before you pulled this stunt."

Lander's head reeled. His stranglehold on the chair whitened his knuckles.

"Did you threaten Russ?"

"I don't know, maybe."

"If I let you stay here, things must change. No more public displays of despicable behavior. No drinking outdoors in your courtyard." Milbourne shot a look at Lander. "Even though you don't like Russ, you will make a supreme effort to get along with him."

"I hate whiners like him." At Milbourne's glare, Lander mumbled, "I'll try."

Milbourne sipped his water. "I recently read about a vacancy for an admin officer in the USSR. Somewhere in the far northeast of vast, frozen Siberia." He slowly turned in Lander's direction. "Now where was that? Shall I look into it for you?"

"No, sir."

"I thought not." Milbourne shoved his plate aside. "Well, you've imperiled our tea sales and probably angered the palace. If the foreign secretary wants a sign of our continued good will, I'll sacrifice you in a minute."

The telephone on the table rang and Lander covered his ears. Without the support of the chair, he crumpled to the patio floor.

"Good morning, Excellency. How are you this fine, sunny day? No, you're not calling too early." Milbourne listened.

When the call ended, he rose and poked Lander's arm with his shoe. "I saved your sorry ass, George. We've agreed you were sick, but this is your last chance. Next time, you're gone!"

Milbourne considered Lander while he replaced his jacket. Who'd stoop to hiding a bottle in a flowerpot? Scotch was to be savored, especially in private. He'd learned that the hard way.

He lifted the water pitcher and poured the remainder across Lander's chest. His underling groaned and struggled to stand as Milbourne left the patio.

Russ parked in front of Khalid's home and smiled at the similarities of their dusty lanes. He knocked to enter the diwaniya. When Khalid opened the door, Russ spoke in Arabic. "I've brought roses from my courtyard. My houseboy tends an old bush."

Khalid shook Russ's hand and smelled the small bundle. "Roses are rare in Kuwait. Thank you, my friend. Please relax. Remove your shoes if it pleases you."

Barefoot and without his keffiyeh, Khalid touched the scar beside the curly dark hair that framed his brown eyes.

Russ removed his boots and sat on one of the divans that lined the walls. "This is my first time in a diwaniya." An incense burner sat in a corner next to a *sheesha*, or water pipe. Bedouin cloths draped the legless sofas. A decorative wooden screen concealed a doorway.

"Please refresh yourself." Khalid gestured toward the brass table holding a platter of fruits and cheeses and an ibrik of coffee. "Men come to a diwaniya to relax and discuss issues of concern. It is much the same in England's men's clubs. Our women withdraw into a harem."

After chatting about life in Kuwait, Khalid turned to business. "We have been tasked with the oil well problem. The Allies wish to plug them to keep them from the Wehrmacht. We need them open to supply revenue for our treasury."

"How many wells are we talking about?"

"Fourteen, all in the Burgan field. We refine crude at Al Ahmadi from three of those."

"Why aren't you using the other eleven?"

"Not enough refinery capacity and too few trained workers. But those other wells are ready to go with a turn of the handle."

"I'm surprised at your willingness to share this information with me."

"I do so at some risk that others may hear about our friendship. For instance, many of our tribal chieftains chafe at Britain's influence over our government. The elders want all the infidels out of the country." Khalid rubbed a hand across his eyes. "They want to return Kuwait to how it was before the discovery of oil, when all authority was held within individual tribes. They are repulsed by the mere idea of a centralized government."

"But Kuwait can't exist in the modern world without a centralized government. Good governments bring fresh ideas, change, and improvements."

"Exactly. They don't want fresh ideas and change. They complain that our merchant ships bring new ways from faraway shores. These old Bedouins have heads as hard as camels' knees. They see no need for improvements."

"Traditions are essential for a country, but Kuwait can't rely on seafarers and desert dwellers. Prosperity could bring fresh water, for instance. But I'm sure you know that."

"I do, but oil wealth won't bring internal peace. Our tribes live by barter and debts, not by buying and selling with money. Currency use means foreign banks." Khalid's eyes smoldered like charcoal in a brazier. "Remember that the elders view the world from the narrow openings of their tents. All they see are the sands and the scraggly bushes of the An Nafud." He slumped against the pillows. "They're not impressed by progress."

"If the elders don't want the oil to change the country, why will they object to plugging them for the duration of the war?"

"The oil is here, and they've accepted that. But agreeing to plug the wells is another instance of foreign domination."

"I see. Your uncles are in a difficult spot." Russ paused. "So, what do you suggest?"

"Let's visit the wells in the Burgan field and then inspect the refinery at Al Ahmadi. Then we'll talk more."

"Good idea." With a glance at the inner door behind the screen, Russ switched to English.

"Our governments must work together to defeat the Fascists." He leaned closer to Khalid and lowered his voice. "The ambassador has asked me to study issues that don't fall within the normal responsibilities of the officers at our Legation. One of these is oil, but I'm also interested in how Kuwait's people live their daily lives. I've observed your need to import water, inconsistent medical care, and lack of educational opportunities. Please don't take my observations as criticism of how your uncles are caring for their countrymen. Providing a good way of life requires money. Oil will bring you great wealth in the future, but right now the world is at war. Can my government do anything for your uncles to help?"

Khalid's eyes had widened as Russ spoke. Now a smile teased the ends of his lips. "Thanks for making this easy. My uncles refrained from discussing our finances with your ambassador as they'd planned to do because, frankly, they disliked him." Khalid sighed. "Forgive me, Russ, but I must trust their instincts on this."

"Oh, don't apologize, Khalid, I can't blame them. I hardly know him and I'm already worried." Russ fell back against the divan. "So, you could use some financial support until the oil wells start producing. How much do you need?"

Khalid hesitated. "A loan of fifty thousand U.S. dollars per month."

"You consider this a loan, not a direct payment?"

"Yes. Think of it as an investment in the future of our two countries."

"Excellent description. I can present my idea to the ambassador as an investment in the form of a loan. If I can convince him, we'll involve Washington."

Russ and Khalid switched back to Arabic as they talked about their lives before the war. Khalid spoke about his experiences in England at Oxford, and Russ talked of his life in Kansas. Near the end of his visit, Russ switched to English again. "Have your uncles shared with you the closely held strategy for the Allies in this region?"

Khalid nodded. "Your governments are concerned about the Germans, but my uncles are equally concerned about the tribal leaders. Knowledge of our cooperation in the security of the Soviet supply line must remain inside the palace walls. Everything we do must be cloaked in the appearance of protecting our country, not helping the infidels."

"Absolutely. But the amir and the sheikh must be aware of the German threat to Kuwait and your oil. If General Rommel captures Cairo, he's only a thousand miles away from your country. If his forward patrols successfully cross the An Nafud, his regular army will follow."

"I've not been told of this threat." Khalid dropped his cup onto its saucer. "Surely my uncles are already acting. How does this affect your plans for the supply line?"

"Well, after your explanation of the problems posed by the tribal elders, we might have to revisit our plans, but I'll tell you what we have so far."

Russ concluded his review with a new concern. "How will your uncles view arming the Bedouins against Rommel's advance units? Will they want tribal chiefs to have weapons they could use elsewhere?"

"Oh, they'll argue about it. One will say we can't arm them, and one will see beyond the threat to the palace. I think the sheikh will carry the point because he knows the Royal Guard, the police, and most of the citizens of Kuwait City are loyal to the Al Sabahs. I believe he'll convince the amir. But we'll see."

A servant appeared to refresh the coffee, but Khalid waved him away. "Come, Russ, let's retire to the roof. It'll be much cooler in the evening air."

With his back against a bagdir, Khalid stared at the stars while

Russ organized his thoughts. "Does the sheikh interact with his counterparts along both coasts of the Gulf?"

Khalid tilted his head toward Russ with a questioning look. "He handles all matters of foreign interest for the palace, both with our Arab neighbors and with the Western governments. Why do you ask?"

Russ took a deep breath and dove into the problem of protecting the Persian Gulf along its entire length, not just along Kuwaiti shores. When he finished, Khalid was no longer lounging against the wind tower.

"The sheikh will have to gain the approval of all the countries affected, particularly the House of Saud, before involving the tribes along the Gulf. I've already caught the attention of the Saudis with my discussions of the oil seep in the neutral area. I'm not sure how they'll view this new involvement in Kuwait's affairs."

"Perhaps it can be presented as a protection scheme for all their countries without mentioning the supply line to Russia."

Khalid laughed. "Don't look so grim. My uncles enjoy crafting political deals. That's their job. They need to earn their keep somehow."

"You're definitely related to the amir." Russ joined Khalid's laughter. "Tell me more about this oil in Saudi territory."

"Well, I'm glad you asked." Khalid's smile broadened. "A shepherd grazing his flock stumbled across a black sludge near some rocks. The shepherd went to his tribal chief who told a caravan meister. The caravan arrived at the Safat, and a merchant who heard the story passed it to a vendor who sells water tins at my office."

"So, you're interested in a black puddle you heard about four or five times removed from some shepherd stumbling in the desert?" Russ shook his head.

Khalid nodded. "The news has traveled in this way for centuries."

"And you've already talked about it with the Saudis. What do the Brits think?"

"Oh, we haven't mentioned this trivial matter to Mr. Smythe. In fact, the amir believes the British colonial empire is crumbling. He's watching the rise of countries with material and financial wealth, like the United States. When the amir declares independence, he hopes America will support us. We'll encourage that support by selling our oil to American companies, and by repaying your loan. Then you'll aid us if we're attacked by a greedy neighbor."

Russ held his head to keep it from spinning. "That's quite a bit to take in all at once."

"Do you know an American oil man named Wendell Fox?" When Russ shook his head, Khalid continued. "Fox was an American diplomat before he converted to Islam. He's advised the amir for many years on deals with Western countries. Your ambassador may know him."

"He sounds like someone I'd enjoy talking with."

"You can do that when we go into the desert to survey the oil seepage. I'd be interested in your impressions of Mr. Fox."

"Are you inviting me to go look at your puddle of oil with you?"

"Yes. When the weather cools, we'll take a caravan into the great An Nafud. Imagine camels and horses and sand and sun. It'll be like a Hollywood adventure movie!"

Chapter 14

September 1941. FDR asks Congress for billions more in Lend-Lease aid.

"THE AXIS FORCES need oil to wage war. That is the prize we protect here in Kuwait. Let's ensure the safety of each other. Inform your supervisors if you suspect anything is wrong."

Congratulating himself on his deft handling of his presentation, Milbourne closed his portfolio. He had instilled in the local employees the need for increased vigilance without mentioning the supply line to the Soviets.

"Any questions?" Mariah scanned the small crowd at the foot of the main stairs.

A hand in the back row shot up. "Sir, I've worked here for sixteen years. I like American food, but the snack bar should be renovated top to bottom. I know you're busy, but could you look into it?" The man dropped into his seat amid encouraging murmurs.

Another man blurted, "He's right, sir. Come and see for yourself."

Milbourne shot Mariah a look of annoyance before plastering on a smile. "When time allows, I'll visit the snack bar. Meanwhile, I'll discuss this issue with Mr. Lander."

Later, in his limousine, he fumed. "Mariah, you know I hate

being blindsided. Don't volunteer me for questioning, especially by the locals. They're Lander's responsibility."

"As you wish." Catching Milbourne's eye, Mariah nodded at the back of Hassan's head.

Ignoring her, Milbourne's face darkened with fury. "And, Russ, why wasn't the snack bar on your list of issues for country team?"

Russ swiveled in the front seat. "I included only those items of immediate concern. But George's inattention to our personal comfort is an endless complaint. Here are the highlights." Before Milbourne could protest, Russ continued. "George's last report to the Department read like we live in the Garden of Eden. Everyone needs an R & R. It's not just the locals who hate the snack bar, we all do. Then there's mail delivery. Too slow, too irregular. Give us access to the army's post office for personal mail. On to our homes. When it rains, our mud-brick walls sag to the point of collapse. No running water. Our commodes reek. Look at your conveniences at the residence and then come to my home. Surely something can be done for the rest of us."

"Russ is right." Mariah faced Milbourne. "George does very little for us."

"And what about our emergency action plan?" Russ said. "George hasn't so much as glanced at that. Be prepared for someone to mention it later at the residence."

Milbourne threw up his hands and turned toward the window.

❦

The Americans sat in a semicircle in the shaded area of the residence patio. Russ glanced at the thermometer. It was already 109 degrees in the sun.

Lander lounged in the back row, puffing on a cigarette.

Milbourne stood before the group. "Ladies and gentlemen, I just had a productive meeting with the local staff. Here's what I told them."

At the end of his remarks, Opal Lodge raised her hand. "Kuwait seems to be in a precarious situation. If we need to evacuate, where would we go and how would we get there?"

"You're correct, Mrs. Lodge. If the Brits can't hold off the Axis powers, we might have to run for our lives. George will review our evacuation plan. I'm sure it needs to be updated since the outbreak of hostilities in Europe. I won't even hazard a guess about where we'd go or how. Once we update our plan, we'll meet again on this topic."

Lander sat up at the first mention of the EAP.

Spencer raised his hand. "I'd like to discuss refurbishing the snack bar."

Lander moved to the edge of his seat.

As complaints rolled over Milbourne, he turned to Lander. "Perhaps, George, you could take the lead on these administrative concerns?"

Lander cleared his throat. "Everyone needs to remember Kuwait is a very backward country. We do what we can."

The ambassador flushed. "I'm sure we can do better, George. Let's meet in my office tomorrow at eight. We'll lunch later in the snack bar." Milbourne waved his audience toward the buffet. "You'll feel better about your lives on a full stomach."

The next morning, Russ and Catherine listened to the raised voices from the ambassador's office. Catherine tapped her pencil. "They've been in there a long time. George will be furious."

Lander swooped out. He pointed a finger at Russ. "I'll get you for this, you little snitch!"

Russ knocked on the ambassador's open door. "Excuse me, sir. Did you hear that?"

"Take a seat, Russ." Milbourne folded his hands on his desk. "I told George he needs to make a strong effort to get along with you. I want you to do the same with him."

"I will, sir." Russ flipped a page in his steno pad. "After the dust settles, maybe this afternoon, I'd like to tell you about my conversation with Khalid Ali."

Milbourne scanned his calendar. "How about at three?"

At precisely noon, Duncan Milbourne III, resplendent in his custom-made Savile Row suit, strode down the center stairs. "Have you calmed down?"

"Yes, sir." Lander stood in the lobby, and together they continued to the basement.

Milbourne glanced at the lighting. "Can't we get some brighter bulbs down here? This is the dreariest place I've ever been in. And it smells of old grease."

With head held high, Milbourne walked to the order window. He nodded to Ossama. "Duncan Milbourne. Pleased to meet you. What do you recommend today?"

The head cook's cigarette fell from his mouth to the floor. "Ossama, sir. The shawarma is very good, perhaps with some peas and a cucumber and tomato salad."

"That sounds fine. George, what do you want?"

"A burger well done and fried potatoes."

After Milbourne took a seat, he poured his Coca-Cola into a glass.

"George, where's your list? We need new refrigerators, freezers, grill, and a vertical lamb spit. Better exhaust ventilation from the kitchen. New paint, new tile, one more ceiling fan, new tables and chairs. Toss the old posters of the national parks and get Bedouin weavings. Buy new plants, then have the gardener keep them outdoors except when the snack bar is actually open."

Milbourne smiled as Ossama brought his food. "Thank you, it looks delicious."

Lander lifted the bun and peered at his hamburger.

"Just eat it. It won't kill you. Any germs will die of alcohol poisoning." Milbourne tasted his lunch. "When this place is ready, we'll eat here again."

After lunch, Ossama approached their table and inclined his head. "It is good for you to come."

"I was just telling Mr. Lander that we need to brighten up the place and give you some better equipment. I want the staff to have a nice area to enjoy your delicious food."

"Oh, thank you, sir. Thank you!"

Milbourne walked out with Lander in his wake. "By tomorrow, it'll be all over the compound that we intend to improve this place. Why, you'll have this dungeon looking like an indoor garden in no time."

Lander merely nodded. He needed a cigarette and a drink, not necessarily in that order.

Chapter 15

THE DEEP BARITONE of the muezzin called the faithful to prayer. On the office balcony, Milbourne passed Russ a tumbler of single malt. "What do you have for me from Khalid?"

"Sir, we'll start with oil." Russ reviewed their conversation. "We'll tour the Burgan field and the Al Ahmadi refinery so we can formulate a plugging strategy."

"That sounds like a workable plan. What else?"

Russ flipped a page. "We talked at length about the security of the supply corridor. Khalid mentioned the potential danger to the amir's government of arming the tribal leaders."

"Hmm, I never considered that angle. I'm sure the Brits hadn't either."

"Khalid believes the threat is remote, so the amir will probably cooperate with the protection scheme, both in the desert and on the Gulf."

Milbourne eyed Russ's steno pad. "Is there more?"

"Just a few items, sir. When we discussed my job responsibilities, you asked me to keep an eye on things beyond the Legation's normal mandate. I believe the Kuwaiti government is struggling with their finances. I brought this up with Khalid, and he confirmed my belief. We discussed a loan to help Kuwait through the war."

Milbourne sipped his Scotch. "How much do they want?"

"Khalid suggested fifty thousand a month."

"Fifty thousand!" Milbourne sputtered. "Listen, the amir is an important ally, but the isolationists at home won't like his hand in our wallet. Neither do I." The ambassador held out his tumbler. "Before we get into that, I need a refresher."

Russ carried their empty glasses into the office. An invoice with Garfinkel's logo, a department store in Washington, D.C., peeked out from a stack of papers sitting on the credenza. Slowly pouring the Scotch, Russ read the attached note.

Mr. Ambassador, we apologize for the delay. I personally mailed your gift and card to the address on the attached invoice. As always, it's been a pleasure doing business with you.
> *Sincerely,*
> *Miss Veronica,*
> *Foundations Manager*

Russ slid the note aside and peeked at the invoice. Lavender satin, size ten, pricey.

Back on the balcony, Russ continued. "Sir, if the Kuwaiti financial system collapses, the royal family won't be able to support the supply line. Then what do we do?"

"I assume you have a suggestion for me to consider?"

"Yes, sir, you mentioned a private cable channel to the president."

"No, that's for matters I deem of immediate concern. We should be able to figure this out without pestering the president with Falcon Wing."

Russ considered. "Then let's mention it as part of a report on your initial calls."

"Go on." Milbourne turned to face Russ.

"Let's see." Russ hesitated. "While assessing the situation here, you realized the government is nearly broke. You're concerned about neighboring countries taking over Kuwait should the palace default on its obligations. To prevent that, we'd have to send military personnel to maintain security for the supply corridor effort. We can fix the problem with money instead of the lives of our soldiers."

"That sounds like it may work." Milbourne sat forward on his chair.

"If we route this cable to the right agencies, sir, you'll look like a genius for solving a problem before it leads to trouble instead of a failure when the Legation has to close."

"Here's the way we'll do it. Take this down in your steno pad."

Russ smiled to himself and flipped to a blank page.

"You said fifty thousand?" Milbourne glanced at Russ. "Let's double it to ensure we get half. Shoot for the moon and ask for one hundred thousand."

"Yes, sir." Russ scribbled in his notepad. "There are a few more things."

Milbourne sighed and dropped back in his chair. "Proceed."

"Khalid said the amir plans to declare independence from the Brits."

"Good lord!" Milbourne drained his tumbler. "Alan Smythe would have a conniption, not to mention Churchill's reaction." He pointed to the office. "Bring out the bottle this time."

Returning with the Scotch, Russ picked up his notes. "There's an oil seep that Khalid wants to survey. It's west of Kuwait, in the neutral zone they share with the Saudis."

"More oil. Why do we care?"

"Well, if the amir breaks with Great Britain, that oil could be awarded to the United States as a separate concession."

Milbourne stroked his chin. "That's a very astute geopolitical move for the Kuwaitis."

"Exactly." Russ glanced at his notes. "Do you know a former diplomat named Wendell Fox? He's advised the amir for over fifteen years."

Milbourne's jaw tightened. "The name sounds vaguely familiar."

"Khalid thinks we should meet with him."

"Hold on. Fox may have gone native. You know how that works. An officer resigns because he believes our government's policies are at odds with the country he favors. He moves to that country as an advisor, then acts to thwart the White House. You see them in Washington, wearing local garb like they've just crawled out of the bush." Milbourne frowned. "You have to ask yourself where their loyalties lie."

"But sir, it doesn't cost us anything to meet with him."

"Never go into a game without studying your opponent. Who's paying Fox to line up the U.S. with an oil concession? It might be the Dutch or even the Germans. Besides, FDR said not to get involved in Kuwaiti oil at this time." Milbourne drained the bottle into his tumbler. "I hope we've reached the end of your list. I'm beginning to regret broadening your responsibilities."

"Yes, sir." Russ ran his eyes over his steno pad. "Enormous amounts of money, the end of the British Empire, and a disloyal American advisor to the amir. That's all I've come up with for today."

When Russ raised his eyes, he caught the last of a smile that had twitched the corners of Milbourne's mouth.

The ambassador waved his tumbler at the door. "You're dismissed."

At the end of the day, only Catherine and Russ remained in the front office. She sat on the edge of his desk, displaying her legs to their best advantage, while Russ furiously typed.

"This looks serious, lover boy. Did you learn anything interesting over your Scotch?"

"As a matter of fact, I saw an invoice from a fancy department store in Washington. Do you know what these are?" He pointed at his notes. "I don't even know how to pronounce this word."

Her feet hit the floor as she studied his scrawl. "A peignoir is a fancy dressing gown that quickly falls away when love is on a woman's mind. A negligée is the sheer nightgown underneath the peignoir. Mules are slippers with little feathers on top that women wear while dressing. Or undressing!"

Russ grinned. "Do you have a pen-wow thing?"

"Maybe." Catherine put her hands on her hips. "Out with the details."

"Okay, I'll get some food at Fuad's and meet you on my roof. Can you keep a secret?"

"I'm insulted by the question." Catherine stuck her nose in the air and walked out.

Two hours later, they sipped chilled white wine on the roof. "A Georgetown address, huh? That's in northwest D.C. The Milbournes live in Virginia." Catherine tapped Russ's note. "I don't know M. Jessup." She shook her head. "I think the ambassador has girl trouble."

Chapter 16

September 1941. Through Enigma decoding, the USSR and Britain learn of Wehrmacht plans to attack Moscow.

THE GRAY SKY matched the mood of Thaddeus Rockefeller, the desk officer for Kuwait and the Trucial States. He held Russ's cable in one hand and his coffee mug in the other while he puffed on a cigarette. One hundred thousand a month? Did they think he was running a bank? Sitting his mug down, he lifted the pile of papers in his wire basket and slid the cable to the very bottom.

Across the street at the White House, Russ's cable generated a far different response. FDR thought the loan, the survey of the producing oil wells, and the strategy of the defensive plan were brilliant. Exploration in the neutral zone held no interest for him.

It was 133 degrees in the direct sun at the aerodrome when Milbourne and the sheikh arrived in their chauffeur-driven limousines. They stepped onto the hard-packed gravel, shook hands, and peered at the western horizon as the roar of an airplane broke the silence.

It taxied near the carpet-covered sand, and a ladder dropped from the side.

Senator Billy Dalton, a Democrat from Georgia, descended the ladder. He had bright blue eyes and a winning smile. He shook hands with the sheikh and the ambassador.

Congressman Homer Titus, an Alabama boy, weighed at least 240 pounds. Sweating profusely, he joined the senator on the oriental carpet.

Russ introduced himself to the staffers. "Lanny Wilkes, Senator Dalton's chief of staff. This is Hiram Flowers, Congressman Titus's special assistant."

After dinner, Milbourne relaxed with a Scotch at the patio table while the visitors savored Jack Daniels. Senator Dalton swept his eyes along the boulder field to the north of the residence. "This is a godforsaken country. What the hell are you doing here, Duncan?"

"When the president asks in a time of national need, you answer the call. I had hoped for the NEA assistant secretary job, but I'm patient and my friends will find a way."

Titus slugged his bourbon. "Now, I don't doubt you're qualified, but Billy said you barely got through your confirmation hearing with your ass intact."

Milbourne's lips thinned to a tight white line. "You're right, Homer, they did mention my departure from Baghdad. But FDR wanted me here, and here I am."

"What'd the Legation staff say about the hearings?"

"My friends in the NEA Bureau intercepted the transcripts and copies of the *Washington Post* and the *New York Times*. No need to diminish my authority with the staff."

"Well, a few of my political cronies back in Montgomery were mighty unhappy with your confirmation. Those old boys recalled all that nonsense about Iraq. You best be careful here. One misstep and you'll never see the inside of the assistant secretary's office."

"Don't threaten me, Homer." Milbourne flushed scarlet. "Or remind me of my personal faults. I am in control and there'll be no problems at this post. The NEA job will be mine after the hard-ships I suffer here."

Titus turned to look at the marble mansion behind them, where Mohammed and Yasser, the chief butler, waited by the French doors. "Interesting definition of hardship. Poor Lanny and Hiram are stuck at some fleabag they wouldn't let their hound dogs stay in."

"I haven't been to the Safir. Next time, the amir will find room for them at the palace."

Dalton held up his hand. "Okay, Duncan. I'm sure Homer didn't mean any harm." He stood and stretched. "Thanks for the hospitality, but I'm turning in. Good night."

Titus looked at Milbourne. "Where's Bitsy?"

"She hopes I'll be named the assistant secretary soon and return home." Milbourne gritted his teeth. "Besides, she's had little time to organize the management of our farm."

"Maybe she'll come for a visit, say for the holidays?"

"As you know, transportation across the Atlantic is growing more difficult." Milbourne stood. "We've got a busy day tomorrow. Goodnight."

After refilling his tumbler, Titus ambled across the patio and listened to the waves rinsing the shore of the Gulf below. A zephyr raced across the waters, bringing humidity in its wake. The sand sparkled in the light of a crescent moon, casting in relief a black triangle beneath the low wall. Titus thought it might be an abandoned well.

Settling into the patio chair, he considered Milbourne. When he returned to D.C., he'd visit a buddy in the State Department. He finished the Jack Daniels and dozed until sunrise.

⁓❦⁓

"What a night!" said Wilkes. "After my sponge bath, I opened the window and the flies swarmed in. Has no one heard of screens around here?"

Russ listened to the complaints from the front seat of the staff automobile.

Flowers jumped in. "My bed had more bumps and dips than a county road back home. Just when my whiskey bottle sent me to sleep, the holy guy started his wakeup call."

Wilkes picked it up. "I'm still annoyed the ambassador didn't offer us a room at his marble palace. What kind of a boss is he, Russ?"

"Honestly, he's arrogant and petulant. He's already offended the palace. He likes a schedule and hates surprises. He's not interested in teamwork." He shrugged. "You asked."

"Well, that's an earful. What'd you think of his confirmation hearing?"

Russ swiveled to face the back seat. "Never saw it. What happened?"

"They grilled Milbourne about his departure from Baghdad, particularly about an escapade with a female officer. Senator Dalton was unhappy FDR sent up a flawed candidate."

Russ chewed his lip. "Odd that the report never crossed my desk. I wonder if that escapade had anything to do with his wife not coming to Kuwait."

Flowers snapped his fingers. "Tell you what. We'll send you a copy."

While the palace luncheon was underway, Russ sat beneath a canvas awning with the drivers. Although miffed the ambassador had omitted his name from the guest list, he was happy with his canteen and a peanut butter and jelly sandwich.

Khalid strolled up. "My uncles noticed your absence. Anything wrong?"

"No, nothing unusual. Did you leave early?"

"I'll not be missed." Khalid eyed Russ's sandwich. "I've made plans for our trip to the oil field and refinery for next week. We'll go at sunrise. It's the best time in the desert."

Back at the limousine, Milbourne waved Russ over. "I'm taking my visitors to the residence for a nap. They're fading fast after three weeks on the road. What time do we have to be at the aerodrome tomorrow morning?"

"The plane must leave by six, when it's cool enough to help with the lift. I suggest we get there at five thirty."

"Five thirty! Damn it all, Russ, these visits are tiresome." Milbourne looked old and weary. "Just meet us there with the staff boys. No need to drive over together."

The next morning, the plane stood silently on the apron. When the limousines approached the tarmac, it was already eighty degrees in the shade.

Senator Dalton shook Milbourne's hand. "Thank you for an enlightening and well-organized visit. Your staff did an excellent job, especially that Russell guy."

Milbourne clamped down on a scowl. "I'm glad I could give you a brief but illuminating look at this very strategic country. My staff have learned to follow my instructions."

The foreign secretary arrived to deliver routine farewell remarks. Afterward, Dalton walked toward the plane beside Milbourne. Titus and the sheikh followed.

"Mr. Foreign Secretary, may I ask you for a rather delicate opinion?" Titus said, his voice low. "What do you think of the ambassador as our envoy to the amir's court?"

The sheikh's eyes narrowed. "As a close friend of your president, he seems satisfactory."

"While I appreciate your careful appraisal, I hoped for a more candid assessment."

The sheikh stroked his beard. "I don't understand."

"Let me be frank. Has the ambassador done anything that caused you concern about his professional or personal behavior?"

"Ah, not yet." The sheikh stopped and pulled at the skin beneath his right eye with his index finger. "But the amir and I are careful leaders." Then he offered his hand. "May you have a safe journey. Inshallah. Go with Allah and ride with the wind."

Chapter 17

September 1941. In London, the Atlantic Charter, as drafted by Prime Minister Churchill and President Roosevelt, is endorsed by fifteen nations.

WITH THE RISING sun behind them, Russ and Lodge cruised along the gravel track to the amir's date farm in the village of Al Jahra, twenty miles west of Kuwait City. Russ glanced at his drowsy passenger. "Did you see a transcript from the ambassador's confirmation hearing?"

"No, why?"

"Well, I haven't either. The CODEL staff said there was a problem with the ambassador's departure from his last post in Iraq."

"Yes, there was something." Lodge straightened in his seat. "Baghdad. Let me think."

"Flowers is sending me a copy. Once our buddies in the Department reply to our letters, we'll have some interesting reading."

"Can't wait." Lodge stared out the open window at the featureless landscape.

"Do you know an officer named M. Jessup? I saw that name in his office and then again on a message envelope from the secretary of state's staff."

"Jessup. Sounds familiar. Talk to Mariah. She was Milbourne's DCM in Baghdad and knows everyone who works the region."

Russ squinted into the horizon. "You know, Al Jahra might be a stop for the Wehrmacht on their way to Kuwait City."

"Ah, our spymaster. We'll ask the manager to monitor the western approaches."

Russ turned onto a side road and parked next to a white-washed building of mud bricks. A middle-aged man of average height wearing a friendly smile stepped out. Hopping out of the car, Russ and Lodge extended their hands.

"Welcome." Rashid clasped each hand in turn.

The farm manager led Russ and Lodge through the concentric circles of date palms planted around one of the few oases in Kuwait.

"Only the female trees produce dates," explained Rashid. "In good years, we harvest a thousand dates from each cluster. A single tree gives about five hundred pounds of fruit."

"I've read that the date is mostly sugar."

"That's correct, Mr. Lodge. Sugar, fat, protein, and minerals for good health. Dates have been a food staple of our culture since the beginning of time. It's a perfect tree for the desert."

Lodge looked at the canopy of fronds waving beneath the deep blue heavens. "I imagine you also value them for the shade they provide to your homes and animals."

Rashid smiled. "In the desert, shade is a luxury and the true gift of these majestic trees. The Bedouins create shade with their tents, but the air inside those tents isn't pleasant."

As they walked, Russ pointed to a young man in a roof tower. "Is he using field glasses?"

"Yes, he's a lookout. We're quite alone in the sands, and there's no wall around our village. Many caravans and Bedouin traders visit us, but we fear the brigands of the desert."

With coffee and dates for refreshment, the men sat under the shade of the tall palms. Before long, the talk turned to the war.

"You know everyone who passes from the west, sir. You're in a perfect position to help the amir secure the country's borders."

"Ah, Mr. Mark, I'm but a poor man with a lowly position. What can I do?"

Russ cajoled Rashid with compliments until he agreed to participate in the network of observers. "Although I'm a humble worker, I'll be a watcher of the tracks out of the desert."

Back at the Legation, Sergeant Benevento stopped Russ at Post One. "Careful, Mr. Russell. Mr. Lander is on the warpath, and your scalp is his prize."

"Great." Russ pulled his wet shirt away from his back. "After a long drive across the desert, I'm parched and covered with sand. Now, Lander. Thanks a bunch."

"Come in for a minute, Russ," Milbourne called from his office. "You look beat." The ambassador reached into his credenza and handed Russ a crisp dress shirt. "Go get cleaned up. We have some things to discuss with George when you're ready."

Russ steamed as he changed in the hall men's room, imagining them lying in wait. When he returned to Milbourne's office, Lander lounged in a chair.

"George got a call from the Safir. Wilkes and Flowers didn't pay for their incidentals."

Lander jumped in. "I'm sick of cleaning up the mess left after these damned junkets. Did those knuckleheads say anything on the way to the aerodrome?"

"Not a word. They were barely awake. Did the front desk clerk ask them about it?"

"Nah, the manager said the clerk was dozing and didn't see them leave."

Milbourne interrupted. "Did you ask them if they were square with the hotel? They know that the restaurant and laundry charges were out of their pockets."

"No, I figured they were experienced travelers and knew the direct-bill procedure."

Lander scowled. "Are you going to pay the four dollars those nitwits stiffed the Safir?"

"Enough!" Milbourne held up both hands. "George, your cashier will pay the hotel. Russ, ask the men for reimbursement."

Russ ripped a fiver from his money clip. "Keep the change."

"Flowers tossed a bottle of bourbon in the trash can in his room. George had to apologize profusely." Milbourne glanced at Lander. "As you know, apologizing isn't George's style."

Lander and Russ glared at each other, but the ambassador continued. "After George's incident at the Safat, we can't afford any more liquor offenses, even from visitors."

"I've learned my lesson," Russ said. "Next time, I'll make sure nothing's left behind."

"Next time, I'll be the control officer." Lander sneered.

"The visit went fine, George." Milbourne waved Russ back into his chair. "By the way, I requested six bottles of Jack Daniels specifically for Dalton's visit. I got five."

"Really?" Lander cleared his throat. "I was sure there were six. Can't recall now."

Russ smirked. "It was only a few days ago."

"Maybe one of the servants swiped one."

"Nice try, George. I'll expect reimbursement for the missing bottle."

Russ mumbled, "At least you weren't puking in public this time."

Before Lander was completely out of his chair, Milbourne struck the desk with his fist. "Enough, both of you. George, sit back down and be calm or leave."

Lander threw open the office door and bolted.

Milbourne turned to his assistant. "And you, Russ. Watch your mouth or you'll be out of the front office."

"Yes, sir. Not another word."

Back at his desk, Russ thought about his career. With the ambassador's warning still burning his ears, he drew out his notes to update them for his next evaluation.

In the inner office, Milbourne added to his own notes in two files.

Chapter 18

September 1941. U-371 is the first German U-boat to pass into the Mediterranean Sea at the Strait of Gibraltar.

"Hi, Trick, what's new?" Russ joined Spencer in the courtyard.

"Well, Kimball and I've been working on our plans for the ambassador. We'll need London to cough up the equipment. But the big question is, will one of us go alone to meet the chiefs, will the palace send an emissary with us, or will we have a big conference here first?"

Russ shook his head. "If you get fifty chieftains at a big powwow at the palace, you'll wind up with sixty proposals."

"You're right. Too many people, too many opinions. On the other hand, a meeting at the palace would have a bigger impact than one of us wandering into a village."

"Time's running short. Visiting all the tribes along both shores would take forever."

"That's the truth," Spencer said. "Oh, hey, I got that list of local employees from Lander, but only after I asked the old man to call him. The major at Special Branch glanced at it and marked three names. Didn't even have to check his records first."

"Really? Who were they?"

"Ali, the assistant cook; Mehmet, the local boss in General Services; and your favorite residence manager, Mohammed. The major said no one from the Legation has run the names in his thirteen years at the Interior Ministry. Still, those three characters jumped out at him. Interesting, huh?"

Russ sighed. "Everyone at a sleepy post grows complacent. What'd the major say?"

"He tagged black market activity for Mehmet and Ali. They both belong to some Egyptian tribe from a Nile River town called Al Minya. Maybe they're funneling money back home. Wanted to know if he should pull them in for questioning. I declined."

"Good call." Russ bit his lower lip. "I'd bet it has something to do with our booze in that warehouse. We need to watch them to get some proof. What about Mohammed?"

"Now that's where it gets interesting. You've heard of the Wahhabis, right?"

"Yeah, they're Islamic traditionalists, religious fundamentalists of the worst kind."

"Exactly. They hate Europeans living in the lands of the Prophet. Mohammed's tribe is connected to the Wahhabis."

"Oh, boy!" Russ grimaced. "Where better to hear everything than at the residence."

Spencer nodded. "The Wahhabis aren't exactly pro-Axis, but they still hate us."

Pulling out a pad from his pocket, Russ jotted a note. "I'm going to spring an audit of Mohammed's books on him. Might learn something we can take to the old man."

Spencer grimaced. "Who'd replace Mohammed if he's fired?"

"Who knows? That smiling Egyptian's been around so long he's become indispensable." Russ grunted. "Too much about the local staff is murky."

Spencer laughed. "My agency loves murky. The murkier, the better."

"If Mehmet and Ali are into something with Mohammed, funneling money to the Wahhabis or whatever, we need to take our time. Allow them to remain complacent. Mass firings could scare them and lead to savvier replacements. At this point, the devils we know are better than new recruits."

Chapter 19

October 1941. German armies commence Operation Typhoon, the assault on Moscow.

RUSS WIPED HIS face with a soggy towel. "Bit muggy today."

Khalid shielded his eyes from the unrelenting sun. "The desert can be beautiful or harsh. Today isn't a time of beauty."

In the early morning, Khalid and Russ had journeyed thirty miles into the An Nafud Desert. They stopped at the Burgan field, a vast expanse of gravel floating on a lake of oil. They stood amid "Christmas tree" wellheads trailing pipes in all directions.

"I'd hoped camouflaging the wellheads would get you back into production quickly after the war. Now I see that won't work. We'll need a new idea."

Rubbing his temples with his fingers, Russ looked at the wells. "Let's think about this from the German point of view. They aren't interested in crude oil."

"They want refined petroleum." Khalid turned Russ toward the waiting car. "Let's move on to Al Ahmadi. My manager there will walk you through the refining process."

As they approached the side road to the refinery, another car sped past them toward Kuwait City. They pulled into the narrow, dusty road and parked near a white building with a Kuwait Oil Company sign at the corner. A tall, slender man stood waiting.

Khalid stepped out and pointed to the dust left by the other car. "Bakri, who was that?"

"Mr. Fox. I wasn't expecting him. When I told him you were on your way, he said he couldn't wait and finished his photographs."

"Photographs? Why was he taking photographs?"

Bakri began to stammer an apology. "Sir, I'm sorry, but…"

"Oh, don't worry, you're not at fault. Although I find it curious that I was unaware we needed photographs of our oil refinery." Khalid slid his eyes toward Russ, who merely lifted an eyebrow. "By the way, Bakri, this is Mr. Russell from the American Legation."

Russ shook hands with the refinery manager, who seemed to find his bearings during the formality of introductions. "I understand Mr. Fox is an expert in oil. Perhaps you could show me, Bakri, the areas that Mr. Fox was photographing, since they must be the most important."

"Of course, sir, that would be easy." Bakri bowed and swept his hand toward the maze of metal catwalks, tanks, and fencing. "Mr. Fox started here and went along this way. I'll tell you what you're looking at as we go. If that's okay with you, sir?" Bakri glanced at Khalid.

"Of course, lead the way."

As Bakri narrated the tour, he stopped periodically and indicated where Fox had taken a shot. "Tell me," Russ said, "why would Mr. Fox need a photo of that particular juncture with that type of valve?"

"I don't know, sir, but he said he was taking photos of the refinery for historical reference. He was afraid the war might damage the structures and we would need to rebuild."

Khalid rubbed his chin. "Did he mention what he was going to do with the photos?"

Bakri eagerly nodded. "Oh, yes, he will keep them safe. I know because he called someone named Huber. I put the call through for him. It was to the Swiss embassy. Although he spoke in German, I understood some of what he said. He'll put the photos in the Swiss vault next week. They'll be very safe there." Bakri beamed his happiness at this good news.

They continued their tour until Russ was lost in the maze of gauges, brackets, and walkways. "Khalid, how can anyone decipher what pipe goes with which valve and why?"

"At university, I studied the basics of refinery design, but even I can't explain what happens in detail. That's why we paid European engineers to make it work efficiently. Now that they've evacuated, our managers hope to maintain the equipment without disruption."

"What happens when a part breaks? Do you have to shut down while you send to England or America for a replacement?"

"Oh no, we handle it ourselves." Bakri gestured at a hunk of metal. "See that piece to the left of the pipe junction? When it failed, we had spare parts for most of it. We sent the rest to the metal craftsmen in the suq. A few days later, they sent back replacements. They may not look like the originals, but they work. Our finest metal artisans have replaced parts throughout the refinery."

Russ ran a hand over a replacement part. "How interesting, Bakri. Thank you for your tour." He looked at Khalid. "It's been very informative."

While they drove across the sands to Kuwait City, Russ told Khalid about his idea. "If you sabotage the pipeline, Rommel's engineers will patch it. But if you sabotage the refinery, the Germans won't be able to make the repairs if you—"

"—remove the parts made in the suq!" Khalid tapped his palm against the steering wheel. "We'll identify the unique parts beforehand, so the refinery can continue production until the last minute. Then we'll remove those parts and hide them away."

He punched Khalid's arm. "You won't have to plug your wells. The palace can continue to earn revenue from the refined petroleum. If Rommel threatens, you shut it down."

Russ remembered Khalid's surprise at Fox's visit. "You were

alarmed when you heard about Fox's photography project. Could your uncle have sent him? And why involve the Swiss?"

Khalid drove for a few more miles before replying.

"I've been concerned about Mr. Fox's influence over the amir for some time. Some of his advice and suggestions confused me, so I spoke to the sheikh about them. He told me in confidence that he'd noticed things that went beyond oil. Apparently, Uncle Abdullah has put in place some sort of action about Fox, but he hasn't shared the details with me. He hasn't told the amir about this plan in case it doesn't turn out as he suspects it will. That's all I know." Khalid slowed and pulled over to a stop. "Of course, I trust you won't tell anyone, especially anyone at the Legation, about this plan. I'm telling you only because I saw that you immediately knew something wasn't right about the photo session."

Chewing his lower lip, Russ nodded along. "Absolutely. Bakri heard in your voice that you were alarmed. That's why I stepped in and diverted his attention. You'd better tell him not to confide in Fox about marking and removing the homemade parts."

"Oh, I intend to have a long talk with Bakri about many things and to remind him that everything must be cleared through me."

"So, what's the Swiss embassy doing with Fox?"

"I have no idea, but it can't be a good thing. And the sheikh will be furious with Fox for dealing with another country's diplomats without his knowledge. Although Mr. Huber may have no idea what is going on either. He might simply be doing Fox a favor. You may be sure that I'll immediately tell Uncle Abdullah about all we've learned. He and Mr. Huber are very good friends. I know he'll manage to reacquire the photographs without raising doubts in Mr. Huber's mind if the sheikh believes him to be innocent of some hidden agenda. If not, then we'll know more than we do now. In either case, the sheikh will get the photos."

"Well, you better hope that Mr. Huber is merely a dupe in Fox's plan. Otherwise, Fox will try to take the pictures again, and he'll be warned when Bakri doesn't allow him access."

"I know." Khalid wiped the sweat on his brow with the end of his keffiyeh.

They were lost in their own thoughts until Kuwait City appeared through the heat haze. "I almost forgot to tell you. I've talked with my uncles about Mr. Spencer and Captain Kimball's ideas on how to organize everyone to protect the supply line. Visiting all the villages along the coasts will take too long. And it may be months before all the Bedouin tribes pass through Kuwait City."

"So, a big meeting at the palace, then."

"That's right. They'll ask about sixty men to attend."

Russ frowned. "How will the amir control such a large group?"

"I don't know. It'll test his political skills, but he'll have help. The foreign secretary is an expert politician and negotiator."

"Okay. We better arrange for the delivery of the equipment we'll use to train the men. I'll get on that when I return to the Legation."

Later that same day, FDR sipped a martini with aide Harry Hopkins in the Oval Room on the second floor of the White House.

"Did you see Duncan's three cables on the situation in Kuwait? His staff is on top of this business and ready to try new strategies."

"Yes, sir. I passed the hat around to get the Kuwaitis their one hundred thousand dollars. Stimson at War chipped in forty thousand, twenty came from Hull next door at State, and twenty from Bill Donovan over at COI."

"Unless my arithmetic is off, that's only eighty thousand. Are you pitching in the rest yourself?" FDR slapped his knee and pointed his martini glass at Hopkins.

"Nope, because I knew you'd like to contribute the last twenty from your nonaccountable emergency funds." Hopkins raised an eyebrow.

"Remind me to watch the pot the next time you try to fleece me at poker."

Hopkins sipped his martini. "I assume you're keeping this from the Hill. No need to start a fight, Mr. President."

"You worry too much. Those crusty isolationists wouldn't understand what we're doing if I drew stick figures for them. These funds are merely a loan to the Kuwaitis until they develop their oil industry. Besides, I like the amir. He's our ace in the hole."

Chapter 20

October 1941. With rumors of an impending capture by the German Wehrmacht, thousands of Muscovites flee the Soviet capital.

"I'm telling you, we should've heard something by now. Why did I let you talk me into that insane amount of money?" Milbourne stood at his credenza, refilling his tumbler.

"But, sir, they're busy in Washington."

Catherine sashayed in with a manila envelope marked *SECRET Eyes only for Ambassador.* She winked at Russ as Milbourne scanned the cablegram.

PM and I agree on logistical support, excluding uniformed forces. Expect flight from U.K. with equipment. $100,000 monthly loan arranged and will begin soon. Do not forget desert to your west. Persian Corridor is key to strengthening Eastern Front.

Roosevelt

Milbourne tossed the cable to Russ.

"Well, that's good timing." Russ scanned it. "And they gave us everything we asked for."

"We'll meet with the Brits at the palace to share the good news. Have Lodge set it up for us to arrive early to tell the amir about the loan before Smythe and Heath-Fleming get there."

⁓ⳠⳠ⁓

"Gentlemen, it comforts me to know that two great leaders of the world are on our side." The amir smiled at the Americans and Brits gathered in the reception room at Dasman Palace. "May Allah give our small country the strength to do its part."

Milbourne nodded. "Excellencies, our duties are easier to bear when shared with strong colleagues."

The sheikh discussed the logistics of training their countrymen on the U.S. equipment. They listened as Smythe and Heath-Fleming explained the lack of Iranian infrastructure, and how it must be improved before supplies could be offloaded and transported north to the Soviets outside of Tehran. The foreign minister reviewed the choices on how best to ensure cooperation of the coastal tribes, the sea captains, and the Bedouins in the great desert. And where to do it.

"Aren't you afraid a big meeting here may offer troublemakers the opportunity to band together to challenge your wishes?" Milbourne asked.

"True, true." The amir turned to Russ. "Perhaps your young aide would like to address that issue?"

Startled when all eyes turned to him, Russ hesitated. "Yes, you've made a good point, sir." He nodded to Milbourne and took a deep breath. "But the amir could invite those potential dissenters to the palace for a private audience before the big meeting." He turned to the amir. "You and the sheikh could tailor your approach to each one of them, emphasizing his importance to the vital security effort for the entire area."

When the amir nodded, Russ continued. "With a little flattery, a dissenter could be turned into a supporter. I'd bet on you two against one chief any day of the week."

Laughing, the sheikh turned to his brother. "At the same time, we can renew old alliances with distant tribal leaders. Once we know from the early meetings who will give us trouble and for what reason, we can formulate a plan to control the situation within the larger group."

"Each tribe will choose their best men to accompany their leader to the palace." The amir rubbed his hands together. "While we talk, the men will take instruction on the equipment and the reporting methods so they can teach their countrymen back home. Excellent, excellent."

"Any further discussion, gentlemen?" The amir stood. "If not, we have much to do."

The sheikh steered Milbourne into the hallway while Khalid escorted the Brits to their car. The amir paused. "A moment, if you will, Mr. Russell."

Russ followed the amir along the colonnades. "Forgive me for placing you in an awkward position just now. Khalid trusts you, and my brother and I will follow his lead. We had already formulated a plan very similar to your suggestion, but we wanted to see if you, Mr. Milbourne, or Mr. Smythe had any other ideas. When no one else spoke after your suggestion, I knew we were on the correct path."

The amir stopped and turned to Russ. "We also wanted to gauge Mr. Milbourne's reaction to the question and responses. After he pointed out the danger of a big meeting, he was noticeably silent regarding remedies. This concerns my brother more than it does me because I'm more interested in his interaction with his own employees and with the Brits. We're a small country dealing with large countries with many different alliances and potential agendas.

"We have our own internal problems…" The amir shook his head and drew in a big breath. "So, we need to tread lightly and know who we can rely on."

"I believe I understand, sir. I hope you can rely on me, but if my current role ever causes you a problem with the tribal leaders or with the Brits, you'll tell me, won't you?"

"The tribal leaders cause their own problems." The amir resumed walking. "You understand we're not used to dealing with matters of state independent of the Brits. We must learn new ways and adjust our thinking." The amir gave a thin smile. "Khalid keeps prodding us like elderly camels." He stopped at the doorway. "I hope you'll continue to provide him with your wise counsel. Now I must allow you to join the ambassador. I fear our lengthy conversation may already have caused too much trouble for you."

Chapter 21

October 1941. Muscovites finish the construction of trenches and anti-tank moats.

"AVERELL HARRIMAN IS inspecting the railways and roads in Iran," Milbourne said, picking a piece of lint from his sleeve. "He'll pay us a quick visit the day after tomorrow on his way home. He wants a meeting with the sheikh at the aerodrome, a short audience with the amir, and an evening with the Brits."

"Isn't he the new Lend-Lease administrator?" Russ jotted a note.

"Yes, he started his career in railroads, so FDR's smart to have him look at the situation in Iran." Milbourne pushed his intercom button and asked Catherine to summon the others.

After explaining Harriman's visit, Milbourne scanned the assembled. "We'll need a control officer." Milbourne eyed Lander. "After the Dalton visit, you asked for it, so it's yours. No surprises with too many whiskey bottles, George, or too few."

At the end of the meeting, Lander asked Russ and Catherine to follow him to his office. He dictated to Catherine arrangements for menus and the reception. "I'll be at the airport, so I'll need you two at the residence. Have the guard awake and Mohammed ready with plenty of ice and cool drinks."

"Look, let's bury our past," Russ said. "We can start a new page with this visit."

"Okay, Russ, I'm willing. We need to do a better job in front of the old man." Lander leaned back in his red leather desk chair. "As long as you don't mess with my turf."

"Great, let's get along. What about you, Catherine?"

"I'm all for making the front office run smoothly."

"Good." Lander rubbed his eyes. "His demands for the residence and snack bar have me running in circles, but I haven't forgotten your housing problems."

Afterward, Russ steered Catherine into the courtyard. "Lander looks beat, but did you notice he even smiled a little when we offered to smooth over the past and work with him?" He glanced around the area. "Did you get a good look at his ceiling fan, wood paneling, and leather chair?"

"Yeah, his office looks better than Mariah's." Catherine turned in a circle. "Who are you looking for?"

"Spies! I'm copying Spencer."

"Why would anyone spy on us? Unless you're planning to do something naughty with me." She fluffed her hair and leaned toward him. "You may whisper endearments in my ear."

Russ reddened. "I'm going to bite it off." He pushed her away. "Can you be serious?"

"Sorry, you're right." Catherine adjusted her skirt. "Yes, George looks worse than usual. It doesn't pay to be too close to the old man. Did you smell him?"

"You mean the booze? Yeah, George is well-oiled all the time now."

⁂

Two days later, as the Brits and Americans filtered in for the reception, Catherine and Russ sipped lemonade on the half wall bordering the residence patio. In the shade of the promontory, the thermometer read a mere eighty degrees. A breeze drifted off the peak.

"So far, so good. Even George is less frazzled than his usual tormented self," Russ said.

Catherine touched his arm. "Come to my house for a meal after the plane leaves tomorrow. We'll eat on the roof and watch the sunset. We'll have fun." She pinched his cheek.

Just then, Milbourne strode onto the patio with their aristocratic guest. "Ladies and gentlemen, I'd like to introduce Averell Harriman."

Harriman offered the assembled a warm smile. "Thank you, Mr. Ambassador. I appreciate your hospitality and this fine reception on short notice. I'll come straight to the topic that's on all our minds. I spoke to the president at Hyde Park and with the prime minister at Chequers. They're absolutely committed to providing military equipment to the Red Army as soon as the facilities in Iran are ready."

Murmurs of approval rose as his audience gathered closer.

"The Wehrmacht is beating Marshal Stalin's troops to a pulp. They've just encircled Kiev, a mere two thousand miles to your north. The Japanese advance through Asia from the east, and General Rommel is breathing on Cairo." Harriman swept his hand toward the calm sea beyond. "To the captain of a U-boat, your placid waters are a big arrow pointed at our main harbor in Iran. I pray the enemy never gets this far. If they do, you'll be running for your lives."

Russ felt Catherine stiffen. He slipped his hand along her skirt and touched her fingers.

Nearing his conclusion, Harriman frowned. "The pity of this operation is that you, this handful of brave souls, bear one of the greater tasks in this war. Yet I'd be hard pressed to find the same number of people in Washington who know the existence of a country called Kuwait.

"As Lend-Lease administrator, I'll get the supplies to Marshal Stalin. But I cannot sound the alarm should Axis vessels appear in these waters. I cannot watch for Herr Rommel's advance units in the An Nafud Desert to your west. Those are your jobs. The Allies count on you."

He stepped in front of the small bar. "Let's have a drink, what say? I mix a good martini. Any takers?" Milbourne was first in line for his usual Scotch.

Catherine and Russ brought up the rear. Harriman winked at her and then looked at Russ. "I didn't catch your name."

"Mark Russell, sir. Ambassador Milbourne's assistant."

"Of course. You served in Moscow. We have a friend in common."

Milbourne steered Harriman away. "Averell, I'd like you to meet a few people."

"Did you see that wink? Quite the ladies' man, I bet." Catherine turned to Russ, hands on her hips. "And who's your common friend in Moscow?"

"Have no idea." Russ smirked. "Could be anyone."

"Don't try that line on me. Who is she?"

Just then, Mariah rushed past them for the nearest bathroom. Catherine touched Russ's arm. "Tell me later. I'll see to Mariah. I'd hoped she was on the mend."

Milbourne motioned to Russ, pointing at Harriman's empty glass.

Russ glared at the residence manager, who was hovering at Harriman's elbow instead of supervising the waitstaff. Mohammed crept away. Russ lifted a drink from the tray of a passing waiter and approached Harriman, catching the gist of the conversation.

"I know I need to visit Iran, but Mariah's been out ill. What with introductory calls, a CODEL, and planning sessions with the palace and the Brits, I just haven't had the time."

"You should find it soon, Duncan, just to comprehend the problems facing the troops."

"It looks like Alan Smythe is leaving." Milbourne left Harriman and walked with a deliberate pace to the door.

Mohammed approached Harriman. "Need anything, sir?"

"No, thanks."

Mohammed slipped away, with Russ right behind him.

"Stay a minute," Harriman called after Russ. He led them away from the others. "The president and I have been impressed with your series of cables on the initial planning with the Brits and the palace on the security measures."

"Thank you, sir. I wasn't aware the president read cables until I saw his response."

"He reads what he's interested in, so always give your best effort." Harriman nodded toward Milbourne. "Now, there's a puzzle. Duncan was always so energetic. What's going on?"

Russ tipped an imaginary glass.

"That's nothing new." Harriman shook his head. "I must get something from my room, but when I return, perhaps you'll join me for a nightcap?"

"Certainly, sir."

Russ took the opportunity to find Mohammed. "You were making a nuisance of yourself with our visitor. You're to supervise the waiters, not station yourself close enough to Mr. Harriman to hear his words. Next time, bring a pencil and paper."

"No nuisance, sir." Mohammed gave his brilliant smile. "No need for a pencil, sir."

"The ambassador saw. You don't want to make him mad. Next time I won't warn you. I'll heave you over that wall. Understand?"

"Yes, sir. No problems. All is good." Mohammed scurried off when Harriman returned.

"I appreciate this moment of your time, sir, because I have something to ask your counsel on." Russ poured two glasses of cognac. "How important is Kuwait's oil potential to our government?" He summarized Khalid's possible discovery of oil in the neutral zone.

"Right now, Franklin is focused on England and the war. He can't spare a moment for oil, although our refineries are at capacity. The world will be a different place after the end of hostilities, so maybe it's not too early to think about which countries will still be allied with us then. But Kuwait and oil?" Harriman twirled the cognac. "Definitely worth thinking about."

"The ambassador is like the president with his fixation on the supply corridor. Of course, that's the most critical issue, but I don't want to miss an opportunity here." Russ sighed.

"Look, Russ, I'm interested." He clasped Russ on the shoulder. "Duncan Milbourne has known Franklin a long while, but I'm the insider now. I can walk into the Oval Office at any time." Harriman turned his drink napkin over and wrote down a number. "This is my home telephone. Leave a message there with whatever concerns you, and I promise to call."

"That's swell." Russ tucked the number away. "I feel better already."

Harriman pulled something from his pocket. "I'm to put this directly into your hand."

Russ held the yellow envelope. "You know Rhonda?"

"Since the thirties in Bern, long before she married Preston."

"I met her just before I transferred from Moscow." Russ stared at the envelope.

"What did you think of her?"

"Very smart, attractive. Not happy as a Foreign Service wife."

Harriman grinned as he sipped his cognac. "And there we have the problem. Who trades the life of an international attorney to be the wife of a diplomat?" He shook his head. "I know she hates herself for that decision."

"She's kind of stuck now."

"Yeah, and it's too bad. She's the sort we should be promoting into business management and government. She'd make a terrific diplomat." Harriman hoisted his glass. "Here's to Rhonda and the women of the future."

⸎

Russ climbed up to Catherine's roof. She waited with food from Fuad's and two bottles of wine. After their meal, they leaned against the bagdir.

Russ twirled a wisp of Catherine's hair around his finger. "After reading that transcript about Milbourne's exploits with women, you might be careful around him."

"I'll avoid being alone with him, especially when he's too far into his bottle." She fiddled with his shirt buttons. "I'm glad I have you to talk to."

"Don't you think it odd that Mariah was his DCM in Baghdad when he attacked that female officer, but she was still willing to be his DCM here?"

"You're right. And why would he want her around?" He kissed her forehead. "She knows too much. She would have become chargé after he was sent home from Baghdad."

"I've invited her for dinner next week to convince her she needs to fly to Jerusalem for a thorough checkup. I know she's frightened. Maybe she'll go now that the ambassador's arrived."

"While she's here, tell her about our concerns with Milbourne. See what she says, woman to woman. Especially the part about what happened with that gal in Baghdad."

"Okay." She snuggled beneath his arm. "Averell Harriman frightened me with his talk about the Wehrmacht coming to Kuwait. What if the ambassador and George are drunk when they get here? Who'll be in charge?"

He trailed his fingers along a breast. "We still have the marines and the Brits."

"Sometimes I'm so scared, I can barely sleep."

Russ drew her in. "Maybe I can help with that."

"Maybe." She lifted her face for a kiss. "You've always looked after me. These moments help me forget for a while."

When Catherine rested her hand on his chest, he closed his eyes and thought about another on the frozen tundra. "You help me forget, too. We're both lonely. You'll find someone who'll treasure you. Maybe there's someone out there for me, too."

She moved above him, and he slipped his hands under her blouse. She murmured with pleasure. When the sun rose, they were wrapped in the blanket, and each other.

Chapter 22

*October 1941. Soviet troops from Siberia arrive at the
Moscow front.*

OUTSIDE THE WILLARD Hotel, a gust of wind tossed litter about
the feet of a tall woman dressed in a gray suit. She ducked through
the hotel's European style columns. Pausing before a gilded mirror,
she patted her curly black hair into place and looked around. Crystal chandeliers and oriental carpets. The perfect place to meet the
wife of an ambassador for lunch.

Across the expanse of marble floors, a woman read the *Washington Post.* She had tied her silver hair at the nape of her neck with
a slender ribbon of robin's egg blue.

"Mrs. Milbourne?" The young woman extended a hand. "I'm
Piper Burton."

"You may call me Bitsy, dear." Her confident smile reached her
striking green eyes. Bitsy lifted the cane that balanced against her
chair and led Piper to the dining room.

Maurice, the maître d', offered his arm to Bitsy and guided
them to the best table.

Bitsy held Piper's gaze across the rim of her crystal goblet. "I'm
sure we'll see each other often once we're both in Kuwait. But I'm

glad you agreed to meet me now. Perhaps you'd like to tell me a little about yourself."

Piper sipped the excellent wine while considering what to confide. "Right now, I'm finishing my Arabic classes, but my last post was Marseille."

"Ah, France. My husband was sent to Paris after the Great War. Marseille is lovely."

"Yes, ma'am. I'm fluent in French, so I was lucky to get posted there rather than some colonial outpost."

"You're so right." Bitsy laughed. "So many French speakers get sent to Africa. Did you speak French at home?"

"Mais oui. My mother is French." Piper gave a small smile.

"How did you come by your name?" Bitsy folded her napkin. "It's quite pretty."

"Thank you. Mother named me after the small shorebirds that fly over the coast of western France. She loves her homeland and still misses her family."

"She must be very concerned for France."

"She worries all the time. So do I. Both of us have left so much behind." Piper took another sip of wine. "You've seen so much, with all your travel during your husband's career. So many different cultures. I can't imagine what such a wonderful life would be like."

"I hate to disillusion you, but the diplomatic world expects a woman to remain one step to the rear of the important man. It has been slow to accept the value a woman can bring to the issues." Bitsy grimaced. "Frankly, I'm sick of it all, especially the Middle East. This is the last time I'll support Duncan's efforts to become the next assistant secretary in NEA. I'm going to Kuwait only for the holidays. Then I'll scoot right back to my Middleburg farm and my Arabians." She sighed. "Sorry, my dear, perhaps it will be different for you in a career position."

Piper barely whispered. "I hope so, although so far, I'm not doing very well."

"I understand you're on a medical hold," Bitsy said. "I trust you're feeling better now?"

"Yes, thank you. I was unaware my situation was common knowledge."

"Oh, I'm sure it's not." Bitsy touched her napkin to her lips. "But I have many friends in the Department and try to be familiar with all aspects of my husband's staff."

She poured more coffee from the silver carafe. "So, allow me to share what I know about the Legation. Mariah McCarry was Duncan's DCM in Baghdad and was posted to Kuwait before Duncan received his assignment from Franklin. Catherine Cushard is the office secretary. She's been in the Department at least a dozen years and knows her way around.

"One man to watch out for, besides my husband, is George Lander, the administrative officer. He drinks, to the consternation of his sweet wife, Doris, who's also the post nurse."

Piper interrupted in alarm, "Why do I need to watch out for your husband?"

"Sorry, that slipped out. George and Duncan are longtime drinking buddies. Both rely on alcohol to handle the pressure. Never, ever, let Duncan tell you he can help your career.

"But, to continue. Are you leaving a boyfriend behind when you go to Kuwait? If not, COI has a new single officer at post. Radley Spencer."

"No," Piper placed her fork across her plate. "I didn't join the service to husband hunt."

Bitsy held her napkin to her lips again, eyes smiling. "Well, I'll get the bill and join you in the lobby."

Near the door, Piper reflected on the lunch. The tightness in her chest eased a bit. She'd handled the questions pretty well. It sounded like Kuwait had far fewer temptations than France. She could avoid drunks and brand-new officers while she put her head down and worked her new job.

When Bitsy arrived at the door, Piper said, "Thank you for lunch and the summary of the people I'll meet. I look forward to my job as a consular officer at a quiet post with few male distractions, your husband and George Lander included."

"Well, good for you, but don't say I didn't warn you." Bitsy patted Piper's arm. "I've decided to enjoy Kuwait, too. Maybe a final fling will make the awful trip across the ocean worthwhile."

Piper stared openmouthed as Bitsy was handed into the back seat of her car.

At her home in Middleburg, Bitsy finished her correspondence with a personal letter to her friend in Moscow. She hadn't heard from Rhonda in a long time and wondered if her own letters ever reached their destination. She reread the final page of her blue stationery.

Even though I've dithered, I'm finally reconciled to going to Kuwait. I plan to make the most of it, even for the brief time I'm there. I'm resolved to find at least one person who entertains me.

Today, I lunched with a female consular officer who's on her way there. She has a unique past, which she keeps to herself. That's okay because I already know all about it. I thought she might be an addition to our little band but reconsidered once I met her in person. She'll be competent at her job, but she's much too insecure to teach anyone about life. She's still struggling with finding herself and, from what I've learned from my sources, she's willing to latch on to whoever makes her feel safe.

Try to stay warm there in the ice capital of that bleak country.

Bitsy

At the same time, frost varnished the windows of a flat in Moscow, and the gurgling radiators barely held the chill at bay. Rhonda pulled her robe closer.

My dearest Russ,

I miss everything about you. I can hardly believe it's been three years since we met. Preston's extended here for another year, and I fear I'll never escape. Winter is early and time has slowed to a crawl. I dream of running barefoot on the green grass of spring like we once did together.

I know life is very harsh there, a furnace-like version of our subarctic steppe. You must be lonely, but I forbid you to despair. There will be someone for you. You'll be ready to love and respect her. You'll know exactly what to do and say. You have my unwavering confidence.

My friends envy my darling silver earrings. I explained that they are tiny ibriks from the desert land of Kuwait. They mean more to me than you'll ever know.

I hope to hear from you soon. Your letters give me a reason to live. I worry that you're not even getting mine. The already poor mail service deteriorates more each week.

You are always on my mind,

Rhonda

Chapter 23

October 1941. Leading the defense of Moscow against the German army is General Georgy Zhukov, already a Hero of the Soviet Union.

IN HER FOGGY Bottom apartment, Piper dipped a tea bag while she stared through her kitchen window. Bitsy Milbourne's words played over and over in her mind, undermining her newly reclaimed confidence. She dropped her tea bag in her cup and reached for her pen.

My dearest Francine,

It's been too long since I've written to you. I so enjoy your letters and hope you forgive me for my negligence. You've been my friend as well as my trusted advisor.

My recovery from my baby blues and the loss of Michel continues. I was doing well until I met the wife of the ambassador at my next post in Kuwait. She dwelt on the odd characters that populate the Legation, including her husband. He sounds like a drunk and woman chaser. But she also circled around my own life as though she knew much about me. She even mentioned her intention to have a fling at post. That shook me up, especially after Michel and all the consequences that followed. She reminded me of the emotions that sent me home early from France.

I spent the afternoon thinking of Michel. He was so handsome, so confident, so romantic. He made me feel secure. When I confessed to Michel about my previous infatuation with Henri at my first post in Shanghai, he waved that away. Michel made me happy. Then, I was so miserable when I learned about Brielle and Chloe. I never imagined Michel had so large a secret.

You helped me understand how many men have mistresses, and often their wives accept it. So very French, isn't it? I was able to control my emotions after you convinced me to try again with Michel, until Simone. She changed everything. Then I had to transfer.

Sorry, Francine, I know I'm rambling about things you already know. All in all, I continue to be hopeful. I'll always love Michel, but now I understand he is part of what I left behind.

While I linger in the past, you are overwhelmed with the present. Aunty Laycie writes that the beautiful beaches of Capbreton have been ruined by the Nazis' building defensive blockhouses. And Marseille's wonderful Old Port was so severely damaged! I'm frightened for all of you. At least I'm going to a small, little-known post. I should be safe there.

Please be careful, darling. You're so important to me. I'll be leaving on the ocean liner very soon, so don't expect to hear from me until after I arrive in Kuwait. I've included my new address. Check on Simone and Aunty Laycie when you can.

Much love and many hugs,
Piper

Chapter 24

A CARAVANSERAI HAD sprung up outside the walls of Dasman Palace. Representatives from neighboring Gulf countries, the Shuwaikh harbor master, the sea captains whose vessels sailed the aquamarine waters, and the Bedouins of the western desert milled about the tents, sharing the news. The air was pungent with coffee, roasting lamb, and animals.

A British military transport plane on its way to Iran had dropped off the training equipment in Kuwait. While the men learned to use the weapons and other gear, the amir and his brother met with each tribal leader to explain the Allied plan to protect the Gulf.

In the shade of a colonnade, the amir was exasperated. Time to wind up this long and fruitless discussion. "Yousef, we've ridden across the An Nafud since we were youngsters. Kuwait can't face the Nazis alone. We need to work as one for the safety of our tribes."

"Ahmad, we'll always be brothers, but I'm entitled to my opinions." Yousef folded his arms across his chest. "The Nazis will never cross our desert. They'll die trying. The Allies are interested in our oil. More Europeans will come to our land. They're infidel devils who expose our people to corruption."

The sheikh raised a hand. "Please. We need the infidels to train us on the weaponry. Won't you join us? Sounding the alarm is what neighbors do for one another."

"Bah!" Yousef spat on the seashells. "Abdullah, the infidels will overrun us. They'll disrupt our traditions and ignore the word of the Prophet."

The amir gripped the arms of his chair. "It's the Nazis who will overrun us. If the German general breaks free of the British in Libya, he'll head for our oil. Then our traditional lives will crumble under the Nazi jackboot!"

Yousef waved his hand in dismissal. "You worry too much."

"We'll honor your wishes." The sheikh bowed his head. "If you change your mind, please let us know. But I ask you to hold in confidence what we've discussed here today."

Yousef shook hands. "My brothers, beware the European infidels. Thank you, Ahmad and Abdullah, for your hospitality. You're both welcome in my tent."

The amir disappeared through a teak door, but Yousef placed a hand on the sheikh's arm. "A moment, Abdullah. Several years ago, you saved my tribe from starvation by providing many bags of rice when we didn't have goats to trade at the suq."

"Yes, I remember. It's not important. We have worries bigger than your small debt."

"It's important to my honor to follow the code of the desert. Now I will repay my debt."

"As you wish, Yousef."

"I've presented to your stable a bay stallion. He is young, smart, and spirited. Once he's tamed, he'll ride with the wind. May Allah allow him to provide you great loyalty."

"Thank you, my brother. Your debt is paid in full. Does this horse have a name?"

"Sharif."

Chapter 25

October 1941. The U.S. Navy loses its first warship, the destroyer Reuben James, *to a U-boat attack off the coast of Iceland.*

AFTER DINNER, CATHERINE followed Mariah to the roof. "I'm sorry to keep nagging, Mariah, but you've got to fly to Jerusalem for a thorough checkup. You can't fight this fever and diarrhea forever. Talk to Doris again."

"To be honest, I'm scared. I've been in the Middle East for so long, with all the strange food, foul water, flies, and dirt. Who knows what I've caught?"

"Well, don't wait too long." Catherine draped a blanket over Mariah's thin shoulders. "I just read the transcript of the ambassador's confirmation hearing. It didn't go well."

"So I heard." Mariah sipped her wine. "The president's cronies really pinned him down about that female officer's complaint."

"Would you mind telling me about it?"

Mariah sighed. "It was May 1938, and Duncan had just finished mesmerizing a congressional delegation with his expert presentation on Middle Eastern politics. Trixie was a new consular officer. Cute, young, and very well-endowed. Just Duncan's type.

"I was upstairs at the residence with one of the congressional wives when I heard a commotion downstairs. Just as I reached the bottom of the steps, Trixie fled through the front door, her blouse hanging off one shoulder. Duncan stood on the patio with a hand over his eye and blood trickling from his nose."

"Trixie hit him?" Catherine's eyes widened.

"You betcha. He missed the CODEL departure the next day, so I covered it. The congressman told me he'd seen everything from the balcony. He planned to report Duncan's drunken behavior to the secretary."

"What did the ambassador say when he returned to the office?"

"He worked at the residence until his shiner dimmed. When he returned, he never mentioned it. Probably didn't remember." Mariah snickered. "Soon he was on his way home."

"Did you write up anything about what you saw?"

"The director general asked me to, but I knew if I sent it in, one of the Black Dragons would tell Duncan about it and it'd probably just disappear."

"Did you know the ambassador before Baghdad?"

Mariah nodded. "I met Duncan at American University in Beirut. He was an alumnus who told us to concentrate on Arabic languages and politics." She snuggled deeper into the blanket. "Even in those days, he enjoyed his Scotch and thought he was a ladies' man."

Catherine frowned. "It's a wonder he's lasted this long."

"Don't forget, Duncan has the Black Dragons on his side. At least most of the time. They're all getting old, and they're tired of covering for him. The Dragons won't hesitate to blackmail him if they must. Such is life in the halls of diplomacy." Mariah chuckled.

"Sad." Catherine reached for a quilt and tucked it around her boss's legs. "What was Marvella Jessup's role in this Baghdad melodrama? I saw her name in the transcript."

Mariah's shoulders sagged. "Marvella is a gorgeous redhead with blue eyes. She was Baghdad's head of Political Section. Her husband, Frank, was retired and accompanied her to Iraq, but she completely ignored him. Marvella and Duncan started up while Bitsy

Milbourne was still at post. I think their affair was the reason Bitsy left so abruptly."

"What did Frank say about all this? Did he even know?"

"I'm not sure. He got sick and died in Baghdad. Marvella was returning to the States with his body when Duncan tried it on with Trixie."

Catherine shook her head. "Did you know the ambassador was coming here?"

"No, I thought the Black Dragons hoped to resurrect his career to eventually place him in the assistant secretary's job."

"Does it bother you to have him as a boss?"

"Not really. I know what I'm getting in Duncan. Besides, I've enough documentation about Ambassador Duncan Milbourne III to protect myself. And he knows it."

"Isn't there something you can do to control his drinking? It must be affecting his work, and Russ told me it's complicated relations with the palace."

Mariah sighed. "I wish I had the energy to tackle Duncan, but it's all I can do to drag myself to the office every day."

"I understand. That's why you must seek help in Jerusalem." Catherine held Mariah's thin hand in her own. "Maybe his wife could control him. Do you think she'll come here?"

Mariah shrugged. "You never know what Bitsy will do."

Chapter 26

November 1941. Joseph Grew, the American ambassa-dor in Tokyo, urges America to be alert to a surprise Japanese attack.

Russ chose a day to visit the residence when he knew Milbourne would be lunching with Smythe. Beneath the patio umbrella, Russ studied Mohammed's ledgers. "Explain this entry for wine, the one where five bottles are missing."

"I may have miscounted, sir." Mohammed's smile had vanished. "I'll check again."

While he was gone, Russ thumbed through the remaining ledgers.

Mohammed returned with two bottles. "These were in the pantry behind the rice."

"Behind the rice?" Russ eyed the residence manager. "Why hide them? Maybe to steal?"

"No! No stealing. It was a mistake." Mohammed mopped his brow with his handkerchief.

"You're still three bottles short. Mr. Lander will subtract their cost from your pay."

During the next two hours, the discrepancies mounted. Mohammed's handkerchief appeared again and again. Finally, Russ stacked the ledgers and put away his notes.

"Mohammed, how long have you known Ossama and Ali from the snack bar?"

"They're very good people. We all started here about the same time. Ossama is Sudanese. I didn't know him before."

"But you knew Ali?"

"Yes, sir."

"Where is he from?"

"Al Minya, in Egypt."

"Is anyone else from Al Minya? How about you?"

"Mehmet from General Services. I come from the village of Damaris."

"What is the nearest town to Damaris?"

The residence manager paused. "Al Minya, sir."

"What's your branch of Islam?"

"It's a minor sect, sir, small, very, very small." Out came the handkerchief.

Finally, Russ allowed Mohammed to scuttle home. He remained on the patio, mulling over the information he'd pulled from the residence manager.

When Yasser, the chief butler, approached with a glass of guava juice, Russ grabbed the opportunity to talk without Mohammed around. "How are things with the ambassador?"

"Very good, sir. We like how he speaks to us in Arabic."

"How is Mohammed adjusting? Any problems?"

A flicker of anxiety skipped across Yasser's face. "Mohammed is very experienced, sir."

"I know." Russ pushed out a chair. "Sit down, Yasser. I'd like to talk with you."

It took nearly an hour for Russ to grasp the inner workings of the household. Only Mohammed and Mehmet handled deliveries and inventory. Only Mohammed interacted with the ambassador. When pressed, Yasser said Mohammed listened to Milbourne's telephone calls. He confessed that Mohammed extracted a percentage of the staff wages to insure continued employment.

A series of shacks dotted the west end of the Shuwaikh port, home to the poorest of Kuwait's foreign workers. Ali, the assistant cook, slept in the corner of a shack on a reed mat with a patched camel blanket. He survived on the free meal he ate at the Legation snack bar and the scraps discarded from the plates of customers.

That night, a candle flickered behind Mehmet and Mohammed, who huddled on two crates. Ali hovered in the shadows. "Russell did an audit today and found problems in the liquor orders." Mohammed shuddered. "He's getting too nosy. We must be more careful."

Mehmet blew cigarette smoke in Mohammed's face. "It's you who must be more careful. I told you to adjust your inventory to avoid problems."

Mohammed recoiled. "I was too busy during the ambassador's arrival. But with all the liquor coming into the residence now, it'll be easier to conceal our actions."

Although he helped Ossama uncrate the liquor orders under the watchful eyes of an American wife and later gave the boxes to Mehmet for delivery to the residence, Ali had no voice in this meeting. He was important only as the carrier of Mehmet's envelopes to the captain of an Egyptian trading vessel that sailed between Cairo and Kuwait City. He watched as Mehmet spoke to Mohammed as though to a dimwitted child.

"Infidels cannot continue to overrun our country, you fool. The drunken ambassador is just one of many who pollute our people. Our leaders in Al Minya must secure this region for true Islam. If Russell learns what we do, we'll lose our jobs. We'll endanger our families in Egypt." With that warning, Mehmet left.

Five minutes later, Mohammed melted into the darkness. On the Gulf, a gust of wind churned the surface of the water. The residence manager made a small prayer to Allah to calm the waters and to protect him from danger. Allah was not listening at that moment.

⁂

"How'd the search go?" Russ sat in Spencer's office before their meeting with Milbourne. "Learn anything we can use?"

"Well, I rifled Mehmet's warehouse office. Stuck to the bottom of the desk's left pull-out, I found lists of wine and whiskey. Taped to the back of one of the desk drawers were orders from Al Minya for money transfers to the steamer captains and their docking schedules. These guys need to go."

⁂

"Why are you just now telling me this?" Russ and Spencer sat in front of the ambassador's desk, watching a vein pulse on Milbourne's reddened brow. "Did you discuss the interrogation of my staff with me? Did you file a report on your visit to Special Branch? Did you ask for authorization for an investigation? No! No! And no! I am the ambassador, and I will be told everything *before* it happens!"

"Sir, as an intelligence professional, I believe we have a major problem. We cannot afford to compromise our internal security."

The ambassador slammed his fist on the desktop. "I'm the only professional at this post. You, Mr. Spencer, are a rank amateur!"

Spencer stiffened. "Any information that points to radicals employed at this mission, especially in your own house, is cause for concern. These men belong to an extremely dangerous Islamic sect. They resell our booze to send money to Egypt. Mohammed listens to your conversations. What else are they doing that we know nothing about?"

Russ cleared his throat. "Sir, Mohammed's connection to a fundamentalist form of religion in Egypt has implications for the State of Kuwait beyond this mission. The amir's more modern ideas would inflame anyone who follows a strict interpretation of Islam. We can't afford to lose a strategically located ally to a regional Islamic insurrection. Sir, I respectfully recommend we act now rather than react later in an emergency."

Russ watched the color drain from the ambassador's face. He finally had Milbourne's attention. "Sir, we must gather as much information as quickly as we can. I propose we interrogate them and then fire all three."

"No firings!" Milbourne spit the words through a clenched jaw. "It's not as though these locals threaten me, or, for that matter, the rest of you. Besides, who would harm a diplomat?"

He gawked at Milbourne. "Those interested in our secrets. Anyone who'd want to rid their lands of infidels. That's who. We're targets in any country, even in Washington."

"Russ, Russ, you're spending too much time with Spencer. His twisted thinking is leading you through one too many turns, and you'll wind up looking up your own tail end. Besides, I have more on my mind than worrying about spies or some conspiracy."

Waving Spencer back into his chair with "I've heard all I want from you," Milbourne spread his hands on the desk. "Okay, this is what will happen. George will review the alcohol procedures. I'll be more aware of Mohammed when I'm talking with visitors or on the telephone to Washington. You'll leave this in my hands. Do you understand, Mr. Spencer?"

At that moment, Catherine walked in. "Sir, sorry to interrupt, but an IMMEDIATE cable from Cape Town came, first person from the consul general. I think you should read it." On her way out, she winked at Russ.

Milbourne read the message. "Oh, great! Bitsy's coming."

Chapter 27

November 1941. With no oil of its own, Japan eyes the oil-rich Dutch East Indies.

BEHIND LARGE SUNGLASSES and a gaily printed silk scarf, Bitsy Milbourne stood at the railing of the coastal steamer. Stevedores gathered her collection of luggage, trunks, and cases. She spied her husband and raised her hand in greeting. When he merely nodded, she sighed.

"Bitsy, my dear, I'm so glad you're here."

She leaned heavily on her cane as they moved toward the motorcar. "Well, Duncan, everything is organized at the farm, so I thought I'd come while I could still book passage."

"You were lucky to avoid German U-boats." Duncan frowned. "Where's your hijab? You know the rules here."

"I had lunch with the Kuwaiti ambassador last month. He said European women needn't conform to old traditions." Bitsy turned her attention to the servant who opened her car door.

"Welcome, Mrs. Milbourne. I am Mohammed. I am pleased to make you comfortable." He bowed in the fading light.

Later at dinner, Milbourne fingered his goblet. "Any idea how long you'll stay?"

"Not really, but at least through the holidays." She traced the rim of her goblet. "Once I return home, will I need to politic on your behalf with the Department? Maybe talk to the Dragons about the assistant secretary position? If you still want it, that is."

"Oh, I still want it. But right now, I'm supporting the president."

"Loyalty is admirable, but you need to come home. You do realize the current occupant at NEA is finishing his retirement paperwork."

"Yes, but I'm preparing for war. They'll hold the job for me."

Bitsy considered her husband with fresh perspective. The skin under his eyes sagged, and new veins mottled his face. He was thinner and his step was slower. He had even lost his quick and often acerbic conversational skills. He appeared a decade older than his fifty-eight years. "You look tired, Duncan. You're under tremendous pressure here. If the rest of the staff is as ill-prepared to shoulder their responsibilities as George Lander, you'll be lucky to hold on to the remnants of your reputation."

He sighed. "I'm managing."

"Thirty years in the Foreign Service is enough! Stay here for a respectable amount of time and then come home."

"C'mon, Bitsy. You've barely set foot in Kuwait and you're telling me what to do."

"I'm not telling you what to do, only reminding you of the truth." She leaned over her plate. "Okay. I'll be the dutiful Foreign Service wife, but after the holidays, I'm leaving."

"Good, we got that out of the way." His head lolled against the back of the chair.

Bitsy chewed her lip. She reached across the expanse of white linen to touch his hand. "We could recapture what we used to have when we were young. Let's try. Will you help me?"

Duncan's eyes blinked open. "I don't know, Bitsy." He stood. "It's been a long day, and I'm tired."

As he stumbled through the door, she shook her head. *He isn't hiding his dependency as well. A major mistake will cost him his last shreds of dignity.* She extinguished the candles and moved to the balcony where a breeze whispered among the curtains.

Three days later, Milbourne drank the last of his coffee as his limousine pulled up to the front of the house. "Good morning, Russ. Is something going on?"

"No, sir. Just thought I'd ride out with Hassan." He cast an inquisitive glance at Bitsy.

"I'm Bitsy Milbourne." She extended her hand.

Retrieving his briefcase, Milbourne turned. "This is Mark Russell, my assistant."

"Pleased to meet you, ma'am." His hand still rested in hers. "Folks call me Russ. If there's anything I can do to help you settle in, please let me know."

Releasing his hand, Bitsy smiled. "Why, thank you, Russ. And you can call me Bitsy."

"Russ, are you coming?"

Two days after that, Bitsy heard Russ talking with Mohammed on the patio. Lingering near the door from the den to the patio, she studied Russ's lanky frame and wavy brown hair. Once the residence manager entered the kitchen, she stepped onto the patio.

"Oh, hello, ma'am. Hope I'm not intruding."

"Not at all." She propped her cane against a chair. "Join me for a glass of wine?" She rang the crystal bell. "Duncan is dining with the sheikh this evening."

"Yes, ma'am."

"Remember, it's Bitsy." She smiled when he held her gaze.

"I hope you're settling in okay."

"As a matter of fact." Exasperation tightened her voice. "I'm sure your house is a lot worse than this place, but I'm having a terrible time with my work orders."

"Maybe I can speed up the process. Give me an idea what needs to be done."

"Let's go upstairs, and I'll show you."

When Mohammed delivered Russ's wine, she told him to dismiss everyone for the evening.

As Mohammed bowed his way out, his eyes slid to Russ, a smirk on his face.

She led the way to the second floor of the mansion.

When they finished their tour, Bitsy opened her balcony door to the evening breeze. The muezzin's deep, melodic chant echoed in the distance. "I'll put on some music."

Bitsy lit some candles and patted the Victorian sofa next to her. "Now tell me the sad truth about staff housing. I need to know if I'm to be of any help."

The candles flickered while he talked about life at the Legation. "Anyway, George doesn't care about our problems."

"I'm sorry to hear that but not at all surprised. The head of administration back in D.C. is an old friend of mine. So is the director general of personnel. Maybe I'll have lunch with both and fill them in on the difficulties here at the Legation."

"That'd be swell. We'd appreciate anything you can do for us."

"They owe me a few favors. It's not what you know in D.C., but whom." Bitsy brushed a piece of lint from her custom-tailored wool slacks. "Now tell me, what does a nice-looking single man do after hours around here?"

"Not much. I read a lot." Russ laughed. "Of course, there's the Marine House. Occasionally the British secretary allows me to take her for a meal."

"Sounds bleak. Maybe a girl waits for you in D.C., or perhaps back home?"

"No, no one's pining away for me back in the States."

"You sound a bit sad. Perhaps a lost love, then?"

"I guess you could say that." He sighed. "Someone meant a great deal to me once."

"I love romance." She held out her goblet for a refill. "Tell me about her."

He returned with their refills and sat with his elbows on his knees, looking into the candle flame. "She was older. I mean, not a girl, a woman. She was interested in the world and everyone in it. She taught me so much about life and love."

Bitsy nodded. "You can learn a lot from a woman like that."

"I know, and I did."

"You miss her, don't you?"

"She haunts my memories." He quickly shook his head and jumped from the sofa. "Sorry, I sound like some Kansas hayseed. I should go."

"That's okay. I'm glad you shared her with me."

As the last of the light receded behind the promontory, Russ left the residence.

Shortly before eight o'clock, Hassan steered the heavy automobile to the front door. Milbourne joined Bitsy at the patio table with a bottle of Chianti.

He poured himself a glass. "What did you do with yourself while I was gone?"

"Your assistant met with Mohammed, and when he was done making notes, I joined him. He's a nice young man."

"Russ doesn't go anywhere without his steno pad. But that's an improvement. When I first arrived, he wrote everything on the back of an envelope." He ran a finger over the rim of his glass. "Since I'll be away much of the time, you should arrange for evenings with some of the wives. You've already met Jane Smythe."

"I didn't risk my life to cross the ocean to spend time with dotty spouses." Bitsy leaned across the glass table. "You need to make some time for me, for us."

"You knew when you came here that I'd be busy with plans for the security of Kuwait." Milbourne tossed back his wine.

"Yes, I did. But we have so much to work through. And we have this big empty house to play in. I need someone to play with."

"Settle down. You've been here a week."

"You're right." She crossed her arms. "I've been here a week and already I see how tired you are. You're depending on alcohol to get you through your days again. Have you learned nothing? Break this assignment and come home. If you don't, this won't end well."

When he pushed himself from his chair, she caught his arm. "I remember what's happened before when you lose your way to drink. And I'm not talking about your job. I won't tolerate another dame. Daddy isn't here any longer to tell me how great you are.

With his money safely tucked away, I don't need you. I'll feed you to the company lawyers, and when they're done with you, you'll have to work until you're ninety just to pay your bills."

He pulled his arm away from her grasp. "Ahh, a new twist in your lording it over me. Don't you ever rest?"

As he left the patio, she called after him. "I won't be the only one ruining your life. Franklin will crucify you."

Chapter 28

November 1941. Marshal Stalin urges the Allies to establish a second front.

"To sum up, Mr. President, Kuwait's leaders are eager to help us."

FDR placed a cigarette in his holder. "A good review, gentlemen. Anything else I should know?" The president looked from Billy Dalton to Homer Titus.

Titus nodded to Dalton. "We're not sure Milbourne is the safest bet in this game."

The president's grin faded as Dalton and Titus aired their misgivings, including the sheikh's signal at the aerodrome that something was amiss with Milbourne.

"Well, that was an earful. To be honest, I needed an Arabist for Kuwait in a hurry, and Duncan was available." FDR stubbed out his cigarette. "He's loyal and I value that. If he redeems himself along the Gulf, I might nominate him for NEA. Besides, he sent a brilliant series of cables outlining his strategy for the protection of the Gulf before his feet were hardly on the ground in Kuwait."

"Mr. President, he has a sharp young assistant named Mark Russell. I'd bet my life he drafted those cables, not Milbourne."

Titus placed a hand on Dalton's arm. "Let me tell you a story about Russell, Mr. President."

When the congressman finished his tale of Russ saving the life of the amir's nephew, FDR's good humor had returned. "Russell is the kind of officer we need in our diplomatic corps. I'd like to meet him some day.

"I appreciate your candor about Duncan. Frankly I'm not surprised. I talked with Bitsy Milbourne before she left for Kuwait, and I hope she'll help him avoid the pitfalls of his past."

Homer Titus shifted his bulk to the edge of the couch. "We've overstayed our time, sir. Thank you for listening to our concerns."

As Dalton and Titus left the Oval Office, FDR moved to the Map Room where his next visitor waited. "Hello, Averell. What do you have for me today?"

FDR poured two glasses of bourbon while Harriman recounted his trip to Europe, the USSR, and the Middle East, ending with his Kuwait stop. "The Legation and the British are ready for their part in your plans. I've never seen a more dedicated group of people."

Scanning a map of the lands around the Persian Gulf, Harriman talked of the Kuwaitis' discovery of a new oil field. "That means a new concession agreement, which could be good for American oil business after the war."

"Duncan is keeping an eye on the oil for us."

Harriman shook his head. "I don't think so, Mr. President. When I mentioned it to him on the morning I left, he was angry that his assistant brought it to my attention. We can't let this concession slip away because of Duncan's bruised ego."

"Look, Averell, I told Duncan in this very room to avoid Kuwaiti oil unless it's handed to us on a silver platter. The Brits are our allies. Still, I don't want the U.S. to lose out." He passed a hand over his eyes. "I've a lot on my mind. Maybe you'll watch this one for me?"

"Be glad to. I told his young assistant to contact me if his source inside the Kuwait Oil Company brings him anything interesting."

"Would this be Mark Russell?"

"Exactly." Harriman laughed. "I should have known you'd already heard the name."

"I have my sources." FDR leaned toward his advisor. "How's Duncan doing?"

Harriman provided an unvarnished account of his visit with the president's ambassador to Kuwait. "I know he's busy settling in, but he can't protect what he doesn't understand. Iran is the reason you sent him there. But what really troubles me is Duncan's resistance to the team effort. No one else can have a promising idea."

"Yes, I've heard that elsewhere."

As Carenza Nasmith walked along F Street near Garfinkel's, she hailed Senator Dalton. "Hello, Senator. Do you have time for a drink at the Old Ebbitt Grill? I'll buy."

"Why, Carenza, how's my favorite foreign correspondent for the *Washington Post*? Where are you off to next?"

The willowy blond offered her cheek for a kiss and tucked her arm through Dalton's. "London followed by North Africa. Got to keep an eye on that Wehrmacht general Rommel."

Built in the 1850s, the Old Ebbitt had long been a gathering place for presidents, politicos, and newspapermen. Carenza scanned the crowd to see who her colleagues were drinking with. "Have you been anywhere interesting? Somewhere I could write about?"

"Nah, just showing the American flag to our allies. It was a real grind. England, Russia, Egypt, Kuwait. We just got home."

"Kuwait? That tiny country on the Persian Gulf? What's your interest there?"

"Right now, it's just a big sandbox, but someday they'll produce barrels of oil."

"Who's the ambassador over there?"

"Duncan Milbourne, one of Franklin's old friends."

"Milbourne." She tapped a finger to her chin. "Oh, right. He barely survived his confirmation hearings."

Later that evening, Carenza called her editor on the Foreign Desk. He added a new stop to her itinerary.

Chapter 29

November 10, 1941. On the birthday of the United States Marine Corps, Yugoslavia's two partisan groups attack each other, weakening opposition to the Nazis.

RED, WHITE, AND blue crepe paper streamers draped the palms, and lanterns edged the wall. Programs with the Marine Corps globe and anchor rested next to small U.S. and red-and-yellow Marine Corps flags at each place setting. The entire detachment lined up to welcome their guests. In dress blues, white covers, and spit-shined shoes, they represented the oldest and the best fighting force in the American military.

Descending the center stairs of the residence, Bitsy wore an evening gown from the House of Chanel. The sleeveless sheath draped her curves in a shimmering robin's-egg blue. A fiery opal pendant nestled between her breasts and smaller opals dangled from her ears. In low-heeled silver sandals, she navigated the steps without a cane. The women murmured their appreciation of her gown. The men were struck mute.

Russ, in his best suit and red tie, stood along the patio wall beside Catherine, lovely in a black evening dress and pearls.

The sergeant cued up "The Star-Spangled Banner." Detachment

Commander Gunnery Sergeant Grady stepped forward at exactly eight o'clock. "Ambassador and Mrs. Milbourne, His Majesty's Political Agent and Mrs. Smythe, and distinguished guests, welcome to this ceremony honoring the one hundred sixty-sixth birthday of the United States Marine Corps. Please stand for the playing of our national anthem."

All remained standing while "From the halls of Montezuma to the shores of Tripoli…" floated through the palms. Russ squeezed Catherine's arm. She looked up at him with shining eyes.

At the conclusion of the music, the gunny introduced the detachment. "Ladies and gentlemen, by tradition we ask the oldest marine present to pass the first piece of cake to the youngest marine." The gunny cut the cake with a sword. "Will Mr. Lodge step forward?"

At a gasp from the crowd, Malcom Lodge smiled at his wife and struggled to his feet. He sucked in his stomach, buttoned his coat, and held his head high. After a salute to the rumpled civilian, the gunny asked Lance Corporal Clemmons to step forward. The youngest marine took a symbolic bite of cake, and the two men shook hands.

Russ noticed Mariah as she made her way across the patio. He fell in beside her. "You look nice this evening. Feeling any better?"

"Not really. I'm planning to fly to Jerusalem." She continued to the parking area.

Catherine grabbed his hand. "Come on, you old stick-in-the-mud, let's dance."

When she stepped into his embrace, Russ recalled dancing with Rhonda so long ago.

"Bitsy is very intimidating in that dress, but she's nice to talk to."

"Yes. We chatted the other day, mostly about problems with George and work orders."

Catherine whispered, "The ambassador doesn't seem happy to have her here."

"Yeah, his fuse is shorter than usual."

"Something's off with them. Be careful, lover boy."

He stopped dancing. "What do you mean by that?"

"Look, you're single and good-looking. She's had her eye on you the entire evening."

When his face reddened, Catherine smiled. "If you want to get promoted, leave the ambassador's wife to the ambassador."

Duncan Milbourne, in a Savile Row tuxedo, finished his circuit of the tables and stopped near the patio wall, where Russ sat with Catherine. He tipped his Scotch to the pair. "I'm thoroughly enjoying myself. How about you?"

"Very much so, sir. The marines and Mrs. Milbourne did a swell job."

They watched the gunny guide Bitsy in a slow dance. When Corporal Clayton cut in, Bitsy laid her cheek against his. Milbourne's jaw tightened before he slugged more Scotch. Next, it was Sergeant Temple's turn. She tossed her silver hair and laughed. Milbourne stomped off.

"Remember my words, lover boy." Catherine moved away when Bitsy joined them.

"Why aren't you dancing?"

"Catherine and I were taking a break." He whistled softly. "I sure do like your dress."

"You're so sweet." As the soft melody of "A Nightingale Sang in Berkeley Square" floated across the patio, she pulled him to the dance floor and pressed her body to his.

Catherine and her friend Pamela watched from their table. When the song ended, Russ stepped back and gave a small bow.

Milbourne glowered and headed in their direction but was diverted by Spencer. Milbourne waved him off and snagged another Scotch from a passing waiter. He caught up with Russ having a chat with Reginald Heath-Fleming.

"You and those young marines better watch yourselves with Bitsy." The vein in Milbourne's brow throbbed. "I know about your affair with Rhonda Pierson in Moscow."

"You don't know anything!" Russ lowered his voice and stuck his face close to Milbourne's. "Where did you get your mistaken information about Rhonda?"

Heath-Fleming quickly stepped away just as Milbourne sat hard on the edge of the wall. Before he could tumble backward, Russ grabbed his arm and steered him to a chair. "You better sober up before you fall over the cliff."

Bitsy swooped in, frowned at her husband, and grabbed Russ's arm.

Russ mumbled into her ear, "Your husband doesn't like your dance partners."

"Good." Bitsy rubbed the back of his neck. "But he won't remember anything in the morning." She spun out of his arm. "Excuse me. I see some guests are readying to leave."

While the ambassador stumbled through his farewells, Bitsy stepped onto the upstairs balcony. With her hair streaming in the Gulf breeze and her blue gown catching the parlor lights, she drew a bow across the strings of her violin. A bittersweet Celtic tune floated on the air.

Everyone turned to the balcony. Some swayed to the haunting melody, but Catherine stood on tiptoe and kissed Russ with passion.

⁓✦⁓

During the celebration of the Marine Corps birthday, American officers handled Legation security. George Lander had just handed off Post One to Trent Hedges, Spencer's newly arrived deputy. He fanned the door to clear out the reek of Scotch and cigarettes.

At twenty-six, Hedges had pale brown hair and wore spectacles. He spoke French and German. COI recruiters were impressed by his even temper under pressure and his problem-solving skills. He was a good foil to Spencer's quick-thinking exuberance.

At a quarter to nine, the local guard buzzed Hedges on the gate intercom. "Sir, there's a man here who wants to speak to an American."

"Okay, search him first." Hedges observed the local guard frisking the visitor. He recalled his COI training about walk-ins. Was this guy seeking asylum, selling information for profit, testing Legation security, or passing information to a friendly nation? He checked his Smith & Wesson revolver. Six rounds in the cylinder.

The walk-in offered his passport. Prominent on the cover was a Nazi swastika.

Hedges motioned the walk-in to a chair. "Do you speak English?"

"Little. What's your job here?" The man exuded a powerful odor of sweat.

"I'm Tom, a consular officer. I can help you." Hedges switched to German. "How much time do you have? Is anyone missing you?" Hedges beat a staccato with his pencil.

"I have all evening. No one waits for me."

"Your Reich passport was issued in 1934 to Gunther Mayerik, a telegraph operator." Glancing at Mayerik, who nodded, Hedges continued. "Where do you live?"

"We moved to Tehran in 1909 when I was seven years old, but I spent summers in Hessen with my aunt. I used to work in the Central Iranian Telegraph Office."

The pencil stopped. "Used to?"

"When the Soviets and the British placed the new shah on the throne, he kicked the Germans out. Now I'm without a job or a place to live. I do not wish to live in Germany under Hitler. I want to go to a country where there is always freedom, like yours."

While Mayerik rambled on, Hedges slid a pack of cigarettes across the desk to the visitor.

"So, Herr Mayerik, you met the Abwehr chief of the Reich's Tehran embassy while playing chess at a café. What did you talk about?"

"Yes, Winebrenner." Mayerik shrugged. "Many things, but mostly about why the Allies are building up in the south of Iran. Herr Winebrenner believes the Allies will push north from southern Iran to reach the oil fields of Azerbaijan before the Nazis get there."

Hedges paused his pencil. "The oil fields of Azerbaijan?"

Mayerik stared at Hedges. "If the Wehrmacht break through

the Russian defenses and move south to Azerbaijan, Hitler will have oil. If the Allies reach Azerbaijan first, the Nazis will be denied the oil fields."

Back at home, Russ pulled off his suit and flopped on his sagging sofa. He tugged over a small chest and lifted out his legal pad and an envelope.

My darling,

I'm sorry it's been so long since my last letter. The arrival of the new ambassador led to a series of meetings with the palace and the Brits. This sleepy sandbox country is about to make a major statement in the world at war. There's so much going on with all the new people, I hardly know where to begin.

But first I want to tell you how much I miss you and how often I remember our time in Moscow. Tonight, at the Legation's Marine birthday celebration, I remembered our first dance at the Marine Bar. I was afraid someone would see us. But you were so confident. And then when you showed up at my door that Saturday morning, all decked out in your fur coat and boots, you woke me from the stupor I had fallen into. I was terrified and bewildered.

Chapter 30

December 1938. At the beginning of the year, oil is discovered 1,900 miles to the south of Moscow in a country called Kuwait.

MAYBE HE HAD frozen to death during the night. That tapping sound must be someone nailing shut his coffin lid. He moved his head. Maybe he hadn't died after all. He forced open one eye and tried to hear out of one ear. He struggled to throw off the pile of blankets, but his mind refused to thaw. The tapping grew louder.

His eyes popped open. He put his right foot in the wrong fur-lined slipper as he reached for the telephone. The duty officer or one of the marines must be calling. Nope, not the phone.

He swung his head toward the door. When he opened it, she was standing there, glamorous in a mink-lined parka and matching commissar hat. Her eyes sparkled.

"You're wasting daylight."

It was eight o'clock in the morning. Her breath formed little puffs of vapor.

"May I come in?" She marched past him.

"Mrs. Pierson, it's Saturday. What I'm wasting is sleep." Russ was annoyed. "I hope the concierge didn't get a look at you." He glanced down the hall.

"Remember, it's Rhonda. Preston's at the embassy reading cables, so I have until noon. Let's go for a walk. We'll get tea and strudel down the street."

He gawked at her. "Tea and strudel?"

"Get dressed. You'll freeze running around in your jammies."

Russ shuffled into the bedroom, grabbed clothes and a heavy sweater, and headed for the bathroom. When he splashed his face, the icy water shocked him into reality. He was unprepared to deal with his reviewing officer's wife at this hour of the morning. Still, he was intrigued. Why on earth was she here?

Leaning against the sink in his flannel pajama bottoms, he smelled orchids. He looked in the mirror and saw her standing in the doorway.

"Mind if I watch? I'm amazed how little we know about those who matter most to us."

"How can I possibly matter to you?"

"You'll see." There was that cute grin again.

"I'm a little worried about being here, in my own flat, I might add, with you."

"Don't be. We're safe. Here, let me fix your collar."

Her soft fingers straightened his flannel shirt and patted his neck. She held open the bottom of his sweater, and he slid in his arms. As he ran his hands through his hair, he eyed her.

"Come, let's sit on your sofa a bit before we leave."

Russ stared at his hands, trying to quiet his alarm.

"You can look at me. What's going through your mind?"

"Mostly panic. What are you doing here?"

"I'm making a start. Saturday mornings are the best time for me to get away."

"A start on what?"

Rhonda touched his wrist. "Getting to know you better. Telling my stories. Teaching you some important life lessons. We'll have fun. You'll see."

"Life lessons?"

"That's right. Lessons on how to treat women. That is, if you want to learn." She picked up his hand and rubbed its palm. "What do you think?"

"I think I need coffee." He went to his kitchen just to put some distance between them.

He rattled around with mugs, water, and the pot. When he returned with the mugs, Rhonda stood before his tiny library of baseball, Russian history, Steinbeck, Stalin's biography.

She wrapped her fingers around the mug and sipped. "Umm, good and hot." She met his eyes, and he looked away again. "Don't skitter away when a woman looks at you. Hold my gaze until you understand what I might be telling you."

"I'll work on that as soon as I sort out what's happening."

They sipped in silence until Rhonda put her mug aside. "Feeling better? I didn't mean to scare you with my sudden appearance. You'll learn that I'm very enthusiastic when I'm pursuing a great idea."

He blew across his mug. "I'll watch out for your great ideas in the future."

She laughed out loud, stood, and reached for his hand. "Now let's get that strudel."

Russ grabbed his keys and shrugged into his parka. He met Rhonda at his door.

When she turned around, a mischievous grin played across her face. "See, we're having fun already. You may kiss me now." She leaned toward him with her hand on his chest.

His mouth dropped open. "Is this one of your great ideas?"

"Don't you want to kiss me?"

"I hope you're not disappointed."

She closed her eyes. When he brushed her lips and pulled back, she blinked. "Needs practice."

He pulled her in and kissed her deeply.

She lingered in his embrace and looked at him with dewy eyes. "So much better."

"Maybe I just need the right teacher."

"I'm available."

"Rhonda, you're married."

"I know that." Her eyes flashed like spring storms in the Kansas grasslands. "We're safe if we're discreet. I'll never hurt you. You must trust me."

Glancing at the concierge's closed door as they tiptoed down the hallway, Russ remembered the NKVD eavesdropping device he had removed from the hollowed bottom of his ashtray. He hoped it hadn't been replaced. His spirits sank as he imagined their glee at Dzerzhinsky Square.

His nasal passages shrank with the cold, but Rhonda marched down the steps. At the bottom, she slid her arm through his as they struggled with the glazed sidewalk. She pointed away from the embassy. When they entered a small arcade, he checked for NKVD tails.

A babushka in a white headscarf and a dingy apron produced two slabs of apple strudel and two chipped mugs of black tea. Rhonda opened a coin pouch and gave her some kopeks.

She cut a bite from her strudel. "Tell me about your past with women."

"My past with women?" Russ watched her eat. "There's not much to tell. All the girls in high school talked about marriage and I wanted to see the world." He tasted his strudel, hoping to settle his stomach. "Are you doing some kind of research?"

"Not exactly." She patted his hand. "What's your dream woman? A friend, a lifelong companion, someone to roll around with in bed?"

"Who knows?" He squinted into the distance. "But if I had to decide, I'd say I'd want all that but in just one person." He looked at her. "But, let's face it, the Foreign Service is hard on women. Not many girls want to leave the familiar, step out of the normal, and wind up back in Kansas when I retire."

"Don't worry about retirement." She took his hand. "Focus on the beginning of a relationship. The early months will set the tone for the rest of your married life."

"My married life, huh?" He finished his strudel and lit a Pall

Mall. "What about your married life? How does it bring you to me?"

"Not now, Russ." She touched his lips with a single finger. "We're discussing your dreams. Let's just say I'm living one of mine. I promise I'll tell you about me, and I keep my promises. Never forget that." Her maple syrup eyes flashed. "Now, move on from high school."

"I've had my share of relationships." He ground out his cigarette. "Do you want a scorecard of my conquests?"

"No, I'm not interested in that." She tilted her head. "I'm interested in how you think, what you want."

He lit another cigarette. "I'll be back in D.C. next summer for Arabic language training. Maybe I'll meet someone who's interested in overseas life."

She checked her watch. "We've got a lot to talk about next time. Gotta run."

"Next time? When?"

"I'll let you know. You'll have to allow me to set the dates because, as you've reminded me, I'm married." At the arcade door, Rhonda's mink flared in the frigid wind. Russ watched as a tall Russian woman standing at a nearby kiosk folded her newspaper and followed. He wondered why the NKVD would tail an embassy wife.

⁂

Russ went to happy hour on the next two Fridays. Rhonda never showed.

On the third Sunday, he rose early and headed to the corner where a crowded bus, belching black fumes, lurched to a stop. He exited at Sparrow Hills, in southwest Moscow, and climbed to an overlook that was supposed to be the best in the city.

From a bench at the overlook, he followed the sweeping curve of the Moscow River past a park cloaked in a haze of coal smoke. When he smelled orchids, he turned, and she was there. This time, he wasn't surprised. "When did you arrive?"

"I'm not telling." She giggled and joined him on the bench. "What were you thinking about?" She scooted closer when he put his arm around her.

"I was wondering how the Russians built such a city in this harsh land." He raised his eyebrows and grinned. "Actually, I was thinking of you."

She smiled. "Glad I made an impression on you."

"Oh, you made an impression!" He turned to scan the overlook. "I've done little except try to figure you out. My brain hurts. I keep trying to rationalize what we're doing. You know, telling right from wrong."

She tilted her head to meet his eyes. "We're taking a gamble, for sure. But I want to do this, and I want to do it with you. I hope the reward is worth the risk."

"My career is on the line if we're caught in an affair, not to mention your marriage."

"This isn't an affair, Russ, although it may look like one from the outside. You must understand that we will not become lovers. Can you be comfortable with what we're doing?"

"I'm willing to try." He turned to look at her. "You're about the most amazing woman I've ever met. Smart, funny, confident. You scare me, but you're a breath of fresh air amid all this coal smoke."

"Don't stop, tell me more, especially the amazing part."

"When I thought about you during the last two weeks, I realized I was lonely. I needed someone to talk to and laugh with. And if I learn something along the way, so much the better."

"Good," Rhonda said. "I know Preston bothers you, but I can manage him. He keeps an eye on me, but I've learned how to carve out time for things I want to do without raising his suspicions."

"Maybe he's right to be suspicious."

"He hasn't had a single reason to be until I met you. Our relationship is more complicated than you're imagining." She sighed. "I'll tell you more over time, but for now understand that Preston wants a pretty wife who doesn't participate in cocktail chatter, because women can't possibly understand obscure references to Soviet history." She held his gaze. "Never do that to a woman. Respect her as your intellectual equal."

"Most of the time I don't want to discuss Soviet history, so that won't be a problem." He chuckled and threw his arm across her shoulders. "What do you like to talk about?"

"I like baseball." Flexing her arm beneath her mink, she tossed an imaginary ball. "And I can throw a curveball better than most men."

"I bet you can." He pulled her beneath his arm again. "Well, I won't be writing to Mom about you, but my last six months in Moscow will be a lot less dreary with you in them."

"Forget your mom. Stick with me and you'll be ready to treat women the way they want to be treated. They'll thank me. We'll make Moscow the post you'll always remember."

"I knew from the moment I danced with you I'd never forget my time in Moscow."

"Good. Before we go warm up in that coffee bar, you may kiss me."

"Here?" He glanced around.

"People kiss here all the time."

"You've been here before?"

She held a finger to his lips and rested her other hand lightly on his chest. "You may need a little more practice."

Russ pulled her to him and breathed her in. She was intoxicating.

When she drew away, her eyes shone. "That was wonderful. But if we're to continue practicing, you must lose the cigarettes."

"I've smoked forever. It's relaxing. Something to do with my hands."

She touched his chest again. "You won't need cigarettes where I'm taking you. Soon you'll crave only me. I'll make you dizzy with anticipation and breathless for more." She caressed his cheek. "If you want me, no cigarettes."

"Okay, I'll try."

"No, Russ, you decide. Cigarettes or me."

He rose and tossed the Pall Malls into a trash bin beside the bench.

At the coffee bar, Russ played with his napkin.

Rhonda rested her chin in her hand. "Having second thoughts already?"

"Just getting my bearings. I hardly saw you at the embassy, and now this." He waved his hand between them.

She leaned across the small table. "But I saw you. I know how you think, how others respond to you. How you take time to consider."

"You were watching me?"

She leaned back in the chair. "Look, your participation in this is completely voluntary. I can vanish as quickly as I appeared." A fleeting sadness passed over her face. "But consider what you'd miss. We can do this. I know we can. All you have to do is believe in me and in yourself."

After a moment, he reached for her hand. "I believe in you. Stay with me. I'll listen to you and gaze into your eyes. I'll kiss you and hold you in my arms."

When a ray of sunlight touched her face, he reached out and caressed the lines at the corners of her eyes. His hand followed the curve of her face.

"I had forgotten how much I like to be touched." She swiped at a tear forming in her eye. "I have to go."

Outside in the biting cold, he pulled her into the shadow of a balcony. His kiss lingered until she stepped from his embrace.

When Rhonda approached an idling bus, a tall woman in a black leather coat crossed the street. She watched Rhonda queueing at the front door. She quickly hopped on the bus at the rear door. When she scanned the passengers, Rhonda was nowhere to be seen.

***

That night while Preston read a history of the Great War, Rhonda retrieved her lap desk and yellow stationery. She addressed an envelope to a lady friend in the States. She wrote of Moscow's bleak days and frigid nights and how she longed for spring. In the final paragraphs, she wrote of Russ.

I've found someone. Like most young men, women confuse him, although he has definite ideas about marriage and, can you believe it, retirement. He's a great candidate.

I made him wait for two weeks before reappearing. He thinks I'm an apparition. He's very lonely. I'm confident he'll learn quickly.

I hope the rolling hills are covered with a picturesque blanket of snow and the cardinals are at your feeders. I wish for a letter from you soon.

Affectionately,
Rhonda

Chapter 31

January 1939. German submarine U-47 penetrates the British naval base at Scapa Flow and sinks the battle-ship HMS Royal Oak.

On a Sunday, Rhonda laced Preston's tea with brandy and put him to bed with a heavy cold. Soon he was fast asleep. She changed into her warmest clothes, threw on her mink-lined parka and commissar hat, grabbed her bag, and ran down the stairs. She tiptoed across the ice-slickened sidewalk and climbed aboard an old belch-fire bus when it lurched to a stop.

Later, she randomly strolled around the block near his building, using shop windows to check for a tail. Must be too cold for Elena, her svelte NKVD shadow.

The old woman's door stood open and opera music floated down the hall. She smiled when she saw the empty light fixture in the stairwell. Removing her boots, she climbed to the second floor and padded down the hall. She steadily tapped until she heard his footsteps. His eyes lit up when he opened the door.

"Rhonda, I hoped it was you!"

"What do you have that will warm me up?"

He laughed. "How about a cognac?"

Glass in hand, she glanced at a book on the end table, *Ten Days That Shook the World* by journalist John Reed.

"You know, Reed's buried beside the Kremlin Wall, behind Lenin's tomb." She tucked her feet beneath her. "It's an interesting story about—"

"No kidding? An American buried here? Do you want to go see his grave next Sunday?"

"Maybe we should start with a quick lesson and chat about John Reed later." She patted the sofa next to her. "What do you know about women and their friends?"

"Not much. The girls I knew back in Kansas traveled in bunches, cried a lot, and got mad for no reason." His smile faded when he saw her serious expression. "But I suppose you aren't talking about high school girls. Doesn't matter, though, women are mysterious."

"Well, you may be right." She laughed. "Sometimes we're mysteries even to ourselves."

"So, what do I need to know about this mysterious subject?"

"What did your mother do when she was worried about something?"

"She visited with her best friends, Mabel and Cora. They talked over the fence or while they picked vegetables from their gardens." Russ stared into space, remembering. "After Mom finished the dishes, she went out the back door with our border collie, Gertie, and kicked off her shoes."

Rhonda settled into the couch to listen.

"That was long before the Depression even started, but they were still tough times. Anyway, while Gertie rooted for varmints, the women talked." Russ shrugged. "That's all I remember. I was long gone through the back gate with my brother and our friends."

He touched her hair, breathing in the warmth of orchids. He whispered into her ear, "What do women talking to one another have to do with me?"

"Your mother and her neighbors must have been devoted friends. They'd formed a bond like a silk thread, soft and pliable and nearly indestructible. Devoted friends know when to listen. That's your lesson. Be a caring listener to the woman you love. Don't interrupt, don't shift the conversation to yourself, hear what's being said."

Russ dropped his hand and sat back. "So, this is about my interrupting you when you were going to tell me an interesting story about Reed. I should've listened."

"Yes, Russ, you might learn something about your woman, like why she thinks the story she's telling is interesting enough to share it with you." She held his hand. "And sometimes you learn even more. Sometimes she's actually telling you something about herself." She picked up her cognac. "You'll never know unless you listen long enough to let her finish."

She glanced at her wristwatch. "Look at the hour. I must leave soon."

"But you just got here. How about some kissing practice?"

Afterward she placed her hand on his chest. "Whew! You may not need more practice."

He traced her lips with his finger. "I want to know everything about you. I live for these moments. You told me I wouldn't need cigarettes and you were right." He nuzzled her neck and caressed her cheek. Then he touched his lips to hers until she broke their embrace.

"Stop, Russ. I must be going." She stood, grabbed her mink, and left before she could change her mind.

Sunday found Russ, shivering and miserable, standing before John Reed's grave in Red Square. He felt a hand brush his and turned to find Rhonda by his side. Her glowing happiness banished the gray from his day.

"I'm ready to hear your story about him, now, if you'd like to tell me."

She nodded and snuggled beneath Russ's enclosing arm. "Well, I found Reed's life interesting, particularly his early years. You know, I'm sure, that he was a journalist, Communist, and friend of Lenin, but did you know he was born into wealth and favor? He was in poor health as a child, surrounded by nurses and servants. His mother handpicked his playmates and associates. Still, he broke away and chose his own path, one that some say he regretted before he suffered an early death.

"Shall we walk?" She passed him her canvas shopping bag and tucked her arm through his. "Even though his family and his health held him to an expected path, he made life-changing decisions when he became an adult that took him beyond the normal and routine. He broke free from his past and stepped out into a world of his own choosing." She squeezed Russ's arm. "I read about John Reed when I was younger. Putting aside his political activism, his life story made me think about what a person, even a woman, could do if she was determined."

"I think you could do anything you wanted if you were determined, Rhonda." He pulled her closer for a moment and looked into her eyes.

She met his gaze and nodded. "Someday I'll tell you more."

They strolled toward St. Basil's Cathedral, at the south end of Red Square. The church, a symbol of old Russia, was adorned with fairy-tale architectural elements. The sun's intermittent rays dappled the onion domes in golden light and cast the nooks and alcoves in deep shadows.

"You never leave my thoughts," Russ whispered in Rhonda's ear.

She rested her hand on his chest. "Where shall we go?"

At her touch, his heart warmed. "It doesn't make any difference."

They wandered along the Kremlin Wall to the west of Red Square, joining clusters of families braving the bitter air. A group of well-dressed people in front of St. Basil's caught his eye. He stopped short and squinted into the distance.

"What's wrong, Russ?" Rhonda followed his line of sight. "Is that Horace Wyman? Is he staring at us? I don't see Sadie."

Russ pulled Rhonda into a larger group of strollers. "She's there too."

She peeked over Russ's shoulder. "Oh, I see her now. She's poking his chest. I wonder what she's saying."

"What do we do?" Russ guided Rhonda behind a statue near the wall.

"I don't know. Maybe I'll mention seeing her and she'll tell me about their conversation."

"This was too good to be true." He sagged against the wall.

"Don't talk like that. It may turn out to be nothing." She shook his arm. "Let's continue as we have been. Here, in Washington, in New York City, or wherever our paths cross."

"We have to be more careful." Russ looked at the scudding clouds. "I'll have to tell the truth if Horace asks."

"What is the truth? You leaned down to say something because it's noisy here. Maybe your arm was around my waist. We didn't kiss." Rhonda shook his arm again. "Think of the fix Horace is in. Will he feel compelled to tell Preston, his boss, that he saw something about his wife? Based on a glimpse in Red Square from over a hundred yards away? I think not."

Russ winced and shook his head. "But what about my career? He may not tell your husband, but we both know how Horace thinks. He may believe the worst."

"We're not sleeping together. You can truthfully deny that." She pulled him away from the wall. "I say we ride out the storm, if there is one." She led him along the river until they found a bench.

"Look what I found at GUM." She opened her canvas bag and removed red wine, cheese, and black bread. "I'm hungry. Are you?" She squeezed his hand. "Let's forget Horace."

"I'll try." Russ checked behind them and then breathed a big sigh. "Let me open the wine while you tell me about your childhood."

"I'm from Norfolk, Virginia. I have one sis, Bernice. Momma died when I was thirteen."

"I'm sorry. Girls need their mothers at that age."

"If you only knew. Those were bad years. Daddy raised us by himself, and he had a tough time of it."

"What did you your dad do?"

"He was a civilian auditor for the Navy."

"How about college? Was it in Norfolk?"

"No, Williamsburg, Virginia. I graduated from William and Mary with a degree in European history and a minor in languages. Then I went on to the Women's Law Class in D.C., specializing in international contract law."

"You're a lawyer?"

"Yes, I'm a lawyer." She stared at him. "You needn't sound so surprised."

"Well, not many Foreign Service wives have careers, especially important ones like law."

"See, there's another lesson. Women can do anything men can do. We're not *just* wives. If you think that way, you'll miss so much."

Russ rubbed his chin. "I know women can do anything they set their minds to, but you must have struggled in a bureaucracy full of men."

"One of my first jobs was with Nestlé, in Bern, and then in Manhattan, at Bill Donovan's law firm." She leaned against the bench and stared into space. "Most of my partners treated me like I was a glorified secretary, not a real lawyer. They expected me to make coffee for our meetings and then take shorthand."

"I bet that didn't sit well. How long was it before they realized you were to be taken seriously?"

"Too long, but they got it in the end. Well, not all of them. Some weren't willing to give up their medieval system." She tore off a bit of bread with a snap of her wrist. "And it never ends. Just look at our embassy. The men treat their fellow female officers like secretaries even though most are better educated and worked harder for the job than they did.

"And while I'm on my soapbox, show secretaries some respect. Make your own coffee. Type your own reports. Share the work. You might be surprised at their reactions."

"Got it. Make them my allies." He grinned. "Maybe they'll even like me."

"Don't try that hard." She punched his arm and offered her best stare.

"You're a lawyer. And here I thought you were just another pretty woman."

"You're on thin ice, buster." She wagged a finger at him.

He pulled it toward him and kissed the tip.

She pulled it back. "Behave."

"Okay. Where did Preston show up?"

"In England. We were both on holiday. We married in 1935. The next year, we sailed to Lisbon, where he was head of the Political Section. Then we went to D.C. for home leave before Moscow. And here we are." She shivered. "I'll fill in the blanks sometime when we're not freezing." She winked. "In private."

Russ brushed aside the wisp of hair blowing from beneath her hat. His hand dropped to her neck. He gently pushed her against the bench. When he leaned over, her lips parted.

❦

Two days later, Nadine stood in Russ's office doorway.

"Horace wants to see you."

Russ could feel his pulse quickening as he walked the short distance to Wyman's office.

"Yes, sir?"

Wyman waved him to a chair. "We need to discuss what was going on in Red Square on Sunday with you and Mrs. Pierson."

"Yes, sir, of course. I thought I saw you but wasn't sure from that distance."

Wyman tapped his pencil against Russ's file. "Even from that distance, I saw you hugging her."

"Oh, no, sir. You're mistaken. I had gone there to view John Reed's grave. Mrs. Pierson was shopping at GUM. She saw me in Red Square. She said something about the coincidence, and I couldn't hear her. You might remember it was noisy. I may have leaned down to hear her better. That may have been what you saw."

Wyman crossed his arms. "Noisy, huh? Are you two having an affair?"

"No, sir." Russ swallowed the taste of her lips on his. "We've run across each other socially the past few months, ever since I first met her at your apartment."

"Socially." Wyman rubbed his chin. "That's it, huh?" He picked up his pen. "I'm noting this conversation in your file. Remember, your evaluation is coming up."

"I realize that, sir. I hope you won't let this color your perception of my work here."

Wyman frowned. "You're playing with fire. Mrs. Pierson may be good-looking and smart, but she's married to my boss and your reviewing officer."

"Sir, Rhonda Pierson and I are friends. We're not lovers. We've done nothing to bring shame to the Political Section or the front office."

Wyman closed the file. "You must live with yourself. Does Preston know his wife has a 'friend'?"

"I wouldn't know. If you've found my reporting or any other aspect of my work dissatisfactory, I would appreciate it if you'd tell me."

"No, you're doing a respectable job."

"Thank you, sir. I'll bear in mind your advice by being more circumspect in my appearances with single, or married, female friends."

"Okay, we're through."

Russ fell into his desk chair, gritting his teeth as he reviewed the conversation with Wyman. Had he saved himself? He had skirted the truth. While they weren't lovers, Rhonda was more than a social friend. Was she worth it? He needed to see her. Talk it through with her. Could he risk seeing her again? Could he survive not seeing her again?

Chapter 32

*November 1941. The Wehrmacht takes Yalta, in the
Crimea.*

Duncan and Bitsy studied the gear piled on the bed, then considered the space in the kit bags on the floor. "I hoped the amir would forget this trek into the desert," Duncan said.

"At least the temperature has moderated." She held the bag while he latched its flap.

"Can you keep yourself occupied for the next two days?"

"Of course. I have a desk full of correspondence. Maybe one of the wives will take me to the suq for some Christmas shopping."

Duncan pecked her cheek as Mohammed hauled the bags to the motorcar.

While Hassan drove Milbourne to the palace, Bitsy rang the bell. "Mohammed, you may give the staff the weekend off."

She lifted the receiver. "Jane, this is Bitsy. Why don't we go shopping tomorrow? I'd like to be back home before the afternoon heat."

At four o'clock, Russ stood on the patio with his steno pad. He knew he wasn't at the residence on a weekend, with the ambassador out of town, just so he could review the progress of the upstairs renovation. When he learned she'd dismissed the staff, he recalled Catherine's warning.

"Thanks for coming. George's meisters spend more time returning to their shop for the proper tools than they do working."

Russ shrugged. "That's the way they do business here."

Bitsy wore tailored slacks and a sweater. Her hair was tied with the familiar blue ribbon. The combination of a pencil behind her ear, reading glasses hanging around her neck, and a legal pad in her hand somewhat eased Russ's concern. Maybe she really did intend to work.

They began downstairs. After an hour, their work order listed twenty-three new items. "I think I'll avoid delivering this list to George Lander in person. His reaction will be awful."

"I don't care. I've known George for years. When he and Doris arrived in Tunis, he was already a serious drinker. But he catered to Duncan's every whim, so Duncan wrote him glowing evaluations. He wasn't so bad then, but now I can't abide the man. I won't let him oversee the work orders, so I rely on you to run interference for me."

In the distance, the faint call of the muezzin notified the faithful of the day's end. The sun fell behind the peak, leaving the patio in shadow.

Bitsy dropped her legal pad and pencil on a table. "Look, it's almost six. Why don't you stay? We'll make sandwiches."

"Okay. I never turn down a free meal."

They prepared their food, bumping into each other and dropping utensils on the counter, bantering all the while. Carrying a tray out to the patio, Bitsy walked to the low wall. "Let's pull our chairs over here and watch the changing colors on the Gulf."

"Mais oui, Madame." Russ pirouetted from the table and joined her with glasses and a bottle of wine.

They ate and talked of embassy life and the hardships of living in the desert. Bitsy pushed her empty plate aside and shivered. "Would you get my shawl from the parlor, and pick up another bottle of wine from the kitchen?"

When Russ returned, he sat on the wall and watched the fading horizon. "The moon's about to come up. Want to walk to the beach?"

She grabbed her cane. At the boulevard, they waved to the guard and strolled past a crescent-shaped rock formation in the sand. "Come on. Let's wade in the surf."

He steadied her while she removed her shoes. She untied the blue ribbon and shook out her hair. She left her cane on the sand, and they walked into the water.

"You miss your friend from Moscow, don't you?" She placed a hand on his back.

"Yes. She haunts me still."

"I can help you to not miss her so much." Bitsy took his hand.

Russ removed it. "I don't think I want to start something new."

"Come on. We'll enjoy each other before I return to the States. Pass the time and have some fun. What can it hurt?"

"Plenty and I know it. Besides I don't want to be a player in a game with your husband."

"It's not a game. I'm trying to decide if it's time to leave him. You can help me."

Russ looked out to sea. "You know you're attractive, Bitsy. But I don't need trouble."

"We'll be discreet. No one will suspect a thing."

With shoes in hand, they passed the sleeping guard at the bottom of the drive. At the foot of the stairs Bitsy turned to Russ. She pulled his head down and kissed him slowly. "It'll be okay. Why don't you let me show you things only an older woman can know?"

Standing in a cloud of sandalwood perfume, Russ let Catherine's warning evaporate on the breeze. He allowed himself to be led up the stairs of the marble palace.

The next morning, a cool breeze wafted through the lace curtains of Bitsy's bedroom. With his arms crossed behind his head, Russ watched her at her vanity as she brushed her hair.

Catching his eye in the mirror, she turned. "Good morning, sleepyhead." She perched on the edge of the bed. "You know, I'm friends with the head of Personnel. I may take him to lunch and mention your sterling attributes. Maybe I can help get you promoted."

"Would you like to see more of my sterling attributes?" He turned on his side and reached into her blue kimono.

Later they rested. "If you don't mind my asking, what happened to your leg?"

Bitsy rolled over and snuggled into his arms. "It was a long time ago, after a Department cocktail party. Duncan was drunk. He ran us off the frozen highway. I should have had surgery, but I'm afraid of waking up helpless. My therapist works with me, and I swim because it helps relieve the pain."

"Does your husband blame himself?"

"Not really. He says he doesn't remember it, and he's convinced himself he swerved to avoid hitting something, so it couldn't have been his fault." She twirled a finger in his chest hair. "You know, it doesn't matter now. I just live with it."

Russ brushed the hair from her face. "You're beautiful, and certainly young enough to have a good life. Why stay in an unhappy marriage?"

She scooted to the edge of the bed and stood. "I've thought about leaving Duncan many times, but my father liked Duncan, liked to drink with him." She returned to the vanity. "Now that Daddy's gone, and I've come into my own money, I'm free to consider my future."

Russ glanced at the bedside clock. "Yikes. As much as I've enjoyed sharing your world, I've got to be heading home." He sat on the edge of the bed and pulled on his pants.

She joined him there and ran her hands through his hair. "Before you go, I have a confession. I have a friend. We share a mission. We want women to have better lives. We believe we can do that by helping men learn how to be better husbands and lovers."

He stopped her hand with his.

"You know her too."

His chest tightened and he closed his eyes. "Rhonda."

Chapter 33

April 1939. Research continues on the Reich's V-2 guided ballistic missile at its Peenemünde Army Research Center, on an island in the Baltic Sea.

RUSS ANSWERED THE door in his jammies.

"We're wasting daylight. Preston is visiting the consulate general in Leningrad. We have this glorious Saturday to ourselves!" She wore a leather jacket and khaki pants. Her gold barrette peeked from beneath her beret. "Let's drive to Novodevichy Convent."

With the convent's red and white crenellated battlements towering above them, she motioned Russ to pose before the oldest structure on the grounds, the five-domed Smolensky Cathedral. "Now take my photograph." She raised her arms in joy and twirled on the spring green grass. "I no longer have to bundle up like a Siberian babushka."

In the quiet lanes of the cemetery's old section, lichens draped the gray stone crypts of the half sister and first wife of Peter the Great. Birds twittered high in the branches over Moscow's premier interment site. "Look, my love, how the sun dapples the grave of Chekhov!"

On a wooden bench under a stately tree, they shared their lunch. No one else wandered in the gardens. They were completely alone in a world away. Using her jacket as a pillow, Rhonda closed her eyes. Rays of sunshine tiptoed across her face in the quiet garden.

While Rhonda dozed, Russ explored lanes lined with the tangled brambles of old roses. White clouds towered before a backdrop of cerulean sky. He returned to the bench just as Rhonda stretched. Yawning, she turned sideways and put her head in his lap.

With one finger, he moved a strand of hair and caressed her cheek. Soon he would leave Moscow. Would she write to him, or let him pass into memory? Could he bear the separation?

What began as a respite from loneliness in a far-off land had become something more for him. A lot more. She still seemed intent on making him a more confident man around women, but she had relaxed her reserve and allowed him to offer her a bit of contentment. He thought he could make her happy. But how? Would she let him? For her, he would do anything.

Later, they strolled the convent's grounds. "Many women of the Russian royal family were forced to take the veil here. Although we're near the heart of Moscow, they might as well have been cloistered in Siberia. What occupied their endless days?" She wiped her eyes. "When their quiet lives led to the silence of the grave, were they buried by a lone gravedigger holding a lantern in the frigid gloom of a long winter night?"

As if in sympathy, the sun passed behind a cloud.

Russ pulled her to his side. "I'm sure these women reached out to one another, sharing their stories. Just like my mother and her friends. Maybe right here in these gardens."

"You remembered!" She brushed his lips with hers. "These pathways offered them sanctuary, a place to wander and converse outside the restrictions of the convent."

She spun out of his arms. "Enough sadness. I'm hungry. Let's find a coffee bar."

When she pulled her Peugeot to the side of the road near a tiny café, Russ looked in one direction and Rhonda in the other. They smiled at their freedom and entered the cozy shop. Two elderly

Russian women glanced at them before returning to their conversation.

Rhonda ordered black tea while Russ selected coffee.

She looked at the offerings. "Am I too fat for an order of *syrniki?*"

"I don't know what those are. Besides, you're not fat; you're fluffy."

She smacked his arm. "Very funny. Syrniki are pancakes made from flour, cheese, and sugar. Crispy on the outside and creamy on the inside. Lovely and delicious."

Russ dabbed the powdered sugar from her lips. "I don't know anything about your lady friends. Do you have any, considering how often we must move around?"

"I do. One of my dearest friends is Treva. I met her a long time ago in a small hotel on the Isle of Skye. She has silver hair and the most amazing cornflower blue eyes. We began talking and before we knew it, we were like old friends." She laughed. "I think we knew more about each other than some married couples know in a lifetime."

"Treva sounds wonderful. Maybe you'll introduce me someday." He toyed with his napkin. "Do we have a someday?" He raised hopeful eyes.

"Darling, we've talked about this before. You'll find someone. You'll charm her with all the things you've learned from me."

"I've already found her." He leaned his head against hers.

"I know." She stroked his cheek. "But it can't be like you want, darling. You know that."

"Why, Rhonda?" He clutched her fingers. "I know you feel the same."

She touched his lips. "You'll interrupt those ladies' afternoon chat."

"I don't care." He shook off her finger. "I knew you were married. It didn't matter when we began, but now I want to spend every minute with you. I love you, Rhonda."

With a final glance at the old women, she gathered her things and led him into the street. "Hush now, let's not ruin a wonderful day." She grabbed his hand. "Let's go for a walk."

He pulled his hand away and stood still. "I ache for you. I want to possess you. I want to turn my life over to you. You want it, too. I know you do."

She closed her eyes for a few moments before turning and walking away. When he followed, she turned into a small park with two benches on either side of a tall sculpture dripping with water. "Ah, roses, my favorite." She bent to sniff the petals.

He stood without touching her. "Come on, Rhonda. You can't just walk away from this. You can't leave me hanging here without saying something. Anything."

She sighed. "I know. I just needed a moment." She turned to face him. "In the beginning, I never considered what might happen. I thought I could keep our lessons lighthearted and fun. Something an older woman could give to a younger man to make his life better for his future." She gripped the sides of her head and pulled at her hair. "But then I got to know you. The real you, not just some smart young man who could be led through a series of steps."

He pulled her hands away from her hair and held them. "And you didn't think I'd see the real you, Rhonda. The woman who wants so much and gets so little. A woman who needs to be loved. A woman who's not afraid of much, except what will set her free."

She blinked away tears. "You're right, I'm afraid. Without Preston, who am I? I no longer practice law and don't work for Bill Donovan, at least not in the normal way." She waved that aside. "Without Preston, I can't be what I am, do what I do. As much as I want my freedom, I can't have it. As much as I love you, Russ, and I do, I also love my life. The one separate from Preston."

He brushed away her tears and led her to a bench. "I don't know what you're talking about. Why can't you have a life without Preston? I can you give a life."

"Ahhh!" Her hands were back at her hair again. "You can't, you can't." She hit his chest. "You're too young. Too new." She dropped her hands into her lap. "You just can't."

"Okay, Rhonda, okay." He pulled her close and made soothing sounds in her ear. "I don't know what to say, what to tell you, because I don't know what just happened." He petted her hair back in place and whispered, "At least I know you love me too, and want me as badly as I want you. It's a start, and we can try to figure out the rest later." He held her until she stopped sobbing.

"Thank you, Russ. Sorry I'm such a mess." She blew her nose on his handkerchief. "You'll leave Moscow soon. Maybe we need time and distance to see a way through this. Maybe you'll find your perfect woman." She touched his cheek. "Until then, I'll continue to love you. I'll find you wherever you go. Like a ghost, my darling, I'll always be nearby."

Chapter 34

May 1939. Norway, Sweden, and Finland reject the
Nazis' offer of a nonaggression pact.

ONE LATE SPRING evening, Rhonda appeared on his doorstep. "Come on, Russ! We're going for a ride." Her eyes sparkled with anticipation. "You'd better hurry."

She steered her Peugeot 402 out of Moscow. When they slowed for the village of Severny, Russ looked into a hut squatting on a dirt lane. A single candle illuminated an old woman pouring water into a teacup. A black-and-white cat tiptoed through the weeds below the open window. The air was redolent of humus, livestock, and honeysuckle.

In a few miles, they crossed over a dam onto a dirt road. "This is Pirogovskaya Reservoir."

She backed under a tree and turned off the ignition. A full moon illuminated the vast and silent steppe. The chirp of crickets surrounded them and, once, the wing beats of a night bird passed overhead. Something splashed at the edge of the water, thirty feet down the slope.

Russ threw out a blanket, and Rhonda opened a bottle of wine. "This may be our last time together before Hitler finishes rolling over Europe and turns on Stalin. He hates Communism almost as much as he hates the Jews."

She lounged in his arms. "How'd you like to kiss me by the light of the moon and tell me you'll desperately miss me when you transfer?"

"I'll miss you desperately when I leave Moscow." His hand crept beneath her blouse.

She pulled it away. "Behave. If we don't talk first, we may never get to what I want to tell you. And we have so little time left."

He fell against the blanket. "Okay, I'm listening."

"You deserve a woman with a sense of joy. Someone with spunk, joie de vivre."

"You're spunky, Rhonda." His hand strayed to her waist.

She giggled and slapped it away. "I am. Now pay attention.

"Give her small gifts. Women in distress need chocolate. Make her smile. Kiss her in public. And most importantly, challenge her mind, and she'll give you her heart."

Russ sat with his arms around his knees, staring at the reservoir. "All we ever talk about is my future with someone else. What about my present, with you?"

She closed her eyes and her lids fluttered. "After my breakdown at Novodevichy Convent, I hoped we could return to the old way of being together. I'm still not ready to admit even to you that I haven't figured it all out."

"Maybe I could help if I knew more. Why won't you trust me with your secrets?" He blew out his breath and turned to her. "I know you have them, Rhonda."

"I'll try." She sat up, crossed her legs, and leaned forward. "Remember I told you I worked for Nestlé when I lived in Bern, Switzerland?"

He nodded and rolled to his back with his arms crossed beneath his head.

"Well, I met a lawyer there who worked with American companies. Colonel Bill Donovan. We spent many days together over a few weeks on a company project. When we finished, he offered me a job handling international contracts for his Manhattan law firm." She poked at him. "Are you awake?"

"Yep. Just picturing you as a single woman with a career."

"Anyway, Colonel Donovan and Franklin Roosevelt were fellow law students at Columbia. They remained friends after FDR became president. They often met to discuss our country's isolationism and the rise of this little thug Hitler."

"I'd like to have been a fly on the wall for those conversations."

"Sometime about 1933, Colonel Donovan approached FDR about creating an agency for collecting information about other countries. The president wasn't interested. Too much to do, what with the Depression and all. The colonel persisted until he'd convinced the president to allow him to set up a rudimentary agency. The colonel would handle everything from his offices in Manhattan. No one in the government would have to know about it. The colonel knew FDR loved intrigue, so he spun the agency as men and women following rumors and ferreting out secrets. FDR was sold."

Russ rolled up on one elbow. "While this is interesting, what about your career as a lawyer in Manhattan?"

"Hang on, I'm getting there." She pushed him down on the blanket. "Colonel Donovan looked over his group of bright young East Coast attorneys. He selected a few for specialized training. I was one of them."

"You're kidding. What kind of specialized training? Where did you go?"

"Patience." She watched his face. "I traveled by ocean liner to Liverpool. From there, I went to the Isle of Skye, off the northwest coast of Scotland."

"Skye? That's where you met Treva. What an odd place for training."

"I know." She laughed. "I was so excited. When I left Manhattan, I'd never heard of Skye. I had no idea what the training involved. It was all a big mystery.

"Everyone lodged in this little inn in Portree. The desk clerk passed us instructions for where to report the next morning." She hesitated. "You know you must never tell anyone about what I'm about to tell you."

Russ was sitting up now. When he nodded, she continued.

"The colonel had several friends who'd retired from Britain's SIS. These men traveled to Skye to teach us their methods. One of them actually lived there, so he was able to deflect any local interest in our group."

"Are you a spy?" Russ stared at her.

"Silly boy." Her eyes twinkled. "I'm a woman. Can you imagine a woman spy? Perish the thought."

"Right, you're not a spy. You just do extra work for the colonel, based on your training from retired intel officers." Russ slapped his thigh. "That's why a mere wife gets a tail from the NKVD!"

"Maybe, maybe not."

"Everything makes sense now. You have a car when most of us don't. You've been to all kinds of unusual places. Like this reservoir. Delightful place to meet a contact, or a lover. You're always scanning a room. I've seen you in the embassy library reading Soviet newspapers and magazines." He glared at her. "You're putting your life in danger!"

"I know and I'm careful. I just poke around, talking to people and reading newspapers."

When he rubbed a hand across his face, she took it. "There's more."

"More than being a spy? I can't imagine where you're going next." He flopped on the blanket. "Okay, I'm ready."

"I met Rupert on the Isle of Skye. He'd been in His Majesty's service until a broken leg from a parachute jump led to early retirement. He was one of Donovan's friends and an instructor. We trained by day and gathered with our instructors in the evenings at an old pub to share a pint. One evening, Rupert and I found ourselves alone after the others had left."

Russ smiled. "Hmm. I wonder if that was Rupert's idea."

"Maybe. He was a handsome widower. He invited me to sightsee around the island. We spent many evenings together and gradually became more than student and instructor. By the end of the course, we were lovers." Rhonda paused to glance at Russ.

"Don't stop now. What happened to Rupert? And how did you wind up with Preston?"

She rose and walked to the edge of the slope. "This view reminds me of our favorite place on Skye. We'd drive through the gloaming to a tiny car park at Kilt Rock. We walked along a small brook that burbled its way through emerald-green grass to the cliff. At the edge, he steadied me while I leaned out to watch the water fling itself over the brink, turning to mist as it touched the sea."

"That sounds wonderful." He reached for her hand and pulled her back to the blanket.

"I'd love to show you that waterfall." Rhonda leaned into Russ's arm. "Skye was like a fairy tale. I was still so young and dazzled with life.

"When it came time to return to Manhattan, Rupert drove me through a pouring rain to the ferry for a trip across the Sound of Sleat. We promised to write, to make plans."

She hung her head and closed her eyes. When Russ's arm tightened around her, she sighed and gave him a small smile.

"What happened, darling?"

"I never heard from Rupert. I waited for weeks. I believed him when he told me he loved me. How had I made such a mistake?"

"Oh no. Did you try to find him?"

"Yes. He had run off a cliff on the rain-slickened road on his return from dropping me off. I was devastated. Bill Donovan noticed the change in my behavior and pried out my story. Then he sent me away until I recovered."

"What a tragedy. I'm so sorry, Rhonda."

"I met Preston in England. He was looking for a wife to make him more suitable for advancement in the Foreign Service. I was a proper candidate. He was nice and very gentle. He never pushed himself on me. I barely noticed his lack of interest in me as a woman. I thought he was being considerate because I was still reeling from losing Rupert."

"You know I've wondered about Preston." Russ wiped her damp cheeks with his flannel shirttail. "Why do you stay with him if he can't love you like you want?"

"I had accepted it as my life until I met you. Still, the marriage is convenient for both of us. I'm the wife he needs to advance. He provides the cover I need to pursue my unofficial career. Through Preston, I have access to embassies and parties and the whole Foreign Service world. Our first post as a married couple was Lisbon. I learned so much about the Nazi threat there. Then we moved to Moscow." She tried a small smile. "And I found you."

"I get it now." Russ rubbed his eyes with the palms of his hands. "That's why you can't have a life without Preston. He's got enough rank to get you into the places you need to go. You said that I'm too young. I'm too new. What you meant was I'm too junior. You don't love Preston. You love your job as a spy for Donovan."

"Yes. I work for Donovan. I attend functions with high-ranking officials of various governments. I listen to chitchat. What happens if Hitler attacks Stalin? Will the Soviets become allies of Britain and America? I also look for people to join us. Call it spotting and assessing."

He pulled her on top of his lap. "Did you spot and assess me?"

Her finger was at his lips. "You are not part of my work for Donovan. I spotted you as a decent guy who could learn how to treat women." Her lips were on his. "I assessed your kissing skills."

"Well, I got more than I expected." Russ smiled. "I'm not surprised. I knew you weren't just another wife. I'm glad you told me. Especially about Rupert and how you wound up with Preston. Although it will take me some time to digest it all."

"You know, Colonel Donovan wants to form a federal intelligence agency for the coming war. If you don't get promoted, you might consider joining it. You'd be perfect."

"Would you write me a good reference?"

"A glowing one, darling."

"I'll keep that in my pocket for a rainy day."

"Let's not waste the rest of our last night here on the steppe." She rested her hand on his chest. "You've been very patient, and I know it hasn't been easy."

She unbuttoned his shirt and kissed him with passion. "We must do this my way, okay?"

Russ lifted her blouse and pulled her alongside him. When he was ready, she helped him with her firm grasp.

He trailed his finger along her thigh. "What about you?"

"Yes, please." She took his hand and guided it to her warm spot. "Just here," she breathed, "and here."

Later, they lay beneath the canopy of stars. Russ ran his fingers through her hair. "Maybe someday, you'll let us do more. Is that possible?"

"I don't know, Russ. I have another secret. When I'm ready I'll tell you, and then you'll understand why you must be satisfied with what I can offer."

"I am. I'll wait." He sat up. "Are you seeing me off at the train station?"

"Probably not. Preston has a reception that evening, and I must work while acting as the wife of an important man. At least the ambassador has arrived, so his wife can take over the hostess duties I've been covering. Preston's spirits have improved now that he has less responsibility."

"Well, we survived the worst that General Winter could throw at us. Thanks in great part to the warmth you brought to my life." He pulled the blanket around them, and they slept until a rooster greeted the dawn.

Rhonda stretched and wiggled her toes. She whispered, "Thank you for understanding me, Russ. I don't know how I'll survive without you."

"It'll be a torture to be away from you, but I'm grateful for this time we've had. I love you. I'll always love you, Rhonda."

As her car crept once again through Severny, wisps of white

smoke trailed above the hut Russ had noticed before. Through the open window, he glimpsed the old woman bent over a cooking fire. The black-and-white cat perched on the sill, licking milk from its paw.

Chapter 35

June 1939. The president and Mrs. Roosevelt host the king and queen of the United Kingdom at Hyde Park, where they serve hot dogs and beer.

No one would describe Horace Wyman as a cheerful man, but he looked grimmer than usual.

"You have a future in the service." He cleared his throat. "However, your liaison with Mrs. Pierson still troubles me." He tapped Russ's performance evaluation.

"I've never denied that we're friends." Russ held Wyman's gaze.

"Well, Preston's comments on his section of your evaluation were favorable. He doesn't appear to be bothered if he's even aware. Maybe I'm imagining things."

Wyman fiddled with a pencil. "Sadie saw me wrestling with this and encouraged me to take the long view. I did and modified my wording. It's a gift you may not get from others."

"I see."

"Your job performance was excellent. I saw great progress in your skills while you were here. But you must learn to protect your classified better, especially on that cluttered desk of yours." Wyman passed the document. "Write your section, and we'll put it in the next pouch."

Russ later read Wyman's review statements and shook his head. No matter how glowing the job-performance section, Wyman's personal observations would cost Russ his promotion.

⌒—✴✴✴—⌒

The next evening, Russ squeezed through the throngs to the train station counter to have his ticket stamped with the proper crimson bureaucratic ink. A voice over the tinny loudspeaker announced a one-hour delay for his train's departure. "Next information—thirty minutes."

Russ wandered over to a vendor for an orange soda and cheese sandwich. He told the old man to keep the change. "I won't need kopeks where I'm going."

Shriveled women and wizened men occupied the benches. Russ leaned against a light pole. A boy approached with a tray of trinkets and fruit. Russ shook his head.

He sighed, suffering the lonely torture of the Foreign Service.

In the dim recesses of the platform, soldiers shared a bottle of vodka. Babushkas in dark scarves and stockings sat among bundles piled high on the grimy floor.

A cloud of steam venting from his train's engine startled Russ. Through the vapor, another babushka limped toward him, leaning heavily on a cane. A drab gray scarf covered most of her auburn hair, although a barrette peeked out. She headed directly for his lonely light pole.

She reached up and caressed his cheek. "I couldn't let you leave this godforsaken country alone, and in the night."

"I've been hoping." He kissed her, inhaling orchids. "That's quite a disguise."

"You'd better appreciate this getup. Didn't want my minder along." Her eyes twinkled beneath the scarf. "Preston said he gave you a good evaluation. How about Horace?"

He grimaced. "It was great until the comments section where

he used the word 'generally.' That's the kiss of death for promotions. He hasn't forgotten Red Square."

"I'm not surprised. Remember Sadie told me the next day that Horace was shocked about the indiscretion. She couldn't have cared less."

"Whatever happens, I'll deal with it in Washington and Kuwait. I just wonder why he's so bothered by what he saw."

"Apparently, he had a disastrous first marriage. His wife's flings were not discreet. Also, he had a strict religious upbringing. I can't see how Sadie fits with him, but then the same could be said of Preston and me."

She squeezed Russ's arm. "I'm so sorry, darling. I thought we were careful. I worked hard to make sure Preston never suspected a thing."

Russ pulled her over to a bench vacated by a stooped couple.

The loudspeaker came alive. "Delay. Next information in thirty minutes."

A young soldier stood with his girl beneath the light pole. She hid her face in his uniform tunic and cried. Russ recognized the picture of goodbye.

"Before my train's announced, here's a gift for you." He retrieved a small tissue-wrapped box from his satchel. "This will remind you of all the moments we shared."

She pulled the simple knot of yellow ribbon to reveal a lacquered box. "It's beautiful." She peered inside at a piece of cloth nestled amid tissue paper. "What's this? I can't see in this light." She held the folded square beneath the lamp.

"It's a little hankie I made for you. Something to dry your tears on."

"Oh, Russ." She dabbed her eyes. "It's from one of your flannel cowboy shirts."

The loudspeaker crackled and announced his departure. He held his babushka close.

"I'll find you in D.C." She sniffled. "When I transfer home, we'll be together again."

"I love you. I hope you don't forget me."

When Russ slid his lips from hers, she clung to him before stepping away.

He leaned from the window of his compartment and saw her hunched beneath the lamp pole. He waved as she faded into the sea of babushkas.

⁓≭≭≭⁓

Rhonda once again bent her head over her lap desk.

Sir, in my duties of spotting and assessing, I've become friends with a young embassy officer who would serve our government well in the future. His name is Mark Russell, and he has many attributes we can use.

Chapter 36

November 1941. Churchill states that Britain would declare war on Japan within the hour should Japan attack the United States.

A TALL WOMAN clung to the ship's rail as she scanned the mass of people. When she spied an American man moving through the throng, she made her way down the bouncing gangway.

At the bottom, the young man offered his hand. "Miss Burton, Radley Spencer. Welcome to the State of Kuwait."

"I'm Piper." She smiled. "I was so happy to see your face in this crowd."

"People call me Trick. I'm your welcome officer. I'll show you around later, but I'm sure you want to head home right now."

"You're so right. I want a hot bath and a good meal."

"Well, only the ambassador has running water, but I've hired a houseboy for you. I'm sure he'll have a hot bath waiting." Spencer shrugged. "Welcome to the Middle East."

She laughed. "It'll take me a few days to adjust to life at a hardship post."

"Bassam will bring your luggage. So, if you're ready, we'll be off."

Spencer drove through the dusty lanes to her house. "Kuwait's a simple land. We lead a quiet life here."

"I'm looking forward to a little simplicity. I plan to have a good tour."

"That's the spirit."

Piper gazed out her window at the passing buildings and people, absorbing all the new sights and trying to get her bearings. On a dusty lane, Spencer pulled up to a whitewashed one-story house made of mud bricks. Surrounding the property was a wooden fence. Inside, her gaze fell on a rose bush in the courtyard. A light from the other half of her house perfectly illuminated its velvety petals.

"Oh, look. A yellow rose, out here in all this gravel."

Spencer turned. "That's Russ's pride and joy."

Piper smiled at him. "Thanks for getting me here in one piece."

"You're welcome. I'll pick you up for work tomorrow morning."

Piper smiled again when she heard him whistling as he headed toward his auto.

Later she sat on the edge of her bed with baby booties clutched to her cheek.

Oh, Simone, I can still smell your baby scent. I hope you're safe with Aunty Laycie. Those Nazis are getting close to Capbreton. But my counselor said I shouldn't worry about what I can't control. Someday, darling, you'll be in my arms again. But for now, you're in my heart.

⸻❦⸻

Russ turned when a woman with curly dark hair walked into the front office. "Well, hello. We've been expecting you. I'm Mark Russell, the ambassador's assistant. Welcome."

"Piper Burton." She proffered a sheet of paper. "I need initials on my check-in sheet."

"You know we're neighbors."

"Trick told me. I like your rose bush." A small smile edged her lips.

"Thanks. The ambassador and DCM are at the palace. Catherine, our secretary, should be back in a minute."

Catherine swooped in, holding a stack of items from the code room.

"Look who's here. Piper Burton."

She dropped the papers and clapped her hands. "At last, another woman."

Russ tilted his head toward Catherine. "She's the big boss up here. At least we let her think that."

Catherine shook her fist and laughed. "Listen, buster, you're already on thin ice."

Piper chuckled. "Sounds like he may need a bit of bossing."

"Most days." Catherine grabbed the sheet from Russ's hand and initialed the boxes. "I'm going to like you."

Piper's gold earrings and pendant caught the morning light as she left the office.

"Well, lover boy, what do you think?"

"Refined, nice clothes and jewelry, small scar at her hairline. Good sense of humor. And you're right, someone new to talk to."

At lunchtime, Russ sat in the snack bar paging through the *International Herald Tribune*. U-boats had sunk the British *Ark Royal*, leaving the Mediterranean without an Allied carrier. Russian battlefield temps dropped to minus four. Congress amended the Neutrality Act to allow U.S. merchant ships to unload munitions at British ports. No mention of Rommel taking Cairo.

"May I join you?" Piper stood there with her lunch tray.

"Please do." Scrambling to his feet, he held out a chair. "Have you sorted out your section yet?"

"It wasn't so bad." She tucked a strand of hair behind her ear and bit into her shawarma. "My locals know the job better than I do. Their English is excellent, but I need to use my Arabic or I'll lose it." She dabbed at her chin with her napkin. "It's Mark, right?"

"Everyone calls me Russ."

"Oh? What does your mother call you?"

"Mark."

"Then Mark it'll be." Her hair flopped over her scar again. "I'll need a car if I'm to get out and mingle with the locals."

"I'm going to the port this weekend to talk to the dhow meister. We'll be speaking Arabic. You can ride along if you want."

"That'd be great. Thanks."

As they drove toward the port, Russ pointed out the landmarks. "That's Smythe's home, the British political agent. It's been in their inventory for decades."

Piper gazed at the white house trimmed in blue. "I can't imagine what it must have been like for those families years ago having to leave England's humidity for this desert."

"Probably just like it is now. Kuwait hasn't changed much in the last century!" He stopped at a building with large windows, open doors, and a flat roof that extended far over the walls. "You asked for local color." He waved his arm toward the entrance. "The fish market."

Piper held the back of her hand against her nose and leaned in to hear what Russ said.

"When the boats come in, this place is bedlam. In the heat of summer, the fish go bad in a hurry. That's why the roof hangs so far over. It keeps out the sun as long as possible."

They moved along tables burdened with piles of fish, some still twitching. When Piper slipped, Russ took her elbow. "Careful, now, the floor's a mess."

Back in his old Ford, they continued west along the waterfront, where men and boys caulked vessels from rickety scaffolds. "This looks like a shantytown from the Dust Bowl."

"The shipbuilders live in those dilapidated hovels."

After Russ parked next to a hut, an old man tossed aside the flap over its entrance and stepped out. He stumbled over his rudimentary English. "Mr. Mark, welcome."

Russ replied in Arabic. "Ghadir, my friend, this is Piper Burton, a new officer at the Legation. Piper, Ghadir is considered by many, including the amir, to be the best dhow meister in Kuwait."

"Welcome, Miss Piper." He gave a slight bow. "I'm honored to meet you."

"Thank you, Mr. Ghadir. It is I who am honored."

Ghadir inclined his head. "Your Arabic is very good, Miss Piper. Please come and sit." The meister directed the pair to boxes beneath a wooden frame covered in torn sailcloth. Up rushed a chai boy. Ghadir whispered in his ear, and the child ran toward a shack down the road.

Russ opened the conversation, and Ghadir relaxed into the ceremony of introductions. When the chai boy returned, Ghadir passed glass cups on porcelain saucers.

"Seeing Mr. Mark, and now you, Miss Piper, is the highlight of my day. Talking to friends is time well spent."

Russ flipped open his steno pad. "The ambassador has asked me to write a report to our government about the importance of shipbuilding here in Kuwait."

The old man puffed out his chest. "Miss Piper, the amir is an old friend, and we have our tea together when he comes to visit." He paused, waiting for Piper's nod of understanding. "He told me of Mr. Mark bringing your new ambassador to the palace and of his wise counsel for the amir's nephew Khalid, an important official in our oil company." Ghadir leaned in. "Do you know Mr. Mark is a hero?"

"I didn't, Mr. Ghadir. Would you tell me about it?"

"Yes, yes, a very inspiring story repeated every day in the suq, in the An Nafud Desert to the west, and in the foreign ports where these dhows dock. Mr. Mark is the infidel who saved the life of Khalid while risking his own, receiving many serious injuries."

When Ghadir finished, he grinned at Piper and then nodded at Russ. "A very brave man."

"That's an interesting tale." She glanced at Russ. "Thank you for sharing it, sir."

"Khalid would have done the same for me." Russ removed the pencil from behind his ear. "Perhaps we should talk about shipbuilding?"

"Ah, yes, Mr. Mark, your report." Ghadir looked at the dhow towering above their heads. "I learned my trade from my father, who learned it at the knee of his father."

As they followed the old man up the wobbly steps along the side of the dhow, Russ whispered to Piper, "He keeps everything in his head. No blueprints."

"You see, Miss Piper, I design the ship and guide the young men in the work. Each of the curved pieces of the hull fits into the keel just as one of Ibrahim's swords fits into a scabbard."

After their tour, the old shipwright grinned. "I'll soon build a dhow with a long table and benches. There'll be two sleeping compartments in the hold, with portholes and inside toilets."

Russ tucked away his notebook. "Who wants this nice vessel?"

"Well, I talked with a Mr. George, but he was speaking for your ambassador."

"Oh, really?" After a few more minutes of conversation, Russ stood. "We must be going, Ghadir. We enjoyed our visit."

Ghadir turned to Piper. "It's been a pleasure. May Allah smile upon you."

On the way to the car, Russ halted behind a stack of boxes. "Wait a minute."

"Why?" Piper peered over his shoulder. "Who are they? What's wrong?"

"That's Mehmet, George Lander's chief local, and Mohammed, the residence manager, coming out of that shack. I wonder who lives there." While they watched the men move between the shanties, Russ explained about the suspicious activity with the tea sales and about Mehmet, Mohammed, and Ali's connections to the Wahhabi fundamentalists in Egypt. "I can't wait to tell Trick about this."

A lone cloud blocked the sun, and dust choked the lanes between the shacks.

At home, Russ opened the pedestrian door to their courtyard. "I hope you enjoyed your tour. It was nice having another officer on my visit."

"I did." Piper blocked the sun with her purse. "I learned more about Kuwait in one afternoon than I ever did in predeparture briefings. And I used my Arabic."

In her half of their house, Piper dropped her bag and thought about Mark. Midwestern ease, confident, nothing strange. Still, it was too early to get comfortable with him.

Inside his half, Russ splashed water on his face and changed his shirt. He glanced into his small mirror and thought about Piper. Good Arabic, natural ease around the locals, curious about other cultures. Smart. A good officer for the Foreign Service.

Russ finished his Campbell's bean with bacon soup and headed for the office. He typed a draft on shipbuilding and then rolled a clean sheet of paper into the platen. He detailed his sighting of the two local employees at the port and tucked the memo into a folder in his safe.

In Lander's empty first-floor office, Russ searched the *Foreign Affairs Manual.* He tapped the pages with his index finger. Just as he thought. Lander needed departmental approval for big purchases like a dhow.

They're buying a boat, and our houses don't have running water.

Chapter 37

November 1941. Thirteen hundred miles north of Kuwait as the falcon flies, the Wehrmacht occupies Rostov-on-Don, a gateway to the oil of the Caucasus.

CARENZA NASMITH JOLTED awake as her plane taxied to a stop. She flipped pages in her steno pad, looking for her schedule. Dressed in an RAF flight suit, a Washington Senators baseball cap, and aviator Ray-Bans, she stuck her head out and cringed at the endless gray desert floor. "Where the hell am I?"

Malcolm Lodge ambled out of the shadows of the navigation hut. "You're in Kuwait." Lodge extended a hand. "Good afternoon, Carenza. It's good to see you again."

"Thanks for meeting me." She handed him a typewriter case and pointed with a sheepish grin at two large duffels being tossed to the ground by the crew chief.

When Lodge shepherded Carenza into Milbourne's office, the ambassador held her hand. "Welcome to Kuwait, Carenza. You'll stay at the residence with Bitsy and me."

"Thank you, Duncan." Carenza hardly recognized him. His clothes hung on his gaunt body, and his normally pale complexion was blotchy with broken veins. His formerly striking white hair had thinned and dulled. What had happened to the robust diplomat she knew?

Lodge cleared his throat. "Now don't get me wrong, you're welcome here, but Kuwait's a little off the beaten path for a famous correspondent like you."

"Oh, Malcolm, you're such a charmer."

"Right. So why are you here?"

"Well, I ran into Senator Dalton, and his visit to Kuwait piqued my interest. What could possibly draw the attention of someone on the Foreign Relations Committee?"

"It was personal, Carenza," Milbourne said. "His wife, Charlotte, and Bitsy were college roommates."

She tilted her head. "But Charlotte didn't make the trip."

"That's because Bitsy was still in the States."

"I see, I guess." She gave him her cutest little-girl grin. "Besides, my editor called my room at the White House to say he looked forward to my dispatches from here."

Lodge rolled his eyes. "Let me introduce you to the rest of the front office." He gestured to the almost empty room. "Mariah, our DCM, is at home with an illness. But this is Mark Russell and Catherine Cushard."

Carenza considered Russ before she followed Lodge to Post One. "So, Catherine is a secretary, but what does Mark Russell do?"

"He's the assistant to the ambassador."

"Kind of a small post for an ambassador to need an assistant, isn't it?"

"The previous minister was a political appointee who had sufficient clout to demand one. Russ speaks excellent Arabic and moves quite easily in this society. He ensures against mistakes."

"But Duncan is a Middle East expert. Is Russ still ensuring against mistakes?"

Lodge just shrugged.

After plenty of wine at dinner, Bitsy was at her desk working on her correspondence. Milbourne and Carenza sat at the patio table, wrapped against the cool air coming off the Gulf. Carenza sipped a glass of Beaujolais while Milbourne had his usual Scotch.

"What do you do here all day, Duncan? Why aren't you in London or Cairo?"

He covered her hand with his. "Kuwait is a small place finding its way into this century. It's strategically important to us for the future."

She freed her hand by moving her chair closer. "You're talking about oil after the war, but what about now?"

Milbourne smiled. "FDR likes his sources as close to the ground as he can get." He pointed at her steno pad. "May I?" Milbourne drew a map of Azerbaijan to the north, Cairo to the west, and India to the east. He pushed the pad back. "Now, connect the dots. Where do they intersect?"

Carenza drew three lines. "I see. Kuwait's right in the line of fire." She patted his arm. "Oh, Duncan, you're so brave. You're alone here in the Gulf with the Nazis and Imperial Japan just over the horizon."

"Now, dear, you see why FDR wanted my experience amidst all this oil."

After a few more questions, she realized flattery was getting her no closer to the big story that had to be lurking here somewhere. She could taste it. Perhaps the Brit and the foreign secretary would be more forthcoming.

"Well, I've been up since dawn, and tomorrow's another long day. I'm turning in."

As she climbed the stairs of the marble mansion, she smirked. *I bet the old goat is down there trying to figure out how to turn my visit to Kuwait to his advantage. He knows I have a room at the White House. He knows I hobnob with all the actors on the political stage. He'd love to see his name under my byline. We'll see.*

Feeling revived by a decent night's sleep, Carenza inhaled her breakfast and ducked out before Bitsy and Milbourne had barely begun theirs. "Gotta run. Deadlines to meet."

Lodge guided Carenza through her appointments at the Foreign Ministry and the British Political Agency. Back in the car, she snapped shut her steno pad and threw her pencil into her purse. "Gosh, almighty. Must I run naked through the suq to get a story around here?"

Guffawing, Lodge wiped his eyes. "As much as I'd like to see that, you've given me an idea. Maybe you'd like to do some shopping before you leave."

"Sure, send the little woman to the bazaar. Distract her with baubles. Why not?"

Carenza was rapidly filling a notebook while a breathless translator tried to keep up with two merchants regaling her with a tale of courage and sacrifice. She looked up to see Lodge pushing through a crowd who'd gathered to watch her. "Are you here already?"

"It's been a couple hours. I thought you'd be done shopping."

"Shopping? Are you kidding me? I've finally found my story. Bravery, friendship, culture clash. My editor is going to lap it up. Find me Mr. Mark!"

Back at the residence, Carenza was deep into her notes before a stack of blank typing paper when she heard Bitsy clear her throat.

"Aren't you coming to the dinner that the Lodges are hosting for you? Captain Kimball and Russ will be there. They're both good dinner companions."

"I talked with Russ today. Honestly, I don't have time for a dinner party."

Bitsy swung her eyes to her husband, who was sitting on the sofa next to Carenza.

"Bitsy, darling, Carenza's working on a big story and her deadline is tomorrow morning."

"Duncan, I told you I don't need help." Carenza edged closer to her typewriter perched on the coffee table. "But he's right, Bitsy, I'm on deadline. Please give my apologies to Opal Lodge."

"Carenza won't reveal the topic of her story. Still, I'm responsible for our foreign policy in Kuwait and must assure myself that she has the facts correct."

"But I've told you, my story has nothing to do with foreign

policy!" Carenza pushed Milbourne toward Bitsy. "Go! Look at her. She's all dressed up and wanting an escort."

"That's okay, my dear. I'm fine on my own." Bitsy glared at Duncan before spinning on her heel and walking out.

At the Lodges', Bitsy dismissed Hassan for the evening. She laughed and chatted and enjoyed herself much more than if her husband had come. As the evening wound down, she caught Russ's eye. "Mind if I beg a ride home with you? I seem to be left all alone."

She scooted next to him as he started his old Ford. "Are you up for a little adventure?"

"Sure." He placed his hand over hers, where it rested on his leg. "I'm all yours."

As they headed out of Kuwait City, she pointed to a spot just before the last curve to the residence. "See that pile of rubble? There's an alcove above it. Turn off your lights and pull in."

Bitsy leaned on Russ's arm as they walked up to the recess overlooking the road and the beach. He spread a blanket between two boulders. While she unbuttoned his shirt, he pulled her sweater over her head. Clinging together in a passionate kiss, he stretched her out on the blanket. She eased off her skirt while he kicked out of his pants. She ran her hands along his work-hardened muscles. They moved together until Bitsy arched her back and cried out.

Later, their damp bodies cooled in the sea breeze. When Bitsy shivered, he stood. "I'll run to the car to see if I have anything warmer." Russ threw on his clothes and trotted to the Ford.

He returned with a small bundle. "It's one of my old flannel shirts." He dropped it over her arms. "You never know when you need to cover your face in a dust storm."

When Bitsy tiptoed through the front door, she was surprised to see light pouring from the parlor. She studied Carenza, sitting on the couch in pink pajamas printed with blue teddy bears. Her fingers flew over the typewriter keys. "Carenza."

The reporter jumped a foot. "Good grief. You scared me!"

"Where's Duncan?"

"He finally staggered off to bed." She met Bitsy's eyes. "You know he drinks too much."

Bitsy sighed. "He likes his Scotch. How's the story going?"

"Just about finished." Carenza tapped out a few more sentences and sat back. "Done."

"Are you going to show it to him?"

"No, it's not about the Legation. It's about Duncan's assistant, Mark Russell. Did you know that he rescued the amir's nephew from an automobile accident? It's all everyone at the suq wanted to talk about."

The memory of Russ's hard body flitted through Bitsy's mind. "Yes, I've heard that story. It's just as well Duncan didn't get to read it. He's more than a little jealous of Russ."

Carenza noted Bitsy's bare legs, rumpled hair, and inverted sweater. "Did you have a good time?" She pulled her sleeve down. "You know, Duncan was interested in more than my article."

"That doesn't surprise me." Bitsy picked up her shoes and stood. "Was he successful?"

"Hell no." Carenza bit her lip until Bitsy threw her head back and laughed.

"Good for you."

Chapter 38

November 1941. The Japanese Pearl Harbor task force steams from the Kurile Islands.

"THE INTERIOR MINISTRY says they've got a man with an American passport in the Al Ahmadi jail, but he may be German. Go down there with Russ. You may need his Arabic."

"What's the charge?" Piper accepted the notes Mariah passed to her.

"Internal security threat. Claims to be a freelance journalist taking pictures for a book, but he was photographing an off-limits area, the refinery up the road from the jail."

Piper promised Russ a pleasant ride along the coastal road in her Chevy. They parked before a grim one-story structure with barred windows. She marched in and spoke to the duty officer, who handed her the prisoner's passport.

A guard led them through a steel door into a courtyard. "I'm going to put your chair a little off to the side, Mark. That way you can watch his reactions while I question him."

She flipped through the American passport. "This looks genuine."

The guard led a man in dirty clothes to the chair across from Piper and threw a pack of cigarettes on the table.

"I'm Miss Burton from the American Legation, and this is Mr. Russell."

"Paul Guderian." His English was heavily accented.

Piper compared the passport picture to the blond, blue-eyed, stocky prisoner before her. "This says you were born May 1, 1912, in Germany. How do you possess a U.S. passport?"

Over the next hour, Guderian rambled on about his birth in Giessen in the state of Hessen. His parents were German, but he eventually moved to New York to live with relatives. After trade school, he received a cartography certificate and worked for Rand McNally in Manhattan. Pursuing his love of photography, he became a freelance photographer and illustrator in 1936. For the next three years, he worked for several news agencies in Manhattan, taking pictures and drawing maps to complement their feature stories.

"Mr. Guderian, have you ever applied for a U.S. passport and been denied?"

He fumbled with his cigarette and mumbled, "No."

"Other country passports?"

"No." His eyes slid away from hers.

Piper smacked the table with her notepad. "I'm here to offer you help. The least you can do is look at me when I ask you a question."

He stubbed out his butt and lifted his eyes. "Sorry."

"In Manhattan, did you associate with other Germans. Men, or maybe women?"

"I drank a few beers with men in the German bars on the Lower East Side."

"Names?"

He shrugged. "Didn't know them that well." His gaze settled on the cigarette pack.

"Mr. Guderian, have you ever been arrested in the United States or in another country?"

"Is this an interrogation?" he snarled.

Piper bristled. "Perhaps I'll return another day." She gathered up her notes.

"No, wait." He drew in a deep breath. "Why all the questions?"

"I'm pursuing the standard inquiry for an American incarcerated in a foreign jail."

Guderian grunted and lit another cigarette.

Piper repeated her question.

"No, no arrests in other countries."

She reopened her notebook. "You were born in Germany. Where is your Reich passport?"

"I left it in London in a safe deposit box."

"Where does your father work?"

"At the Reich Foreign Ministry, as a chauffeur for Herr Ribbentrop."

Out of the corner of her eye, Piper saw Russ lean forward. "Is he in the Nazi Party?"

"Yes, but only because his job requires it."

"Are you?"

Guderian lifted his eyes and snapped, "No."

"Do you speak Arabic? Or maybe Russian? Italian?"

"Only German and English."

"Please tell us about your life from 1939 to now."

"I worked in London for Rand McNally and a few British news agencies. In 1941, my editor asked me to do a photo book about the Middle East. That's why I'm in Kuwait. It's for a chapter on the people of the Gulf region."

Once again, she thumbed through the passport. "Where else have you been?"

"I started in Cairo, then Damascus and Baghdad. Now here."

"Why were you arrested?"

"A mother camel sat before the refinery with her baby. When I tried to move them, the mother snarled at me." He ran his fingers through his dirty hair. "So, I snapped the picture, and the soldiers guarding the refinery took me into custody."

"We just drove by the refinery. It's well posted with signs forbidding photography."

Guderian shrugged. "I wanted the photo."

Piper closed her notebook.

"Wait!" Guderian jumped up. "Is that all? You're leaving?"

"Yes. You've no special status and have committed a crime." She paused. "Why didn't you stop in Tehran, a city of beauty and history that would be perfect for your book?"

He slumped in his chair. "I've already been there."

"You failed to mention that, and there's no Iranian visa or entry stamp in your passport."

Guderian sighed. "I was on a bus from Baghdad. No officials or questions."

"Who did you meet in Iran? Friends? Government officials? Other Germans?"

"There was a man named Gunther who worked at the telegraph office."

Piper asked a few more questions, but Guderian maintained that he knew little more about Gunther. She closed her notebook. "Mr. Guderian, have you told the truth today?"

Guderian dropped his cigarette to the ground. "I have."

"Okay. You'll hear from the Legation about legal counsel. Goodbye, Mr. Guderian."

On the coast road, Piper glanced at Russ. "So, what did you think?"

"He's not a very good liar."

"Right. I'll cable the Department tomorrow. Trick and Trent will be interested in his reference to Foreign Minister Ribbentrop, not to mention the German expatriate Gunther."

"They'll be doing handstands. On the night of the Marine Corps birthday party, Trent interviewed a walk-in named Gunther Mayerik. A former telegraph operator from Tehran."

"Oh, really! So maybe our photographer will fill in a missing piece to a jigsaw puzzle?"

"Very likely. I don't believe in coincidences, especially Germans in Iran."

"I couldn't determine if he objected to an interview by a woman or if he was just difficult."

"Probably both. He certainly acted suspicious."

They drove for a few miles until Russ broke the silence. "How do you like this Chevy?"

"It runs well. I appreciate Khalid's help in finding it for me."

Just then a plume of smoke snaked across the windshield. "Uh-oh. Spoke too soon."

Russ propped open the hood and poked around. "I think it's the thermostat. We'll wait for the engine to cool so I can remove it." He took the toolbox from the trunk.

"I remembered what you said about travel in the desert and packed a small picnic just in case. I hope you like lamb sandwiches and water."

"Swell." He put aside one of the canteens. "We'll save that one for the radiator."

"Are you a mechanic?"

"I worked for a while at a Chevy dealership when I lived in Kansas. I changed oil, washed cars, fixed flats, all the simple stuff." He dropped into the shade of the Chevy.

Piper sat on the running board. "Do you miss Kansas?"

He chewed on his lower lip. "Hays is home and Mom still lives in the house where we grew up, but no one in Hays has heard of the State Department." He turned to Piper. "When I'm in Hays, I miss the travel and D.C. So, I'm ready to get back on the train and head out."

"In suburban D.C., where I'm from, the Foreign Service is just another agency loaded with overeducated liberals who act like the tweedy college professors we all had."

"Where'd you go to college?"

"Georgetown University. I majored in English with a minor in history." She offered a small smile as she stretched out her long legs. "I've had tours in Shanghai and Marseille."

"Very different places. If you had a choice, where would you live?"

Piper rubbed her chin. "Maybe the South of France, the Atlantic coast."

"I've never been. Do you have some connection there?"

"Yes, my mother's sister, Aunty Laycie. Mother took me for the summer several times when I was young. It's heaven on earth. Ocean breezes, lush gardens, beautiful sunsets." She shook off the sadness that touched her voice. "Now, tell me about your other posts."

"Just Moscow, I'm afraid."

"Moscow, wow. How long did it take you to thaw out?"

He laughed. "You've no idea. In the winter, we all looked like penguins waddling around." He gazed across the gravel of the desert. "A friend of mine loved the arrival of spring there. When we got out of parkas, she was ready to dance barefoot in the green grass."

He stood. "Time to check that engine."

As Piper repacked the picnic basket, Russ removed the thermostat. Fifteen minutes later, he slammed the hood. "Ready to go. I'll drive if you want to enjoy the countryside, such as it is."

"Great." She smiled. "You saved the day."

Motoring north into the fading light, Piper studied Mark Russell, then turned back to the window. *He seems normal. But then, they all start out that way.*

When they reached their house, Russ jumped out. "There's enough cloud cover for a beautiful sunset. Let's go up on the roof and watch."

As the sun slipped below the horizon, its beams sliced through the scattered silver clouds like the spines of a Chinese fan. The colors of the canopy turned from pale blue to sapphire. The desert floor darkened and cooled, as it had done since before the birth of the Prophet. Where the desert met the sea, the day was done.

Russ took Piper's hand as they descended from the roof and said goodnight in the courtyard.

In her bedroom, Piper held the baby booties. She thought about Simone as she fingered the lace. Would she ever see her secret treasure again?

Chapter 39

*November 1941. Secretary of State Cordell Hull de-
mands that Japan abandon Indochina and China.*

REGINALD HEATH-FLEMING PUFFED on his pipe while Spencer
held court at the COI office. Piper had her notes from the jail, and
Russ flipped open his steno pad. Hedges twirled his pencil.

"Our headquarters ran Guderian's name. He's a naturalized
American citizen with no political or criminal history. Reginald's
man says Guderian's publisher is legit, but they'll check the employment records for more information."

Hedges drummed the desktop. "Ribbentrop had a chauffeur
named Hans Guderian, party membership unknown. I wonder if
he was employed by the Gestapo."

Spencer rocked back on his chair legs. "Maybe Reginald and I
should pay our friend a little visit at the jail and ask some different
questions. See if we can turn him."

"Maybe we should follow up on the Guderian link with Gunther Mayerik." Russ checked his steno pad. "What do we know
about the intelligence chief at the German embassy in Tehran, that
Winebrenner guy Mayerik mentioned?"

"General Horst Winebrenner is career Abwehr," Heath-Fleming said. "Been in Tehran about two years. Speaks Farsi and Arabic.

A widower. Friend of Admiral Canaris, the head of Abwehr. He's a professional intelligence officer, not some Nazi goon playing at the spy game."

"Any weaknesses?" Hedges said.

"He likes young women and aged whiskey."

Piper snickered, "Sounds like a description of Milbourne."

Russ rubbed his hand across his face. "Look, we've got our jailbird Paul Guderian and the possibilities in Berlin through his father and Ribbentrop. We've got our walk-in Gunther Mayerik and the possibilities in Tehran with the Abwehr chief Winebrenner. Ribbentrop is the bigger fish, but with more security. Winebrenner is closer geographically and a lot closer to our supply route. If Guderian would rather remain in jail than talk, should we still pursue Mayerik?"

Piper stuck her hand in the air. "Gentlemen, you're the professionals, but Guderian really bothers me. There are too many gaps in his history and too many things he conveniently forgot."

"She's right, you know. Guderian left his Reich passport in London, but he still got into Iran. He says he doesn't know what Ribbentrop does. Does he think we're fools?" Heath-Fleming exhaled a smoke ring. "And Guderian knew Mayerik in Tehran!"

They looked at one another until Piper offered, "A legitimate photographer would be panting to get out of jail. Guderian volunteered his life story until after he left London. Then he made me pull every answer from him." She turned to Russ. "You couldn't see from where you sat, but when I asked if he was telling the truth, his eyes hardened into what looked like hatred."

"I heard it in his voice. Sometimes he was compliant and other times he was defiant." Russ studied his notes. "He waited until late afternoon, when the light on the refinery is at its best, to take his photos. Why hazard jail for a camel? He plainly knew the risks, but he wanted those photos. What was he photographing before that? The oil fields at Burgan, the ports in Iran? Has anyone developed his film yet?"

"On the other hand," Piper broke in, "he has a valid American passport, and the information about his father seems to be the truth. So, is he just stupid or is he a provocateur?"

"Provoke us into what, Piper?"

She leveled her gaze on Spencer. "You guys are in covered positions. If you go to the jail, he'll know you're spies. If he has a contact here in Kuwait, he'll identify you."

"She's got a point, Reginald. Even if we use false names, Guderian will have our descriptions. Then we might as well go home."

Hedges stopped drumming. "I'll cable headquarters for more background on Guderian. Reginald, get your man on Guderian's employment at the publishing house."

"Let's remember that Guderian and Mayerik grew up in German towns less than ten miles apart," Russ said. "Is that just another coincidence? I doubt it."

Heath-Fleming took a deep breath. "I'll wire our headquarters to see if there's anything unusual about that area in Germany."

Hedges stuck his pencil behind his ear. "Two suspicious characters wash up on our shore in a little over a week. And they just happened to bump into each other at a telegraph office in Tehran? Nonsense!" He rubbed his hands together. "I love this business."

The British officer lit his pipe. "Let's not forget a point that's always on Alan Smythe's mind. We're focused on security for the supply line to Stalin, but maybe our German friends aren't even aware of that yet. Maybe they're looking farther afield. Maybe India."

Russ snapped his fingers. "I just remembered that Guderian told Piper he spoke only German and English." He glanced at Piper, who nodded. "While she fetched the guard, I commented on the weather to Guderian in Arabic. He didn't understand. Then in Russian I threw out an insult about Moscow weather. He laughed before he caught himself."

Chapter 40

November 1941. The Red Army retakes Rostov-on-Don.

MARIAH STARED AT the rain pounding against the office windows. "How will I ever make it home?"

Russ appeared at her door. "What's the matter?"

"Oh, Russ." She sagged against her desk. "I didn't know anyone was still here."

"Come on. I'll drive you." As he helped her negotiate the steps, he wondered when she had become so frail.

At home, Mariah collapsed across the bed. Russ called Doris Lander, the nurse, and Catherine. It was seven in the evening.

Russ watched from the doorway while Doris did a quick assessment.

Catherine hurried in. She brushed Russ's cheek as she ran past.

Half an hour later, Doris found Russ perched on a chair. "We're going to spend the night with her. You may as well go home." She sent him into the dripping darkness.

Three hours later, they assisted Mariah to the car. At the clinic, Doris stood across from Doctor Husayn as he examined the sick woman. "Mrs. Lander, she's barely responsive. I'm concerned about her elevated temperature. How long has she been ill?"

"Since June. It started slowly, but she's much worse lately."

At midnight, the amir's personal physician joined Doctor Husayn at the clinic. While Catherine held Mariah's thin hand, the two men stepped into the hall with Doris.

"Mrs. Lander," said Dr. Husayn, "amebiasis is common here. The parasite enters the body through tainted food or drink. Flies and cockroaches transmit the disease, and we have many of these insects in Kuwait. If only the intestines are involved, we manage the disease with drugs. In Miss McCarry's case, the disease may have spread to her lungs. We've started a regimen of sulfa drugs, but she's in serious trouble. She must go to the hospital run by the American Colony in Jerusalem. They have a laboratory that can perform the necessary tests."

At two in the morning, Doris phoned her husband. "Mariah's at the clinic. She's desperately ill and needs to go to Jerusalem today."

"Who is this? Wha-a-at day is it?"

"It's Doris. Call the Regional Medical Office in Jerusalem for a verbal authorization for a medevac flight. I'll be home in a few minutes to pack a bag."

Lander dropped the phone. He was snoring before his head hit the pillow.

Doris stopped haranguing her husband long enough to stuff a duffel bag with clothes, toiletries, and her passport. Before she emptied her husband's wallet, she called Captain Kimball at home. "I need a plane."

Doris paced until Kimball called back. "We're in luck. There's a weekly mail plane to our Army Liaison Mission in Abadan. They leave at one this afternoon for Cairo. I'll have the plane diverted for Mariah. I'll call you later with the details."

Russ awoke before six and arrived at the clinic to find Doris asleep in a chair in the hall. Catherine dozed beside the bed, still holding Mariah's hand. He considered what might have been if Mariah had been healthy enough to temper the behavior of Milbourne and Lander.

Doris stirred and blinked herself awake. "Captain Kimball's arranged a plane for this afternoon. The palace is providing an ambulance. I'll fly with Mariah to Jerusalem."

"You've done a terrific job. Thanks, from all of us who work with Mariah."

"Catherine's falling to pieces. She'll need your help with all this."

"I'll take care of Catherine. You worry about Mariah."

"If she lives, she'll be sent to D.C. for treatment. Her overseas career is finished."

"It won't be the same in the front office without her." Russ shook his head. "Malcolm will have to fill in as DCM until someone can get out here."

"I hope the Department picks someone not coming out of exile. Or prone to drink."

"I'm sorry for you, Doris."

She dropped her head against the back of the chair. "Before Tunis, George was very good at his job. It all went bad with Duncan. At our last post, George was sent home early. They called it declining performance, but it was really the bottle. Kuwait was his chance to prove himself capable at a smaller post." She snickered. "He's always kept his pay grade, though. What does that tell you about the Foreign Service?"

"Jeez, I didn't know all that."

"And then George was Bitsy's dupe in a game she played for Duncan's benefit."

Russ wiped sweat from his forehead. "Ah, yes, Bitsy." He sighed.

"Don't get me wrong. Fooling around wasn't new for George. Bitsy was. That strumpet is shameless. She looked me straight in the eye whenever we met. I could barely stand to be in the same room with her. But she's not interested in George anymore. I wonder who she's using to get at Duncan this time?" Doris directed a considered look at Russ.

He squirmed beneath her stare. "How long do you think you'll be in Jerusalem?"

"Until Mariah's out of danger. Maybe I'll escort her on to the States. George was worthless tonight. I'm about done with him, and with the Foreign Service. My kids have their own lives. Maybe it's time I took care of myself."

At ten o'clock in the morning, Mariah awoke. She nudged Catherine. "Take my house key from my purse. Go over there with Russ. Taped to the back of my bedroom mirror is a white envelope detailing Duncan's misbehavior in Baghdad, including his attempted rape of a consular officer. You'll also find a letter to the director general. I'll no longer need them to protect me, but you two should hang on to them." She gripped Catherine's hand, her voice fading. "Take my jewelry box and my personal papers in the teak box under the vanity. Hold them for now and send them when you pack me out later. I won't be back."

When Catherine began to cry, Mariah loosened her grip. With the last of her reserves, she whispered, "It's okay, Catherine. I'll see you in D.C." She closed her eyes and slept.

The Army Air Force pilot squinted at the horizon, where the clouds were the same gray as the runway. When the plane cleared the ground, Russ and Catherine waved goodbye to Mariah.

At Mariah's house, George Lander sat at the table with a bottle of Kentucky bourbon at his elbow. "What are you two doing here?"

Russ grabbed Catherine's arm before she could strike Lander.

"Whoa, Catherine, let's calm down." Lander tilted the chair on its rear legs. "Mariah won't be back, so I'm doing an inventory of her house." He brandished a clipboard.

His chair hit the floor when Russ elbowed Catherine in the direction of the bedroom. "Hey, where's she going?"

"Mariah asked her to gather her jewelry and personal papers." Russ pulled out another chair. "Why are you here? Mariah just took off, and you're doing an inventory?"

"Regulations, Russ, regulations. I'm just following orders."

"Is drinking Mariah's bourbon in the middle of the afternoon in the regulations?" Russ clenched his fists. "You're sick, and that goes for the ambassador, too."

Russ escorted Catherine to the door so she wouldn't do bodily harm to Lander.

Chapter 41

"DON'T KNOW HOW you stay upright with all this bounce." Milbourne clung to the rail.

"It's rough, but Captain Kimball's in his element." Russ pointed forward. "Look at him out there leaning into the wind."

Under a dingy sky, the boat left the Gulf and moved up the Shatt al-Arab River. As the sun slipped behind the clouds, Kimball pointed to an orange glow. "That's gas flaring from the twin towers of the Anglo-Iranian oil refinery at Abadan. Rommel would love to get this far."

At the dock, the men hefted their duffels and moved down the gangplank. An officer in a brown wool uniform with a Colt .45 pistol on his hip offered his hand. "I'm Colonel Sherm Griffith, commander of the U.S. Army Liaison Mission. Welcome to Abadan."

They followed Griffith to two jeeps. At a fenced compound topped with barbed wire, an Iranian guard swung open the crossbar under the watchful eye of an American MP standing in the door of a tiny booth. Down the fence line, a man in a white T-shirt and apron bent over a galvanized garbage can, handing food scraps through the fence to a gaggle of grimy urchins.

Russ looked around. "Colonel, how big is this compound?"

"About a hundred yards square. It houses our Corps of Engineers liaison group of fifty-three officers and enlisted."

"Are you an engineer?"

"Yep, civil. There are two more of us; some structural engineers who know bridges, tunnels, and roadways; a unit of railway experts; and a few officers who understand the port equipment needed to unload cargo. Add our complement of MPs, medics, clerks, cooks, carpenters, electricians, mechanics, plus one chaplain, and you have our merry little band."

Griffith was slender with close-cropped brown hair speckled with gray and wire-rimmed spectacles. "You'll bunk in the Persian Palace. That's where General Ray Wheeler slept a few weeks ago. It's just a big tent with six cots on a dirt floor. We have outdoor latrines and showers, and the chai boy will bring you cold water for the washbasins."

Thirty minutes later, Griffith began his briefing around a conference table made from shipping crates. "Gentlemen, our liaison group was sent here a few months back to assess the state of the Iranian transportation system. On paper, the Gulf is the best route to the Soviets. On the ground, General Wheeler will have to move mountains to make this operation work."

Milbourne swiped the dirt from his shoes while Russ jotted in his steno pad.

"But before I talk about infrastructure, let me give you a quick recap of the recent history of Iran so you know what we're up against. When the Brits and Soviets became allies, they expelled the Germans, removed the old shah, and installed his son on the Peacock Throne. All this to protect Iran's oil from the Germans. We're standing in the southern half of Iran, under British control. The Soviets occupy the northern half."

Captain Kimball noted the piles of equipment lining the tent as Griffith walked to a map and pointed. "You may remember that Soviet Russia was until recently in a nonaggression pact with her sworn enemy Nazi Germany, a convenience that allowed each of them to carve out spheres of influence in Europe. For now the Soviets fight on the side of the Allies, but who knows what way the wind will blow after the armistice?"

Griffith tapped their location on the map. "The Soviets have agreed to leave this garden spot after the war, but they might be inclined to stay. If they do, they'll have something they've always coveted: warm water ports at Abadan and Bandar Shahpur. Then they'll cast their eyes down the beach toward Kuwait, Bahrain, and Oman, all countries with ports, not to mention lots of oil. And remember, from the Gulf it's not far to the Khyber Pass and the Jewel in the Crown."

Griffith sat down. "That's it in a nutshell."

Milbourne tapped his pen against a small leather notebook. "So, this supply line will operate under the shadow of serious political issues. If the Soviets stay, they'll control this fertile crescent of petroleum without firing a shot. How does all that affect the supply corridor?"

"You've got it, Mr. Ambassador." The colonel ran a hand through his hair. "The Russkies demand that we offload everything we import at a rail yard near Tehran. Then the Red Army reloads all that tonnage on Soviet trains for points north."

"How much matériel are we talking about?" Milbourne said.

"I can't begin to guess. There are millions of Russian soldiers."

"Can Iran's rail system handle all the traffic?"

"Good question, Russell. It's the most modern in this region, especially since it was just finished in '38. It'll improve once we replace all the tracks, engines, and rolling stock." Griffith waved toward the outdoors. "We'll have to deal with weather, rugged terrain, washouts and rockslides, theft, corruption, and sabotage. The mountain tribes demand tribute in the form of rifles to allow passage for the meager supplies that are already arriving. Who knows what they'll want when they see airplanes and tanks?"

Later, the men joined a chow line on one side of a tilted, V-shaped, corrugated sheet metal trough. Butane heaters were spaced every three feet beneath the wedge. Two cooks stood on crates at the top of the trough, opening tins with meat cleavers. The food slid down the slope of the red-hot metal and fell into the tray of the soldier standing at the bottom. The man across from him stuck his tray beneath the first to catch the overflow.

Griffith collected the steaming concoction, threw a biscuit on his tray, and grabbed a piece of cherry pie. Kimball winked at Russ and nodded toward the ambassador as Milbourne took his turn at the trough, his face a mask of resignation.

While the ambassador rooted around on his tray, Griffith told them, "Now, imagine round-the-clock meals for thousands of soldiers, contractors, and local help. The mess hall operations for this supply line will be enormous.

"The locals are starving because the Brits buy and the Russians confiscate everything their farms produce. When we pulled in, you saw our cook slipping the poor kids a few scraps."

Kimball eyed the cherry pie. "That looks almost as good as store-bought."

Griffith howled. "The crust is handmade, but the canned cherries are government surplus and tend to be a little gray. So, our creative baker improves the color with beet juice."

On the way back to the tents, Griffith pointed to the telegraph poles along the train track. "The Iranians shimmy up the poles to swipe the wire. They sell it to local coppersmiths who make it into handicrafts for the suq. They also steal railroad spikes, ties, and even the rails themselves. Pilfering our improvements is big business for the locals."

"I'm certainly glad I made this trip," Milbourne said.

"I bet it's not what you expected, right?"

Milbourne nodded. "The president likes to hear what's happening as close to the ground as he can get it. He's counting on this supply line to alter the outcome of this war, not to mention the future of this region. I have his ear and will report everything you've told me and everything I've seen here."

"Please quote me to my commander in chief, Mr. Ambassador. Iran is it. We have no other choice!"

Chapter 42

December 5, 1941. Hitler stops the Moscow assault due to harsh weather.

ON THE MORNING of December 5, Russ huddled in his trench coat in the courtyard of the Al Ahmadi jail. In ragged trousers and a thin overshirt, Guderian shivered in the chill air.

Russ began in Russian. When Guderian refused to understand, Russ rose as if to leave.

"Wait, I will talk with you." Guderian's Russian was excellent.

"Smart decision. Tell me about your trip to Egypt."

"I photographed people around the pyramids, in the suq, and in the villages along the Nile. Children, old women, that sort of thing."

"Tell me about the villages along the Nile."

"What do you want to know? I went to Luxor, Aswan, Beni Suef, and Al Minya."

Russ jotted "AM" in his notebook. He pulled out a Hershey bar. "Comrade Guderian, do you like chocolate?"

Guderian held out a dirty palm.

"Tell me how your Russian is so good." Russ dropped a square of chocolate into Guderian's hand.

"My parents were born in Russia. They grew up with both languages."

"But your passport says you were born in Germany."

Guderian held out his hand for more chocolate. "I was born in Kiev, but Lenin did not like Germans. He expelled all of us. I was only nine when we moved back to Hessen. My father was a skilled mechanic, so the authorities gave us new identity papers."

"Hessen is far away from Berlin, where you said your father works."

"Can I have a cigarette?" Guderian hunched in his chair. "My father moved with my mother and baby sister to Berlin in 1933. The Nazi Party was on the rise and there was a great demand for skilled mechanics and drivers."

"You didn't accompany your family to Berlin?"

"No, I went with my older sister to New York to live with relatives. My father feared the Nazis and didn't want us to become involved with the coming war."

"Is your family still in Germany?"

Guderian stared into space.

Russ repeated his question. When Guderian remained silent, Russ slapped his steno pad on the table. "I asked about your family. Are they still in Germany?"

"No, they're dead. The Gestapo murdered my mother and my little sister."

"Why would they do that?"

"They were visiting at another child's home when the Gestapo raided the building. They burst in and sprayed bullets everywhere. The Nazis are animals!"

Russ placed another chocolate square on the table. "You know, Comrade Guderian, the Nazis might win the war. Russia is struggling. It might fall to Hitler."

Guderian gripped the table edge. "That is not possible. Marshal Stalin will beat Hitler. We Russians are a strong and determined people! I will celebrate when Hitler is dead."

"Perhaps you'd like to write to someone." Russ pushed a tablet, pen, and envelopes across the table. "I'll mail your letters for you."

The prisoner stared at the paper. "I could write to my sister. She lives in Cincinnati now."

While the prisoner penned his letter, Russ waited near the guard booth. Then he returned to the courtyard, where Guderian handed him two envelopes. As he pocketed them, Russ said in Arabic, "Two weeks from now, you'll be executed."

The blood drained from Guderian's face. "So soon?"

Russ placed the remainder of the Hershey bar on the table.

⌁

That afternoon, Russ, Spencer, Hedges, Piper, and Heath-Fleming met again.

"COI headquarters confirms Guderian's father is still alive in Germany. But Paul Guderian's not working for the Nazis," Spencer said. "They suspect he's a rogue Russian agent."

"That fits perfectly with what I got from our prisoner. When I suggested the Russians might lose to the Germans, he became angry. He really hates the Nazis."

Spencer tipped his chair back. "Good pickup on Guderian understanding Arabic. So, our prisoner floats down the Nile to villages where Islamic fundamentalism is strong. He even goes to Al Minya, hometown to our favorite local misfits, Mehmet and Ali!"

Everyone nodded except Heath-Fleming. "What's this about Islamic fundamentalism? Are we talking about the Wahhabi sect in Egypt?"

Hedges told the Brit about the Legation's trio of locals who might be funneling money to the Wahhabis. "We're tossing around ideas about the Wahhabis, unwittingly or knowingly, playing into Soviet dreams of controlling the Gulf region."

"Let me get this straight." Heath-Fleming chewed on his pipe stem. "You think Guderian's got a role in a Soviet plan to toss the Kuwaiti government into the rubbish bin by helping religious nuts from Egypt?"

"Exactly." Hedges snapped his pencil. "If the Soviets have oil, they can fuel their industrial machine. If they can berth their ships in the ports of Muslim fundamentalist regimes along the Gulf, they can sail directly to all the ports of the Crown, including India."

"But why would the Wahhabis work with the Russians? They'd be trading one set of Europeans for another. Doesn't make sense."

"You're right." Hedges pulled another pencil from his pocket. "That's why it's just a theory for now. We're working on it."

Piper waved aside all the conjecture. "Let's focus on what we know. Guderian's letters. Someone needs to interview this sister in Cincinnati. She can tell us more about the family's life in Germany. Someone needs to watch that post office box in D.C. See who shows up." She snapped her fingers. "Better yet, see who's on the rental card for that box."

"You're right. Everything else is speculation. I'll ask our headquarters to get the FBI to interview the sister and look at the rental card for the PO box." Spencer wrote a note.

"Maybe you should visit Guderian one last time, Russ."

"I don't know. Seemed like he was done talking. He'll take the sword before he'll tell us anything about the real reason he's in Kuwait."

"Yeah, and when he's dead, what happens next?" Spencer made another note. "I wonder who will miss him? Will the Gestapo or the NKVD react?"

Piper nodded. "And does he have a handler right here in Kuwait?"

Chapter 43

*December 7, 1941. The United States of America loses
its innocence in world affairs.*

TALKS THAT HAD started in April with the government of Japan
had broken off without resolution. On December 6, Secretary of
State Cordell Hull cabled all U.S. missions.

At 2:00 a.m. in Kuwait, Duty Officer Radley Spencer was sum-
moned to the Legation. The code clerk handed over Hull's cable,
and Spencer left for the ambassador's residence.

Milbourne read the cable aloud to Bitsy.

*The days of negotiation are over. All diplomatic and consular
posts are directed to prepare for war. Specific instructions con-
cerning each post will follow in separate cablegrams. Good
luck and Godspeed.*

Hull

"Damn! Now I'm stuck in this hellhole." He tossed the cable
aside.

With a trembling hand, Bitsy dabbed her eyes with a hankie.
"I'll stay through the holidays and then I'm done. I hope I can find
a way out of here."

Milbourne fell hard into a chair. "I may as well kiss the NEA job goodbye."

"FDR and Churchill are still watching you. Even Averell Harriman and Alan Smythe. The security for the supply line is squarely on your shoulders."

"*My* shoulders? I'm not in this alone."

"No. But your mistakes will jeopardize the Allied cause. You better not mess this up."

Spencer repeated his early-morning trip to the Legation code room on December 8, 1941. His hand shook as he handed over the latest SECRET cable to the ambassador at the residence.

JAPAN ATTACKS U.S. FLEET AT PEARL HARBOR

At eight o'clock, Russ sat at his desk reviewing his calendar when he heard Milbourne ask Catherine to call everyone to the conference room. Clutching a damp hankie, Bitsy appeared in his doorway and shook her head. Russ felt a chill run down his back as he stood and walked with her to join the others.

"We're assembling on such short notice because I have terrible news," Milbourne said. "Japan has bombed our fleet at Pearl Harbor, Hawaii."

Russ's thoughts flew to his brother. He turned toward Catherine when he felt her touch his arm.

The ambassador continued. "Today the president will ask Congress for a declaration of war against the Empire of Japan. War in Europe will surely follow." He ran his eyes over the assembled. "If you have problems locating loved tones, contacting your family, or with the state of your own spirits, please let my wife know. Does anyone have relatives in immediate danger at Pearl Harbor?"

"Sir, my brother, Craig, is a marine radio operator stationed there."

Milbourne pointed at Kimball. "Captain, send an IMMEDIATE cable asking for the status on Russ's brother." Milbourne looked back at Russ. "We'll find him."

Back at his desk, Russ tried to quell the scenes of disaster that ran through his mind. He shuffled papers, stared out the window, and finally drew a diagram in his steno pad with Guderian in the middle. Lines flowed to the words *Moscow*, *Al Minya*, *Ribbentrop*, *Mayerik*, *Winebrenner*, *Cincinnati*, *Mohammed*, and *Mehmet*. He concentrated on the puzzle. Should he add a line to Kuwait with a question mark?

Catherine brought him a coffee and stroked his hair. "I'm sure your brother is one tough marine. He'll know how to survive."

"What'll I tell Mom if he's wounded, or dead?"

"Let's wait. It may take a while, though. Everyone must be cabling Pearl about family."

After Catherine went to her desk, Piper strolled in. "How are you holding up?"

"I dunno. It's tough waiting for news."

"Are you close to your brother?"

"We were best friends growing up. I guess we still are."

"Maybe you should eat something." She turned toward the door. "Anything sound good to you? I'll make a trip to the snack bar."

"Whatever. Don't be too long. I want you here if I hear anything."

Catherine fielded phone calls while munching on her lunch from home. Milbourne and Bitsy had retired to the residence, so Piper and Russ ate their lunch in his quiet office. Shortly before noon, the sound of hurried footsteps in the reception area broke the silence. Russ stiffened and rose.

Captain Kimball stood in the doorway with a smile on his face. "Good news, buddy. Marine Corporal Craig Russell suffered a slight concussion during the initial attack. He's okay and is currently on duty."

Piper threw her arms around Russ and patted his back. Catherine joined the celebration.

"I kept imagining the worst." He let out a long sigh. "Thanks for the fast service, sir. I need to cable Mom."

Kimball shook Russ's hand and left. Catherine returned to the ringing phones. Piper pecked Russ's cheek, and he grabbed her for a hug. "Thanks."

When Milbourne returned from lunch, Russ handed him an envelope marked "Eyes only for ambassador."

Milbourne slid out a Falcon Wing stamped SECRET, scanned the single sheet, and passed it to Russ.

Duncan, Averell has made the Soviet supply line a top priority of Lend-Lease. The Allied nations and the occupied peoples of the world count on you. Be ready. Your thin line must hold!
Roosevelt

"I may be stuck here, but FDR still supports me."

"Ready or not, we're out of time. Maybe we can still turn the tide on the Eastern Front." Russ rubbed his hands together. "Let's get cracking."

❦

Bitsy did her best, but no one was in the mood for celebrating Christmas Eve at the residence. The buffet of local delicacies and desserts moldered in the parlor, though the bar was crowded. Hankies were a constant presence while the wives talked of home. Cigarette smoke wafted over the patio from the men who discussed the coming war.

Malcolm and Opal Lodge made their apologies to Bitsy and departed early.

Trick and Trent huddled with Captain Kimball. They had already secured the burn barrels on the roof of the Legation building. Nothing would prevent the fertilizer from quickly igniting should they need to destroy classified documents in a hurry. They ran over their plans again, assuring themselves they had thought of every eventuality.

The gunny stood with his detachment by the half wall. They had inventoried their stores of C rations and water. He assigned a corporal to check again on the gas masks and extra ammunition, should they have to defend the Legation. Warring despots from three compass points could have Kuwait in their sights. The Legation's defenses were few.

Russ turned from Piper when he saw Catherine struggling up the driveway with a cable dangling from her hand. She had remained at the Legation to cover the front office until Washington closed at noon for the Christmas holiday. He opened his arms as she walked into them, tears streaming down her face. He read aloud the shocking news.

We regret to inform you that Kuwait DCM Mariah McCarry died at 1100 hours at the American Colony Hospital in Jerusalem. Cause of death was complications of amebiasis. In attendance was Kuwait Legation nurse Doris Lander. The staff of Consulate General Jerusalem extends deepest sympathies in the loss of a fine officer. Mariah was known to all in the Middle East as a caring professional and an Arabist of consummate skill. She will be missed. Mrs. Lander will handle arrangements.

"I'm so sorry, Catherine." Piper patted Catherine's back as she sobbed in Russ's arms.

"What's happened?" Bitsy limped across the patio tiles. "Is it Mariah?"

"She's dead," Catherine wailed. She wiped her face on Russ's sleeve.

Bitsy called the remaining guests together. "Let us bow our heads to remember Mariah, a true Irish gal." She reached for her violin lying on the half wall. Irish ballads evoked windswept highlands and cloudy shores scoured by the sea.

Catherine sniffled. "I should have insisted she go to Jerusalem sooner."

"It's not your fault. Mariah was dedicated to the job."

"Mark is right, Catherine, you did your best."

"I knew she was really sick, but I wasn't prepared to lose her."

"We're never prepared to lose loved ones."

"Mariah was our last hope to temper the old man and Lander." Russ closed his eyes and shook his head.

All three of them turned toward the far corner of the patio where Milbourne poured another round for himself and Lander.

Chapter 44

'TWAS THE NIGHT before Christmas and all through the White House...

In the biting air, carolers held hands and moved around the Christmas tree on the south lawn. Franklin Roosevelt and Winston Churchill appeared on the Blue Room balcony and waved to the crowd. The prime minister approached the array of microphones.

Let the children have their night of fun and laughter. Let the gifts of Father Christmas delight their play. Let us grown-ups share to the full in their unstinted pleasures before we turn again to the stern task and formidable years that lie before us, resolved that, by our sacrifice and daring, these same children shall not be robbed of their inheritance or denied the right to live in a free and decent world. And so, in God's mercy, a happy Christmas to you all.

Later, Churchill padded down the hall in a dressing gown to join FDR, who sat before the fireplace with a shawl around his shoulders. "My embassy just delivered another teletype from our friend Uncle Joe." Churchill rubbed a hand across his jowls. "Stalin wants to know when the war matériel will begin arriving. He must think we're miracle workers!"

FDR scanned the teletype. "My ambassador in Kuwait returned from a trip to Iran, and he confirms that we're starting from scratch over there. I hope he's got it under control by now.

"Say, Eleanor's journalist friend has just returned from the Middle East. She's with the *Washington Post*. We'll ask her about Milbourne and the other players along the Gulf."

"Good idea. How about tomorrow after lunch?" Churchill clasped his hands across his midsection. "Send me copies of her dispatches, so I'm up to snuff."

⁂

When Wembley escorted Carenza into the Oval Office, Churchill held out his hand. "It's good of you to join us during the holidays, Miss Nasmith. I've read your articles about the Middle East. Franklin and I welcome insights from those with experience on the ground. Please have a seat."

Carenza bit down on her nervous giggle. "I'm flattered, Mr. Prime Minister."

"You understand that this is not an interview for publication." When she nodded, he turned to FDR. "Franklin, perhaps a libation would smooth the flow of her narrative?"

While FDR served drinks, Carenza launched into a summary of her travels, concluding with Kuwait. "I met with Ambassador Milbourne and your Mr. Smythe. I had an appointment with the foreign secretary. I shopped in the suq. What parts are you most interested in?"

Churchill gazed into the fire as he chose his words. "Let us start with personnel. Miss Nasmith, I've known Smythe for some time. Did he impress you as the right man for the job?"

Carenza nodded. "His depth of knowledge is remarkable, but he's very worried about the fate of your colonies, especially India."

The prime minister gave a quick nod of his head. "He should be."

FDR chimed in. "What's your opinion of the foreign secretary?"

"Mr. President, the sheikh is well-read on international affairs and has a detailed understanding of the Allied concerns for the future of the region. He's also very charming. He complains how his brother makes him sweep the floors at the Foreign Ministry."

"And what about Ambassador Milbourne?" Churchill chewed on his cigar.

"His wife, Bitsy, is a friend, so I already knew him through her. Duncan has a good grasp of the Middle East and speaks the language." She glanced at Roosevelt. "He enjoys his whiskey."

"A man after my own heart." Churchill raised his tumbler. "I trust it's in moderation."

Her eyes dropped. "I can't say I never saw him drunk."

"We appreciate your candor, Miss Nasmith." Churchill held a newspaper clipping in his hand. "Your article on this young American officer caught my eye."

"Thank you, sir." She took the article and smiled. "I chanced upon those old merchants in the suq. I enjoy writing about the personal sacrifices of our diplomats."

"Perhaps you could elaborate on your article for us?"

"Certainly, Mr. President." With great enthusiasm, Carenza recounted a detailed rendition of the rescue of Khalid. She noted Roosevelt's rapt attention and Churchill's closed eyes. Maybe the prime minister saw himself starring in such a tale.

At the end of her account, the prime minister guided the conversation back to the people on the ground in Kuwait. More comfortable now, Carenza admired how he pulled critical information from her observations without her even realizing how much she knew.

"To be honest, gentlemen, my experience tells me there's something going on in Kuwait. It lurks right below the surface patter everyone gave me. From the palace to the Brits to the Legation, everyone told the same tales, mostly about oil. I left without the real story there."

"Well, sometimes you have to accept what is given in honor of the bigger picture." FDR stuck another cigarette in his holder while glancing at Churchill.

"Yes, Miss Nasmith, Franklin and I appreciate your honesty and the fact that you were persistent, even if you feel you failed. Don't give up. We need people like you with your experience and good instincts."

Carenza let their flattery wash over her. She drew a big breath before she stepped over the line with these important men. "Look, if you and everyone in Kuwait wish to keep whatever is happening quiet until later, I understand that. Much must be riding on the outcome." She drew another breath and plunged in. "But if it's so almighty important, you better take a closer look at the people running the operation." She held the president's gaze. "One of them is buckling under the pressure."

Churchill cast a hard stare in FDR's direction before rising. "Thank you, Miss Nasmith, for your frankness. We will not disregard your warning."

"Gentlemen, I have enjoyed the afternoon." Carenza stood and left the Oval Office.

The prime minister chewed on his cigar before he broke the silence. "That's a very shrewd woman, Franklin. She pointed us at your man without actually naming him."

"Duncan has yet to let me down, Winston." FDR bit down on a stronger retort. "Look, I haven't found a qualified replacement and the supply line effort is under way. I say, let's go with our team since we're out of options.

"In the meantime, I'll call Duncan back for consultations. While he talks, I'll look him over. If I'm dissatisfied, I'll read him the damned riot act."

"Excellent." The Prime Minister sighed. "I hate to spend so much energy on this, but one man can bring the whole thing crashing down."

A frigid wind blew across the south lawn, and it began to snow.

Chapter 45

December 1941. The extreme cold (−40° F) stalls Hitler's offensive in the USSR.

RUSS WAS READING Arabic newspapers when Piper stopped by his office. "Let's pick up some food at Fuad's and eat at my place. At least you won't have to drive home afterward."

"I'm not very good company." He rattled the papers with a grim expression.

"Oh, come on. Take your mind off the war."

Her smile convinced him to chuck the newspapers aside.

Later, Piper stood over her hot plate reheating the lamb and potatoes when Russ walked in from his side, swinging two bottles. "Interested?"

"Sure, and set the table, too." She gave a mischievous grin. "That is, if you know how."

"Very funny." He moved around the tiny space, grabbing dishes and silverware.

Each time he bumped into her, the grin widened. "You'll have to excuse me. Us cowpokes carried only the essentials on the trail. Nothing fancy like wine glasses and candleholders."

"That's a sorry tale." She laughed. "Hope you're hungry. We have lots."

"I'm always hungry." He drew out her chair with a flourish. "Mademoiselle."

"So, am I getting the aw-shucks version of Mark or the French lover? I know both are fakes hiding the real you." She tilted her head and gave him a sidelong look.

"Dagnabbit, I overplayed my hand." He grabbed his fork and stabbed the lamb.

"You know, this place is nothing like I expected from the post report. It's far grimmer than the green oasis I was led to imagine." When Russ snorted over his wine, she dabbed at his chin and continued. "Bitsy Milbourne warned me about the characters here when I met her for lunch before I left D.C. She didn't tell me about our living conditions."

"She probably didn't know. Probably still doesn't, considering her life in her marble mansion. I'd bet the old man has never been in staff housing." Russ rolled up his napkin and tossed it on the table."

"Sorry, you've lived with this longer than I have." She patted his hand. "Maybe we should talk about the war. It might be safer. You look like you might bite me."

"Now that's an excellent idea." He jumped up and made a lunge for her neck.

She held up her hands to ward him off, then on impulse pulled him closer. For a moment she met his eyes and then shoved him away.

'Sorry, I'll have to control my vampire urges."

"No, no, entirely my fault." She hurriedly cleared the table.

"Your mom lives in Bethesda, right?"

"Yeah, ever since I was eight. Dad's a physician."

"Your dad must be busy. Washington's becoming a boomtown."

"I don't know. We lost contact when he found one of his nurses more attractive than Mother. They divorced when I was twelve."

"Sorry. That must've been hard."

"It's tough being disregarded and forgotten, yeah."

"Wanna talk about something else?"

"It's okay." Piper turned her back on him to fill the dishpan from a pot boiling on her hot plate. "Mother never recovered from the betrayal, and, honestly, neither have I."

"And now you're in a profession where women are overlooked."

"That's a subtle way to put it." She laughed. "Men ignore us unless they want to get into our beds."

"I'll bet you get a lot of that." He flushed. "Sorry, that didn't come out right. I meant with your good looks and all." He shook his head. "I'll quit now."

Chuckling, she patted his arm. "Thanks for the compliment. As bad as it is for female officers, the secretaries suffer more. Catherine has shared how hard it is for her."

"Yeah, and it's too bad. She's smart and a good secretary. She's also a great office buddy. She puts up with a lot of my grousing."

"I know I've been lucky to be promoted. Very few consular officers are. What about you?"

"I had a setback at my last post. As terrible as it might sound, I look forward to the coming war. Our critical position here on the Persian Gulf might lead to good material for evaluations and result in promotions for everyone."

"Unless it gets us killed." Piper dumped in the dishes and swirled the suds. "I know Catherine is scared, and so am I."

"We'll be okay as long as the Axis powers don't realize what's happening in Iran." He joined her at the basin and reached for a towel. "Catherine is tough. And don't ever get her mad. Her temper's ferocious. I had to restrain her from throttling George after Mariah died."

"Turn her loose. George needs throttling." She paused with a plate in her hands. "Milbourne and George are completely unreliable. Where would we go if we're evacuated?"

"Not sure. Depends on where the threat comes from. But be prepared. Have your papers in order and some dollars stashed away. Don't forget medicines, a change of clothes, canteens, and some food. Even a Swiss Army knife and flashlight. All in one bag."

At her startled look, he held her arm. "I've had longer to think about this than you. I'll help you, and so will Catherine. The three of us will look after each other." He dried the plate she still held. "When we're finished here, let's go up on the roof and look at the stars."

Wrapped in a quilt, Piper stood at the edge. "It's so quiet here, more so than Marseille."

"It is. Moscow could be quiet too since most of the time we were frozen."

"Ha. Winter must have been awful, but I would have enjoyed the depth and character of Russian culture."

"Yep. It had its characters, many of whom were deep into their vodka by sunset."

"Sounds a lot like here, only with Scotch and sand!"

"You have a great smile, Piper. And you're funny, too."

A bit flustered, she turned back to the desert. "I'm glad you told me about preparing an evacuation bag. I hadn't thought of that."

"Yep. Catherine's had hers ready ever since the old man announced our mission for the Persian Gulf." When she offered a corner of the quilt, he wrapped his arm around her waist and pulled the quilt over his shoulders.

"Sorry to keep returning to the war. I enticed you here to get away from that, didn't I?"

"Yes, but I came so I didn't have to open another can of soup." He pulled her to her feet and into his arms. "How about a dance under the moonlight?"

He began to hum the tune to "The White Cliffs of Dover." As they slowly moved around the rooftop, Piper sang the lyrics.

A chill breeze blew across their roof as Piper sang the final verse. She leaned into his embrace and felt safe and warm. When they parted, she retrieved the quilt. "It's getting cold. Perhaps we should call it a night."

In her half of their house, Piper sat with her feet curled beneath her and sipped red wine. Thinking about the evening, she realized how comfortable she was with Mark. Although he was silly at times, he was also interested in her as a person. So different from her past experiences with men. And he was concerned about her welfare in this dangerous sandbox.

She swallowed the last of her wine and turned back her bed-covers. Feeling safe and relaxed, she held Simone's booties as she fell asleep.

Chapter 46

December 1941. In the besieged city of Leningrad, three thousand die each day.

"Sir, Post One here. Fuad wants to see you about your dinner order."

When Russ entered the restaurant, Fuad was sweeping the floor while two old men sipped coffee and played backgammon in the corner. "I'm here about my dinner order."

Fuad glanced at the corner. "Mr. Mark, two European strangers ate lunch here. They spoke very bad Arabic. They wore dirty suits and said they came from Baghdad. I offered to help them during their stay. They said they were archeologists and were interested in the Red Fort."

"Did they ask about the Legation or its activities?"

"No, but they watched your building and wrote down who came and went."

Russ jotted down their descriptions. "What first made you suspicious about these men?"

"The way they spoke to each other in a low voice when they thought I could not hear. I recognized their language. It was German!"

The next afternoon in Spencer's office, Russ gave Heath-Fleming, Piper, and Hedges time to digest Fuad's report on the archeologists. "Trick, anything from your end?"

"As a matter of fact, Major Khoury from the Interior Ministry called this morning. He'd picked up the pair during a routine sweep of foreigners. They carried Austrian passports and academic references to verify their archeology story. Khoury was inclined to let them go about their business until one of them mentioned an acquaintance with Admiral Canaris, head of German military intelligence. He seemed to think that would impress Khoury, but all it did was get them an escort to Cairo for further interrogation."

"At least you know Fuad is paying attention, Russ. That was a good pickup on his part." Heath-Fleming chewed on his pipe. "And I'm impressed that the Interior Ministry is on the ball with their random sweeps."

"I don't know." Hedges tapped his pencil. "We've got our walk-in, Gunther Mayerik. A photographer, Paul Guderian. And now two archeologists. Who else has slipped by a café owner and occasional sweeps of foreigners?"

Spencer sighed. "You want to come with me to tell the old man, Russ?"

"Not particularly, but I won't let you brave that scene by yourself."

⚜

Two British counterintelligence officers finished their fruitless interrogation of photographer Paul Guderian. They filed their report and flew from Kuwait to Cairo. Two possible spies calling themselves archeologists awaited a chance to be more cooperative.

A few days later, Spencer, Hedges, and Heath-Fleming trained a camera through the jail office window at a blindfolded man. With his hands bound behind his back, Paul Guderian knelt in the dust. In his final words, he railed in Russian against the oppression of the workers.

A Kuwaiti guard raised a curved sword above his head. The

honed blade sliced through Guderian's neck, sending his head to the dirt with a muffled *thunk*. The body tilted and fell forward, ending the Allied effort to fathom Guderian's mind.

After the execution, Hedges sorted Guderian's few belongings. "A pencil, a small notebook with scribbles about camera settings, a Ronson lighter, a few coins."

"That doesn't tell us much about this character." Spencer ran his hands through his hair. "Of course, we're still waiting for the FBI reports on interviewing his sister and on that postal box in Washington, D.C. What takes them so long? We're supposed to be on the same side."

Hedges hefted a small package wrapped in a piece of German newspaper. "This is odd." Flecks like pepper escaped the brittle paper as he unwrapped the bundle. "It's dirt!"

"Some people fear dying away from their country." Heath-Fleming lifted the parcel from Hedges's hand. "Dirt symbolizes the earth of their homeland. They'll abandon all else but never lose sight of their package of dirt."

Spencer photographed the contents. "Who does that?"

Heath-Fleming grimaced. "Russians."

Chapter 47

*January 1942. The Allies agree to refrain from negoti-
ating a separate peace agreement.*

MILBOURNE'S MIND WANDERED as he watched Khalid. *That upstart
rattles on and on. And Russ scribbles away as if there were a big cable coming out of this ridiculous meeting.* He raised a hand to muffle
a yawn.

"In summary, Mr. Ambassador, KOC believes this is a major
oil find in the neutral zone. We want to start production as soon as
hostilities have ceased."

"I understand oil will be an important economic asset to your
country. But I can't see how it'll benefit the United States."

"Mr. Ambassador, in as simple terms as possible, oil is in the
future of the world. Our little country will have it in excess. We'll
repay our allies for their protection by exporting it to them. I've
been authorized by my government to extend to your government
the first chance to reap the benefits of our exploration."

"What about your traditional KOC associates, Gulf Oil and
British Petroleum?"

"KOC hopes to extend its marketing beyond our established
partners. We need more efficient technology and hope Texas Energy will be interested in cooperating with us."

Russ drove the point home. "So, you're giving Tex-En a chance to develop a field of unknown size for the benefit of both KOC and the United States?"

Khalid smiled. "That's it."

Russ turned to Milbourne. "Do you have any questions about the offer, sir?"

"No." Milbourne rose. "You know, the president is too busy with important matters to be bothered with potential oil in an uncertain future with some vague idea about benefits."

Khalid stiffened and gathered his papers.

With a glance at Khalid's expression, Russ offered, "I'm sure the ambassador will appreciate the details of your presentation once we're back at the Legation and have time to discuss it." He turned to Milbourne with widened eyes. "Isn't that right, sir?"

Milbourne nodded. "Perhaps."

"Okay, then." Khalid rose. "I plan a research expedition to a very promising sector when the weather clears. I'd like to have Russ along as an observer."

Milbourne gave a quick nod. "Take him."

⁂

Early the next afternoon, the phone rang in Russ's office. "Mr. Russell, this is Wendell Fox, advisor to the amir. We haven't had an occasion to meet."

"No, sir. How may I help you?"

"I've heard from the amir about Khalid's meeting with your ambassador. He's asked me to renew my acquaintance with Duncan to follow up on the oil seep in the neutral zone. Can you arrange a meeting with him?"

Russ recalled his previous discussion with Milbourne about Fox. "I'll call after I talk with him. When did you know the ambassador, sir?"

"We served together in the Istanbul embassy in 1910. Unless

he's changed, I don't expect much from talking with him, but the amir has insisted."

At the end of the day, Milbourne led Russ onto his balcony. "Look, I've listened to Khalid, and he said he spoke for the amir. You're drafting a cable to Washington on his proposal. Why should I meet with an advisor?"

"Because the amir is pushing it. Besides, it's an opportunity to understand Fox's function in the Kuwaiti government."

"You meet with him. Tell him I'm too busy." He waved Russ out.

As the muezzin's last call echoed along the dusty lanes, sunlit motes drifted into the shadows of the storefronts. The ambassador sat on the balcony and nursed his Scotch as he thought about the oil problem. *Why am I being forced to deal with some royal relative? The foreign minister should be addressing me. And now Fox. I need a DCM. Marvella would know how to deal with Fox. She could move into the residence. Plenty of room.*

⁓⟨⟩⁓

Back at the office, Russ found a note from Catherine. *Ibrahim called. Your jewelry is ready.*

Russ strode along the rows of darkened shops. He found the old silversmith stooped over a pendant. "Hello, Ibrahim." He bent over the tray. "That's a beautiful piece. Is it an order from the palace?"

Ibrahim inclined his head. "It is beautiful, but alas, it belongs to no one. Maybe one day someone important will appreciate my small effort. You're the first to see it."

Russ picked up a piece of silver shaped like a dhow. "These tiny sails and awning over the wheel are magnificent."

"Another piece without a home." Ibrahim peered at the pendant. "I need to add filigree swirls along the hull on both sides, like the waves of the Gulf."

"My friend, you left a message for me. What have you observed?"

"Ah, yes. This morning, a man of about forty years with light brown hair and large build came in." Ibrahim held his hand higher than his head. "He wanted a bauble for his wife. He wore European clothes."

"Was another stranger shopping nearby?"

"No. Mustafa said the same. No one else."

Russ lifted a pencil and pad from his pocket. "Can you tell me any more?"

"Over chai, he said he worked for a London newspaper. He traveled through Baghdad on assignment." Ibrahim smirked. "His English was very bad, but he spoke very good Arabic."

"Did he use any other languages?"

"No, but he asked if I had seen other men like him in the suq recently. I told him I had not but would ask my friends."

The old man reached into a pocket of his dishdasha and retrieved a piece of paper. He tapped Russ's notebook with his finger. "Write this down, Mr. Russ. The stranger seeks a man about six feet tall with thinning hair by the name of Paul."

⚜

The next day, Russ followed a stout man in a gleaming white dishdasha through his luxurious private quarters in Dasman Palace. In flawless Arabic, Wendell Fox ordered a servant to bring juices, cheese, and British biscuits.

"I'm glad I was able to take this meeting on behalf of Ambassador Milbourne, Mr. Fox."

"Yes, yes, I know how this meeting occurred, Mr. Russell. Both of us must comply with our bosses' wishes."

Over refreshments the men relaxed into less formal conversation before getting to the matter at hand.

"Do you understand the geopolitical impact of this find, Russ?"

"I do. Oil will alter Kuwait's standing along the Gulf."

"Exactly, but it goes beyond that. Kuwait will have the economic power to align itself with powerful countries like the United States."

"And that will allow Kuwait to break with Britain." Russ exhaled.

"I see you've thought about this." Fox moved his bulk deeper into the chair. "Look, I was once like you, full of piss and vinegar. When I joined the Foreign Service, I hoped to make a difference, maybe change the antiquated policies we supported then."

"When was that, sir?"

"Back in 1904. By 1915, I was disgusted with our refusal to see the eventual collapse of the British Empire." Fox shook his head. "I left the Foreign Service and spent the next nine years in Texas as an international oil consultant. During several visits to Kuwait to lay the groundwork for oil exploration, I became fluent in Arabic. I also fostered a friendship with the amir. He appreciated my political savvy."

"Yes, the amir would see you as a valuable resource for his plans."

"Right again. When he offered me a job in his court in '26, I accepted. Same job, better pay, no U.S. income taxes." Fox lowered his head and raised an eyebrow in Russ's direction. "So, you're joining us on Khalid's expedition into the An Nafud?"

Russ nodded. "Yes, I'm eager to get out of the Legation, and the ambassador agreed."

"Excellent." Fox laced his hands across his ample midsection. "I'll share some stories about the good ol' days of diplomacy, back when Duncan and I were in our glory. He was quite a player, and I'm not talking about foreign policy, if you get my meaning."

Chapter 48

January 1942. Japanese advances in Borneo meet with little opposition.

RUSS STUDIED THE map while Piper arranged their provisions in the bottom of their rented fishing boat. "Ready for a moderate adventure to a little-known place?"

"Sure. If it isn't scary, I'm ready."

"Nah! It's all about history and beauty. Khalid recommends the island."

"Will it be like our visit to the Red Fort?" She tied a scarf around her curls and stepped into the boat. "I loved those little green bee-eaters flitting about the acacia tree in the fort's courtyard."

"No migrating birds today. Maybe a bustard. Their wingspans are enormous. But it is another fort, only this one is Portuguese."

"You're amazing, Mark. You know so many odd things."

"Thanks, I guess. I specialize in odd." He started the motor and angled the boat toward the open Gulf.

They bounced along the choppy water, the noise of the motor dampening any attempts at talk. Russ steered the boat toward a barren strip of land and turned off the motor when the hull touched the beach.

They hiked to a promontory overlooking the Persian Gulf. With a hand shading her eyes, Piper peered at the endless horizon. "It's a magnificent view, but it's very lonely out here."

"Faylakah is mostly windswept scrub and sand." Russ scanned the northeastern horizon, where clouds were beginning to swell. "The fort's over there. Let's have our picnic in the ruins."

He grabbed their gear while Piper picked up the canteens and an old army blanket. The wind shifted direction as the clouds darkened with portent. Keeping an eye on the horizon, he arranged the blanket inside the fort's bleached sandstone walls.

She climbed to the top of one of them. The freshening wind blew through her hair.

"It's getting muggier." Russ joined her on the wall. "Think your aunty in France would like my choice of a picnic place?"

"I doubt it." Piper jumped from the wall and sat on the blanket. "She's more of a champagne and caviar kinda gal." She sighed. "I try not to think about the dangers they face. The Nazis are building beach fortifications just a hundred yards away from her bungalow.

"Is there something wrong, Mark?" She reached up and pulled him onto the blanket beside her. "You look worried."

He nodded at the towering thunderheads. "Back in Kansas, those types of clouds meant danger and death."

"Oh." She shivered. "Well, let's finish our lunch and pack up in case it rains."

After they stowed away the picnic supplies, they leaned against the warm wall of the fort's central plaza. "This was fun. Thank you for showing me the sights in this barren land."

"Well, it's better to explore with someone else." He reached out and touched her hand.

When she twined her fingers in his, he brushed them with his lips. She placed her other hand around his neck and pulled him in for a kiss.

"Tell me more about the young you in Kansas."

Piper leaned against his shoulder while he talked about growing up on the Great Plains. She laughed at his horse stories and mourned with him as he talked about his father's death in a ravine during a blizzard.

Lightning forked over the water and a crack of thunder reverberated around the ruins. Russ jumped to his feet and looked beyond the ruined wall. "That's too close. Did you see any shelter?" He pulled her to his side.

Amethyst thunderheads underpinned with ochre scudded overhead. "That looks serious." She pointed to a space beneath an open stairwell. "Maybe over there."

When he failed to answer, she shook his arm. "Mark, it'll be okay. We'll just get wet." She ducked into the small space beneath the stairs with an armful of their stuff.

Thunder rolled around them, and dancing raindrops turned into torrents that flooded the sand. The skyline became a memory.

With her free hand, Piper pulled him in beside her. "We're okay. It's just a storm."

He jumped at the sound of a wall collapsing along the stairwell. Water rushed into a crevice beneath their legs. He huddled in the small space and mumbled, "Angie."

Wind whipped the blanket Piper held across the opening in a fruitless effort to shield them from the worst of the onslaught. She glanced at Mark and dropped a corner to caress his cheek. "Mark, stay with me. It'll be okay."

He grabbed her hand and crushed her fingers in his. "I won't let anything happen to you. I'll never let go." He shoved Piper deeper into the alcove and pressed his body to hers.

Sandstone rained down on their heads when lightning split the darkness. Thunder echoed across the island.

And then, it was over. The torrent turned to a drizzle and the sun broke through the clouds. In moments, a breeze gently riffled the puddles.

Russ crawled out and turned to pull Piper to her feet. Both stretched away their tension. "I think we survived." He glanced at her. "I don't like storms."

"I got that impression." She took his arm. "Are you feeling better? You had me a little worried."

"Sorry." Russ took a deep breath. "When we were nine years old, my friend Angie and I sneaked away from a neighborhood carry-in supper. We skipped and played through the tall grass until we heard thunder. We were too far from home, so we sheltered beneath a rock ledge near a creek. Suddenly, the sky darkened, and the wind raged all around us. Bits and pieces of wood and rock twirled by, and the rain pounded. And then, just as suddenly, it was still. Angie stepped into the open and reached back for me. Just as I touched her fingers, the rain started up again. For a moment I held her hand, but then she was gone. The wind lifted her off the ground and into the pitch-black sky. I never saw her again."

"Oh my God." Piper grasped his arms and held tight.

"Later, the adults found me lying on the ground near the ledge with a huge lump on the back of my head. I was unconscious, and the arm I'd held out to Angie was broken."

"Did they find Angie?"

"No." He shuddered. "I hunted off and on for years, long after the search teams gave up. She had vanished."

"This storm brought it all back, didn't it?"

When he didn't respond, she shook his arm. "Mark, it was just an accident. A terrible, awful tragedy. But it wasn't your fault." She brushed the hair off his face. "You know that, don't you? You were only nine."

"Yeah, everyone said it wasn't my fault. Still…" He shrugged. "When her parents moved away, I felt bad. I guess they had too many memories."

"Probably so." Piper wrapped her arms around Russ and held him. "You protected me this time, Mark. Even when you were the most upset, you found enough courage to shield me with your body. You kept me safe." She squeezed him tighter. "Maybe it's time you forgave yourself for Angie."

"Maybe." He whispered into her hair. "I didn't want to lose you."

"I know." She kissed his forehead and released him. "Let's check on the fishing boat."

Russ bailed water with an old tin bait bucket he found in the bottom. The motor gasped and wheezed and finally sputtered to life. Beneath a bright sun, they puttered across the twenty-five miles of open water to the Shuwaikh port. Piper lay against Russ and dozed until they slowed at the dock.

Chapter 49

January 1942. The Red Army attacks German forces along the Eastern Front.

THE BASEMENT MAIL room was as dingy as the snack bar. Russ walked in and grabbed the front office stack as well as the pile for consular.

Back upstairs, he asked the secretary, "Is Miss Piper in?"

"Yes, sir. Go in, please."

Russ knocked on her open door. "Mail boy here."

Piper waved him in. "Hey, it's good to see you. How are you after yesterday?"

"You mean our near-death experience on Faylakah?" He laughed. "I'm good. Actually, very good. Maybe I needed another storm to come to terms with those memories."

"We all need to forgive ourselves at one time or another." She sighed. "And we all struggle with our pasts. I know that more than some."

The secretary knocked on her door. "Mr. Lander phoned about your furniture requisition. He did not sound happy. He's on his way here."

When Russ moved to leave, Piper stopped him with a hand

on his arm. "No, stay. I don't know what's on his mind, but I might need a witness."

Russ took the chair in the corner just as Lander swept past the secretary. He tossed a scowl in Russ's direction and dropped a sheet of paper on Piper's desk.

"What's going on, George?"

He looked around her office. "Your furniture looks fine to me. Same as everybody else's. Besides, I don't have funds for anything on your requisition."

"When will you get them?"

"Who knows? We'll see what the year-end money looks like."

"Okay, then I'll tap into them. Unless they're already spoken for?"

"Not so far." He looked around again. "Just like Doris, wanting to pretty everything up, and for what? No one sees this place except some Kuwaitis."

Piper stood and leaned across her desk. "Exactly, Kuwaitis see everything. This office looks like it was furnished with junk from a rummage sale. Take some pride. Even here, we represent the United States of America."

"She's right." Russ joined Piper on her side of the desk. "While you're at it, change my work order to fix the walls in my house to tap into year-end funds. I'll mention it to the others with similar problems."

"Stay out of this, Russ." Lander spun on his heel and left.

Later, Russ and Piper ate a meal from Fuad's. Then Russ grabbed a blanket and they climbed to their shared roof.

"Did you see the look on George's face when you stood by my side in the office today?"

"I did. I thought we were in for another near-death experience." Russ bared his teeth and flexed his bicep. "But I was ready."

Piper pushed back her sleeve and flexed her own muscle. "Me too!'

He pulled her to him and laughed. "We make a pretty good team, don't we?"

Piper raised her face and kissed him.

After a moment, he kissed her back. When he slipped his arm around her waist, he began to hum "A Nightingale Sang in Berkeley Square."

Piper nestled into his embrace and sang softly.

Chapter 50

January 1942. The Japanese take Kuala Lumpur, Malaysia.

MILBOURNE DROPPED HIS briefcase on the hall table and doffed his suit coat. "The president's recalling me for consultations."

"Oh, good!" Bitsy exclaimed. "I can get the hell out of here. When do we leave?"

"Not so fast." He headed for the bar and pulled out a fresh bottle of Scotch. "Kimball's arranged transport on a mail plane to Cairo. There's one jump seat. It's mine."

"Can't they toss out some mail and put in another seat?"

"No, Bitsy, they can't. Some poor soldiers won't get their mail as it is."

"Never mind." Her green eyes flashed. "I'll make my own calls."

"Don't bother. I'll arrange it in D.C. at the Army Air Force. I want you out of here, too."

Bitsy bit down on a laugh. The old goat hadn't realized what he said.

"All right, Duncan. When do you leave?"

"Tomorrow I'm going to Iran for a last-minute check on the conditions there. I'll leave the next afternoon."

When Milbourne returned from Iran, his luggage was parked at the foot of the stairs. "Well, I wasn't expecting that. Are you eager to get rid of me?"

"Just trying to help." She handed him a Scotch. "Are you going to be a good boy?"

"Of course, what about you?" Milbourne tossed back the Scotch and refilled his glass. "Going to try it on with one of the marines? Or maybe Russ? Chew him up and spit him out. Then I'll fire him."

"You're delusional," Bitsy said. "Your carrot-topped hussy, Marvella, will be sorely disappointed once she gets you in the sack. You've lost it, lover boy!"

Milbourne sank into a chair with his elbows on his knees. "Don't you ever let up? I'm so tired of you and your needling."

"Look, I traveled thousands of miles to give our marriage another chance. And where did you spend your time? Drinking with George, that's where. No one cared if he wasn't at home because, you might have noticed, Doris never returned after Mariah's death. And I don't blame her one damned bit."

"I've had enough, Bitsy. Work on our marriage by yourself." Milbourne grabbed the Scotch bottle and turned on his heel, giving a swift kick to his luggage on the way up the stairs.

⚬———⚬

Bundled up on a chilly early morning, Milbourne strode the few blocks from the Willard Hotel to the White House. He dropped his card at the West Wing lobby before crossing West Executive Avenue to the State, War, and Navy Building.

Looking across the desk at the assistant secretary of state, another aging Black Dragon, Milbourne came right to the point. "I need a new DCM to replace Mariah."

"Yeah, we've heard. Have anyone in mind?"

"You bet, Marvella Jessup."

"Why would you want her after the grilling you took at your confirmation hearing?"

"Because she's an accomplished Arabist with regional experience. And we get a lot done when we work together."

"I can just imagine that." The Dragon waggled his eyebrows.

"Go ahead. Laugh. From what I hear, all you have left is your imagination."

"All right, Duncan. You've made your point. Doesn't matter anyway. The president will never consider her for your DCM. He's heard too much grief from too many up on the Hill."

"We'll see. He values my opinion enough to bring me all the way back here to discuss the very important mission I'm running at post. That's power."

"If you say so. What does Marvella think?"

"Oh, she'll jump at the chance to get back in the field."

"You might be surprised. She certainly seems happy working on the secretary's staff. Why would she trade that for the hubs of Hades?"

"It might not be up to her. Look, Roosevelt promised me support from State, COI, and War. I intend to hold him to that when I meet him later. Make Marvella happen."

After Milbourne left, the Dragon stared out his window at the White House. He lifted the receiver and dialed a number. "It's me. Let's get together with the others. Duncan Milbourne's picked his DCM. We can't have the old man in the White House turn his eye in our direction."

Within the hour, they had gathered around a conference table. A distinguished Dragon with silver hair started. "Marvella Jessup might be our answer. She's sharp and knows how to manage Milbourne."

The Dragon with the red-and-green rep tie shook his head. "Congressman Titus was snooping around the other day. He confirmed that Duncan's back on the bottle. Bitsy's there now and she hasn't fixed it. What can Jessup do?"

The Dragon in the gray pinstripe suit shrugged. "Probably nothing. Let's just give him the NEA job he wants. We could keep an eye on him if he's down the hall."

The senior Dragon twirled his pencil. "That would antagonize FDR. And the Senate might not let him through this time."

The silver-haired diplomat regained the floor. "How about we pull Duncan out of Kuwait and pack him off to the farm? Give the ambassadorship to Marvella and pick her DCM for her."

The chief Dragon puffed his cheeks. "That's probably the best idea yet. She'd do a better job than he ever will. But that still leaves the president. He chose Duncan, and he won't recognize reason if it comes from us. Let's just wait and see what happens after Duncan's visit with the West Wing."

While they mulled over their choices, an assistant serving coffee slipped away and lifted the receiver. "Long-distance to our Legation in Kuwait. I'd like to speak to Malcolm Lodge."

Wembley strode along beside Milbourne as they neared the Map Room. "He's in there."

"Good afternoon, Mr. President." Milbourne took the seat FDR waved him toward.

"Well, Duncan, I see you weathered the trip." He handed over a glass. "Jasper set me up with the fixings for one of my martini specials. To your health."

Milbourne tilted his glass to FDR. "And to yours."

FDR wheeled his chair beneath a table. "Tell me about Kuwait."

Milbourne coughed into his hand, his leg jittering against the chair. "We're ready, sir. The coast watchers and Bedouin chiefs met at the palace a few months back for training. It went well, except for one rascal of a chief who refused to participate. I devised a plan to cover that chief's sector with Royal Guards from the amir's palace and from the House of Saud."

"Sounds good." FDR blew white puffs toward the ceiling.

"When I was in Iran, our U.S. Army liaison confirmed that Marshal Stalin refuses to let those trains go all the way into Russia. He still wants to offload them onto Soviet trains in Tehran. He doesn't want the folks at home to know where all the supplies are coming from."

"I know. Russia might be our future war." FDR refilled their glasses. "Those COI boys are busy with spy cases, especially that character Guderian. Need more of their officers?"

Milbourne's heel rat-a-tatted against the rug. "Definitely not, sir. We're bursting at the seams as it is. Actually, I considered having their chief recalled for insubordination."

FDR's eyebrows rose. "You don't say?"

"He's an upstart playing junior detective. You read his cable on Guderian before I knew about it. I will not tolerate being left in the dark on activities affecting my mission."

"Easy, Duncan." The president held up his hands. "They're new at their jobs. Work with them. We need all the help we can get to sort out our enemies from our supposed friends."

Milbourne pressed a hand to still his leg, but his temple pulsed with suppressed anger. "I am working with them. But I don't have to like it."

"I've heard about Kuwait from several of my visitors lately. I'm glad I allowed your assistant to remain with you. He seems to be an asset."

The ambassador flushed. "He'll transfer this summer, and I won't need another. I put him to work managing our social events and drafting cables."

"Oh? I heard he's a local hero who's well connected to the amir."

The leg tremor was back with a vengeance. "True, but that was before I arrived. Now I deal with the palace."

"Wasn't he involved in the spy cases?"

"Our female officer needed a man to go with her to the jail to interview Guderian."

FDR frowned. "Did he accompany you to Iran?"

"Yes, he did. But my cablegrams don't go out without my approval and final signature."

"Now Averell told me Russell is onto a possible oil find."

Milbourne stuck a finger under the knot of his tie and pulled.

"Russell needs more experience, so I involve him in several different areas." With an effort he controlled his leg. "If I may ask, sir, what's your interest in him?"

"Oh, I just like to hear about young officers making a difference. The future won't need old fogeys like us." FDR puffed out his cheeks. "Listen, Duncan, about that oil. I've changed my mind. Put Russell on it."

Milbourne put down his glass and gripped the arms of his chair. "With all due respect, Mr. President, I'd like to continue to run my mission as I see fit." His grip tightened. "For as long as I'm ambassador there."

"Of course, you know best." FDR touched his lighter to his cigarette holder. "I trust you learned your lesson in Baghdad and won't repeat your mistakes."

Milbourne's head snapped back. "That's all behind me. I was tired at the end of my career. Now I'm rested and ready." He took a deep breath. "And I believe, after Kuwait, I can contribute next door in NEA."

FDR waved that away. "Right now, I'm concerned with Kuwait. You have a job to do. As you said, for as long as you're ambassador there.

"Tell you what," FDR pushed himself away from the table, "let's continue this tomorrow. I have some ideas I'd like to propose." He pushed a button on his telephone.

When Wembley appeared, the president said, "Duncan will return tomorrow at eight for coffee." He turned to Milbourne. "We both have an idea where things stand now, don't we?"

Stiffly, Milbourne walked from the Map Room. On the street in front of the East Gate, he leaned against a white brick column and wiped his brow. Returning his handkerchief to his pocket, he shuddered. Holy hell, what went wrong? Something had turned the old boy into the wind on Kuwait. Heads would roll when he got back.

In his suite at the Willard, he grabbed a bottle of single malt and took a long pull from it.

The telephone jangled on Mariah's desk. "Malcolm Lodge. Yeah, I'm chargé. Our ambassador's on consultations in your town. Oh, you've seen him?" He propped his feet on the desk. "Haven't heard from you in some time. What's the scuttlebutt?"

"You're kidding me!" Lodge's feet hit the floor. "Jessup!" His face darkened. "If the Dragons want the staff opinion, I offer two words: hell, no!" He listened for a few moments more. "Okay. Thanks for the tip. I owe you."

Catherine waved Russ over. She pointed to Mariah's office and whispered, "He just got a call from someone in D.C. They're talking about Marvella Jessup."

Lodge rose and slammed his fist on the desk. "Good God Almighty! I can't take much more of this." They heard him drop into the chair and dial the phone. "Bitsy, Malcolm here."

Russ and Catherine lingered by the door until Lodge replaced the receiver. They walked in when he called out to them.

"Did you hear any of that?"

Catherine nodded. "We sure did. You look ready to burst a seam."

Lodge dipped his fingers into a glass of water and wiped his florid face. "The old man is pushing the Dragons to replace Mariah with Marvella Jessup."

"The floozy from Baghdad? That'll be the end of the marriage."

"You're so right, Russ. And what about his career?"

Catherine replaced Lodge's water glass. "Maybe Marvella could keep him in line?"

"We can't count on that. He's the ambassador, and Marvella will be careful not to step over the line and have him turn on her." Lodge ran his hands through his hair. "I need a drink."

Russ headed to Milbourne's office and returned with three tumblers and a bottle.

Chapter 51

January 1942. Hitler cancels Operation Sea Lion, the oft-postponed invasion of Britain.

THE NEXT MORNING, Wembley led Milbourne to the Map Room once again. Jasper already had the coffee service set up. The president waved him to the usual chair and poured. "Sorry to meet at such an ungodly hour, but I have a rather busy day."

"No, I'm busy, also." Milbourne accepted the fine porcelain cup with trembling fingers.

"Well, then, let me start with several ideas I have about the supply line."

Milbourne sat back and sipped his coffee while FDR touched on various aspects of the coordination and delivery of the supplies to Stalin. Some of his ideas were worth considering, but several were completely untenable considering the conditions in Iran. Things were going better than he had feared. Probably hadn't needed that fortifying glass of Scotch this morning.

At that moment, the telephone rang. "Ah, Winston. You called at a good time. I have Duncan Milbourne here out of Kuwait. Sure, hold on." He handed the receiver to Milbourne. "The prime minister would like a word."

"Good morning, sir." The leg tremor had returned.

"Mr. Ambassador, I'm sure Franklin is catching you up on our many ideas about the Middle East, so I won't go into any of that. However, I want to ask you about some disturbing comments I've had from my political agent, not to mention others on the ground there." The line was silent for a moment. "We can't have any weak links in aiding Marshal Stalin. To speak bluntly, are you a weak link? Is your weakness Scotch?"

"No, absolutely not." Milbourne jumped up and clutched the receiver in a sweaty hand. "Your sources are mistaken. Frankly, I'm insulted that you'd ask me such a question."

"Be insulted all you want, but we need to keep the Eastern Front open. I know Franklin is an old mate of yours and wants you to succeed, but he understands the ramifications of a failure in Kuwait. And I'm not talking just about the supply line."

"Are you there, Mr. Ambassador? Let me talk to Franklin."

Milbourne nearly collapsed into his chair. He passed the receiver to FDR.

"Well, Winston, I don't know what you said to my ambassador, but he appears rather shaken. I need to finish my meeting here and then we'll talk again later this evening."

FDR stared at Milbourne. "That wasn't about the supply line, was it?"

"No, it wasn't." Milbourne slapped on what he hoped passed for a smile. "There seems to be some misunderstanding about my performance in Kuwait."

"Misunderstanding, huh? It's not only the Brits who are reporting in, Duncan." The president placed his cup in its saucer. "If you don't fix this, I'll have to fix it for you." He ran an eye over Milbourne. "Looks like you've had it for this morning. Perhaps I'll find time to squeeze you in again before you return to Kuwait." FDR touched his buzzer.

Milbourne clutched at the white brick column at the East Gate. He fumbled for his handkerchief and mopped the sweat from his brow. His stomach heaved, and he swallowed hard on the bile that rose to his throat. *I need a drink.* He stumbled toward a taxi and lifted his hand.

That evening, Milbourne waited outside the Willard. A few drinks, a bite of lunch, and a nap had revived him. He shot his white cuffs, smoothed his tie, snugged his collar, and patted his hair. Time to let Marvella soothe his mind. Should he bed her before or after dinner? Both?

When a Chevy pulled up, he got in and pecked the driver on her cheek. "Are we going to your place first, my dear? It's been a while and I've missed you." His eyebrows rose in anticipation.

"No, I've made reservations at a new restaurant in Arlington. They're in demand and I had to take what I could get." Marvella Jessup checked her mirror before pulling into traffic. "Don't worry, Duncan, we'll have plenty of time after dinner."

Milbourne ran his eyes over Marvella as she navigated their way to a spot behind the national cemetery. Her burnished copper hair swung around her face. Her blue eyes sparkled with intelligence. She might be a bit thicker around the middle, but her long legs more than made up for that.

In the elevator, Milbourne nuzzled her neck and breathed in her fragrance. "Ah, lavender, my favorite."

The cloakroom attendant checked her mink and his topcoat. The maître d' led them to a window table with an excellent view of the city.

They reminisced about old times and chatted about the war while they perused the menu and ordered. "You sounded worried about your visit with Franklin. How'd that go?"

"Okay." Milbourne cut into his salmon. "He's planning a trip with Churchill to Casablanca, and he'll drop by Kuwait. He's sending over a navy cruiser to show the flag."

"Have a photographer there. You'll look good with the captain in his dress whites."

"Good idea. I'll call Carenza." The waiter topped off his Scotch. "Then the PM called, and FDR put me on the phone." He slugged back a mouthful. "That was an interesting conversation. But enough about me. Tell me about your job. Ready to get out of there?"

While Marvella by turns groused and bragged about her many responsibilities, Milbourne nodded. Snippets of the morning in FDR's office ran through his head. *Smythe and his cronies carrying tales about the Legation. Churchill threatening me. He's not my boss. But Franklin appeared to know what happened. By God, he set me up.*

"Duncan, did you hear me?" Marvella leaned forward as she pushed away her plate.

"Yes, dear. You were reminding me that you are an insider in the halls of diplomacy while I'm in diplomatic exile." He grimaced and emptied his glass.

She leaned away. "I said nothing of the sort."

He dropped some cash on the table. "Let's skip dessert and go back to your place."

Twenty minutes later, they parked in the alley behind her small Cape Cod in Georgetown.

In her living room, he poured a healthy Scotch and a snifter of brandy for Marvella.

"Why did Bitsy come to Kuwait, Duncan?"

"To save our marriage." He took a swig.

"What's to save?" She sipped her brandy. "What does she do with herself all day?"

"Who knows?" Milbourne sighed. "I don't care what she does."

"She must be bored out of her mind. And that's not her style." Marvella tapped her fingernail against the snifter. "So, she's found someone to entertain her. If not you, then who?"

"A marine, maybe. Definitely not George this time. Maybe my assistant."

"Ah, the famous Mark Russell. Carenza sure likes him. And Averell Harriman. Even Congressman Titus." She peered at him over the rim of her snifter. "I should meet him."

"Enough!" Milbourne threw a pillow across the room. "Stop talking about Russell. I can't escape him even in D.C."

"Okay, okay. He's just a kid." She twirled her brandy. "I've heard rumors at Main State that you're having trouble with the spy guys. I know how much you hate losing control."

"I don't know what's happening anymore." He dropped his head against the sofa back. "I've lost my footing with the palace, and things are moving too fast." He rose and topped off his Scotch. "It's one problem after another." He dropped onto the sofa again.

"Well, there is a war going on." Marvella rose to retrieve the pillow and glanced at the bottle he'd brought with him. "I think your problem is right there in your hand."

She waved away his protests. "Look, Duncan, I've seen it for myself tonight."

"Why are you hounding me, Marvella? Don't I get enough of that from Bitsy? She never lets me forget her richer blood, her connections. She even throws in my face how my dad thought I'd never amount to anything. And yet, here I am. Ambassador to Kuwait."

"Yeah, but for how long? Your cronies at Main State have lost their influence. A younger breed of Arabists is on the scene. Wake up, Duncan! You're throwing away your last chance."

She tossed the pillow on the sofa and stood with her hands on her hips.

Milbourne leaned forward with his elbows on his knees and his head in his hands. He extended an arm to her. "Can't you let me have just one night?"

She dropped her hands and patted Milbourne's head. Her face softened. "All right. Let me show off the lavender lingerie you sent to me."

When she returned to the living room, the glass had dropped from Duncan's hand. The bottle was empty. He was snoring.

She marched into bedroom and tore off the lingerie. She'd save it for the next date with her young protégé. She threw on her clothes. *Didn't even mention the DCM job. That's it. I'm done with the old lush. He had his chance.*

"Wake up, lover boy. Time to go."

"No, no, I want to stay." Milbourne pushed away her helping hand.

"But I don't want you to." She bundled him into her Chevy. The drive to the Willard was quiet. The city was asleep, and so was Milbourne.

Chapter 52

*February 1942. Tactics change as Bomber Command
in London now targets civilian areas in Germany.*

THE PACE AT the harbor slowed while Piper and Russ ate at a waterfront restaurant. Old men played backgammon under the awning of a nearby coffee shop. House servants led donkeys burdened with water tins down the dusty lanes. Two stevedores paused to exchange the news of the day. A spice merchant and a young helper closed their burlap bags of colored spices.

At the end of their meal, they strolled along the dusty lanes to his car. Back at their house, Piper stopped at the stairs to the roof. "If we bundle up, it shouldn't be too cold up there."

When she joined Russ, who was leaning against the bagdir, a furry head popped out of the blanket around her shoulders.

"Whatcha got there?" He scratched behind its ears. "Does it have a name?"

"Oh, I don't even know if I'll keep him."

"He reminds me of the barn cats back home. There were always kittens running around." He laughed when the kitten crawled out of the blanket, settled in his lap, and promptly fell asleep.

Piper stared at the endless stars. "It's a lonely life we lead. Don't you think?"

"Sometimes, yeah. It's hard to remember what my old life was like."

"I remember mine all too well. After Father left us, Mother was so sad. She barely left the house. I crept around hoping I wouldn't cause her to burst into tears."

"She burst into tears when she saw you? What was that all about?"

"I never knew for sure. I look like my father, but it was more than that. I witnessed some awful scenes between them, and she probably felt guilty."

Piper pulled her hair away from her face. "See this scar? Father came home one night from a visit with his mistress. Mother was furious and started a big fight. He slammed a glass of gin to the floor, and a shard flew under the table. Neither of them knew I was under there until I screamed. When Father pulled me from under the tablecloth, my face was covered in blood. Mother was hysterical, but Father refused to take me to a hospital. He was too embarrassed, so he treated it himself." She let her hair fall back into place. "That scar is a physical reminder of the many wounds no one can see."

Russ ran a fingertip along the scar. "It's not so bad."

"I know, and it doesn't bother me, but Mother couldn't bear to look at it."

"Sorry." He put an arm around her.

"Do you know the worst part?" She leaned against his chest and petted the kitten. "She still loves him."

"So, an absent father and a mother who avoided you." He squeezed her against him. "You must have been desperate for love."

"I guess," she whispered. "I know I've made some bad choices. In Shanghai, I fell in love with a French diplomat named Henri. Turned out he had a wife and children. I was merely a fling for him, but it was devastating for me. I'd become the mistress who ruined my family."

Pulling away, she lifted the kitten from his lap. "Probably too much sharing. I'm sorry, Mark."

"No, no, it's okay. I'm glad you felt you could tell me."

"Thanks." She settled back against his shoulder. "Do you want to hear the rest of my sad life?"

He stroked her hair. "Sure, if you're up to it."

"I made a worse mistake at my last post in Marseille. I continued seeing Michel even after I knew he had a family. The guilt affected my work, and I wound up under medical care. That's when the post curtailed my assignment."

"I'd never know if you hadn't told me. You seem so…normal." He rolled his eyes. "Sorry if I'm making a mess of this."

"It was a tough time, but I feel good again." She smiled. "I feel normal when I'm with you." She walked to the wall where she stared into the vast desert. "You're not secretly married with children, are you?"

"Nope, no way." He joined her at the wall.

"Have you had any adventures in love?"

"My first love was Polly. It was in high school, and she was a cheerleader for my ball team. When I left Hays, we lost touch.

"Ow, that hurt." He grabbed her hand before she could pinch him again. "Guess you want to hear about more recent times, huh?"

"You're hard to know, Mark. Sometimes I think you just roll around in life like one of your Kansas tumbleweeds. Do you have any roots?"

"I'm what you might call shy." He bobbed his head up and down. "Honest. I'm closer to my horse Bandit than I've ever been to women."

"I'm dying to hear about Bandit, but later. So, no serious relationships?"

He stuck a hip on the wall and held up one finger. "When I was in college at Lawrence, another student and I eased the grind of Russian language classes with each other. She was more a companion than a lover." He stuck up a second finger. "There was a young gal in D.C. when I worked at Commerce. That was off and on for about a year, but most of the women I saw back there weren't interested in world travel, or in someone like me."

A slow grin crossed his face. "Once I transferred to Main State, life got more interesting. Those women had traveled overseas, spoke different languages, some were even officers themselves."

"Do you have someone back in the States or at another post right now?"

"No, but I met someone I can't forget at my last post, in Moscow. I don't want to forget her. She still haunts my life. We were both lonely and, I guess, a bit lost. She found me and drew me into her world. She opened my eyes about life and love and adventure."

"Do you love her?"

"I'll always love her, but…" He grimaced and turned toward the desert.

"She's married."

"That's right. But it wasn't like your Henri and Michel. I knew it from the start. We never intended to fall in love, at least, she said she didn't. As odd as it sounds, I was more of a project for her. She had a miserable marriage and wanted to help me avoid the mistakes so many men make with their romances." He shook his head. "Sounds nuts, I know."

"Where is she now?"

"Still in Moscow. But we write. Her letters take me away from this furnace."

"I'm glad you told me about her." Softly, she asked, "How long will you wait for her?"

"I don't know." He sighed. "She's all I ever wanted."

"I know what it's like to love a married man. Nothing but heartache. I'll never wait again." She glanced at him beneath her hair. "Perhaps you should think about doing the same."

"I suppose." He sighed again. "Thing is, she wanted me to find someone who would make me happy for my entire life. That was the purpose of her project." He shook his head. "But that sort of got lost in the time we spent together."

He shook off the memories and turned to Piper. "Now, do you want to hear about Bandit?"

Piper laughed and nearly pushed him off the wall. "No."

"Aw, c'mon. He likes to drink beer."

"Sounds like the perfect horse for you."

"He is. I've slept with Bandit more than with all those women combined."

He wrapped his arms around her from behind. "Honestly, I've led a typical romantic life, aside from Moscow. I wasn't ready to settle down, so I've never been in the wife-hunting business." He turned her around and held her gaze. "Maybe I'm ready to change."

Piper caressed his cheek. "Maybe my luck with men will improve."

She stepped away from the wall and scooped up the kitten. "But first we have to make it through the war."

In her side of the house, Piper tucked the kitten into a shoebox lined with an old hand towel. Lying in bed, she reached under her pillow and brought out the baby booties trimmed in lace. *Oh, Simone, my sweet baby girl. Be good for Aunty Laycie and God bless.* She held the booties against her cheek until sleep gave her peace.

In his half of their house, Russ kicked off his boots and flopped on his bed. He reached under his pillow to retrieve a yellow envelope. He read again Rhonda's letter about her plans to return to the States and set up house in Georgetown. *Why haven't I heard from you for so long?*

❦

Rhonda was surprised to find actual mail in the embassy mail room. Delivery had become so erratic recently, and she suspected little of her personal correspondence was arriving in a timely manner. She left Preston's mail for his secretary to gather and settled in a café with only one robin's-egg blue envelope.

> *Rhonda, darling,*
>
> *Thanks for your encouraging words in my struggle with Duncan. Divorce is not something I want, but I see little else left to me. But you must consider if it is right for you. There*

are many pitfalls. Divorce for women of our social standing harms us but not the men. They're held blameless while we're considered fast and loose.

Many will wonder who the other man is. Do you believe it is Russ? Have you considered the age difference? Society's disdain of such a match?

Preston may not be the man you thought you married, but at least he has none of Duncan's weaknesses. Most of my friends believe they know what went on behind the scenes in our marriage. But people will wonder about yours. Why were there no children?

We're both intelligent women who have retained our good looks, and we're too young to be stuck with husbands that hold us back from a wonderful life of possibilities. I've sorted through all the unhappy consequences of starting over and made my decision. I'll be interested to see what you decide.

May your garden come alive with opportunities for a happy future.

Bitsy

Chapter 53

*March 1942. All Jewish residences must be clearly
marked throughout areas controlled by Germany.*

ON A RAINY night in Washington, D.C., Rhonda watched as her
husband was feted at a reception in his honor at the Soviet embassy on Sixteenth Street NW. Preston Pierson was the new chief
of the Soviet desk at the State Department. From the back of the
room, she saw him accept congratulations and shake hands. He had
checked another box on his career list. No one seemed to notice
that she wasn't at his side, but she could feel his eyes on her.

Back at home and tucked into her Turkish robe, Rhonda lingered in the kitchen, warming her icy fingers near the sputtering
teakettle. An evening spent with all those Russians had reminded
her of Elena Zhukova, her NKVD minder.

On an overcast and bitterly cold day a month before, Rhonda
had walked into the lobby of the Metropol Hotel, where Elena
embraced her. Arm in arm, they followed the maître d' to a table
near the fountain.

"Are you afraid to be seen with me in such a public place?"
Rhonda accepted the linen napkin the waiter offered.

"No. I'm not bound by the usual constraints of the NKVD
Guards Directorate." Her eyes twinkled as she accepted a menu

from the waiter. "But then, you knew that before you approached me that first time, didn't you?"

Rhonda grinned. "I knew that your mother, Maria Kostantinovna Zhukova, was the elder sister to Georgy Zhukov, a general of your army. Your family is among the most powerful in the country. I was pleased to be under the care of a member of such a patrician family."

"You're right, my family is rather important, but I still had to earn my way. When I was young, Uncle Georgy suggested to my mother that I should join the Border Troops." She shuddered. "Those were some terrible months. The training was rigorous. I cried myself to sleep many nights.

"My first assignment was in Petropavlovsk in the Far East. Living on the peninsula of Kamchatsky is like living on the moon. Complete isolation from the rest of the country. I'm told winters in Petropavlovsk are warmer than in Siberia, but I'm not sure I believe it!" She shivered. "After that I took bodyguard training and later volunteered to be a diplomatic minder."

"Are you still close with your uncle?"

"Oh, yes. From the time he took me to Marshal Stalin's dacha in Kuntsevo, he's looked out for me. I've always been fearless with my career because I know Uncle Georgy is on my side. No one would dare suggest a luncheon such as ours is inappropriate." She tossed her head. "Besides, our countries are allies."

"And so are we, Elena. I've depended on your discretion during my stay here in Moscow. As you know, I wasn't always doing my job when you followed me."

"You were very skilled at evading me during those private times. My mistakes in losing you then will help me in the future."

"See, I was helping you further your career." Rhonda grinned. "You're a strong woman in a tough world of men. You could go as far as you want." She retrieved a piece of paper from her purse. "I'll be in Washington for a while. You can write to me at the Foreign Service Lounge at this address."

Elena penned her address on a paper doily. "This is at the old Lubyanka Prison."

"I appreciate all the times you helped me. Remember when I fell on that icy sidewalk? You rushed over and got me into your car. Or that time when those two young toughs tried to rob me?" She laughed at the memory. "When you strode up, gun drawn and pointed at them, they ran in the opposite direction."

Elena muffled her laughter with her napkin. "And I thought it was my grim expression that scared them away."

Rhonda paused while a waiter poured red wine into their crystal goblets. "If I'm ever again in Russia, could you manage to be my minder? It'd be great to catch up with you."

"Sure, just ask for me through your official channels."

The women retrieved their coats and walked into the frigid air. "Would you like a ride to your embassy? Once more for old time's sake?"

Rhonda took Elena's arm in hers. "That would be lovely, my dear."

Seated in the back of the car, Elena felt on the floor until she found the Kodak Retina camera she used in surveillance. "We'll ask the driver to take a photograph of us. I'll send a copy to you."

Standing on the sidewalk before the embassy, Rhonda said, "If you're ever in Washington, D.C., you must look me up."

Rhonda blinked away the memories and placed her teacup in its saucer. She touched Elena's face before returning the photograph to a drawer in her correspondence desk. She ran her finger over the last letter from Russ. It had been so long since she'd heard from him.

Preston was moving forward with his career, and it was time she did the same. She thought of her meeting tomorrow and smiled as she climbed into bed, alone.

The next morning, Rhonda sat across from COI director Colonel Bill Donovan. His office was tucked away from the bustle of pedestrian traffic on Twenty-Third Street NW.

"Glad to have you back in town, Rhonda. I've found the perfect cover to allow you to continue your work with us. You'll be on the Swiss desk at the State Department, at least on paper. You'll really work in this building. Fair enough?"

"Sounds perfect. I know I'm not your typical hire, but I really needed to strike out on my own. I can't use Preston here in D.C. as I did in our overseas postings. I always thought I'd return to practicing law someday, but this is the best move for me now."

"I agree." He laughed. "It's time you have a real position with COI. And you know I don't believe in typical when it comes to hiring the best for my new service." He stood and shook Rhonda's hand. "Welcome to COI."

Chapter 54

THE CAPITAL AWAKENED to the glories of spring. Tiny leaves misted the trees. Cherry blossoms dotted the Tidal Basin. Mockingbirds dive-bombed pedestrians on Sixteenth Street NW.

Russ sipped a Coke in his tiny apartment in Arlington's Potomac Village. He grabbed his keys and downed the rest of the cola. Time to clear his head of Arabic clutter.

On the far side of the bridge across U.S. Route 50, he hopped a low fence. The sun cast shadows on the green grass, and insects floated on the warm breeze. Russ meandered among the graves of the Civil War dead on the hallowed grounds of Arlington National Cemetery.

He knelt before the marker of a Union Army corporal who had died at the worst of all battles, Antietam. Russ imagined the shouted commands, the crack of rifles, the whinnies of terrified horses, the screams of the wounded, and the final gasps of the dying. *Will I ever be tested as they were? Will I be as brave?*

He rose and drifted up a small rise. In a grove of trees, a woman perched on a bench. Radiant beneath a straw hat in a simple dress of white lace, her maple syrup eyes sparkled.

Savoring this moment of enchantment, Russ slowly approached. "Waiting for me?"

"Always and forever." Rhonda brushed his cheek with a kiss.

"Why are you here in D.C.?"

"Preston had to come back to learn how he's expected to act with the Russians during the coming war. It would have been so simple if he hadn't extended, but he thought it might enhance his career. Of course, that means I'll be in Moscow another year also, so I thought I'd console myself by coming with him to the States. And I can talk with Bill Donovan about how my role has changed now that war is inevitable. But the truth is, I wanted to see you. I wanted it to be a surprise, so I didn't tell you before. Were you surprised?"

"Definitely. I love surprises."

"I told you I'll find you wherever you go. Like a ghost, I'll always be nearby."

Hand in hand, they strolled through the cemetery. She paused and looked into his eyes. "Romantic places make me hungry."

He laughed. "Where shall we eat?"

"We could have dinner at my hotel."

At the Willard with Russ in tow, she breezed through the lobby and up the elevator to her corner suite. "Let's order room service so no one interrupts us. What do you want?"

He stood with his arms wrapped around her from behind. "I'm holding what I want."

She wiggled her bottom. "Okay, I'll order for both of us.

"And there's no hurry." She replaced the receiver and led him into the bedroom.

"Should I expect Preston to suddenly appear?" Russ glanced around for a bolt hole.

"No, silly. He's in New York City for at least three days. He's meeting with Brits who are setting up an organization to protect their interests in the western hemisphere. We have the suite to ourselves." She wrapped up in a robe. In the bathroom, she drew a bath.

From the swooning couch, Russ watched her languidly drop the robe and step into the tub. She slid beneath the steamy water and beckoned. He accepted the washcloth and drew lazy circles on her back while she rearranged the lustrous bubbles. "Want some company in there?"

"No, thank you." Rhonda rose and replaced the robe. "Now it's your turn."

Russ leaned forward while she made soap patterns on his back.

At a knock on the door, Rhonda pattered across the tile. She reappeared pushing a room-service cart to a table by the bedroom window.

Russ dried off and draped himself in a second robe.

She lifted a champaign flute. "Here's to a love that spans lands and time."

While they ate, they watched evening descend on the capital. She lit lamps on either side of the four-poster bed. "I'm willing to delay dessert if you are."

She pulled an envelope from beneath her pillow. "Do you remember this day?"

He removed a picture of a man in a garden dappled with sunlight. "Novodevichy Convent! I never forget those days. I was so happy. My snapshot of you sits next to my bed."

He dropped down and put his head on the pillow. Reaching behind him, he pulled out a bedraggled teddy bear. "Look what I found."

"Give him to me." She snuggled the bear. "I've had him since childhood. He'll help me tell you about that time in my life." She peered over the bear's head. "Are you interested?"

"Of course I am. You've only ever shared the most basic facts. I'm eager to hear more."

"Well, I was raised in a small house in Norfolk's Colonial Place neighborhood. The city was lovely, with parks, a beach, and an amusement park. Occasionally, Momma took us to Smith and Welton's, the big department store. We ate piquant cheese sandwiches in their tearoom."

"So, you loved to eat even then." He ducked when she swatted at him with the teddy.

"My older sister, Bernice, was golden haired and slim, Momma's favorite. I was a daddy's girl. Bernice struggled after Momma's death, so Daddy focused his attention on her."

"What about you? How did you handle it?"

"I felt abandoned." Rhonda smoothed the teddy's fur. "Bernice wound up pregnant at the end of high school. Murray was a loser, but his parents and Daddy forced them to marry for the sake of the baby. They moved in with his parents. Soon after Charlene was born, Murray's father died. They lost the house."

"Did Bernice and Murray move in with you then?"

"Not a chance, Bernice hated Daddy for forcing her to marry Murray. They moved into a tiny apartment over a filling station where Murray found a job. I can't recall what happened to his mother."

"Did you lose contact with your sister over all this?"

"No, she visited when Daddy wasn't home. Before long, I realized she came whenever things were particularly bad at the apartment. Sometimes her face was bruised, or she carried Charlene only on one side because she was sore where Murray had hit her."

Russ grimaced. "Did you tell your dad?"

"She begged me not to." Rhonda bounced her teddy. "One night, Daddy went bowling. Bernice arrived with a swollen eye, a bleeding lip, and a torn dress. Charlene was screaming."

Rhonda met Russ's gaze. "Remember back at the reservoir outside Moscow when I told you I had a secret, one that I'd tell you someday?" When he nodded, she drew a deep breath and squeezed her teddy. "Well, that night, I climbed the stairs to Daddy's closet where he hid an old revolver. I took it to the kitchen and placed it on the kitchen counter next to the stove. I put water on to boil. I told Bernice to watch the kettle while I went outside for some fresh air. When I returned, they were gone. So was the gun." She used the teddy's paw to wipe her eye.

Russ pulled her close. "I don't need to hear any more."

"No, I have to finish this." She exhaled. "The police showed up that night. Bernice had shot Murray six times. She claimed she remembered nothing after the first shot."

"Oh no, what happened to her? What about the baby?"

"Bernice got life in prison. A couple who knew Daddy adopted Charlene."

"Jeez, Rhonda. What about you? What did you do?"

"I'd just graduated from high school." Rhonda turned to Russ. "I wanted a different life. I used my half of Momma's life insurance for college. Then I worked nights, weekends, and summers to go to law school in D.C. After that, I ran as far from home as I could. That's how I wound up at Nestlé in Bern. That was in 1931."

"Those must have been tough years. But you got away. Made something of yourself."

"I did." She nodded. "With a good salary, I traveled all over Europe for the company and for pleasure. I saw fairy-tale castles, quaint canals, and majestic cathedrals. All the romantic places I'd only read about before. I allowed counts, playboys, and handsome attorneys to wine and dine me in fancy hotels." She glanced at Russ. "Those were my heedless days."

"Sounds glorious. What happened?"

"I came to my senses." She pulled her teddy close. "I looked in the mirror and didn't like what I saw. I was getting fat and I suffered with hangover headaches. I was no longer a heroine in my own romantic novel." She punched the teddy. "I was the wanton wench."

Russ removed the teddy from her abuse. "Then?"

"Then Colonel Donovan showed up. It was 1933. I already told you about that."

He returned the teddy to her embrace. "Do you stay in contact with Bernice?"

She sighed. "I do, but not as much as I should. I feel so guilty about everything. Bernice never told anyone about how she got the gun. The authorities assumed she had planned it all out, especially since she emptied the revolver into Murray. She certainly couldn't claim self-defense after that." She punched the teddy again. "If I'd thought it through, I would have loaded only two bullets. Or maybe I shouldn't have given her the gun at all." Rhonda took a deep breath. "If Daddy had known about Murray, he would've been the one in prison."

She turned to Russ and chewed her lower lip. "Now you know my secret. I helped my sister kill her husband." She held her breath while she met his eyes.

He pulled her into his arms and smoothed her hair. "It doesn't matter, Rhonda. You can't blame yourself for what Bernice did. You provided the gun, but she's the one who decided to use it. You were just a kid in a tough situation. You loved your sister. And she and Charlene were in danger if they continued to stay with Murray. You can't live with that guilt."

"I know, and I've reconciled with my part in the murder. But Bernice's actions, even before that, have stayed with me ever since. If she hadn't gotten pregnant, she wouldn't have been forced to marry Murray. Because of the baby, she remained in the marriage." She twisted the teddy's legs and pulled at its arms. "I don't want a baby to force me to stay with a man."

"I'm sorry, but I'm a bit lost here. What baby?"

She tossed the teddy to the end of the bed. "Look Russ, we both know my marriage is a sham. Preston isn't interested in women. I provide cover for him. No one wonders about him when he has a bauble at his side. But he gives me no comfort, no attention, no love."

"Why would he care if you took a lover, then?"

"Oh, but he would. That's something I had to learn the hard way. Even when he appears to be unaware of my movements around a room, he's watching."

"Are you sure? How do you know?"

"In order to gather information for Colonel Donovan, I have to listen to conversations without being conspicuous. I hover around groups of men. It happened first in Lisbon. Preston accused me of trying to catch another man's eye. I thought he was jealous, but that didn't make sense since he wasn't interested in sex with me. Then I thought he was just trying to save himself embarrassment in case someone else commented that I always hung around the men. But finally, I realized that Preston is extremely possessive. Even if I'm only a convenience for him, he doesn't want to share me." Rhonda exhaled slowly. "What I and others like me do for Donovan is a secret, even from our spouses. So, Preston never knew about my work. He knew I was up to something, but he couldn't figure it out and that made him crazy. He grew more watchful and more possessive. I tell you, Russ, it was a real trial trying to work a room while avoiding Preston's scrutiny."

"And yet, you were so unafraid when you started your project with me."

"That's right. What I had with you was different from my circulating in a room with Preston watching me. I told you I knew how to manage him, and I did. He never knew about us. Still doesn't. Never will. Unless I make the mistake Bernice made.

"Even if I wanted to leave him, he'd never give me a divorce. He'd pass the baby off as his, but he'd never love it as his own. I couldn't live like that. I couldn't do that to a child."

They sat in silence for a long time. Finally, Russ hopped off the bed and picked up the teddy bear. Placing it in her arms, he left the bedroom. "I know what will make you feel better."

In moments, Russ returned with the room service cart. "This is a good time for dessert."

Clapping her hands, Rhonda dropped the teddy and threw her arms around his neck.

Later, she lay against the pillows with closed eyes. "There's nothing quite like a six-layer chocolate cake with chocolate frosting."

Russ bent over Rhonda and wiped chocolate from her lips, and then he bent to kiss those lips. "I can think of something better than cake." He rolled over and pulled her to his side. "Don't worry, Rhonda. We'll do only what you want."

She kissed him and took his hand in hers. "Touch me here."

Chapter 55

February 1942. German casualties in the USSR in-
clude over one hundred thousand cases of frostbite.

MILBOURNE HELD ON to his hat. Where was Hassan? Freezing cold and there was no one to meet him. What the hell?

He slammed into the residence and threw his luggage to the floor.

Bitsy turned in her wingback chair. "Well, hello to you, too."

"Don't start. The limousine broke down on the way to the aerodrome so Hassan was late. Then it stopped again on the way home. Damn Kuwaitis can't even service a car." He scowled at her state of dress. "And you couldn't bother to throw on some clothes and meet me at the plane?"

"Do you blame me?" She turned back to her newspaper. "When you're in a better mood, you can tell me how your trip went."

"What'd you do with yourself while I was gone? Entertain much?"

"No, I was a saint, as always." She turned to face him once again. "How about you?"

"Me? Never left my suite."

"Did that floozy accept the job as DCM?"

"I don't know what you're talking about."

"Oh, c'mon. It was all over the Department. Have you forgotten my contacts?"

"How can I? You're always rubbing them in." He kicked his luggage. "Where's Mohammed and the rest of the servants?"

"I gave them some time off. I wanted to be alone."

"I'll bet."

As he headed for the stairs, he thought about Marvella. Had he talked to her about being DCM? The Dragons had never gotten back to him. He needed a drink.

Bitsy called out to him, "You promised to arrange my flight out of here. Any luck?" When he didn't answer, she sighed.

Dinner was a chilly affair. Bitsy broke the ice. "Your COI guy Trent sat at my table at the Marine House last week."

His mouth fell open. "You went to the Marine House?"

"Yes, part of my job as morale officer. Don't forget, the marines will save your pitiful backside faster than any of your striped-pants colleagues. I want to keep them happy."

"Yeah, I can I imagine that," he mumbled into his napkin. "So, what about Mr. Hedges?"

"We talked about espionage."

He stifled a yawn. "He loves that stuff. Get to the point, Bitsy."

"Trent said something odd that got me to thinking."

Milbourne stayed his hand on the wine glass. "Odd?"

"Religious fanatics are spying on us."

"That's ridiculous." Milbourne sneered. "Those COI guys are idiots."

"It's not ridiculous. Maybe we're vulnerable right here in this house. Most of the staff aren't bright enough to be spies, but what about Mohammed?" She leaned forward with her elbows on the table. "Could he be a zealot? I've never trusted him. He can hear all your conversations and phone calls. His smile gives me the creeps."

"You don't like his smile?" Milbourne smirked at her expression.

"I'll bet George hasn't investigated him, or anyone else. What are their religious beliefs? Where do they come from? What does the palace say about them?"

"Slow down. What do you imagine happening here?"

"Let's start by firing Mohammed. We'd be better off without him."

"You sound like those COI knuckleheads. I'm not firing Mohammed." He tossed his napkin on the table. "Stop listening to cocktail chatter from sniveling amateurs. They should know better than to scare wives."

"You're so wrong!" Bitsy gripped the table edge. "They should be warned. Wives chatter without thinking about what they're saying or what they know."

"Wives never know anything." He pushed his chair back.

"I beg your pardon! We know more about a post than you and your pompous, condescending bureaucrats." Her green eyes blazed with anger. "We notice everything. We can figure out what's going on without a roadmap." Her chair tipped over when she fled the room.

⁓⟊⟊⟊⁓

Late the next morning, Milbourne thundered at Spencer and Hedges. "Never, ever discuss your work with my wife! Or with any wife, for that matter."

"Easy, Trent." Spencer touched Hedge's arm. "Listen, Mr. Ambassador, counterespionage is part of our job. Spies within the Legation are as dangerous as Axis probes in the An Nafud Desert or along the Gulf."

Milbourne looked deliberately at his watch. "Let's wrap this up, Spencer."

"Mayerik, Guderian, two archeologists, a man asking the silver seller in the suq about someone named Paul." Spencer counted off on his fingers. "All identified threats. But what about those we don't know about? Say, your residence manager?"

Milbourne swallowed hard on his words. *Mohammed again. Am I missing something?* He shook his head. He'd made his position clear. Now he just had to hope Mohammed didn't burn down the residence. "Thank you for coming. I'm busy after my long trip to consult with the president." As the COI guys rose to leave, he said, "Remember, no talking to wives. I will not be undermined at my own post."

Covering her typewriter, Catherine called, "Russ, want anything from the snack bar?"

"Sure, whatever looks good and a Coke."

Later, Catherine collected their tableware. She peered over his shoulder. "What's that?"

"It's a personal project."

She sat on the edge of his desk and slowly crossed her legs. "Tell all, cutie."

"It's a report on everything that's going on here. Mismanagement, neglect of staff housing, building a luxury dhow, alienating the palace. I'm giving it to the post inspectors."

"Are you crazy? Milbourne will be furious."

"Yeah, yeah, the old man isn't going to promote me anyway. May as well go out with a clear conscience."

"Be very, very careful." She shook a finger at him. "Inspectors are usually longtime buddies with career ambassadors. Their report will whitewash everything. You'll sacrifice your career and Milbourne will continue unscathed."

"I know." He pulled at his hair. "But I have to try."

She reviewed the pages he had already typed. "What can I do to help?"

"Thanks, Catherine." He gripped her arm. "Check my facts. Summarize Mariah's notes from behind her mirror. The inspectors can't ignore actual evidence."

"But much of Mariah's testimony can't be corroborated. Even though it's all disgusting, only she and Milbourne were there. He'll just deny everything."

"We must try. Maybe it'll catch someone's notice. Harriman

told me our stuff is widely read, sometimes making its way to the Oval Office."

When Catherine dropped the pages, Russ laughed. "Don't worry, my name will be the only one on the document."

<hr>

On the weekend, Russ and Piper wandered the fence in front of the covered grandstand at the camel racing track outside Kuwait City. "Who sits in the overstuffed chairs?" Piper asked.

"The amir and members of the royal family. Everyone else sits on the wooden risers."

As the camels milled around, Khalid approached. "Ah, Russ and Piper, please join me." He led them to chairs behind his uncles. "Camel racing is extremely competitive. The owners chase the camels on horseback from behind that dirt berm, urging them on with much yelling."

At the crack of a distant rifle, he passed his field glasses to Piper.

Two camels shared the lead as they raced toward the grandstand. When the outside camel picked up a half-length and won by a nose, Khalid collapsed in his chair.

Piper leaned over him. "Are you okay?"

"That's the sheikh's camel. He'll not let us forget the win for a long time. Come." Khalid escorted Piper and Russ to the front of the grandstand. "Uncle, congratulations on your tremendous victory."

When the amir joined their group, Khalid introduced Piper.

"I'm honored, Excellency. I enjoyed the victory of the sheikh's beautiful camel."

The amir ignored his beaming brother. "Miss Burton, it was I who bought this camel for my brother. If it were not for me, he wouldn't have the winner's trophy today!"

The sheikh replied, "It's true. I don't earn enough at the Foreign Ministry to afford such luxuries as a racing camel."

While everyone laughed at the brothers' usual banter, the amir placed a strong hand on Russ's shoulder. "The expedition to the neutral zone is especially important for both of our countries. I hope you plan to join Khalid."

"Yes, Excellency, I've received permission from Ambassador Milbourne."

"Walk with me a bit, Mr. Russell." The amir led him away from the others. "As you know, Khalid is very favored in my heart. He's smart and eager. Sometimes too eager. There is a time to talk and a time to listen. I know you are of the same generation as him, but I believe you're cautious and thoughtful."

"Thank you, sir. I know Khalid has a lot on his mind. He understands his duty to find the oil that will improve the lives of all Kuwaitis. How may I be of assistance?"

"I'm not sure." The amir sighed and turned to face Russ. "I'm uneasy about this expedition. I'll feel better with you there by his side. Please be careful."

"Excellency, Khalid and I listen to each other. We'll watch over each other. Trust us to be careful."

"I will." The amir led Russ back to the risers. "May the blessings of Allah be upon you, Miss Burton. Mr. Russell, please enjoy the remaining races." The amir led his bodyguards away.

"He stays for only one race. He has many problems of state to consider each day." Khalid pointed to the risers. "Please enjoy the races, but I too must leave. The expedition into the great wilderness of the An Nafud demands my attention. I worry about many things."

"Will it be dangerous?" Piper asked.

"Anytime you enter the desert, Miss Burton, you must expect some risk along with much beauty. But don't worry, we'll be prepared for everything. Inshallah."

Chapter 56

March 1942. Thousands of Jews are shot by the Germans in Minsk, USSR.

MILBOURNE PUSHED A Falcon Wing across the desk toward Russ. "The president is coming later this month. Malcolm will be the control officer." He rubbed his head. "George will manage lodging and transport. That's all he can handle."

"Looks like two Secret Service agents are en route for the advance." Russ replaced the cable on the desk. "I'd like to volunteer as an Arabic speaker for them."

"It's yours."

Two days later, Russ walked from the shade of the aerodrome radio operator's hut to greet the men. "Good afternoon. I'm the ambassador's assistant, Mark Russell."

"Jim Rowley, and this is Nick Pastorini. Good to meet you." Rowley, a former special agent with the FBI, was tall with thick, wavy hair. Pastorini was younger, slender, and had the black hair and dark brows of someone from Little Italy in the Bronx.

In the lobby of the Safir Hotel, Rowley questioned Russ. "We know a little about your ambassador, but we'd appreciate a frank assessment of how well he'll work with us."

"Milbourne is the epitome of career Foreign Service. He knows how to get things done, especially if it makes him look good. He's intolerant of any deviation from his instructions or of something done without his knowledge. He hopes this visit will enhance his image in the Department. He aspires to be assistant secretary for the Middle East Bureau."

"Okay. Good to know. What about weaknesses."

"He likes his Scotch and has an eye for the ladies. His wife, Bitsy, is still here but wants out as soon as possible."

Pastorini whistled. "Well, we're glad to have you working with us."

"Thanks. I'm looking forward to this experience and will help in any way I can."

At half past four, Russ ushered the two agents into Milbourne's office.

"Mr. Rowley, Mr. Pastorini, I recognize you from my visits with the president."

"Yes, Mr. Ambassador, we remember you as well. Perhaps we may begin?"

"Certainly. Russ, would you please retrieve the single malt and four tumblers?" Milbourne turned to the two agents. "May as well be comfortable."

"We're here to ensure safe surroundings for the president," Rowley said. "We have a rather lengthy list of requirements and realize this is a small post."

"We'll do what we can to accommodate Franklin. Russ will be your liaison."

While Rowley talked and Russ took notes, Pastorini observed.

Later, Russ escorted the agents to Fuad's for dinner. Pastorini leaned in and softly said, "The ambassador drinks with authority. He'd have me under the table in no time."

"I warned you. By day's end, he slurs his words, and he remembers little in the morning."

"Sounds like the administrative guy, George Lander, might be a problem."

Russ shrugged. "When you meet him, you can decide for yourself."

Day two of the advance began with Major Khoury at the Interior Ministry. Everyone knew his role in the security plan. Professionals understood one another.

At the clinic, Dr. Husayn assured the agents that he'd enjoy working with the White House physician, Admiral Ross McIntire.

The amir's personal secretary led them around the meeting areas and grounds at Dasman Palace. The amir was looking forward to meeting the president.

After lunch, the Legation's American staff gathered in the second-floor conference room. Rowley elaborated on the specific aspects of the visit. He began with George Lander. "We'll need the following vehicles and drivers."

Lander interrupted Rowley midway through the list. "We're not running a used car lot here. You're already at ten vehicles. We have two cars, one truck. The Brits have four."

Russ cleared his throat. "I'll ask my contact at the Kuwait Oil Company. He'll be able to manage additional vehicles from KOC and the palace."

Hank Greene, the senior code clerk, and Gunnery Sergeant Grady, the detachment commander, already knew their roles from prior experience.

"We use lapel pins for easy identification of anyone interacting with the president. The traveling staff will wear the same pins. Is that your responsibility, Mr. Lander?"

The administrative officer turned a page in his notebook. "I'll need a month to get this organized. When did you say he's arriving?"

"He leaves later this week for Morocco." Pastorini smiled thinly. "The secretary of state often travels with the president. Secretary Hull's been known to fire an ambassador on the spot if he finds the post is unsupportive." His dark eyes swept the staff. "I'm sure no one in this room will let the president down."

No one batted an eye when Lander stood and walked out.

Early on day three of the advance, the trio sat with Khalid in his office at KOC.

"Russ has informed me of your requirements. The palace will provide police support, vehicles, anything you wish." Khalid scanned his notes. "We can arrange everything." He raised his eyes. "President Roosevelt's visit to our country is a great honor."

"Thank you." Pastorini smiled at Khalid. "It's a pleasure to work with someone who's so cooperative. We appreciate your assistance."

Khalid inclined his head and smiled. "You're fortunate to have Russ as your guide. He speaks excellent Arabic and has the complete trust of the amir."

"Please, Khalid." Russ turned to the two agents. "He gives me far too much credit."

Over lunch at Fuad's, Pastorini asked, "What's your relationship with Khalid?"

Russ washed down a bite of kebab with coffee. "We became friends after he flipped his vehicle on the motorway. That was in the summer of '40 when I'd just arrived. I saw the whole thing. The fuel tank ignited. I got Khalid out before the explosion."

"Sounds serious. Were either of you injured?"

"He had a concussion, a deep cut to his forehead, and a broken arm. My back was peppered with metal shards. The doctor extracted one close to my carotid artery. I was lucky."

Rowley tore off a piece of warm bread. "I can see where that experience could lead to a friendship. So, you met the amir through Khalid?"

"Yes, he presented me with a silver dagger in appreciation of saving Khalid's life. Since then, I went with the ambassador when he presented his credentials. The brothers got into it with Milbourne over capping the oil wells. I suggested that they allow Khalid and me to work it out. The brothers were happy with our solution. I've been to the big meetings at the palace regarding the supply corridor to Russia. It's been busy here if you can believe that."

Pastorini sipped an orange soda. "How does Milbourne like your palace connection?"

"He hates it. The amir enjoys putting me on the spot if there's a sticking point. If I come up with an answer, the ambassador claims it as his own in our cables. It's a tough situation for everyone." Russ pushed aside his plate. "To be honest, I thought my palace connection would advance my career. With this ambassador, I've given up on that hope."

"Well, I'm off to look over the residence." Pastorini pushed back his chair.

"Wait a sec." Russ leaned in. "Watch out for Mohammed, the residence manager. COI has a particular interest in him. And never mention Trick and Trent in front of the ambassador. He hates other agency personnel, particularly COI."

Rowley dropped dinars on the table with a frown on his face. "Well, that was an informative lunch. You'd better head out, Nick. Can't keep the madam of the household waiting. I hope Mrs. Milbourne is friendlier than her husband."

Russ bit his lip and led them to his car.

Chapter 57

March 1942. U.S. citizens of Japanese ancestry are removed from the Pacific coast to inland assembly centers.

BITSY WATCHED FROM the patio table as a handsome man climbed the driveway.

"Thank you for seeing me, Mrs. Milbourne. I'm Nick Pastorini with the Secret Service."

"You're welcome, and please call me Bitsy." She waved him to a chair. "You look familiar. About four years ago, I attended a Democratic fundraiser at the Waldorf Astoria, where Franklin was the speaker. I remember a good-looking sharp dresser. Could that be you?"

"It was and thank you." The young agent met Bitsy's eyes. "You wore a floor-length blue gown with a matching hair ribbon. Quite a showstopper if I may be so bold."

"You may, and thanks for remembering." She glanced at his empty ring finger.

Pastorini opened his notebook. "I understand you'll be speaking for the ambassador on arrangements for the president's lodging here."

"Yes, we agreed I have a better feel for this than Duncan."

"I see. You'll also need to house his staff and accommodate his infirmity. Two Navy stewards help him with that."

Bitsy stood and motioned for him to follow. "About that. There are no bedrooms on this level of the residence, so I recommend we convert the library for his use. He can meet with Harry Hopkins and anyone else right off the library in the dining room." Bitsy moved through the house with Pastorini in tow. "We'll use the parlor for informal buffets and other food, such as snacks for the agents. What do you think?"

Nick looked around and out the windows. "Sounds like a workable solution. Let's walk outside so I can decide where to post our agents."

She smiled when Pastorini took her elbow as they walked the grounds.

He made a line drawing of the property. Frowning, he pointed. "What's up there?"

"Nothing much, except a pleasant view of the water. Should we go up?"

"Sure, but I can do it alone if you'd rather."

"No, I'd enjoy the exercise, and the company." She patted his arm. "While you look around upstairs at the bedrooms where Harry and Dr. McIntire will sleep, I'll change into something more suitable for climbing."

Bitsy, wearing only panties, wandered between her bathroom and closet. If Pastorini looked, he'd be able to see her through the door she'd left ajar. Couldn't hurt to advertise.

Pastorini folded his notebook when Bitsy emerged in cotton pants and a blouse. She'd tied her hair back in a ribbon, and Keds dangled from her hand. "That looks a lot more comfortable," he said. He parked his suit coat on a kitchen chair, loosened his tie, and rolled up his sleeves. "I hope you don't mind."

"Not at all. We'll take some canteens and a pair of field glasses."

At the top of the promontory, Bitsy fanned her blouse and Pastorini wiped his neck. "Whew, that was a lot harder than it looked from below. I admire your stamina."

"You mean for an old gal?" Bitsy grinned at his expression and patted his arm. "It's okay. I have a great deal of stamina." She raised an eyebrow and offered a canteen.

Pastorini studied the waves of sandy desert rolling away from the promontory. "I'm definitely going to need agents up here to watch that approach." He turned to the Gulf. "And we'll have to think about all that water." He raised the field glasses and turned in a circle. "I agree it's a tremendous view." He passed the field glasses to her.

Bitsy watched Mohammed walk along the side of the house. "I plan to give that guy time off while Franklin's here. You never know when he's sneaking around. Our butler, Yasser, is perfectly competent to handle his duties."

"You must be talking about Mohammed, the residence manager."

"You've heard about him?"

"Russ warned us. Glad you'll handle him."

The sun began its slow descent into the west, transfixing the two on the peak.

"Guess we better head down. Your husband will be coming home."

"No, he's going straight from the office to a dinner at the British political agent's house. He'll come home with enough Scotch in him that he'll fall into bed and sleep until morning."

She allowed Pastorini to guide her down the steep slope until they were back on the patio.

"You know, Nick, I'm returning to my farm in Middleburg soon. Maybe you'd like to have dinner with me sometime."

"I surely would." He took a business card from his coat and jotted his home number.

⚜

Pastorini walked into the Marine Bar with his suit coat over one shoulder and his tie hanging loosely around his neck. He was sunburnt and windblown.

Rowley gave him the once-over. "And where have you been, laddie?"

"Working." Pastorini dropped into the nearest chair. "Found some things we didn't plan for. The peak behind the residence will need one Kuwaiti security and one agent. It was a hike up to the top. And we'll need a destroyer off the beach."

Spencer passed Pastorini a slim file. "We were discussing the Mohammed problem. I've already shown that to Jim."

"Bitsy plans to give him time off while the president visits."

Rowley sipped his drink and eyed Pastorini. "Bitsy, huh?"

Pastorini shrugged.

Spencer whistled. "I bet the ambassador will nix that plan."

"What objection can he possibly have to Mohammed having a few days off?" Rowley pulled out his notebook. "Okay, someone mentioned the ambassador's limo boiled over last month. We can't trust it. Russ, can you call your friend Khalid again?"

"First thing in the morning. It won't be a problem."

Pastorini stood. "The next round's on me. Any takers?"

All raised their glasses.

⚜

On the morning of day four, Lodge walked into the conference room waving two cables.

"Domestic political problems in Britain are keeping Churchill at home, so the Casablanca stop is postponed. The president will still come to Kuwait and Iran, only two days early."

Rowley glanced over the second cable. "FDR wants a cruise along the Gulf to Iran. If that can't be arranged, he wants to drive into the An Nafud Desert."

In the hallway, Pastorini shook his head. "Am I going to have to ride a camel?"

Rowley glanced at his colleague. "We'd have to tear you away from the residence first. How much more time do you need out there?"

The young agent winked at Rowley. "Are we still having fun?"

That evening, Lander and Milbourne sat on the residence patio, watching the sunset.

"This advance is a pain in the ass." Milbourne fingered his Scotch glass. "Look at what they're doing to my home."

Lander glanced at the cables snaking through a window and down the drive to a telephone pole at the road. Maps, field radios, shotguns, and ammo cases were stacked in the sunroom. "Hank Greene and his commo guys are sure making a mess."

"Get some field latrines in for the agents and staff. I don't want them using the toilet in the servant's area. It doesn't have running water and will stink to high heaven."

"Where would I get field latrines this late in the day?" Lander topped off his drink.

"I made a mistake when I gave Bitsy free rein over these arrangements."

"Did you know they've appropriated your limousine?"

"If the president is in my limo, I'll be right there beside him." He burped. "And another thing, I'm not wearing a lapel pin. Everyone knows who I am."

Lander rubbed his tumbler across his aching temple.

After Greene's men left, Pastorini sat in the parlor, checking his notebook.

"Hi, Nick." Bitsy leaned against the parlor doorway. Her hair flowed around her shoulders, and one leg peeked out of her blue kimono. "Is everything ready?"

"We're in pretty good shape." He followed her to the patio. "Very good shape, I'd say."

"George finally left, and Duncan is passed out on his bed. I gave the staff the night off."

She walked to the table where a platter of sandwiches and a bottle of Chianti awaited them. "You looked hungry." In the soft light, her green eyes shimmered.

Pastorini hoisted his goblet. "Here's to beautiful friends in faraway places."

She picked up a sandwich. "I bet someone is eager to have you return to the States."

He shook his head. "There's no time to find that someone special. We're so busy, it's hard to even wedge in a nice dinner with a lady friend."

Bitsy smiled as she refilled their goblets. "No rest for the weary." She extended her long legs. "Let me tell you about a project I'm working on with a few friends. We want to help young men develop into the type of lover who can attract and hold the interest of special women."

Pastorini turned his dark eyes on her. "Are you having any success?"

"Some. Most men don't realize that a woman deserves to be treated as an equal in a marriage. She needs to be valued beyond the physical." She looked at him beneath lowered lashes. "Although the physical is important, too. You might say that's one of my specialties."

He took her hand. "Am I a candidate for your class?"

"You are." She squeezed his fingers. "We'll start the lessons when I return to the States."

He placed a hand on her exposed thigh. "Why wait until then?"

Near dawn, Bitsy stood in the shadows by the main entrance of the residence. Nick bent to kiss her one more time before walking to the motorcar on the road. He touched the KOC driver, who awoke from a doze in the front seat.

From his balcony, Milbourne watched the man move out of the shadows. He saw Bitsy's silver hair shimmering in the last of the moonlight. He clung to the railing, shaking the alcohol haze from his mind. He hadn't recalled Russ's hair being that dark.

Chapter 58

March 1942. The Japanese take the island of Java.

DAY FIVE OF the advance dawned clear and warm. No one seemed to care when both Milbourne and Lander failed to appear at the Legation all day. Russ led the Secret Service agents through their final appointments.

That evening, everyone gathered around two tables on the residence patio. Milbourne topped off his glass from the bottle of Scotch at his elbow. Pastorini placed his chair so he could monitor Mohammed's activities.

Rowley cleared his throat. "Mr. Ambassador, I believe we've waited long enough for Mr. Lander to appear. Perhaps we could get started." He opened his notebook. "I understand the kitchen restroom is off limits to the agents."

"That's my servants' toilet, and it doesn't have running water. It tends to get smelly."

"What are my agents to use?" Rowley tapped his pen against his notebook.

"Mr. Lander is handling that. What next?"

"Did you know the secretary of state frequently reviews our advance reports?" Rowley stilled his pen. "Some ambassadors never attain the higher positions they seek."

Milbourne directed a scowl at the agent. "I don't entertain threats."

Pastorini pushed the box of lapel pins toward Rowley.

Milbourne crossed his arms. "I'll not wear a lapel pin in my own house."

"Their agents won't know you on sight. The pins make their job easier."

"When I want your opinion, Russ, I'll ask for it."

Recoiling from the malevolence of Milbourne's glare, Russ fell back in his chair.

"After last night, you'll be lucky if I don't ship you home. That'll end your career."

That brought Russ to the edge of his chair.

"Oh, don't look so bewildered. I saw you from my window in the early morning hours."

No one noticed Pastorini paling.

Milbourne swung on Rowley. "If there's nothing else, I think this meeting is over."

"You'd be wrong." Rowley leaned forward with hooded eyes. "Sir."

Pastorini took over. "I see you've reinstated Mohammed on the work schedule."

Milbourne interrupted. "I did." He directed another glower at Russ. "Whoever authorized his removal will be on the next plane out of Kuwait."

"That's right, Duncan, I will be on the next plane out." The scent of overheated sandalwood flooded the patio.

Later that night, Rowley called his boss, Mike Reilly, at W-16 in the West Wing.

The next morning, Lodge carried an IMMEDIATE Falcon Wing to the residence, since Milbourne was once again a no-show at the Legation.

Bitsy intercepted the cable and climbed the stairs to Milbourne's bedroom.

Mohammed hovered in the hallway. He didn't need to put his

ear to the door to hear Bitsy yelling at her husband. He scuttled away when she banged open the door.

Taking several deep breaths, Bitsy smoothed her hair and adjusted her sweater. She walked to her bedroom, where she reached for the telephone. "Please place an urgent overseas call to the White House. Tell Mr. Wembley I won't take much of the president's valuable time."

Ninety minutes later, Lodge returned to the residence with another IMMEDIATE Falcon Wing. Bitsy met him at the door. She scanned the cable and smiled.

Presidential Detail Chief Reilly called Rowley from D.C. At the end of that conversation, Rowley wiped his hand across his face and hung up. He shook his head and turned to the group gathered around Catherine's desk.

"Milbourne has done a complete reversal on everything. He's agreed to ride in his own vehicle, which we'll use as a backup, while the president will ride with his personal staff in Khalid's vehicle. The ambassador will wear the lapel pin, allow use of the servants' restroom, and give Mohammed a short vacation. Hell, what a mess!"

Duncan and Bitsy Milbourne stood with the sheikh at the end of the red carpet when the president's plane touched down in Kuwait. The Milbournes accompanied FDR, Henry Hopkins, and Mike Reilly to the residence, where the president freshened up before Milbourne took them to the palace.

FDR regaled the royals with tales of youthful summers sailing the waters off Campobello Island, New Brunswick. The amir and the sheikh traded versions of adventures in the great An Nafud Desert and on the Persian Gulf. The president and the foreign secretary bonded over guava juice and Arab delicacies while the more reserved amir enjoyed their banter.

Driving rain prevented FDR's excursion into the An Nafud

Desert, but he was determined to make the trip by dhow to Iran. However, once he arrived at the port, he agreed that the rolling swells would make everyone seasick. Instead, FDR sat beneath a streaming tarp and visited with Ghadir, the dhow meister.

"Mr. Hopkins, would the president like to see the very special dhow we're building for Ambassador Milbourne?" The old shipbuilder glowed with pride.

"I'm sure he would, but it's been a long day for everyone." Hopkins stood as FDR was wheeled toward the limousine. "Perhaps you would be kind enough to show me your craftsmanship." He touched Milbourne's arm as the ambassador started to follow FDR to the car. "Would you like to join us, Duncan?"

Back at the residence, Pastorini and Russ stood beneath the awning when the limo pulled up. Pastorini stepped forward to open FDR's door. Once FDR was settled into his chair, he stuck out a hand to Russ. "I don't believe we've met."

"Mark Russell, sir. I hope you've enjoyed your day."

"It's been most enlightening, yes, indeed." He continued to pump Russ's hand. "And now I can put a face to the name I've heard from several of my friends."

Before Russ could comment, the ambassador stepped out of his limo and motioned to FDR's aide. "Perhaps we should move indoors out of the damp weather."

Russ stepped back under the awning as Milbourne moved between him and the president. As he did so, he noticed FDR's lips draw down in a frown.

On the final day, Russ and Piper stood with Khalid in the early morning light at the aerodrome. A KOC vehicle wheeled to a stop on the tarmac. Pastorini hopped out and turned to offer a hand to Bitsy. She smiled at everyone and waved as Pastorini walked her to the plane.

When the amir's limousine arrived, Khalid turned to greet his uncles, so he missed the scene that transfixed Piper and Russ. Pastorini said something to Bitsy, and she laughed and kissed him full on the lips. He patted her bottom and helped her into the plane.

Piper snickered and nudged Russ out of his daze. "Wake up, I hear the motorcade."

Flashing lights signaled the arrival. A Navy steward wheeled the president over the sea of Persian carpets to shake hands with his Arab hosts. The amir wished them all a safe journey. At wheels up, Milbourne returned to his car and Lander handed him a glass of Scotch.

On the plane to Cairo, Bitsy dozed. When Harry Hopkins joined FDR for a nightcap, the president said, "Round up some names for me for the next NEA assistant secretary. And keep the Black Dragons out of this one."

"Yes, sir."

"While you're at it, find me some Arab speakers who can fill in at the Legation until I can name a new ambassador. And keep the search close. No Black Dragons."

"Glad to, sir. Maybe I'll touch base with that aide to Cordell. I understand she knows everyone in the field. Name of Jessup."

Chapter 59

March 1942. In Malaysia, Australian nurses are marched into the sea and then machine-gunned.

"THOSE WERE GOOD times in Buenos Aires, Bart."

Perry Showalter and George Lander listened as their bosses, J. Bartholomew Dunbar and Milbourne, reminisced on the residence patio. When Milbourne paused, Showalter offered, "I heard the NEA assistant secretary has moved up his retirement."

"Oh, really? That's good news. Thanks for the tip."

"So, to business." Dunbar leaned toward Milbourne. "We're not here to stir up old dirt. We'll do our interviews and get out. First, tell us about unhappy staff."

"Watch out for Mark Russell." Milbourne topped off his glass. "He forgets his place as my assistant, not my equal."

Dunbar held his glass for a refill. "I know that name. He's in play in Washington, in the Department, and even with FDR. Carenza wrote an exciting story about him."

"Yeah, but everyone's forgotten the stain on his reputation in Moscow. Look it up. Had an affair. Totally unprofessional."

Dunbar sputtered into his Scotch. "Well, Duncan, you know something about that."

When Milbourne slammed his Scotch on the table, Dunbar

held up his hands. "Relax, I get the picture. Why don't you send Russell away on the day of our interviews?"

Milbourne smiled. "Excellent solution. I'll take care of it myself."

The inspection went off without a hitch, and somehow the team managed to preserve Milbourne's dignity. As Dunbar relaxed at the Safir the evening before departure, he heard a knock at his door. "Who are you?"

"Mark Russell, the ambassador's assistant."

"Ah, the man who skipped his appointment. Come in."

"I didn't skip it. I was sent to Iran on urgent business. Turns out I wasn't needed after all. But Lander was to tell you where I was."

Dunbar shrugged. "How can I help you?"

"I'd like to have my interview now, if it isn't too much trouble." He waved a large manila envelope. "And I'd like you to review this when you have time. Perhaps on the plane home."

After a few routine questions, Dunbar stifled a yawn. "I'm tired. I think we have all we need from you." He pointed to the envelope Russ still clutched. "What's in there?"

Russ quickly summarized his report. Noting Dunbar's flagging interest, he wrapped it up. "It's getting late, and I haven't mentioned the ambassador's behavior. He threatens not only relations with the palace but also the security of the post and our mission to protect the supply corridor to Stalin."

Dunbar rubbed his stubble. "Those are very strong, and dangerous, accusations."

"Here's the proof." Russ placed the envelope on the bed.

The inspector's eyes narrowed. "Is this the only copy?"

"Yep." Russ looked Dunbar straight in the eye while remembering Catherine's warning about inspectors being in cahoots with ambassadors.

"I'll be honest with you, Russell. Some of your associates have

voiced similar complaints. We'll certainly take a look at your report."

"Thank you, sir." Russ exhaled. "That's all I ask."

At the aerodrome the next day, Dunbar waited until Showalter left
the limousine. "Listen, Duncan, Russell stopped by my room last
night. He gave me quite an earful and then handed over this envelope. I didn't read it because then I'd have to act on it." He tapped
the envelope on Milbourne's knee. "I'll leave it with you. It was
never in my possession, if you get my meaning."

Milbourne skimmed Russ's summary page. His face paled. Tea
sales, the dhow, the oil concession, and Mohammed. Alcoholic.
The palace. *This could ruin me.* He returned the pages and patted
the envelope. "Leave it to me, Bart. It will never see the light of day.
And thanks."

Chapter 60

March 1942. The Japanese take the island of Java.

Russ lounged on Piper's sofa, the sleeping kitten wedged under his chin and its paw in his ear. "Have you named this ball of fur yet?"

"Earmuff. Fitting, don't you think?" Piper poured wine.

"What's the matter, Piper? You've barely sat down."

"We'll get to that, but first tell me why you're all down-in-the-mouth."

"Last night, I gave the inspector a document that sealed my fate with the State Department. I listed the fraud, drinking, and spies at this Legation. And I didn't mince words."

"You better hope the old man doesn't find out."

"Too late now. At least I was honest about how this place is run."

"As long as we're being honest." She snatched Earmuff from him. "You might have more to worry about than your report. Tell me about Bitsy."

His stomach clenched. "How'd you hear about that?"

"Bitsy bragged about you to Catherine over dinner at the residence. Then Catherine told me at lunch today."

"She did?" Russ let his head fall against the sofa back. "Catherine probably knew anyway. She warned me."

"Apparently you didn't listen. Did the ambassador know?"

"I hope not." Russ sat up and clutched his head. "I knew I was making a mistake from the moment she led me upstairs. But I went anyway."

"Bitsy's your mother's age!" She furiously petted Earmuff. The kitten flattened his ears and jumped to the floor. "And what about me?"

Before Russ could answer, Piper started pacing the small room. "You're just like all the other men. Flattered by a little attention. Wasn't Catherine enough for you?"

"Oh, yeah, she told me about that long ago. But she said the two of you are buddies."

Piper poured a glass of wine, downed it, poured another. "Tell me."

"You weren't even here when this thing with Bitsy started. It doesn't have to affect anything between us. She's gone now."

"You told me you were shy. You told me you had a normal history with women. Except for the one in Moscow. I knew about your buddy relationship with Catherine. But Bitsy! What are you doing, making up for lost time?"

When Russ hung his head, she stopped before him. "What am I to believe, Mark?"

"You know the woman in Moscow is married and I'll never have her." He spread his hands, palms up. "Catherine and I are friends. Bitsy was a mistake. It's over. She's gone."

"But look at it from my perspective. You had Catherine, then moved on to Bitsy, and now you're acting interested in me. What will you do when another woman comes to post? It won't matter if she's young or old because you don't seem to care. You're a jerk."

"Come on, Piper. Give me a chance. You'll have to trust me."

"Trust you? You told me you still love the Moscow woman. What am I to make of that? Am I second-best? A substitute for something you can't have?"

"I guess, no, I don't mean that, but…" He closed his eyes and let out a deep breath.

"If you love her so much, why start something with me?"

"Because she taught me how to find someone to love. Someone that's not her. You might be that someone." He reached for her. "Please. Let's not fight."

"All right." She stepped over Earmuff and opened the door. "Get out!"

Chapter 61

*March 1942. FDR orders General MacArthur to leave
the Philippines.*

At the aerodrome, Carenza Nasmith stepped from the Army
Air Force plane. She wasn't surprised to see the ambassador standing by the landing strip. After all, FDR hadn't been the only one to
ask her to return to Kuwait for the ship visit.

"Welcome, Carenza. You're going to be busy. I hope you brought
lots of film."

The next day, beneath the flags of both countries, Captain Swenson of the light cruiser USS *Juneau* exchanged formal greetings
with the amir of Kuwait. After refreshments on the fantail, he led
the palace entourage on a tour of the ship. Carenza trailed along
with her camera.

Khalid and Russ brought up the rear. "The oil expedition leaves
in ten days. Do you prefer to ride a camel or a horse?"

"Definitely a horse!"

"Excellent. Come soon to the amir's stables to choose your
mount." Khalid placed his hand on Russ's shoulder. "Decide care-
fully. The desert is extremely dangerous. The right horse can save
your life."

When the royal party gathered after the luncheon, Carenza focused her lens on the amir and Captain Swenson. Her camera followed the amir as he broke away and turned to Russ.

"I hoped to see you today. Let's walk."

Carenza continued to click the shutter as the amir and the young diplomat stood against the backdrop of the *Juneau's* superstructure. They were speaking Arabic, so she put away her notebook. She'd get the story later.

"Khalid's ready for the expedition. Are you?"

"Yes, sir. He invited me to your stables to choose my horse for the journey."

"The An Nafud is a perilous place, with many ways to die. It's more difficult for Allah to protect you in the sands." The amir held Russ's eyes. "As director of the oil company, Khalid will lead the expedition. He's experienced in the ways of the desert. But you have the instincts of a Bedouin. Use them out there." The amir dropped his hand. "I trust you'll do your best."

"Khalid will always be in my care, Excellency."

With a swirl of his bisht, the amir walked away.

Still winding her film for the next shot, Carenza headed toward Russ. "Remember me? I'm covering the ship visit for the *Washington Post.*"

"Yes, I remember you." Russ grinned. "Welcome back to Kuwait. And thanks for the terrific story about Khalid's car crash. I'm still trying to live that one down."

She tossed the camera strap over her head. "What's on the amir's mind today?"

"Oh, he was just warning me about the many ways to die in the desert. Windstorms, brigands, dehydration. You know, stuff like that."

"Sounds wonderful." She frowned. "Why's he warning you about the desert?"

"His nephew Khalid is leading an oil exploration trip into the great An Nafud. And I'm going along as an observer."

She removed her pencil from behind her ear and flipped open her notebook. "Are you an observer, or are you looking after the nephew again?"

Russ shrugged. "A little of both, I guess you'd say."

Carenza tried to ignore Milbourne's increasingly animated gestures. Finally, she closed her notebook. "His Eminence beckons. We'll talk more later, okay?"

Once the Kuwaitis left the *Juneau*, Captain Kimball waved the liquor carts onto the fantail. The Americans and Brits relaxed in casual conversation as drinks were passed.

"Don't tell me what I saw, George." Milbourne tossed back one Scotch and poured another. "Russ monopolized the amir and then latched on to Carenza." He clung to the rail as a wave rolled the ship.

"Well, you could always talk to Piper Burton. She's avoiding Russ."

Milbourne followed Lander's gesture. "Nah, she doesn't like me."

Lodge shuffled over. "Gentlemen, you might want to slow down on the alcohol and make a stab at entertaining our guests. Some of the Brits look ready to leave."

"Let 'em go." Milbourne lifted his glass in Smythe's direction and smiled. "We're the leaders on the supply corridor, not the Brits. I'm the one under pressure, not Smythe."

Lodge turned on his heel and walked away.

Captain Swenson nodded his exec toward the ambassador and Lander. "Go over there and peel those two away from the rail. The sea's up, and I don't want anyone falling over. The oily-looking one appears to be turning green."

Lander stared over the rail at the waves. When someone took his arm, he pulled it away. He glared at the ship's exec. "Whadya want?" The ship rolled, and Lander emptied his stomach on Milbourne's shoes.

Alan Smythe and Reginald Heath-Fleming gathered their mates and fled.

Carenza reloaded her camera and kept it trained on Milbourne and Lander.

That evening, Russ sat on his sofa and held a cold beer against his aching head, worrying about the cable Captain Swenson would be sending back to Naval Command.

He looked across his courtyard at the dark window in Piper's half of the house. Another mess. She had made such a show of avoiding him. When his telephone rang, he grabbed the receiver. "I was just thinking about you."

"I'm glad." Carenza's giggle wiped the smile from Russ's face.

"What can I do for you, Carenza?"

"Well, I'm bored." She giggled again. "I made sandwiches for us, hoping Duncan might sober up. He reached for the bottle. I took it from him. When he stood up, he almost fell over the patio wall." She clucked her tongue. "Did you know there's a big opening in the sand just below that wall? Anyway, I just checked on the drunk, and he's passed out on the bed, still in his clothes."

"You're a good person. I'm glad you were there to help with him tonight." Russ stared at the dark window across the courtyard. "Maybe I'll see you tomorrow."

"Well, that's just it. The night's still young. How about a beer at the Marine Bar?"

At the silence from the other end, she offered, "I'll buy."

He checked Piper's window one more time. "Okay, I'll be out there in a few minutes."

Russ grabbed his keys and softly closed his door.

When Piper heard his car start, she wondered which woman he was seeing tonight.

Chapter 62

March 1942. The Cripps Mission fails when it doesn't resolve the question of when India will have self-government.

CATHERINE SAT ON the edge of Russ's desk and swung her legs. When he continued to twirl his office chair back and forth, she leaned down and placed her hand on an arm. "Stop, will you? I know whatever it is must be bad. I used to be able to get your attention when I showed off my legs. Now, not so much." She grinned. "It must be Piper, because you look like a kitten without milk, and she looks like a cat with its fur rubbed the wrong way. Why don't you just spit it out and let me see if I can fix it."

"Fix it?" He squinted at Catherine. "A lot of it's your fault. Why'd you have to tell her about Bitsy? And you told her about us."

"Whoa, sorry. I'm not upset about your dropping me. Why should she be?"

"I didn't drop you, Catherine." He met her eyes. "I was just showing her around, you know, to some of my favorite places, same as I showed you. Anyway, she isn't mad about you. She's mad about Bitsy."

"I can't imagine why." Catherine furrowed her forehead. "I told her it was nothing, just a fling. Bitsy being Bitsy." She glared at Russ. "And you being stupid."

"Thanks a lot."

"Look me in the eye, Russ, and tell me you want a future with Piper."

"I've thought about it." He kicked at his wastepaper basket. "Doesn't matter now. She's avoiding me."

"Like I said. Let me help you fix it." She poked his shoulder. "Is it just Bitsy, or is there something else? I must know if I'm to devise a clever plan."

"Well, she seems stuck on my friend from Moscow."

"Ah, the orchid woman. Well, that could be a problem. Have you figured out what to do about her? Are you going to keep pining away for a married woman you may never see again? Or are you ready to move on?"

Russ swung his chair back and forth, back and forth. He stared out the window and chewed on his lip. He blew out his cheeks and closed his eyes. Finally, he put his head in his hands. "I can't just stop loving her. I may never stop loving her." He raised his head. "But she told me I was meant to find someone else. She was preparing me for that someone. She wanted me to be happy."

"Does Piper make you happy? Is she the right one?"

"Maybe. We have fun. She makes me feel good about myself."

"Okay, then," Catherine said. "Let's get you two back on speaking terms so you can decide if you want to make it work."

They put their heads together and came up with a plan.

⁓❦⁓

"Uncle Ahmad, you wanted to see me?"

"Yes, Khalid. Please join me for coffee."

Khalid stepped onto the palace balcony and took in the sunset before noting the worry beads dangling from his uncle's hand. "Something troubles you on this pleasant evening?"

"How are the preparations for the expedition?"

"Things are coming together. I'm glad Farid agreed to be my caravan meister again."

"So am I. He's very experienced."

Khalid sensed an unease in the air. He gathered his thoughts, then said, "I feel you're not entirely comfortable with the arrangements. Is there something I need to do? Or is it my bringing Russ along?"

"No, Mr. Russell's presence reassures me. I'm glad he's going with you." The amir sat on the edge of the divan. "The last time you went into the desert, things didn't go as planned."

"I remember, uncle." Khalid hung his head. "I didn't act soon enough, and lives were lost." He straightened. "But that was two years ago. I won't make the same mistakes."

"Do you know what those mistakes were, Khalid?"

"Yes. I wanted to prove myself to the men. Even when I was unsure, I didn't ask for help. I didn't seek the advice of those with more experience. I didn't want to appear weak."

"You are a member of my family. You don't need to prove yourself. In any case, seeking the counsel of wise men doesn't show weakness. It's a sign of wisdom.

"I rely on my brother as he does on me. I rule the country and the decisions are mine, but Abdullah and I work better as a team. Remember that when you lead your men. Work with Farid, the captain of the guards, and with Mr. Russell. They'll trust your decisions more if you show them that you value their opinions. Do you understand?"

"Yes, Uncle Ahmad. Thank you for your considered advice. I'll do my best to earn your respect."

The amir pocketed his worry beads and stood. "I know you will." He touched Khalid's shoulder. "Go with Allah."

⁊⊷⧗⊶⁊

The light of late afternoon turned the sea from aquamarine to a slate blue dappled in orange. Russ spread his blanket. Piper laid out their dinner and opened a bottle of wine.

"How's your kitten?"

"He's a little monster. In the morning, he crawls into the pocket of my bathrobe and rides around while I fix breakfast. He's a holy terror and a sweet bumpkin, all in one."

"At least he's company." Russ scuffed the sand with his toe. "I'm glad you came out with me today."

"Clouds are coming in." Without meeting his eyes, she handed him a paper cup of wine and a lamb sandwich.

"Did you enjoy diplomacy on the high seas during the *Juneau's* visit?"

"Not really. You've been to one reception, you've been to them all."

Russ fell silent. He flopped onto the blanket and looked out to sea.

"I especially liked the ambassador getting all upset about your talking to the amir."

He rolled up on one elbow. "Yeah, that was unexpected. But when you're the amir, you do what you want."

"What was bothering him this time?"

"He was worried about the oil expedition. 'Allah will find it more difficult to protect us in the An Nafud. There are many ways to die in the desert.'"

She inhaled sharply. "That doesn't sound good."

"We'll be okay. There's a bunch of us, including Royal Guards. I'm going to the amir's stables next week to pick out my horse."

"Great. Just what we need. More horse stories."

"They're better than camel stories." He inched closer to her. "Wanna come with me?" When she hesitated, he added, "You can see the stables."

"Maybe." She shrugged. "I'll think about it."

They ate their dinner in silence. Finally, she brushed her hair away from her face and sat cross-legged on a corner of the blanket. "Well, Catherine invited me over for dinner. Halfway through our meal, I figured out she was trying to get me to give you a second chance." She sighed. "How do you draw women like a magnet? Even that reporter followed you around."

Russ fiddled with his empty cup. "She wasn't following me."

"I saw her hanging on your arm." She folded her own arms.

"She wanted to know why the amir was talking to me."

"So, what am I going to do with you?" She raised one eyebrow.

"I don't know. Do you want to do something with me?"

"How should I know?" She glared at him. "You're driving me crazy."

"Look," he said, "When this started, I was trying to be an office buddy. Someone to show you the country and help you get comfortable at a new post. Then I learned about all your heartache with past lovers, and I wanted to be your friend. A man you could trust."

She twirled a lock of hair around a finger and stared at the waves.

He touched her fingers. "But then you heard about Bitsy. She's not a woman I'd change my life for. She's gone. You're here." He cocked his head and looked up into her eyes. "I thought you might be interested in me as more than a friend. Was I wrong?"

"No. I'm just scared. I can't rely on my instincts anymore." She twined her fingers with his. "You make me feel safe, Mark. Can I trust you to keep me safe?"

"I think you can. Let me try."

They lay on the blanket and listened to the surf wash the shore. After a time, Piper sat up and started packing the picnic supplies.

Russ got to his feet and stretched. He held her for a moment. "I enjoy being with you."

"Me too." She leaned into him.

He turned to the gulf and squinted into the distance. "Look at that."

Piper followed the direction of his finger. "I thought the *Juneau* left the other day."

A huge warship bristling with guns and cannon loomed out of the dusk. The Stars and Stripes flew above her superstructure.

Sleek and powerful, she was a floating battle platform. And she was heading north toward Iran.

"That's not the *Juneau.*" He ran to the Ford for his field glasses and silhouette cards.

He handed her the glasses. "See if you can spot the number *fifty-two* near the bow." He sorted the cards like a Monaco croupier. "Remember when we took the launch out to the ship? Those numbers were huge, at least four, maybe five feet. Where are they?"

He held various cards up in the dimming light. "See anything?"

"Not really, but the light's pretty bad. Could they have painted the numbers out?"

Russ showed her a card. "It's a German heavy cruiser, a pocket battleship."

She compared the card to the gray behemoth. "You're right!" Her lower lip trembled. "What do we do?"

"Let's find Kimball and Spencer." He tossed the rest of the picnic into his car.

The ship trailed a phosphorescent wake as it slid into the haze. A periscope broke the surface two hundred yards off the ship's starboard stern. It went unnoticed.

Back at the Legation, they hurried to the front office. "You call the ambassador. He might listen to you. I'll call Kimball."

Milbourne picked up after several rings. "This is the ambassador."

"It's Piper, sir."

"Piper? Do you want to come over for a nightcap? I'm all alone here." He snickered.

She hung up. "Forget the old man. He's drunk."

"Not surprised. Kimball didn't answer. Call Trick and Trent. I'll call Heath-Fleming."

"No one's answering. What's going on?"

"Dunno. Maybe they're out playing spies in dark alleys." He dialed Khalid.

"Yes, Russ." He listened while Russ described the situation.

"Meet me at the Interior Ministry command post. I'll head there immediately."

Large posters displayed silhouettes of Allied and Axis ships, planes, and land vehicles. Russ and Piper glanced at the pins dotting the maps of the Gulf that hung from the walls of the ministry.

Khalid pointed at them. "Each pin designates a coast watcher and his radio call sign. Our radio operators listen to traffic and log everything into these books." He lifted the nearest ledger. "According to this, two coast watchers reported sighting a ship flying an American flag. The first came from Al Jubayl, about two hundred miles to the south on the Saudi coast. No hull numbers. The second was from Mina Az Zawr, south of Al Ahmadi and fifty miles from here. No additional comments."

Russ looked at the ledger and shook his head. "Did they check the silhouette cards?"

"Apparently not." Khalid clenched his fists. "We told those sons of jackals to examine each ship. Check the flags, the numbers, the silhouettes. We told them to count the turrets, look out for false flags. Over and over. Aah!" He threw the ledger against the wall.

Russ looked at the maps. "What about transmissions from north of here?"

An operator shook his head. "Nothing but reports of fog."

Khalid frowned. "I need to go to the palace. My uncles will be most unhappy."

"I'll call our man in Iran. Alert him to the danger. See what he can learn." He turned to Piper. "Can you try Kimball again?"

"Sure, but I think we need to cable Washington and London right away. What if this ship decides to lob a few shells on the Iranian ports?"

"All hell would break loose." Russ grabbed Khalid's arm before he could leave for the palace. "Could you ask your guys to raise the alarm farther north? At Nahr-e Owyeh, the town at the mouth of the river."

While the operators began their radio transmissions, Piper tried Kimball again.

"Oh good, you're back. Russ and I are at the Interior Ministry, but we're heading back to the Legation. Meet us there in fifteen minutes. We've spotted a German ship."

"Are you sure?"

"Positive, and it was flying an American flag."

"Damn! I'm on my way."

The young voice that spoke into Colonel Sherm Griffith's receiver was excited. "Duty officer, sir. One of our men just called in from a supply run down at Nahr-e Owyeh. He saw a warship with its string lights illuminated. It was flying an American flag."

Griffith interrupted. "It's probably that light cruiser that was visiting Kuwait."

"No, sir, that ship left two days ago. This one bore German markings on its superstructure. It was ablaze like a Christmas tree. It's at anchor off the town."

"I'll be there in one. Have our operational plans out and ready!"

Two lieutenants had the watch. "Ring the ambassador in Kuwait." Griffith looked at the map. "Lieutenant, get me a boat to the coast. Find the exec and get him over here."

"Sir, we can't raise Kuwait. Only static. Maybe the lines are under repair?"

"Of course, what did I expect? Too much rain. It's a weekend. No one working." He pulled at his hair. "Okay, get me the War Department duty officer."

At the Legation, Piper began a chronology log. Trick, Trent, and Heath-Fleming rushed in. "Kimball alerted us. Where are we?"

Piper waved at Kimball in Mariah's office. "He's drafting a cable for the Department, with info copies to London, the War Department, and COI. One of you needs to alert the commo guys that we'll have an outgoing NIACT IMMEDIATE within the hour."

Russ was on the phone with Lodge. "The old man is drunk, and you're in charge. Here's the scoop." He turned to the others. "He's on the way. Let's check those lines to Iran."

When Lodge arrived, he fell into the ambassador's chair. "I tried Lander before I left home. He's drunk as a skunk. Where's Kimball's cable? I'll sign it." He added a copy to the White House. He lifted the receiver. "I'll try Milbourne one more time, then I'll drive out there."

At 2:00 p.m. local time, the Legation cable hit the desk of the State Department's assistant secretary for Near Eastern Affairs, a chair Milbourne hoped to occupy.

Nearby, Franklin Roosevelt held his copy.

The chief of Naval Operations clutched his back-channel SECRET transmission. Kimball had detailed Milbourne's response to the German ship sighting. The CNO held in his other hand the earlier cable from the captain of the USS *Juneau*.

The assistant secretary of NEA clasped a similar back-channel cable from Lodge. Milbourne would never see the inside of that office.

Back in Kuwait, the code room was busy. A Falcon Wing labeled FLASH had arrived for Milbourne. The clerk had rarely seen a cable with higher precedence than NIACT IMMEDIATE.

Confirm sightings of German battleship. Describe situation, location. First spotter? CNO ordered to send ships to Gulf to confront vessel.

Roosevelt

The second cable was from the NEA assistant secretary. After ordering a review of the post's security posture and Emergency Action Plan, he directed Milbourne to call him.

Lodge tossed the cable on the desk. *Why bother? Milbourne's out of service.*

At 1:00 a.m., Colonel Griffith circled the ghost ship in his launch. He threw up a hand when a searchlight blinded him from the ship's deck. "Pull away and get that light out of my eyes." He compared his silhouette cards with the superstructure of the huge craft and handed them to his exec. "Definitely a German pocket battleship. Take me back to the dock!"

Griffith's launch nearly clipped the periscope that was peering at his exec's glowing cigar. The men in the launch never saw the steel eye.

Twenty minutes later, Griffith was on the line to his duty officer in Abadan. "Lieutenant, I just circled a huge enemy warship. Send this cable to everyone on our emergency list, including the White House." Griffith dictated three paragraphs.

The Navy Department reacted with controlled chaos. Navy planners had to find ships, organize a task force, and steam at flank speed to the Persian Gulf. The stream of curses bouncing off the corridor walls would have caused church ladies to swoon.

Along the Gulf, Iranian fishermen heard the whoosh of air being forced from tanks and diesel engines. Rumors and speculation raced through the suq. Was there a flotilla of German warships ready to pummel the town with shells as large as camels?

The battleship remained at anchor near Iran. It illuminated its string lights at dusk, while at midnight, the ship went dark. The still-unnoticed periscope scanned the shoreline.

Terse IMMEDIATE cables flew among Kuwait, Iran, Washington, and London. A source close to the State Department called the White House to leave a message for Carenza. The next day, the story of the mystery ship was in the *Washington Post*. FDR was furious. He would never know Carenza's informant was Bitsy, by way of Malcolm Lodge.

Milbourne wilted under the mounting pressure. *They want action. They want details. What am I supposed to do? Interview the German captain?* He reached for another bottle.

After three days at anchor off the Iranian coast, the pocket battleship disappeared. One night it was there; the next morning it was gone. Not a single coast watcher saw her departure.

The morning after the German ship vanished, a Navy destroyer and two cruisers, one of which was the *Juneau*, transited the Strait of Hormuz, enroute to Iran. The German battleship paused off the coast of Dubai until the Americans passed the narrowest point of the strait. When the task force steamed up the middle of the Gulf, the Nazi ship weighed anchor and headed out under the cover of darkness. When the task force arrived off the coast of Iran, it was too late.

The sub still cruised beneath the waters of the Gulf. The frightened fishermen abandoned nighttime fishing. No one thought to report the strange noises to the authorities.

In its report to Berlin, the U-boat captain detailed the response time of the Allied task force, its deployment pattern off the coast, and other data for Kriegsmarine naval planners.

When the task force departed, the U-boat followed to the open sea. Then it disappeared. Coast watchers at the Strait of Hormuz reported the arrival and departure of the task force.

✦

"Franklin, Winston here."

"Hello, Winston, how has your Sunday been?"

"Better now. Are you surviving the fallout?"

"Barely. Our defensive perimeter failed its initial test."

"It's the biggest fiddle I've seen in a while. Folks here suggest we ask the Kriegsmarine to conduct maneuvers only in daylight. A promising idea." Winston was his usual snide self.

"Well, much went wrong, but at least one officer did his job. Had his silhouette cards with him and sounded the alarm. You may recall him from your Christmas visit. Mark Russell."

"Yes, the local hero Miss Nasmith featured. Are you doing something about your man Milbourne? Alan Smythe is tearing out his hair over there, and he doesn't have much left."

"As soon as I find a replacement, Duncan will be out of Kuwait. You have my word."

FDR returned the receiver and stared out the window toward the darkened Washington Monument, where only two red lights blinked a warning to aircraft. His was a lonely job.

Chapter 63

April 1942. Hitler orders an offensive against the oil fields in the Caucasus.

TARIQ, THE STABLE meister, greeted Russ and Piper before leading them along the stalls. Khalid brought up the rear.

"Our horses are pure Arabians, Mr. Russell. Curved ears, longer nostrils, dished heads, and elevated tails. They're fine animals."

"I've never ridden an Arabian. I've heard they're temperamental."

"Not temperamental." Tariq shook his head. "They are intelligent, spirited."

Khalid laughed. "Tariq means don't think you're smarter than your horse."

"This one is pretty." Piper pointed to a gray mare.

Tariq smiled at her. "Bedouins prefer mares. They're silent when entering an enemy camp. Stallions show off, calling attention to themselves."

A chestnut mare nuzzled Russ. "I'd like to ride this one and the gray, please."

Tariq inclined his head and waved over two stableboys. "You've chosen steady and experienced desert mounts. Qassem and Jamal will saddle them for you."

When Russ dismounted the second mare, Qassem took the reins. "Sir, there's another horse. Would you like to see him?"

Tariq dismissed the stableboy with a flick of his hand. "Well, sir. What do you think?"

"They're a bit quiet. Are they too old for a long trek?"

The stable meister stiffened. "No, sir. They're fine Arabians."

"Still, I'd like to see a few more."

Qassem stood before the last stall, where a bay made quite a racket. Russ stopped and looked over the rail. "Who's this?"

"A new acquisition, a gift from a Bedouin chief. He's maybe four years old."

Khalid quietly said, "You may recall Yousef, the only chief to decline participation in the defense of the desert. This horse is from his camp."

The horse stomped and bumped the gate as Russ watched. "I'd like to ride him."

Tariq shook his head. "Sir, no one has successfully ridden this horse."

"I exercise him in the big corral twice a day." Qassem ignored Tariq's glare.

"How did he get those welts on his hind quarters?"

"We don't know, but Yousef can be a hard man," Khalid said.

Pulling Qassem's arm, Tariq stepped away when Khalid moved to the rail. "My uncles argue about this horse. The sheikh wants to keep him. The amir wants him gone."

The stallion sniffed Russ's hand. "If he can't be ridden, why does the sheikh want him?"

"He believes he could be the fastest in the stable. But the amir complains the stallion disrupts the care of the other horses."

"He reminds me of some horses back in Kansas. He wants to run."

"There are other horses." Piper wrung her hands. "This one makes me uneasy."

Russ put his arm around Qassem. "Will he take a saddle?"

Qassem beamed. "Yes, sir. I'll bring him to the corral for you."

When they walked into the sun, Khalid said, "I don't want to pick your bones from the ground. Shouldn't you reconsider?"

"You told me to choose my mount with care." Russ nodded toward the stallion. "When I ride him, I'll know if he's right for me."

Khalid turned. "Tariq, a whip."

Russ stopped Tariq with a wave of his hand. "He's felt the whip too much already."

Qassem led the horse into the sun. "His name is Sharif, sir." The horse nickered.

Russ put a foot in the stirrup. Sharif moved away. Russ stepped back. He grabbed the pommel and threw his leg across the saddle. Sharif bucked him off.

Piper jumped to her feet. "Are you okay?"

"I might be a bit rusty." Russ picked himself off the ground and dusted his denims.

Qassem gathered the reins. "Sir, Sharif is not running around. He waits for you. He wants to please you if you'll give him a chance."

Russ threw himself into the saddle. At the gate, Sharif stopped short. Russ flew over the horse's head. "Damn! That hurt." He peeled himself off the rails.

Piper circled the outside of the corral. "Oh, Mark, please. Don't let that horse kill you."

Sharif moved to Russ's side and nuzzled him. "I think he's checking on me." Russ petted the stallion. "I'm okay, Sharif. You haven't scared me off yet. If you let me stay in the saddle, we'll go for a ride."

Sharif tossed his mane and then patiently stood.

The stableboy held the reins. "Give him another chance, sir. Sharif is telling you to open the gate." He whispered, "Sharif trusts me. I want to ride him, but Tariq won't let me."

Sharif whinnied and tossed his head at the gate and freedom.

"Qassem, tell Jamal to open the gate as soon as I mount Sharif."

The child whistled for Jamal. "Be ready, sir. He'll go fast once the gate is open."

Piper chewed her thumb. "What is he doing, Khalid?"

"I don't know. Men from Kansas ride differently than we do."

Russ grabbed the pommel and leaped into the saddle. Sharif reared, but Russ held on. "Not this time, buddy." He slapped Sharif's flank. "Let's go." Sharif rushed the gate just as Jamal threw it open. Russ bent low over the saddle, yelling, "Yee-haw!"

As they tore across the sand, Russ felt Sharif's power. He also felt a resurgence of joy that he hadn't realized was missing. He leaned over the flying mane and became one with the horse. When Sharif approached the water, Russ reined him in.

"You could have gone on forever, couldn't you, boy? It's a good thing we ran out of sand, or we'd be in another country soon."

While Sharif trotted along the water, Russ pumped his arm with excitement. "You're my horse, Sharif." He sat tall in the saddle and yelled over the surf. "Wow, it's great to be alive!"

He turned Sharif toward home. "We'll take it easy for a bit, and then when we're closer, I'll set you free to run like the wind."

When Sharif bobbed his head, Russ said, "I believe you understand me. We're going to make a great team."

Once the stables loomed in the distance, Russ smacked the stallion's rear. "Let's show them what you've got." Sharif reared and was at full gallop when his front legs hit the sands.

Once again, Russ bent low over the horse's mane. "Yee-haw!"

Sharif pounded toward the corral. When he slid to a stop, Russ jumped from the saddle and threw his arms around Qassem. "What a horse!"

In their absence, the amir and the sheikh had joined the party at the corral. Russ nodded in their direction. "Excellencies." Piper was clapping her hands, and Khalid was whooping his delight. The sheikh nudged his brother. "Sharif has allowed an infidel to show us the way."

The amir took the reins from Qassem and coolly stared into the stallion's eyes. "You don't have me fooled. I'm still watching you." He turned to Russ. "Remember what I said on the *Juneau.* Would this horse die so you may live?"

"He would." Russ patted Sharif's flank. "He's the one."

The amir nodded and returned to the palace with his brother.

Qassem approached Khalid. "Excellency, Sharif will need someone to care for him on the expedition." He turned to Russ. "I eat very little."

Everyone laughed, and Khalid looked at Russ. "Okay with you?"

"Sure, what could go wrong?" He turned as a dust devil swirled up across from the corral. "I hope that wasn't a warning." He grinned, and everyone laughed except Khalid.

In the remaining days, Russ went often to the stable to ride Sharif into shape. One day, he stopped near Tariq. "Qassem should learn to ride Sharif. Khalid said you'd need to give the boy permission."

The stable meister waved the child over. "Let's see if you can handle so powerful a horse." With hands formed into a stirrup, he lifted Qassem into the saddle.

Sharif tore out of the gate with Qassem low over his mane.

"He rides well. That horse has accepted him. He may go with you."

When Sharif returned, Russ held the reins while the boy slid from the saddle. "You did great, Qassem. How old are you?"

Qassem beamed. "I have twelve years, sir."

Russ draped an arm across the boy's shoulders. "It will be the three of us braving the great desert."

They turned when the dust devil swirled nearby. Qassem whispered, "Allah is reminding us to be careful."

In Dasman Palace, a telephone's ring broke the silence. Wendell Fox grabbed the receiver and checked the room. When he spotted his servant Hosni moving about the kitchen, he switched to German.

"Herr Langer, how is Amsterdam?" Fox listened and shook his head. "No, that won't happen. I know this ambassador very well, and he won't work with the Kuwaitis."

Fox watched Hosni approach the sidebar. "No, the palace needs a decision and can't wait for the Americans. The process must play itself out. It shouldn't take longer than a few more months. I assume my fee is still agreeable?" Fox gripped the receiver until he heard the answer.

"Okay then. You won't hear from me again until after the expedition to the oil seep. Don't forget to use the Royal Dutch letterhead with their London address in any correspondence for me." Fox replaced the receiver.

Hosni folded his towel and left the kitchen. He had been raised in Iran, where his father worked for the German company building the Trans-Iranian Railway. Hosni's German was flawless. And his loyalty to the sheikh was complete.

Chapter 64

April 1942. The British carrier Hermes *is sunk in Ceylon.*

PIPER LEANED AGAINST the car while Russ donned his dishdasha. When he placed his keffiyeh on his head, he pointed to the other men milling about the area near the stables at Dasman Palace. "Do I look like one of them?"

"Except for your blue eyes and cowboy boots." She snapped his photo.

Slinging his kit bag over one shoulder, he squeezed her hand. "I'll miss you."

She pulled on his arm. "Be safe and come back to me. Please."

Russ waded into the melee of sweating herders, ill-tempered camels, and nervous horses. He found Qassem feeding apples to Sharif. He mussed the child's hair. "Are you excited?"

"Oh, yes, sir." He patted the horse's nose. "But Sharif is very calm."

Khalid strolled over. "You look like T. E. Lawrence."

"I do, don't I?" He eyed the crowd. "When do we leave?"

Waving at the general mayhem, Khalid shrugged. "Who knows? Could be an hour, could be minutes. It's up to Farid, the caravan meister."

"Looks like a big job with so many men, horses, and camels." He eyed Khalid's outstretched arm. "What have you got there?"

"This is a British-made six-shot revolver. Always wear it."

Russ strapped the bandolier across his chest. "I hope I won't need it."

"The desert is a tribal area. Bedouins constantly shift their alliances." Khalid rubbed the back of his neck. "Then there are brigands, outright thieves who are loyal to no one." He slapped Russ's back. "Look. Farid has signaled the scouts to mount up and head into the western desert."

At midday, the column of men and beasts stopped for prayers. Devout Muslims rolled out their prayer rugs and faced the holy city of Mecca. Khalid knelt on a beautiful wool from Kayseri, Turkey. A young Royal Guard scanned the horizon with a telescope.

While watering Sharif, Russ saw Fox leave the camp. "Where's he going?"

"He looks for plants, animals, and rocks. He's a great explorer of the expanses."

As the expedition prepared to resume its journey, Khalid drew Russ aside.

"When we meet the nomads of the An Nafud, we must offer food and water. It's the code of the desert. Some tribes, like Yousef's, hate foreigners. Others are more forgiving, but all will talk. The news of an infidel riding with the caravan of the amir would pass quickly from tent to tent. You should remain out of sight until our guests leave."

"Of course, I understand. But won't your men talk about me to the tribesmen?"

"Not if they want to remain employed by the palace."

"I see. Is there anything else I should avoid?"

"Only quicksand, jackals and wolves, sand fleas and flies." Khalid laughed and then sobered. "Then there's the shamal, the sandstorm of the An Nafud. It can blind you, scour your skin like a stiff brush, and coat your lungs.

"Two years ago, I oversaw an oil exploration into the An Nafud.

There was a shamal. It tore up our camp and killed several in my party."

"Is that why your uncle's so concerned about this trip?"

"Probably. He worries that I didn't act soon enough to protect my men. He may be right." Khalid's face paled. "It's a terrible burden to carry."

"Surely you couldn't be expected to control the wind."

"No, but I hesitated to seek help from those with more experience." Khalid shook his head. "My men murmured among themselves that my leadership cost the lives of good men." He straightened his back and held Russ's eyes. "I won't ever let that happen again."

When the caravan moved out, a young Royal Guard smiled at Russ, who inclined his head. The guard moved to a position at the rear of the line.

Late in the day, the caravan approached the oasis at Al Jahra. Rashid, the date farm manager, shared news over a meal of lamb and rice.

"There's talk among the caravans of a raiding party to the west of Ar Ruqʿi."

"Tell us what you've heard." Khalid leaned forward to catch every word.

"There are six men, some say eight, all speaking an Egyptian dialect. They steal food and sheep. They carry rifles. One caravan saw men on horseback in a wadi. They were conversing with strangers traveling east on camels."

Khalid paced around the tables. "When do they strike?"

"Early in the morning, from the east when the sunrise is behind them."

Khalid stopped pacing. "Do you think they have something to do with the war?"

"German generals need oil. Kuwait has oil." Rashid spread his hands. "The shortest route to the oil is the caravan track across the An Nafud."

"So, the Germans may be sending Arabs into the desert to

search out a way to Kuwait. If you're worried about this raiding party, Rashid, then so am I. I'll warn the Royal Guards."

Khalid inclined his head with his palms together. "Thank you for your hospitality. We'll leave in the morning."

At their camp, Khalid gathered Farid, Fox, and the captain of the guards. He explained Rashid's warning and emphasized the need to be alert.

At the end of a day of blistering sun, Qassem led Sharif away. Russ took a cup of coffee from a grizzled cook and moved to the campfire, where he joined Fox. "The desert looks barren, yet you hunt all over for plants and animals. Do you find anything interesting?"

"Indeed I do. Join me." Fox pointed at a second rolled blanket. "Today I saw an antelope called an oryx in a wadi. I found the tracks of a jerboa. Funny little guys with large ears and a long-tufted tail. They come out only at night."

"Maybe I could tag along on your next hunt, Mr. Fox."

"Call me Wendell. Sure, you'd be welcome." Fox leaned against his saddle. "I've enjoyed this life for a long time. But once I was young and dedicated like you. That's when I knew Duncan." He stretched his short legs toward the fire. "We served together in Political Section at the embassy in Istanbul, from '09 to '11. He was really after the ladies. He bedded anything that wore a skirt." He patted his paunch. "I have a harder time attracting women.

"And could he drink! Everyone swigged that awful stuff called raki. Looks like lighter fluid. We were young and invincible." He sighed. "Those were the days."

"How did he hold his job with all that drinking and women?"

"He always showed up sober, even if he hadn't slept the night before." Fox glanced at Russ. "I guess Duncan's age is finally catching up with him." He stirred the embers with a stick. "How do you get along with him? He could be downright mean if he took against you."

"Yeah, I've seen that side of him on several occasions."

On the afternoon of the fifth day, the caravan reached Ar Ruq'ī, the last village on the edge of the wilderness. They camped near the well.

"Russ, I'm riding into the village. Come along and meet Anwar, the village chief."

A few tired cats skittered down narrow alleys as the horses snorted through the dusty lanes. The evening was pleasant, but Russ wondered how the village survived days when the temperature reached 150 degrees in the sun.

They dismounted in the courtyard before a tall man with a solemn face.

"Anwar, this is my friend Mark Russell. He's the one who saved my life two years ago."

"Welcome, welcome. Please come into my home." Khalid and Anwar shared news of their families in the relaxed conversation of old friends. When the coffee was replenished, Khalid questioned the village chief about the disturbing news he'd heard from Rashid.

"Rashid is correct." Anwar narrowed his gaze. "It is very bad. Six men riding mares. They were last seen north of Linah, about two hundred miles due west of here, on the caravan route straight to Egypt. They claim to be traders bound for the suq in Kuwait City, but there are no camels. After entering a camp, they stack their rifles in an upright circle."

Russ leaned forward. "Sir, has anyone described the rifles?"

Anwar beckoned to a woman "Bring our nephew here." He turned to his guests. "He was in a camp where these men spent the night. He doesn't know how to read, but he is very observant and good at drawing pictures."

They met the young man in the courtyard. "Remember when you were at the camp with the strangers with guns?" Anwar handed him a stick. "Will you draw for our guests what you saw on the rifles?"

Russ studied the lines. "It looks like he's spelling Mauser. That's a German rifle." He squatted at the second drawing. "Here's a *K*. Maybe a Soviet-made Kalashnikov?"

The young man gestured with his arm. "The guns looked like this."

"A curved magazine. Kalashnikov, without a doubt." Russ stood and pointed to the second drawing. "How many of these?"

"Five." He put his stick on the first drawing. "Only one."

"Thank you." Russ smiled at the nephew. "You've been a big help."

Khalid shook hands with Anwar. "We'll stop again on our return to Kuwait City. Thank you for the news."

Anwar followed them to their mounts. He stroked Sharif's head. "This one is smart." He dropped his hand. "Khalid, be very careful. Foul winds blow through the An Nafud this spring. Raiders aren't the only danger. I'll pray to Allah I'm mistaken."

⁓⊰⊱⁓

In the chill before sunrise, they entered the vast and dangerous wilderness. The shepherd who had first spotted the oil seep led them toward a distant uplift. Late in the afternoon, the shepherd dismounted and pointed to a puddle at the base of a rock.

Khalid stuck a finger in the black goo and smelled it. Then he smiled. "We'll need only two days to evaluate the site since the oil is right at the surface. But I already know this is a promising seep. After the war, we'll drill test wells to be sure."

On their return trek, the men were finishing a dinner of roasted oryx when a guard alerted the camp that strangers approached on horseback. The visitors dismounted at a distance and threw sand into the air as a sign of peace. Russ gathered his kit and retreated into the darkness. Khalid called, "Let them pass." He waved Farid to his side.

Six men led their mares out of the gloom. They were armed with rifles. One stepped forward, his black dishdasha and cloak swirling in the breeze. He offered a hand. "I am Habib."

"Welcome to our humble camp. I am Khalid. Please come and rest." He clapped his hands. "Food and drink for the weary travelers." He ushered the strangers inside his tent.

One of the men showed brown and broken teeth. Another wore an eye patch. All reeked of horse and sweat. As they supped, Khalid asked, "Where is your home?"

Habib ran a sleeve across his mouth. "Al Minya, in Egypt. Do you know this place?"

"No, I've never visited Egypt, but I understand it's a country with much history."

At the end of the meal, Habib stood and made a slight bow to Khalid. "We'd like to share your campsite. We'll leave you in peace in the morning."

Khalid inclined his head. "Of course, we would be honored. Three may stay here with me. Three with Farid." He nodded toward the caravan meister.

Farid looked toward the desert. "Have you become separated from your caravan? Should we expect the arrival of the camels carrying your goods for market?"

"No, they'll continue traveling through the night, as they are heavily laden. We saw your fire and smelled the oryx. We wanted to share the news."

While Farid settled the strangers, Khalid found Russ in the darkness, near Sharif. "Did you get a chance to examine their weapons?"

"Yes, they carry one Mauser and five Kalashnikovs."

A cloud of dust swirled as the air turned foul.

⚬⟅⟆⟆

Before dawn, Khalid watched the raiders ride east. He gathered the men. "They'll expect us to go straight for Ar Ruqʿi." Khalid turned to Farid. "What do you advise?"

"Let's pass south of the oasis and then turn back tomorrow afternoon, sir. It'll cost us an extra day but disappearing into the desert might help us avoid the raiders."

"I agree."

Khalid led his gray mare to the tent where Qassem and Russ saddled Sharif. "Fayza needs exercise before we strike camp." He handed his reins to the child. "Why don't you and Russ ride out and look around?"

They galloped along until Russ pulled Sharif up short. He gestured to Qassem to be quiet and pointed to his ears. Qassem listened and nodded. They climbed a dune and shared the field glasses. Qassem gasped and his eyes widened. The machine growl that had reached their ears belonged to the Wehrmacht.

Peering through the glasses, Russ whispered, "They're headed toward Kuwait City. But they're not on the caravan route. Do you think they're lost?"

Qassem shook his head. "They're avoiding Ar Ruq'ī."

"We must be able to describe the vehicles." Russ pulled a small notebook from his denims. "Count the cars and trucks and all the men you can see."

Qassem squinted into the field glasses. "Four heavy trucks, a sign on the front with three spokes. Shovels and large metal tanks. Two long open cars. One shorter open car."

Russ took the glasses and recognized the Mercedes and Fiat emblems. One officer and twenty-six soldiers. While he watched, the Wehrmacht major stood in his vehicle and began yelling and pointing.

"Wonder why he's so agitated?" When Qassem didn't answer, Russ lowered the field glasses. Qassem was on his feet, pointing to the west beyond the Wehrmacht.

"Shamal!"

Chapter 65

April 1942. The Nazi extermination camp at Sobibor, Poland, opens.

RUSS AND QASSEM sprinted for camp. Sharif galloped among the tents, with Fayza right behind, nearly trampling a man lost in the haze of windborne grit. At Khalid's tent, they led the horses through the flap. Qassem tied it down while Russ and Khalid threw off the saddles and forced the horses to kneel in the sand.

Over the shrieking wind, Khalid shouted, "Use your keffiyehs to cover the heads of the horses, then lie down next to them."

Russ knelt against Sharif's flank with his hands over his ears, his mind clear to the danger. He watched Khalid wedge the whimpering Qassem between himself and Fayza. Before he pulled his cloak over their heads, he called to Russ, "With Allah's grace, we'll survive."

The wind snapped the tent poles, and canvas dropped over men and animals. Khalid called out, "Allah is trying to protect us."

While the winds howled through the camp, Russ recalled the storm on Faylakah Island. He realized he was as calm as anyone could be in a shamal.

When the roar diminished to a mere gale, Russ threw off his cloak. *I'm alive.* He patted himself down to confirm he was in one piece. *And I'm not blubbering.* He had lost his fear of storms. He could finally lay Angie to rest.

He watched Khalid gain his feet and shove Qassem into the open. He felt Sharif struggling to rise beneath the collapsed tent canvas.

"Russ." Khalid grabbed his friend's arm. "Help me with the poles, so we can get the horses out."

Men and animals lay amid the devastation. A sandpile shuddered and a man emerged, his face wrapped in his keffiyeh. More sandpiles partially concealed equipment and supplies. Water bladders leaked their precious contents into the sand.

Some piles remained still. A man or a camel rested beneath. The elderly cook stared out of lifeless eyes. Russ knelt and brushed the grit from his face. "I'm so sorry."

He turned at the sound of gasping. The young Royal Guard who'd smiled at him struggled to breathe. Russ cradled his head as he took his last breath. Russ passed a hand over his eyes. *So very young.*

At Sharif's side, Qassem whispered calming words. Russ touched the top of the child's head as he passed by. In a wadi, Russ found two dead horses. He stumbled back into camp and saw Fox and Farid toss back their tent canvas. At the sound of Khalid's voice, Russ approached the small group of men.

"Farid, find the field radio. We need to warn the command post of the shamal."

Russ grabbed Khalid's arm. "Just before it started, Qassem and I saw a German military convoy south of the caravan track. They were headed for Kuwait City."

Farid was back with the radio. "It was buried in the sand just inside my tent. I've cranked the handle, but I fear it's broken."

Russ took the radio, pulled back the housing, and blew out sand. He cranked the handle. Nothing. He shook his head at Khalid.

"Okay." Khalid turned when the captain of the guard approached. "How many?"

"Only three."

"Too few. Everyone will help cover the posts. Draw up a rotation schedule."

Fox said, "Khalid, we should send riders to Ar Ruq'ī."

"That might not be wise." Khalid turned to the captain.

"I agree, we can't spare even one rider."

Fox stepped forward. "Why not?"

"The raiders may have survived the shamal, and now we have to consider the Germans," the captain said. "Only Allah knows who's out there. We must stay together."

"Qassem and I can ride to Ar Ruq'ī," Russ volunteered. "We have two healthy horses."

Khalid turned to Farid. "What do you think?"

The caravan meister shook his head. "Sir, the captain is right. We can't lose any more men or horses."

Khalid bowed his head. Then he met each man's eyes. "We'll stay together to better defend ourselves. We move toward Ar Ruq'ī tomorrow."

In the distance, a lone man spread himself across a dune. With his good eye, he studied the tattered Kuwaiti caravan through his rifle's scope. He counted animals and men. Then he melted into the sands.

That night, Russ stood with Khalid under the stars. "How long did the shamal last? It seemed like forever but also like only moments."

"I don't know," Khalid said. "Probably less than a quarter of an hour, but it could have been longer. Although we were covered in sand and rock, it wasn't very deep. It may become more ferocious as it covers more ground."

At the sound of snarling camels, they drew their weapons. Looming out of the gloom, two scouts fell from their camels' backs. In voices rubbed raw from sand, they reported seeing the German caravan just as the shamal struck. When they rose from the shelter of their mounts, they again saw the trucks and open cars. The surviving Germans abandoned the disabled vehicles, piled into two trucks, and headed back toward Egypt.

Khalid accompanied the scouts to the campfire, leaving Russ alone with his thoughts.

So much loss. How much time do any of us have left? He squatted in the sand and let it run through his fingers. *Time to decide what I want in my life. And who.*

⁂

Dawn touched the edge of night. As the sun crept over the horizon, Habib stared through his scope at his comrades creeping toward the expedition camp. He saw a Royal Guard fall beneath the curved blade at his throat. He watched as three more died. His men inflicted mortal wounds on horses and camels. Habib raised his Mauser and took out a scout before he could raise the alarm.

As the echo of the shot rang against the dunes, Sharif backed away from Qassem and the feed bucket. He reared and ran toward Russ's tent, screaming the alarm.

Khalid stopped a raider who was aiming at Farid.

From the top of the dune, Habib had the fat infidel in his crosshairs. The round tore a hole in Fox's keffiyeh as he bent to retrieve a rifle.

A raider aimed his Kalashnikov at Khalid, but Russ shot him from behind.

Russ spun around when something hit him in the back. He fell hard, striking his head on a rock. As his vision dimmed, he saw One-Eye dismount and walk toward him. "Are you ready to die, infidel?"

Staring at the end of the Kalashnikov, Russ blacked out to the sound of hoofbeats.

The stallion reared and caught the raider in the back. When he reared again, One-Eye rolled over and shot once before Sharif crushed his sternum. The stallion fell to his side.

Khalid fired a round into the middle of One-Eye's forehead. Then he knelt beside Russ. "Allah, don't let him die." He felt Fox grab his arm.

"Three raiders are dead. Shoot the horse. Let's get out of here."

"No, let Sharif live." Qassem pushed Fox aside and stood over Khalid.

"Quick, grab his legs." Qassem helped Khalid drag Russ into a tent.

"Put water over the fire," Khalid yelled at Fox. He tore off Russ's shirt and used it to staunch the blood. "Be strong, Russ."

Qassem said, "Let me help." He left the tent and returned within minutes with a paste. "I saw my mother use this when I still lived with her. She said I should always carry it with me." He nudged Khalid aside.

"What is it?" Khalid took the hot water from Fox.

"I don't know, but it slows the blood." The child smeared the paste into the wound with a spoon. "Help me sit him up."

Qassem wiped away the blood and sand. Together they tightly wound Russ's keffiyeh around his shoulder and under his arm.

Farid threw back the tent flap. "Excellency, now we're only eight: the captain, one cook, and one scout. Only your horse is well. We have three camels."

Khalid lowered Russ to the sand. "I must leave you, Qassem. Stay with him."

He squared his shoulders. "Farid, we leave immediately for Ar Ruq'ī. Find water bladders, dates, and bread. The sniper is still out there. Alert everyone."

"But Excellency, the infidel can't travel."

"Build a litter from arfaj and tent poles. The infidel can die here or on the journey. Only Allah knows. We'll make Ar Ruq'ī tonight."

Once Russ was on the litter, Qassem tucked a partially full water bladder beneath his head. "Be well, Mr. Russ. I'll take care of Sharif."

Khalid found the boy at the stallion's side. "Come, Qassem. We're leaving."

"I can't leave Sharif. Mr. Russ would want us to save him."

"No, Qassem, we must destroy him." He pulled Qassem up. "Bring my rifle."

Qassem shrugged out of Khalid's grasp. "No, Excellency. I won't!"

"Don't speak to me like that."

"I won't leave Sharif."

Khalid's face softened. "I'm sorry, Qassem. We must go if we're to save the infidel."

"I know how to be a nomad. I can survive. If Sharif dies, I'll walk home. Let me try. I'll meet you in Ar Ruq'ī."

"Before Allah, I won't abandon you in this desert of death."

"Go! Save Mr. Russ. I'll save his horse." Brushing away tears, Qassem hugged Sharif. "He's mine, too!"

Farid looked down at the stallion. "Excellency, leave him with the horse. He's a child of the desert. We'll send someone back for him. Now you must save yourself and the others."

Fox pulled Khalid's arm. "You must decide. Move now or die."

Khalid turned away from Qassem and bent over Russ, covering his face with his keffiyeh before the others lifted the litter to the back of the strongest camel.

⚔

When he was alone, Qassem collected scraps of arfaj and lit a fire. Brushing away the flies, he bathed Sharif's wound with hot water and smoothed the paste over the bullet hole. When the horse tried to rise, Qassem helped the stallion regain his feet.

"Good boy." He dragged over a water bladder and found a pottery cup in the sand. He raised the cup to the horse. "Here, try some water."

⚔

At intervals, Farid knelt the camel to allow Khalid to check on Russ. "Stay with us, my friend. We're traveling to the oasis."

Russ surfaced and mumbled, "Qassem? Sharif?"

"Rest easy." Khalid grasped Russ's hand in his own. "All is well."

After sunset, the caravan limped into Ar Ruq'ī. Khalid led Russ's snarling camel into the courtyard of Anwar's home. "Help us. My friend is dying."

The village chief clapped his hands. "Quick! Aisha and the other women."

That night, Qassem wandered his camp alone. He placed thorny bushes and rocks on the faces of the dead to ward off jackals. He dug through the remains of the campsite for food and more water. He piled his small hoard near Sharif.

He recovered Russ's revolver and bandolier. When he opened the cylinder, there were five rounds left. Throwing the bandolier and holster around his shoulder, he stood with Sharif, "The raider won't take us alive."

Qassem fed the stallion and smeared more paste over his wound. He wiped away the blood and flies. "Rest tonight, boy. Tomorrow, we travel." The child leaned against his hoard and fell into an exhausted sleep.

Chapter 66

April 1942. Britain destroys oil fields in Burma.

WITH GENTLE HANDS, Aisha cleaned Russ's wounds while her assistant washed away the sweat and grime. A young girl stood nearby with an apron full of jars and bottles of all colors.

Turning to Khalid, who was hovering in the doorway, Aisha looked grim. "Your friend is very weak. His head doesn't concern me, but this bullet wound is serious. My skills are for laboring women. I'll do what I can, but he needs to be in a clinic. If he lives through the night, he may have a chance." She held Qassem's pasty bandage in her hands. "I haven't seen a poultice like this in years. It's part of our old tribal medicine and may have saved his life. We shall see."

She beckoned to the child with the apron, selecting several bottles. "Go now and bring me boiling water and my grinding stones."

As Aisha applied a new poultice, her assistant continued to drench Russ's body with water. "His temperature rises, Aisha. I can't control it!"

The midwife hurried to find Khalid. "Excellency, your friend is too hot. You must leave soon, in the darkness, when it's still cool."

Khalid located Farid resting in the shadows. "We need to travel before the sun rises. Prepare our departure."

"But, sir, the men are exhausted."

"If Russ is to have a chance, we leave now."

"Certainly, sir." He sighed and rubbed his eyes. "Anwar has replenished our supplies and provided new camels. I'll rouse the men and prepare the infidel's camel."

Khalid woke Anwar. "How can we ever repay your hospitality, sir?"

The village chief inclined his head. "I'll pray for the safe delivery of your European friend." He held up a finger. "But remember, my son, danger still lurks in the silent sands."

Later, Farid walked beside Fayza. "Sir, your horse limps. Perhaps you should dismount."

Khalid bent over Fayza's leg. "Thank you, Farid. My worries for Russ and fear of the raider have consumed me. I was unaware of Fayza's struggle. When do we reach the date farm?"

"Not until tomorrow, I fear. We'll stop only to spell the camels." Farid wiped his face with his keffiyeh and then spat. "They're cursed, these sands."

⚬━✴✴✴━⚬

South of Ar Ruq'i, in the old camp, Qassem awoke to find Sharif standing above him. He jumped up and examined the stallion's wound. After a quick meal of dates and bread, he reapplied the paste and watered Sharif. "Easy, boy. Drink slowly. We leave behind the saddle."

Before the sun touched the horizon, the child stood on the top of a pile of discarded surveying equipment and pulled himself onto the back of the wounded horse. He bent low over Sharif's mane and whispered, "Take us from this death camp." No one noticed their departure.

When Qassem led Sharif into Ar Ruq'i, several children ran ahead with the news to the home of the village chief. "Praise be to Allah! I didn't expect to see you and this horse."

Qassem dropped the reins and sat in the shade of the house. "Are the others here?"

"No, my little one. They left in the cool of night for Al Jahra."

A child offered water to Qassem. Wiping his mouth, he asked, "Does he still live?"

"Yes, but he's gravely ill. Here, come and rest."

Qassem pointed to Sharif. "Do you remember the sheikh's horse, the one that Mr. Russ rode? He saved the infidel's life. He was wounded, and I stayed behind to care for him. He's my horse, too." The child's lip trembled with exhaustion. "Please help him."

Anwar clapped his hands. "Run again for the midwife and her women."

While Qassem slept in Anwar's house, Aisha cared for Sharif.

Near dusk, Qassem awoke and stretched. "Where's my horse?"

A small boy pointed beneath a date palm.

Qassem ran to Sharif and put his head against the stallion's flank. "Are you better? I am."

Pulling the horse's head down, Qassem looked into Sharif's eyes. "Mr. Russ is far ahead of us. We must catch the caravan. Are you ready to leave this tree?"

Anwar found Qassem with Sharif. "We have fresh clothes, food, and water for you. There are bandages and medicine for your horse." He held the stableboy by the shoulder. "I should keep you here, but I know you'd sneak away. May Allah guide you and keep you safe."

Adjusting the heavy bandolier, the boy stepped into the cupped hands of a young man.

With a gentle touch, Qassem urged Sharif into the evening shadows. "Take us home."

⁓❦⁓

At sunset, Khalid touched his patient's forehead. "Not so hot, Farid, but he's unable to stay awake. He seems very confused." He rubbed his eyes. "Perhaps it's too late to save him."

Tightening a litter strap, Farid shook his head. "No, he's strong. We must give him a chance."

Before dawn, Farid heard hoofbeats. Fearing the worst, the men squatted with drawn weapons. When they recognized the lone rider, they stood and cheered.

The stallion trotted into their midst, and Qassem raised his arm in salute.

"How is he?" Qassem slid to the ground at the side of the camel where Russ lay on his litter. Sharif lowered his head and nudged Russ's arm.

"Is that my horse?" Russ's eyes fluttered open.

"Yes, sir, it's Sharif. And me, Qassem."

"How is Sharif?" Khalid ran his hands over the stallion. "Do you think he can still run?"

"Yes, Excellency." Laying his hand on Sharif's flank, Qassem nodded. "He's tired, but the women of Ar Ruqʻi helped him and gave me medicine." He looked up at Khalid. "He's very happy you did not shoot him."

Khalid grimaced. "So am I, Qassem, so am I." He gripped the child's shoulders. "Fayza's gone lame. Sharif won't accept another rider. Will you seek help for Russ?"

The stableboy covered Khalid's hand with his own. "We'll go."

"Farid, move Fayza's saddle to Sharif.

"Qassem, I want you to go directly to Rashid's. Tell him to telephone the palace to send an ambulance for Russ. I hope to meet you at the date farm."

He threw the child into the saddle. "His life is in your hands. But be careful. There's still one raider out there. Don't die in the sands."

Khalid smacked Sharif's flank. "Go with Allah and ride with the wind!"

Sharif reared. When his hooves hit the ground, the stallion galloped to the east.

The men watched as a small boy and a wounded horse carried the infidel's last hope out of sight.

Qassem felt Sharif pull to the right and lift his head to sniff the air. The boy scanned the rocky ridge to the left and saw death swathed in a black robe. He leaned into the flying mane. "Faster, boy!"

The raider pushed his mare down the ridge to intersect with the stallion.

Sharif was drinking the wind when a bullet nicked his ear. Another report from the Kalashnikov echoed on the sand. Qassem's arm went limp at his side. The stallion continued to gallop to the east.

When Qassem checked behind, he saw they had lost the mare. He reined in Sharif by a pile of rubble and dismounted. Using his keffiyeh, he wiped fresh blood from the horse's face and the old wound. He wrapped his arm in the head covering. "We can still do this, Sharif."

He threw the bandolier across Sharif's back and opened the food pack. Nibbling some dates, he looked at the cloudless sky. "I'll walk beside you. Lead the way."

When he could no longer drag himself across the desert, Qassem clambered up some rocks and managed to throw a leg into the saddle. "Go, boy," he whispered into Sharif's ear.

Mile after mile, Sharif carried the child east. Qassem clung to the horse's mane. The fierce sun rose high in the blue sky. The stallion adjusted his gait to help the boy stay on his back. When Sharif stopped, Qassem raised his head. A slight breeze brought the smell of the oasis. Qassem blinked and saw date palms in the distance. "Just a little more, boy."

Peering into the horizon, the lookout rang the bell. "Comes a riderless horse!"

Rashid ran toward the lookout tower. Believing he'd heard thunder, he glanced at the cloudless sky. It was hoofbeats ringing across the sands. A lone horse galloped toward him in the searing heat. Beneath the canopy of palms, Rashid caught the rider as he fell from the saddle. He lowered the boy to the sand. "Who are you?"

"I'm Qassem. The infidel is dying. Call the palace. Excellency Khalid wants the ambulance."

Chapter 67

April 1942. Marshal Stalin asks Churchill to open a second front.

SUNBURNED, FILTHY, AND exhausted, Khalid waited outside the exam room. When Dr. Husayn emerged, he searched the physician's face for any hint of good news. "Tell me."

"Mr. Russell will recover from his concussion. He has a broken collarbone. His pain from the bones moving against each other while riding on the back of a swaying camel must have been terrible. He should have surgery, but I'm unable to do that here. I've set the break as best I can and hope it heals properly. His wounds are badly infected. I'm trying to control his fever. He's weak from blood loss and days in the sun with little to eat or drink." Drawing a deep breath, the doctor rubbed his eyes. "His condition is very serious, Excellency, but his will is strong."

"Can I see him?" Khalid rose and started for Russ's room.

"Only for a minute. He's awake, but he may not know you."

When Khalid pressed a glass to Russ's parched lips, the water dribbled down his chin. "Russ, you're safe now. Please fight to live."

The doctor motioned for the orderly to push Russ's bed out of the exam room.

Khalid turned away. "Where's the child who rode in the ambulance with Russ?"

Another orderly showed Khalid to a room at the end of the hall. Qassem sat on the side of a bed, fatigue shading his face. "How's the infidel? Will he live?"

"Russ is extremely sick, my son. He'll spend many days here recovering." Khalid joined Qassem on the edge of the bed. "How are you?"

Qassem pulled away a corner of the sling cradling his arm. "I'm good. It hurts only a little." The child tried on a smile. "I have to stay here too, until the doctor makes sure my arm doesn't swell." He settled back against the pillow. "Where's Sharif?"

"The sheikh sent a truck to Al Jahra for him, and he's back at our stables. Tariq and Jamal will care for him until you return. Russ will expect you to make sure Sharif is fully recovered when he's ready to ride him again."

"I will, but now I'm very tired." Qassem's eyelids fluttered shut.

Stepping from the stableboy's room, Khalid heard women's voices.

"Where is he? Is he alive? The amir's secretary told us to rush over here." Catherine and Piper were leaning over the front desk, demanding answers from a bewildered clerk. Piper switched to Arabic, and the clerk pointed down the hall.

Khalid intercepted them before they reached Russ's door. "Let me help, Miss Piper."

Piper's already ashen face froze in fear when she saw his expression and appearance. "Oh, Khalid, is he dead?"

Catherine clung to Piper and sobbed. "We're too late!"

"No, no, he's alive." He guided them to chairs in the waiting area. In a reassuring voice, he told them about the death camp and the trek across the desert. "If you're ready, I can take you to see him."

They stood at the foot of his bed and stared in shock at Russ's peeling lips, his sun-scorched face, and the swath of bandage covering his chest and shoulder. An IV line ran into the other arm and a cold compress lay on his forehead. His breathing was hoarse and ragged.

Catherine gasped. "I hardly recognize him."

Piper steadied herself against the bed rails. "We need to be strong. He can't do this alone. We'll take turns staying with him whenever we can get away."

When news reached the Legation, everyone stopped by the clinic. Lodge often relieved whichever woman sat at Russ's bedside. No one expected Milbourne or Lander to appear, and they did not.

Several days later, dawn touched Piper's face. She leafed through a magazine and sipped coffee from a paper cup. The ray of sunlight crept toward Russ's bed.

Russ croaked, "Too bright!" He raised a hand to his face.

Piper jumped up. "You're awake." She stepped around the bed to block the sun. "Now try opening your eyes."

He squinted at her. "Are you an angel?" His eyelids fluttered closed.

"Oh, Mark." She squeezed his hand. "I've been so frightened."

He closed his fingers over hers, and she bent and kissed his cracked lips.

When Piper heard heels in the corridor, she ran to the door. "He's awake. He's talking." She threw her arms around Catherine.

Catherine bent to kiss Russ's forehead. "You had us very worried."

"Hello, Catherine," he croaked. "Another angel."

Piper stepped into the hall and flagged down a nurse. "Please get Dr. Husayn."

The doctor knelt over Russ and shined a light into his eyes. "Mr. Russell, you must stop visiting my clinic. Perhaps you should find a less dangerous way to increase your fame in the suq." He gently prodded Russ's shoulder. "Good, good. Very responsive."

Russ mumbled, "Where's Sharif?" Before they could answer, he drifted to sleep.

When Dr. Husayn completed his examination, he motioned the women into the hall.

"His vital signs are good. His color is better. The overnight nurse reported his wound is clearing the infection. He's had little fever for two days." The doctor smiled. "I have more faith in a full recovery."

When the women started to enter the room, Dr. Husayn stepped in front of them. "The most important thing he needs now is rest. Please, only one at a time and only for five minutes. Would you like me to notify the palace of this development?"

"Oh, yes." Piper nodded. "Khalid will want to know he's better."

As he ushered the women to the front of the clinic, Dr. Husayn shook his head. "He shouldn't have survived this ordeal. Without the midwife's aid, he could have bled to death. He could have died in the scorching sun before reaching the date farm. Without the child who raced across the desert, alerting us to send an ambulance, he could've died. The horse could've foundered and lost his way. And yet, all brought hope. Allah has smiled on Mr. Russell."

In the suq and at the harbor, news of the oil expedition circulated among the Kuwaitis. Mehmet and Mohammed huddled in Ali's hovel, arguing on how to word their message. That evening, Ali delivered an envelope to the captain of a ship bound for Egypt. "The infidel lives. The traitorous nephew lives. Your mission has failed."

When Catherine stopped in at the clinic the next day, she found Russ sitting up in bed. "That's an improvement." She straightened the sheet. "Why the sour look?"

"I need real food, Catherine." He shoved away the food tray. "I'll never recover on this!"

"What do you want? A cheeseburger with pickles and onions, fries, and a chocolate milkshake?" She pushed the tray back and shook her fist. "Don't make me mad."

"Okay." He meekly sipped his guava juice.

Later when Piper walked in, she had a newspaper tucked under her arm. "Ready for a break, Catherine? That scowl on his face looks alarming." She bent and kissed Russ.

"Have you been misbehaving?"

"No, ma'am. I've been an angel, haven't I?" He smiled at Catherine.

"Right." Catherine pecked him on the cheek. "Till next time, you rascal."

Piper scanned the headlines. "Do you want to hear about the war?"

Russ shook his head and slid a bit of lamb into his mouth.

Piper fluffed his pillow. "Finish your lunch. Then it's time for a nap."

The next afternoon, Khalid stuck his head around the doorframe. "Brother, you look much better. I almost recognize you."

"It's been a struggle." Russ sat in a wheelchair before the open window. He patted his bandaged shoulder. "It's tough getting out of bed. But they want me up and about more."

Khalid leaned on the windowsill and whistled. "How about a surprise?"

The stallion poked his head into the room and whinnied. Qassem appeared below the horse's neck.

"Sharif." Russ whispered, "And Qassem. My heroes." He stroked the horse's nose and then clung to the child's hand. "You two saved me."

A nurse entered, and when he saw the horse hanging in the window, he shooed them away and pushed Russ to the side of the bed. "We'll have no more of that. Flies and dirt are not welcome in my clinic."

After the nurse finished bustling about, Khalid sat down in the chair. "When you saved my life on the Fourth Ring Road, I prayed to Allah that I could return the favor. I never expected it would be so difficult."

"I owe you my life, my brother. If you hadn't forced the caravan to Al Jahra, I would have died in the wilderness."

An orderly entered and stuck an arm under Russ's good side. "Time to get back in bed."

With his aid, Russ stood and clutched Khalid. "Thank you."

"You're welcome." Khalid nodded as the orderly lowered Russ into bed.

Piper passed Khalid in the hallway. "How is he today?"

"Very good. He was sitting near the window. Be sure to ask about his surprise."

Piper straightened Russ's bedside table and sat in the chair. "Well, I can see you're bursting to tell me something."

"Khalid brought Qassem and Sharif to see me. They were right there at the window. They both look terrific." He slapped at the sheet. "Makes me want to get out of here."

"Whoa, buster. Slow down. It's far too soon to go riding.

"You know, Mark, Khalid was sick with worry. If you had died, I'm not sure how long it would have taken him to forgive himself."

Russ reached for her hand. "When the one-eyed raider pointed his rifle at me, I thought I was a goner. I saw Sharif rear, and then nothing until here. Everything else is a blur."

"Well, you didn't miss much. Except for the trek across the desert on a litter, the rush to Kuwait City, the suffering and pain." She laughed and patted his knee.

"I have a second chance, Piper, a fresh start. I have a future." He squeezed her hand. "I want someone to share it with."

Piper moved to sit on the bed. She laid her head on his chest. When he stroked her hair, she said, "I'd like to be that someone."

"I hoped you'd say that." He continued to stroke her hair until he fell into a light doze.

Piper slid from the bed and tiptoed from the room. She thought she heard him say, "I'm dreaming of an angel."

Chapter 68

A WEEK LATER, Russ drowsed in the courtyard as a breeze stirred the palm trees. When he awoke, he found Piper sorting their mail. "Hello, darling."

"Hello, sleepyhead. Here's the *Tribune*, all bad war news. Hitler's planning his summer offensive. Wants to capture the oil fields in the Caucasus. That's getting awfully close to us if you ask me."

He watched her eagerly rip open a letter. "International mail?"

Piper nodded. "From my aunty. Somehow it made it past the censors." She scanned the pages and her expression changed.

"Bad news?"

"Not really. I'll read it later." She bent over to retrieve a photo that had fallen from the envelope. "Why don't you close your eyes a little longer while I finish up here?"

"Maybe you're right."

Piper glanced at the photo of a small girl in a pinafore. She dropped the rest of the mail and stood. "I'm going inside for a bit."

After a dinner of Campbell's soup, Russ parked himself in an old folding chair on the roof. He stared across the sands where Rommel's advance unit had labored toward Kuwait City and where

Habib and his raiders had attacked the caravan. He had survived a shamal, killed a man, and nearly died. He shuddered at his memories.

Piper joined him on the roof. "I've brought supplies." She held up a canteen of hot water, bandages, and towels. "Let me help you with your sling and pajama top."

With practiced hands, she soaked loose the dressings and examined the wounds. "Looks good." Ignoring his gritted teeth, she replaced the bandages. "You're a big baby." She buttoned his pajama top and tucked an blanket around his shoulders. "You need to exercise that arm more and start walking around the neighborhood. Otherwise, they'll send you to Jerusalem to finish your recovery."

"No way." He smiled into her hazel eyes. "The nurses in Jerusalem won't be up to my standards." He petted the cat purring in his lap.

A gentle breeze blew across their shared roof.

⚜

Several days later, Piper pulled Russ from his chair in the courtyard. "If you get out of your pajamas, I'll drive us out to see Sharif. Maybe Khalid will be there."

Qassem ran and threw his arm around Russ's waist. "I've missed you. Sharif, too."

"How's our horse?" Russ ran his hand over the stallion's wounds. "He looks good. Really good."

"Do you want to go for a ride, Mr. Russ? I ride Sharif every day, even with this." Qassem held out the arm still in a sling.

Piper held Russ back. "Don't. It's too soon. Just walk him around the corral."

"Miss Piper, Sharif didn't let me fall, even when I was shot by the black rider."

Russ tousled the boy's hair. "Sure, have Jamal saddle him. Come with me. If we're together, Miss Piper will feel better."

He mounted a stool and threw his leg over the stallion. "Okay, Qassem. Let's go."

Piper turned as Khalid approached. "Oh, I wish you'd arrived a few minutes earlier. You might have persuaded Mark not to ride today. He won't listen to me."

"Ah, but I watched from the stables. Sorry, but he needs to ride again."

"I should have known. Men are all alike!" She marched to the table and sat down.

In a few minutes, the amir arrived. "I heard there's excitement at our stables today."

Tariq shared the field glasses. "They're returning, Excellency. They ride side by side."

Glowing with pleasure, Russ slid from the saddle. "Excellency, Qassem convinced me to go for a ride. It was swell."

Khalid and Russ traded stories about the shamal and the battle with the raiders. The amir listened to details he hadn't known before. When he stood to leave, he motioned to Russ.

"Walk with me. It's nice to see you at my stables again, Mr. Russell. I enjoyed hearing you and my nephew talk about your ordeal. I hadn't realized the complete circumstances until now." He paused. "I hadn't understood how many difficult decisions Khalid had to make."

"We survived because of his leadership. He sought the advice of Farid and the captain of the Royal Guards. Even Fox. He considered the choices and then led us out of that desert."

The amir resumed his slow pace toward the palace. "Sometimes Allah decides to test our worthiness. Khalid passed." He nodded to Russ. "As did you."

He paused once again. "That horse is a continued trial for my stable meister. I must decide what to do with him." The amir clasped Russ's good shoulder. "Be well." He strolled into the fading light.

Russ returned to the others, where Piper stood at the fence with Sharif. "You're lucky he didn't throw you."

Sharif nuzzled her neck.

When she brushed Sharif's mane from his eyes, Russ chuckled.

"What's so funny?"

"Oh, nothing. It's just you and Sharif. An unexpected pair."

On the roof, Earmuff jumped from Piper's arms and walked the wall before settling into Russ's lap. Leaning against the bagdir, they gazed at the canopy of stars and sipped their wine.

"Mark, have you decided if you're going to stay on here after your tour is up?"

"Yeah, I know you want me to stay, but I really need to get back to D.C." He rubbed his chin. "I'll have a lot to do there."

"I won't do well without you. I can tolerate Milbourne and Lander, but I still worry about the war reaching us here." She nudged his shoulder. "Besides, I'll get pretty lonely."

He put his arm around her. "I know. But I won't work for the State Department anymore, so I'll need a new job with a different agency. I don't know how hard that will be to find."

"What do you mean?"

"Well, I'll need something we can do as a tandem couple, won't I?"

"I guess." She pouted, then pulled him closer for a kiss. "I know how all this works. Separations are part of the business." She sighed and gave a small smile. "I really do trust that things will work out. It's not the end of the world." She exhaled and seemed to relax.

"That's better," he said. "Don't laugh, Piper, but I've thought about our future far beyond the war. Skip over job considerations, assignments, and housing. Forget the practical stuff. Focus on our honeymoon. Dream a little. You like France. Let's go there. See your aunt. Lie on the beach."

Piper slipped out of his embrace and walked toward the other wall.

"Whoa, what did I say?"

"Oh, nothing."

"Am I moving too fast? I thought…"

"No, no. It's sweet, what you said."

"Maybe it's too soon to dream about life after the war. Maybe you won't want to go back to France and see what damage has been done."

Piper shook her head.

"I don't like seeing you so sad. What can I do?"

"Just leave it, Mark. Okay?"

"Okay." He dropped her arm.

Russ was finally strong enough to return to work. On his first day back, he struggled to stay focused and was glad to lock up his safe. He heard the telephone on Catherine's desk jangle.

"That was the old man. George probably told him you were back. He wants you to stop by the residence on your way home." Catherine stroked his hair. "Poor boy."

"All day I was glad he wasn't here, and now I have to face him after all." He winced.

Mohammed led Russ to the patio table, where Milbourne sat with a bottle of Scotch.

Milbourne eyed his assistant. "You're thinner. Want one, or maybe a lemonade?"

"Sure. Lemonade," Russ said. "It's been a slow recovery."

"Well, now you're back. Since the Nazi warship fiasco in the Gulf, it's been quiet." He topped off his Scotch. "The palace said there was a German advance unit in the desert."

"Yes, sir." Russ gritted his teeth. "I was there."

"Oh, right, right." Milbourne crossed his legs. "Did Khalid learn anything on the trip?"

"He found the oil seep and will drill test wells when hostilities cease. So, they'll probably make an offer to the United States soon. We should be ready for it."

"What do you have in mind?" Milbourne twirled his tumbler.

"You could cable FDR to lay out the details. I'll write the cable for you if you want."

"Let me think about it. We'll talk more later."

The next afternoon, Khalid sat with his two uncles under a shaded archway at the palace. They sipped their coffee and nibbled British biscuits.

"Uncles, believe me. Tex-En is the company that deserves our concession. Their managers and technicians are experienced in modern extraction techniques and marketing. These men came from firms like Standard Oil and Gulf Oil."

The sheikh leaned forward. "Then why haven't we heard back from the ambassador? You laid it all out for him weeks ago."

"I don't know." Khalid stood up and paced. "Russ only just returned to the Legation, and I haven't had a chance to see if he's talked with him."

"Well, I'm about to listen to Wendell. He's steered me toward the Dutch all along. He doesn't like Ambassador Milbourne." The amir flicked his worry beads. "After all, Royal Dutch Shell has submitted the lowest bid."

"You mean the only bid." The sheikh tossed his cup where it rattled around in the saucer.

"Exactly." The amir turned to Khalid.

"I don't know, Uncle Abdul, you know how I feel about Fox. Besides, the Nazis control Holland."

The sheikh stood. "I agree with Khalid, Brother. If the Nazis lose the war, will Holland be able to honor the contract?"

"I need more time," Khalid pleaded. "Let me talk to Russ."

The next day, Russ answered the telephone at his desk.

"Fox here. What's up with Duncan? Catherine told me he hasn't been into the office in days. She said you were back, so I decided to call you."

"Yes, I returned a few days ago. What's going on?"

"The amir wants to finish the paperwork on the concession. He favors the Americans, but other companies are in this, too."

"Sorry, Wendell, during my recuperation I sort of lost track of what's going on. I mentioned to Milbourne about the oil during the one and only time I saw him, but he's still thinking about it. Khalid didn't tell me the clock is running."

"Khalid thinks you aren't ready to tackle Duncan, so he's been working on his uncles to give you more time. I'm telling you, time's up. In fact, I think it may already be too late."

Russ replaced the receiver and fished a telephone number from his wallet. "Averell Harriman, please. Tell him it's Mark Russell calling from Kuwait. I'll hold."

Harriman came on the line, and Russ described the situation. "I believe, sir, that my involvement has tainted the oil concession for the ambassador. He can't figure out how to claim the glory when he knows that everyone has already heard about my relationship with KOC."

"Okay, Russ. Thanks for the call. Let me handle it."

After Harriman left the Oval Office, FDR cabled Milbourne via Falcon Wing.

⸙

Catherine picked up the cable traffic. She scanned a copy of the international telegram from Doris to George. She was so delighted at Lander's future misery, she failed to notice the Falcon Wing from FDR when she stuffed Milbourne's mail into an envelope. She dropped the envelope off at the residence on her way home.

Milbourne balled up the cable and tossed it across the patio.

Damn it all. He's giving me two days to act. He pushed himself out of his chair and lumbered over to retrieve the cable. He smoothed it out and put it in his robe pocket. *I'll deal with it later.*

⁓✻⁓

Ever since Bitsy's late-night phone call about Russ getting shot, Rhonda had barely slept. Her worry escalated when she failed to get any response to her numerous letters to Kuwait. *Why hasn't he answered? Is he that sick?*

She put pen to paper in hopes of receiving good news in return.

My darling, I long to hear from you. Tell me what happened. Tell me you're well. Tell me I'm still in your thoughts. You've never left mine. My world would be empty without you in it. I love you.

Chapter 69

WHEN RUSS RETURNED from lunch, he found Catherine and Piper in a snit.

"Whatcha got there?" He pecked Piper on the cheek.

"The inspectors' report." She tossed it to him.

"Wait! This is a complete whitewash. Where's the fraud? Where's the bad behavior?"

"They'd already made up their minds," Catherine said, "and your report made no difference."

"Maybe they never read it. Now he'll get the NEA job. But at least we'll be rid of him." Piper turned on her heel. "I'm going back to work. If I stay here, I'll start throwing things."

The phone rang on Catherine's desk. She passed the receiver to Russ. "Fox."

"Listen, Russ. I can't reach Duncan. The amir has awarded the oil concession."

"What? Khalid never called me."

"I'm not surprised. They did it and then told him. He's furious."

"Who got it?"

"A European consortium. They'll work out of offices in London."

"So, it's over. Thanks for letting me know." Russ handed the receiver to Catherine.

"Bad news?"

"The worst. I need to call Khalid, but I'll do it at my desk."

"I'm sorry, I can't talk," Khalid said. "Too much going on. I'm into it with my uncles. At least they won't sign the paperwork until the summer. Maybe as late as August."

Russ dropped his head in his hands. *So much work for nothing. And I can't do a thing.*

The next morning, Milbourne strolled into the front office. "Don't look so surprised, Catherine. You know I must come in occasionally."

When Russ returned with a stack of mail, Catherine held a finger to her lips and pointed at the inner office. "He's back."

Russ grabbed his steno pad and walked into Milbourne's office. "Morning, sir. There's been a lot going on. Shall I start with the oil situation?"

"Oil, always oil with you." Milbourne waved his hand. "Sure, start with that."

Russ gave him the overview of Fox's phone call. He looked up from his notes. "How do you want to handle this?"

"Handle what? It's over."

"But you could visit the palace and try to talk some sense into the amir." Russ clutched the edge of Milbourne's desk. "You could talk to Fox. You've got to do something!"

"You're far too excitable. You jump at everything without analyzing it first." Milbourne straightened his tie. "That's where my experience comes in."

"Maybe we should cable the president before he gets wind of the problem."

"Relax, Russ. I'll take care of this. It needs the touch of an ambassador."

Russ dropped his steno pad. When he bent to retrieve it, the ambassador cleared his throat.

"As long as we're talking about what needs fixing, let's get into your annual evaluation and your list of accomplishments. Open that notepad."

Russ leaned back with his pencil poised over a clean page.

"I reviewed what you sent out to the residence with George. There's an extensive paragraph about your work with those COI boys." Milbourne steepled his fingers.

"We uncovered illegal activities involving Mehmet, Mohammed, and Ali."

"And I repeatedly told you there was nothing to it. Let it go."

"But they were directly involved with the killers who stalked us in the An Nafud Desert."

"You can't prove that."

"The raiders were from Al Minya, Mehmet and Ali's hometown. Surely even you can see that it's more than a coincidence we met them in the middle of hell on earth."

"You will lower your voice and watch your mouth."

"Look, Guderian, the Soviet spy who was executed, made a stop in Al Minya before he came here. Everything is tied to Al Minya." Russ gripped the arms of his chair, trying to keep himself in it. "Men from Al Minya tried to kill me!"

"You're jumping to conclusions again." Milbourne adjusted his shirt cuffs. "Better calm down or this meeting is over. Then I'll write what I want without input from you."

Russ simmered but said nothing.

"You wrote how you and Khalid devised a plan to check on the locals involved with monitoring the port, the desert approaches, the suq, and the refinery and oil fields. I don't recall that idea."

"It's something Khalid worked on to make sure those on the reporting end knew we were watching and available to help them if they had questions."

"How come I wasn't told about this?" Milbourne steepled his fingers again.

"It was nothing formal, just a follow-up idea to make sure we missed nothing."

"Sounds like insubordination to me. And it didn't catch the Nazi ship in the Gulf."

Russ's knuckles whitened on the arms of his chair.

"Speaking of the Nazi ship, why would you want to connect yourself to that fiasco?"

"I spotted the ship. I identified it. I sounded the alarm."

"Oh, I'm well aware of that. It was a mess and lasted for weeks. I heard from everyone, even the president. If I were you, I'd stay away from that blunder. If you insist on including it, I'll have to address it. Then it will remind everyone of the post's failure."

Russ bit down on his retort. *Yeah, and your complete collapse.*

"And now you dump the oil concession in my lap for me to fix. That was your responsibility. You were told to keep an eye on it."

Russ jumped to his feet, knocking his chair to the floor. "I did everything I could to get you off your lazy ass and act!"

"Sit back down! This is your final warning."

Russ picked up his chair but stood behind it. "I'll sit when I'm good and ready."

"If you have yourself back under control, we'll continue. While you glorify your accomplishments, you neglect your lapses."

"Lapses?"

"Let's start with Dalton's visit. The palace was upset about all those liquor bottles."

"That's chicken feed compared with your behavior on the *Juneau*. I'm sure the president loved the photographs of you and George on the fantail."

The old man's head snapped up. "What photographs?"

"Don't remember, huh? What do you think Carenza was doing out there?"

With a trembling hand, Milbourne closed Russ's file. "That's it, Russ. Now you've slandered me during our interview. You're done." Milbourne turned to his credenza.

"It's slander only if it's not true." Russ stood. "I wrote everything down. You fixed it with your inspector buddies, but others back in

D.C. may be interested in your mismanagement of post funds, to the detriment of the staff.

"Oh, yeah." Russ sneered. "And there's more. I wrote about your endangerment of our alliance with the palace and the supply corridor security operations. Your enemies at State must be clapping their hands with joy. Wish I could see the president's reaction."

Milbourne's hand froze on its way to the tumblers.

"That stopped you, didn't it? My Department career is over, but I can get a job with any agency I choose." Russ turned on his heel. "You, on the other hand, are done. Finished."

Russ slammed out of the front office and ran down the stairs.

The ambassador reached for the Scotch.

Chapter 70

June to September 1942. In July, Wehrmacht field marshal List is ordered to capture Baku, Azerbaijan, and its oil fields.

"Hi, Catherine, it's me. Russ went to the stables to ride Sharif. I'm tired of sitting out there at the table all alone. How about we have lunch together? I'll cook."

"Great. I'm bored, too. But don't cook. I'll bring something from Fuad's."

When Catherine arrived, she had several bags of food. "I couldn't decide what I wanted, so I got a little of lots."

Piper uncorked a red wine. "At least we won't go hungry."

"Right!" Catherine held out her glass. "We deserve a little fun after our horrible spring. I thought the Nazi ship cruising into the Gulf would be the highlight of excitement around here. Who knew Russ would nearly get killed?"

"Really. I shudder every time I think how close he came to dying. What would I have done without him?" Piper rubbed her arms and shivered.

"Well, you're about to learn. We all know he'll never get promoted after that row he had with the old man the other day. He'll be out of here as soon as the promotion list comes out. Honestly,

I'm surprised he's not gone already." Catherine popped a piece of kebab in her mouth. "So, what's the latest on this romance? If you don't mind my asking."

"I don't mind. After all, you stepped aside and allowed me to get to know Mark." She tilted her head toward her friend. "And I thank you for that."

"So, you think you have a future with him after Kuwait?"

"I think so, although he's not the type of man I thought I'd end up with. I like tall, dark, suave." Piper laughed. "I read too many romance tales in glossy magazines when I was a teenager." She buttered a slab of bread. "But I've had those guys. And they didn't turn out too well." She shuddered again.

"Russ has something special." Catherine laughed. "But I don't need to tell you that."

"No, you don't." Piper unwrapped another paper parcel. "Now, what's in here?"

They ate their way through the bags while they talked about their jobs. Inevitably, the misconduct of the ambassador consumed their conversation. Piper pushed away her plate and said, "Enough talk about the head drunk and his lackey. I'll have indigestion."

"Back to Russ. He's pretty good-looking, in a Midwestern way, and funny," Catherine said. "When did you decide that he might be the one for you?"

"I always enjoyed our field trips into the few sights outside Kuwait City. Mark has a way of making small things seem really interesting." She twirled her hair around a finger.

"That trip to Faylakah Island really opened my eyes to who he is. Even when he was upset in that storm, he found courage enough to protect me." She grimaced. "Actually, I think he forgot it was me. He was reliving his childhood tragedy. But that doesn't matter. He gave his all to make me feel safe. That's something I haven't felt in a long time. Maybe ever."

Catherine nodded. "It's like that time he saved Khalid in that awful accident. Khalid could have burned alive. But Russ just blushes and waves it all off."

"I know, right?" Piper leaned forward. "He just doesn't get that he's really quite terrific in dangerous situations. I think that's why the royals valued his opinion so much. He's calm under pressure. Decisive. And so smart."

"And he's a pretty good kisser." Catherine's grin spread across her face. "Isn't he?"

"Yep." Piper threw her napkin at Catherine.

"So, as long we're on the subject, what do you think of him as a lover?"

Piper raised an eyebrow but said nothing.

"Oh, my God, you haven't taken him to bed yet?" Catherine gawked at Piper.

"The time hasn't been right." Piper rose and drew a trash can their way. "Besides, I like that Mark has taken it slow. My previous encounters always felt rushed." She poked Catherine's arm with a fork. "And I don't have to wonder about his prowess as a lover after all his experience. Rhonda, Bitsy, you. What he didn't know before, he certainly knows now."

"True, true. But I bet you can't wait to have him show you his stuff." Catherine ducked when a hunk of bread flew at her.

"Our time will come. I know it now. I can wait." Piper's face softened. "Did Russ ever dance with you on your roof?"

"No, he did not." Catherine gave a small grin. "Was it wonderful?"

"It was magical. I want to do that all my life."

⌒⟊⟊⟊∽

Summer turned to fall, and Kuwait's heat dissipated. On a cool, clear morning, Catherine held the much-anticipated promotion list in her hands. *Only Piper and me.* She dropped the cable on Milbourne's desk and watched a smile play across his lips.

⌒⟊⟊⟊∽

One evening, Russ visited the suq. He stopped in front of Ibrahim's shuttered shop.

"I miss him, too." Mustafa leaned against the door to his stall.

"I knew he was ill, but his death was so sudden."

Mustafa lowered his head. "He was one of the last lions of the desert."

"I'm leaving Kuwait soon. I've come to say goodbye."

The bespectacled merchant beckoned Russ inside, where he placed a small box on the counter. "Ibrahim left this for you. I buffed it for him when he was no longer able."

Removing the lid, Russ held the silver dhow pendant. "I remember this. He wanted to add the filigree swirls along the hull to look like the waves of the Gulf."

"It was his most accomplished work. He said only you were worthy of this gift. Perhaps you'll give it to your mother." Mustafa removed his spectacles and polished them with the end of his keffiyeh. "You were his favorite customer, Mr. Mark. None of us have known a European such as you. While it's bad to lose customers, it's terrible to lose friends."

"Thank you, my friend, for allowing me to share your days here in the suq."

"The pleasure was ours."

In the palace courtyard, Russ paused to listen to the baritone call of the muezzin. *I'm going to miss that sound when I'm gone.* He turned a corner and spied Khalid.

"My time here is running short. I'm glad to visit today."

Khalid stayed Russ's progress. "Let's pause here before we go to my uncle's. I need to tell you about Wendell Fox."

"Fox? What's happened?"

"He was working with the Nazis out of the Hague. The oil concession he arranged for us wasn't for the Dutch. It was really for the Germans."

"The Germans! How did you find out?"

"The sheikh had reports about information leaking out of the palace. He discussed it with the amir, and they narrowed the possible traitor to a few men, including Fox."

"I talked with him on the expedition and never suspected a thing."

"I've never liked Fox, but none of us foresaw this treachery."

"What happens now? Is the contract binding?"

"Come, my uncles will tell you." Khalid ushered Russ into the amir's private chambers.

The royal brothers stood, and the amir held out his hand. "I'm glad you were able to come here today, Mr. Russell. We know you're busy getting ready to leave."

"I'm always happy to visit with you and your brother. Thank you for inviting me."

"Please join us for some coffee." The amir waved Russ to a chair, then poured from an ibrik. "I trust Khalid has told you about Mr. Fox?"

"Yes, sir. I was surprised to learn of his disloyalty."

"Fox has left Kuwait. I've withdrawn the concession he arranged with the Germans. I'll be entertaining new applicants." He raised an eyebrow. "I understand the leadership of your Legation may soon undergo changes?"

"Yes. It's not official, but all our sources in the Department of State say Mr. Milbourne will also be out of Kuwait soon."

"Perhaps Tex-En, in the United States, will be interested in our news about the oil concession. What do you think, Mr. Russell?"

"I believe that is an exceptionally good possibility. A new ambassador will see the many advantages to repairing our relationship with your country, beginning with the concession."

The amir and the sheikh exchanged a look. "Good. Then we'll await your changes."

"If I may ask, how did you manage to learn about Mr. Fox? He could have slipped away and fled to Germany."

The sheikh took up the story. "I gave Fox a new servant, one who spoke German. We also added palace telephone operators who spoke German. I filtered his incoming and outgoing mail through the Interior Ministry. An expert steamed open his correspondence." The sheikh smoothed his beard. "It's what happens when one becomes too complacent."

The amir laughed. "Anyway, when we learned the full extent of Fox's scheme, we went to Mr. Smythe. He called in Scotland Yard. Fox was very clever. His draft contracts with potential American companies included a large commission for himself. But he would have made much more from the Nazi-backed firm in Holland."

"Two investigators escorted Fox to London, where he'll undergo interrogation." The sheikh rubbed his hands together. "They may learn much about other German plans for this region of the world."

The sheikh turned to his brother, who nodded. "We didn't share our concerns with your ambassador because we didn't know if he was complicit with Mr. Fox. How else could we explain his failure to act on behalf of the United States?"

"I thought Fox was working alone," Khalid said. "I said your ambassador wasn't disloyal, only…" He pointed to his head. "What's the word?"

"I don't know which one you're searching for. Maybe 'crazy,' but mine is 'drunk.'"

"Ah, yes. Perhaps so." The three royals nodded and then shook their heads.

"I'm sorry our ambassador abused your country's gracious hospitality."

The amir placed his hand on Russ's shoulder. "Thank you. London has confirmed that Mr. Fox worked alone. Khalid was right." He gestured to his nephew.

Khalid placed a wooden box on a cushion next to Russ. "Open this."

Russ pulled out a dishdasha, a keffiyeh, and a revolver and bandolier. "My expedition gear!"

The amir smiled. "When you're old, these items will remind you of your great adventure and our friendship. You've taught us much. Although you're an infidel in the eyes of the Prophet, we have learned to trust in your heart."

"Thank you, Excellency. It's been my honor to know you and your brother." Russ turned to Khalid. "And our friendship has been the best part of my time in your country."

"Now, another matter." The amir glanced at his brother. "Remember when I told you to choose your mount wisely? That horse saved your life. So, I'm giving him to you."

"But, your Excellency, he's the sheikh's horse!"

The sheikh smiled. "Never mind, it's arranged. His groom will accompany Sharif all the way to the United States. They'll meet you at the harbor on your departure day."

"And I'll have that horse out of my stable. He's been a continual disruption from his arrival. More so since he recovered from his wounds. He wants more adventures." The amir offered his hand. "May Allah bless you in all that you do."

Khalid led Russ through the maze of rooms and corridors back to the central courtyard. On the way, the friends reminisced about the events that had cemented their bond.

"I can't believe I've been honored with the gift of Sharif."

"He'll be happiest with you. But Qassem is very sad. He's losing both of his friends."

"Will I see you at the port?"

"No, we'll part here." Khalid stopped at the gate. "Our friendship has taught me so much about the heart of an infidel." Khalid touched his own heart and inclined his head.

"Thank you. You, too, will always remain in my heart."

Khalid stepped back. "Go with Allah, my brother, and ride with the wind."

Chapter 71

*September 1942. A U-boat lays mines in the Chesa-
peake Bay.*

RUSS STROLLED INTO the office on his final morning at the Legation. "This is it, Catherine!"

"The old man's working at home today, so you won't have to
face him."

"Thank you for small favors." Russ clasped his hands and looked
to the heavens.

Catherine laughed. "Tell you what, finish packing up here and
go home early."

"Excellent idea."

Before lunch, Catherine wept in Russ's arms. "What will I do
without you?"

"We had a lot of fun, didn't we?" He brushed her hair off her
face. "You helped me survive this post."

She sniffled. "You were a good lover and a better friend."

With a final kiss, Russ whispered in her ear, "Goodbye, Catherine."

The muffled voices of others sitting on their own roofs floated across the still night. Russ and Piper stood near the roof's edge and gazed into the star-studded sky.

"So, Piper, what am I going to do with you?"

"Hey, that's supposed to be my question."

"I know." He took her hand. "It won't be long until we're both in D.C."

"Are you sure you can't stay in Kuwait until my tour is over?"

"We've been through this." He laughed. "Remember about finding a new career?"

"I know. But it was worth one more try."

"I'd like to get things done before the wedding takes over our lives."

"We're not even engaged, Mark."

"I know. I have plans for that." He tilted her chin. "You're going to like them."

"I've always dreamed of a home with a white picket fence." She held up her arms and spread her fingers wide. "A girl in a pinafore and a boy with a baseball glove."

"Sounds good to me. We'll have to work that into our careers."

"I know. And first we must survive the war."

"The war will eventually end, and then we'll be happy."

He wiped her damp eyes. "Have you heard anything about an early transfer?"

"You know Personnel won't give me one, what with my leaving early at my last post. They'll say the needs of the service require them to keep as many personnel here as possible until the new ambassador arrives." She heaved a huge sigh. "That means I'm stuck with the drunk until who knows when."

"Let's hope for a miracle, then."

"At least I'll have Catherine. We'll need each other."

"Just don't let her murder anyone." He pulled her to the reed mat, lifted the blanket over them, and stared at the stars. "Remember these nights, Piper."

In the early morning, the muezzin's melodic chant signaled the start of another day. The unrelenting sun began to bake the sands of the An Nafud.

When Piper opened her eyes, Russ was wrapped around her. Somewhere between them she heard Earmuff's purrs.

⌐∕∕∕∕∕∾

Russ spent his last day in Kuwait in final preparations for his morning departure. He labeled another box, stood back, and dusted off his hands. He strolled into the courtyard and watered his rose bush. Just then, Piper pulled up in front of their house.

"Perfect timing, I'm all through." He pecked her on the cheek. "It's a glorious evening. Why don't we drive out to the stables one last time?"

She sat at the small table and watched as Russ and Qassem saddled Sharif and the gray mare. The Arabians raced toward the beach. Before long, the stallion and mare reappeared on the horizon, neck and neck, their riders low over their manes, drinking the winds.

Russ dismounted and held the child close to his side. "Thank you for everything, Qassem. I'll never forget you."

"Oh, Mr. Russ, I wanted to go with you and Sharif, but Tariq said I'm needed here."

"That's right, the amir wouldn't be happy if you left."

The stableboy swiped his damp eyes. "Will you take care of Sharif for me?"

"Of course, I promise. You can say goodbye to him while you brush him down one last time." Russ held the child again.

When Piper joined Russ at the corral, he pointed into the distance. "Let's climb that rise and watch the sunset."

As the last rays pierced the sky, Russ turned to Piper and dropped to one knee. He held out a small box. "Will you marry me?"

"Yes, yes, I will." She gasped when she opened the box. "Oh, Mark, they're beautiful."

"Ibrahim made them for us. They're silver. I hope you like them."

"I do." She slipped her ring over her finger. "And it fits perfectly."

"Now let's go home and celebrate. I bought champagne."

They stood on their roof and enjoyed the cool night breeze. With his arms wrapped around her from behind, he whispered, "I hope the wait was worth it."

"It was. So romantic with the setting sun. I couldn't have asked for more."

He held out his hand. "I saved the last dance for you."

With her head on his shoulder, he began to sing "We'll Meet Again" by Vera Lynn.

"Won't you join me, Piper?"

She nodded and softly sang.

At the end of the song, he twirled her around and caught her in a low dip. Then he kissed her until she pushed him away. He followed her down the stairs to her side of the house.

With her legs wrapped around his waist, they covered the short distance to the bed in a breathless rush. She tore at his shirt while he fumbled with his pants. In a moment, he had pushed her dress aside and stripped her panties. Pausing to look into her eyes, he entered her when she pulled his hips closer. He buried his face in her shoulder and heard her panting gasps in his ear. Too soon it was over. Still joined, they lay together until he rolled away.

He laughed when she said, "Perhaps we waited too long."

"Perhaps you're right." He rolled up on an elbow. "We won't make that mistake the next time."

"Let's hope we didn't make another kind of mistake already." Piper stood and walked to her bureau. When she returned, she was naked and waving a small packet. "Better use this the next time." She straddled him. With his hands cupping her breasts, they moved together until she fell across his chest with a muffled scream. She lay there until their sweat began to dry.

Beside her, Russ traced the scar at her hairline. "If you give me a few minutes, we can try to do it more slowly. You know. More romantically."

"We'll have all the time in the world to do it more slowly when we're old."

"You're right. Maybe passion is better than romance." Russ let his fingers follow the curve of her belly until he was ready. She opened her legs and accepted him with pleasure.

Chapter 72

September 1942. General Rommel leaves North Africa for medical treatment in Germany.

As Russ's ship steamed down the Gulf, Catherine sat alone in the front office. For the third day in a row, Milbourne remained at home. No ambassador, no DCM, no Russ. Lander still fumed about Mehmet fleeing after rifling his warehouse office.

Spencer breezed in. "Hi, Catherine. I wanted to tell you that Russ got off okay."

Catherine threw a stack of papers onto her desk. "That better be all. I'm not entertaining complaints today." She waved a stapler. "One wrong word and I'll start throwing things."

"Okay, maybe this isn't a good time." He stepped back into the hall.

She replaced the stapler. "Sorry. The old man never shows up, but the work doesn't stop." She fished two envelopes from the mess and waved them in Spencer's face. "This cable will turn his world upside down, and this packet will finish him off. Then there's one from his paramour, Marvella Jessup. I'll drop them off at the residence on my way home."

"Why don't you let me do that? I don't trust you with the old man today."

"You're right." She handed the stack to Spencer. "Thanks, and good luck."

Spencer found Milbourne and Lander on the patio with tumblers in their hands. "Good evening. I knocked, but no one answered. Where's the staff tonight?"

"Well, if you must know, Mohammed didn't show up this morning, and I sent the rest of them packing. Mohammed can deal with it when he slinks back from whatever hellhole he wandered into."

"Okay, glad I asked."

"I suppose those are for me," Milbourne pointed at the mail. "Unless you planned to join us for a little libation in celebration of Russ getting out of my life."

"No, I came out because Catherine said this cable and the packet on top are especially important." Spencer dropped everything on the table and backed away. For the first time he realized how thin Milbourne was. He looked almost cadaverous, with those yellow eyes and sallow skin. He glanced at Lander. He was almost as worn and pale as the old man. "Well, I'm off. Cheers."

Lander sniffed as Spencer walked down the driveway. "He's almost as bad as Russ."

"You're right. Well, let's see what's so important that Catherine had to send that knucklehead out here." Milbourne opened the Falcon Wing.

Duncan, I've accepted your resignation effective at the completion of your replacement's confirmation hearings. Secretary Hull will withhold your pension pending a review of your fiscal management of the Legation.

Roosevelt

Milbourne tossed the cable to Lander.

"Well, you can't be surprised." Lander poured more Scotch.

"Why not? When I was in the White House, I shared cocktails with him. I talked on the phone to the prime minister. His visit to Kuwait went well. The inspectors gave me glowing remarks." He grabbed the cable and crumpled it into a ball. "And to have him turn on me like this?"

Lander eyed his boss. "I warned you about letting Russ stay at post. You should have sent him packing long before the inspectors arrived. Who knows what he told them privately, and what they passed on to those in the know back there?"

With a gasp, Milbourne remembered Russ's report. But Dunbar said he hadn't read it. "No, something else riled FDR up." He held out his glass. "Fill me up.

"Well, I guess I'll just slide into the NEA a bit early."

"You can't be serious." Lander stared at Milbourne across the top of his glass. "You'll never get that job now that the president has taken away your ambassadorship." He smirked. "You'll be heading home to Middleburg and Bitsy.

"But at least you have somewhere to go." Lander dropped his glass on the tabletop and sighed. "I got a letter from the divorce attorney Doris hired."

"Well, you can't be surprised." Milbourne sneered.

"At least Doris didn't screw Russ."

"How do you know?" Milbourne scowled at his flunky. "When the Department looks over my management of this post, they'll run across your name. Does Columbus need a pinsetter in its bowling alley?"

The breeze freshened as Milbourne ripped off the top of the larger packet. While he scanned the contents, Lander slid over the envelope. "Whoa, a law practice in Manhattan. I can't wait to hear what that's about."

The pages slid from Milbourne's hand. Lander picked them up and laughed so hard he nearly spilled his Scotch. "Good for Bitsy.

Her lawyers will eat you alive. Maybe there's two jobs at that bowling alley."

Milbourne grabbed the documents. "Get out of here. I'm sick of you and your insubordination." He emptied the bottle and threw it against the wall.

As Lander lurched toward the driveway, Milbourne rubbed his eyes. *What a mess. Marvella always wanted me to leave Bitsy. Well, I won't have to now. She'll be thrilled to hear we can marry.*

He reached for the small pastel envelope.

Duncan,

 I'm through waiting. You're no longer the man I knew. It's over.

      Marvella

 P.S. I'm putting in for ambassador to Kuwait.

Milbourne's head spun, and he lowered it to the table.

Lightning sizzled over the Gulf. A humid breeze ruffled Milbourne's thin hair.

He pushed himself to his feet and stumbled toward the low wall around the patio. With his tumbler dangling from his hand, he leaned out to look at the whitecaps on the Gulf. Grit blew into his face, and he lifted his free hand to wipe his eyes. His head spun again, and he fell over the wall into the dark slit in the rock face below.

Help me.

Allah did not hear his cry. Darkness surrounded him, and he passed out.

The storm lashed Kuwait with rain, and lightning ripped the sky. Pebbles and sand followed Duncan Milbourne's body into the crevice until all was smooth at the surface. The desert had reclaimed the void.

On the storm-tossed ship, Russ awoke to the roiling seas. Clinging to the rails, he made his way below. The groom was at Sharif's side. Together they steadied the stallion.

Through a driving rain, Russ hurried back to his berth. Shaking water from his shoulders, he studied himself at the tiny mirror. *I'm no longer afraid of storms.* He opened the cabin door and stood in the spray. *Feels good.*

Toweling himself dry, he dropped into his bunk. Piper filled his dreams.

Russ had awakened that morning with his arms around Piper. He gently kissed her until she stirred. This time, their passion was tempered by the tenderness of goodbye.

Later, they stood beneath the awning at the Shuwaikh harbor master's office.

Piper turned when she heard Sharif. "That horse is going with you, and I have to stay here?" She backed away from Russ. "That's not fair."

"Now, honey, I wanted Sharif to be a surprise. He's booked all the way to Kansas! I'll visit with Mom while I find him a place to board." He patted the stallion's side. "Sharif will have a new life, too. We'll see him when we're in Hays. It'll all work out. You'll see."

Piper balled her hands against her eyes and began to sob. She allowed Russ to pull her against his chest. He held her until she spent her frustration.

Standing in the shadows of a shack, Mehmet glared at the American lovers with disgust. Such a shameful public display of affection. He melted into the crowd and boarded a coastal steamer bound for Egypt.

Russ brushed the tears from Piper's face. "Don't worry, I'll look for a job that keeps us together. If I can't find one, I'll follow you until something turns up." He held her shoulders. "Will you write to me?" He tipped her face toward his. "I love you."

"I love you, too." Crying softly, her hand slipped from his.

As the ship left the dock, Russ watched Piper fade into the mass of humanity. His last images of Kuwait were the white donkeys moving through the surf.

Chapter 73

September 1942. A Japanese plane drops incendiaries on Oregon, but with negligible effect.

THE NEXT DAY, Catherine stood in the empty office. Another day and no ambassador. This had to end. She picked up the jangling phone.

"Miss Cushard, Mr. Lander hasn't come into the office. We need someone to sign purchase orders."

Catherine sighed. *I shouldn't have told Piper to take the day off.*

Lander awoke on the dirt floor of a tiny room. He squinted at a window high on a wall. Were those bars? Where the hell was he?

He shuffled across the floor and tried the doorknob. Locked.

He pounded on the door. "Hello? Anyone out there? I'm from the American Legation."

A man peered through the tiny slot in the door and walked away.

"Wait. Come back!" Lander slid to the dust behind the door.

"Hello, Trick. It's me, Catherine. Did you talk to the old man yesterday?"

"Yeah, he was drinking with Lander on the patio. Both looked the worse for wear."

"Great! Did they say anything about coming in today? Neither have shown."

"No, but I'm not surprised. They're probably still passed out. I hope Lander didn't drive home. The wind was fierce last night. Couldn't have been safe on the beach road, even if he was sober. Want me to go out to the residence?"

"No, thanks, I'll call out there and talk with Mohammed."

"Nope. The old man said Mohammed hadn't shown up."

"What? Mehmet and now Mohammed? What's going on?"

"Who knows? I'd bet someone at the Interior Ministry warned them about Special Branch's investigation."

"What investigation? Oh, never mind. So they up and left. How'd they get out of Kuwait?"

"Any number of ways. Probably hopped aboard a coastal steamer headed down the Gulf. Next stop Al Minya, where they'll find their Egyptian religious-nut buddies."

⌁

Piper answered Catherine's call. "Thanks for letting me stay home. I cried myself to sleep." She pressed the receiver to her ear. "What? Criminy! I'll be right in."

She walked into the front office and held up a hand. "Go easy. My head still hurts."

Catherine brought Piper up to date. "Trick thought someone tipped off Mehmet and Mohammed. He called the Interior Ministry, and they confirmed it. That guy's been arrested.

"Wait, it gets better. Lander's missing." She shoved a chair toward Piper. "Better sit down for the best part.

"The old man isn't answering the phone at the residence. Trick drove out there."

Piper's head hit Mariah's desk with a soft thud. When she raised it, she sighed. "We'll wait until Trick calls us from the residence. He might be too far gone to hear the phone. Same for Lander. Maybe someone should go out to his house."

Catherine grabbed the ringing phone. "You're kidding me. Piper's here. I'll tell her.

"Trick said the residence is completely empty. Not even a servant. Just a single glass on the patio table and a bottle smashed against the wall. Soggy mail was blown all over the patio."

"Now that's beyond odd." Piper pulled over a legal pad. "I think we better start an event log. Help me remember the last time anyone saw Lander and Milbourne. And maybe the missing staff."

Catherine lifted the phone again. She listened and then put her hand over the receiver. "It's the sheikh's personal assistant. George wrecked his car last night on the road back from the residence. Missed a curve and ended up on a dune. He's in Al Ahmadi jail. The Kuwaitis will kick him out as persona non grata. He wants to know if we want to talk to George."

"Nope. Let him rot." Piper wrote "jail" next to Lander's name on her list. "Now where's the ambassador?"

⚜

Russ took his coffee mug aft to check on Sharif. He pulled an apple from his jacket and cut it in half with his pocketknife. "Here, buddy, you deserve a treat after that storm. We're in for a long journey. But you'll like Kansas. You'll be a king with a harem of mares in your pasture."

He sat on a coil of rope and sipped his coffee. In the warm sun on a placid sea, his thoughts drifted back to Kuwait. So much had happened in such a brief time.

He fumbled in his jacket pocket for his notebook and pencil. Time to make a list.

POSSIBLE JOBS:

1. LEND-LEASE, Call Averell Harriman. *Might be good throughout the war, but then what?* He added a note.

2. SECRET SERVICE. Call Rowley and Pastorini. *More permanent than Lend-Lease. Lots of traveling and dealing with Milbourne types.* He added a big question mark next to that line.

3. CALL EMIL FAIRFAX. *He has a lot of contacts from his desk on the deputy secretary's staff.*

4. OSS. *Should have talked more to Trick and Trent.* Contact Rhonda. *She'd mentioned talking to someone on my behalf there. Did she do that? How long has it been since I last heard from her?*

He flipped a page and titled it APARTMENTS. *Newspaper ads? Emil for this too? Bulletin board at the State Department Lounge? Surely something will turn up.*

Russ watched the coast slide by as the steamer ran in the warm aquamarine waters.

He flipped to another page. WEDDING. *Mom will be shocked. And thrilled. I'll need more pages for her suggestions. And Piper's mom. Wait! I don't even know her name. Better start a new page.*

QUESTIONS FOR PIPER. Mother's name and address. Aunty Laycie's full name and address in Capbreton, France. He stared at the water. *France always made Piper sad. What troubled her there?* He made a note.

Twenty minutes later, Russ flipped his pages back and forth. He chewed on his pencil while he read his list of questions for Piper. There was a lot he didn't know about his future wife. How'd that happen? Rhonda would shake her finger at him. *Take your time and get to know the woman you'll spend your life with.*

Fingering the tiny box with the silver pendant that he kept in his pocket, Russ closed his eyes and pictured the last time he saw Rhonda. *Maybe I'll stop by to see her. Can I be around her again? Not touch her auburn hair? Not caress her cheek?*

⚜

Rhonda looked up when a secretary dropped off a stack of unclassified mail. "Thanks so much. I hadn't realized how much paper I'd have to shove around. Your name's Blaire, right?"

"Yes, Mrs. Pierson. I'm surprised you know my name."

"Call me Rhonda. Once I get my bearings, I'll be self-sufficient. That'll free you up to humor my fellow *male* officers."

"And they take a lot of care." Blaire chuckled. "I'm still adjusting to a female officer in OSS. Foggy Bottom sure is changing. Tell me if you need anything."

Rhonda lifted a blue envelope from the stack. "Just a sec, Blaire. Did you see who brought this to our office?"

"No, sorry. It just appeared on my desk with your name on it."

Rhonda smiled to herself. She'd made a friend.

Preston would faint if he found out she worked on the Swiss desk at the State Department. So far, he'd believed her cover story about returning to work as an attorney.

She slit the blue envelope and pulled out the single sheet.

Chelsea Pier, New York City. October 21. Passenger liner Cherokee. Cheers,

Bitsy

New York City was a short train ride from D.C.

I'll see him and learn why he's stopped writing. All will be well. There's always hope.

Author's Note

I FOUND MY inspiration for *The Infidel and the Ghost of Moscow* in my father-in-law's journal entries from his World War II army duty. He was assigned to a railway battalion in Iran on the Persian Corridor. In later life, he received a medal from the Russian government for his service in saving their country.

I drew many details from my Secret Service years at the White House and my Foreign Service career, particularly during my last posting in Kuwait. I hope you've enjoyed this work of fiction that began over twenty years ago with an idea I finally put in print.

Many well-known historical figures, like FDR and Churchill, appear in my book, where you will also find lesser-known real-life characters. Ahmad al Sabah, the amir of Kuwait; Averell Harriman; Harry Hopkins; Cordell Hull; Colonel Bill Donovan; Captain Swensen of the USS *Juneau* (CL-52); and Secret Service agent Jim Rowley contributed their efforts to winning the war. While Elena Zhukova, Rhonda's NKVD minder in Moscow, is fictional, her uncle, Marshal Georgy Zhukov, was a key figure in the Soviet battles against the Nazis on the Eastern Front. I based the amir's American oil advisor, Wendell Fox, on British expat H. Saint John Philby. Philby's son Kim worked in MI6 during the war. And as a Soviet spy.

Russ's story continues through the remainder of the war years in forthcoming sequels.

Acknowledgments

Several people contributed to *The Infidel and the Ghost of Moscow*. My project advisor, Suzanna, has been with me from the beginning. My critique group partner, Donna, provided valuable comments for over a decade. Alice Tanner and Janice Sinclair shared their concept art for the book cover. My wife, Linda, helped me understand the motivations and desires of my female characters. Her skills prepared my book for the final contributions by my editor in Tucson, Susan Wenger. Thank you, Susan, for guiding me to a better product.

About the Author

David Tanner began his government career at the White House with the Secret Service. Later he transferred to the Foreign Service in the U.S. Department of State. He had postings in Beijing, Buenos Aires, Ankara, Belgrade, and Kuwait City. He also completed temporary assignments in Bahrain, Jerusalem, Sofia, Budapest, and Bangkok. Dave lives in suburban Atlanta, Georgia.

www.ingramcontent.com/pod-product-compliance
Lightning Source LLC
Chambersburg PA
CBHW021405310726
48971CB00005B/1206